SPECIAL MESSAGE TO READERS

This book is published under the auspices of

THE ULVERSCROFT FOUNDATION
(registered charity No. 264873 UK)

Established in 1972 to provide funds for research, diagnosis and treatment of eye diseases. Examples of contributions made are: —

A Children's Assessment Unit at Moorfield's Hospital, London.

•

Twin operating theatres at the Western Ophthalmic Hospital, London.

•

A Chair of Ophthalmology at the Royal Australian College of Ophthalmologists.

•

The Ulverscroft Children's Eye Unit at the Great Ormond Street Hospital For Sick Children, London.

You can help further the work of the Foundation by making a donation or leaving a legacy. Every contribution, no matter how small, is received with gratitude. Please write for details to:

THE ULVERSCROFT FOUNDATION,
The Green, Bradgate Road, Anstey,
Leicester LE7 7FU, England.
Telephone: (0116) 236 4325

In Australia write to:
THE ULVERSCROFT FOUNDATION,
c/o The Royal Australian College of Ophthalmologists,
27, Commonwealth Street, Sydney,
N.S.W. 2010.

THE ORMER SHELL

It is 1940 and three Guernsey children — Edward and William Dorner and their friend, Ruth, find themselves in England as evacuees. Ruth has an Ormer shell, taken from a tranquil beach the day before, and in the coming years she clings to it — a reminder of her island home. Later, the shell assumes great significance in her growing love for one of the brothers. Edward plans to re-open the family hotel after the war. William wants money and an easy life. Ruth has marriage in mind. Ambitions, jealousy, tragedy and love bind the three lives together.

LLOYD PETERS

THE ORMER SHELL

Complete and Unabridged

ULVERSCROFT
Leicester

First published in Great Britain in 2001

First Large Print Edition
published 2002

British Library CIP Data

Peters, Lloyd
The Ormer shell.—Large print ed.—
Ulverscroft large print series: general fiction
1. Detective and mystery stories
2. Large type books
I. Title
823.9′14 [F]

ISBN 0–7089–4765–4

Published by
F. A. Thorpe (Publishing)
Anstey, Leicestershire

Set by Words & Graphics Ltd.
Anstey, Leicestershire
Printed and bound in Great Britain by
T. J. International Ltd., Padstow, Cornwall

This book is printed on acid-free paper

This novel is dedicated
to my wife Hazel Joan

1

The boy took aim and threw underarm gently. The pebble landed against the shell's rim, fell in and was held.

'There, you'll be lucky in love, Edward,' exclaimed Ruth.

Edward glanced at her, puzzled. 'Can't see how that makes any difference.'

'Girls say that sort of thing — I've heard 'em before, and Ruthie's a girl.'

Ruth looked at the speaker — William — Edward's younger brother. She was always Ruthie to him, but Edward called her Ruth — she liked that better, liked him.

A million yellow suns danced in the placid water of Moulin Huet bay, the haze long since cleared to reveal the large rocky outcrops of the Pea Stacks outlined sharply against the blue. Somewhere a plane droned and Edward searched for it; he'd seen plenty recently, vapour trails in the sky criss-crossing. There had been talk of being at war, but it seemed to him like any other day in Guernsey, apart from there being no visitors to the island which felt strange at that time of the year. He glanced at the granite building set at that end of the bay, their home — The Ormer Hotel. The veranda and terrace, the rockery garden with its low wall overlooking the beach. No one came to stay now, it was very quiet. The family rowing boat lay at the bottom of the steps. Sometimes his father would take them out into the bay beyond Lion Rock for a picnic. He was tired of throwing pebbles and a bit bored.

Ruth picked up the Ormer shell they had used as a target, its inside reflecting rainbow-like and put it into her dress pocket. 'Lets go down to the water.'

She set off running between the rocks that littered the foreshore, some large enough to hide her from sight. Edward rounded one where the shingle turned to sand, but then collided with her. Ruth stumbled backwards, and Edward losing his balance, fell on top of her. He attempted to regain his feet, but momentarily her arms encircled him and tightened. They stared into each other's eyes. Edward was surprised, she wasn't smiling or pretending to be cross and had a funny look on her face. She didn't seem to mind him lying on her.

William caught up with them. 'What are you fighting Ruthie for? You don't fight girls.' Edward scrambled to his feet. 'Don't be stupid, I wasn't, we banged into each other.' He was somewhat irritated by his brother's remark, and William was sure to say something back at the house.

Ruth gazed after them. William was all right but he was younger. Edward was taller and rather thin, not at all silly, and he smiled nicely but not often. She thought about him a lot, usually at night in bed.

The three splashed slowly along the sea's edge, their shadows dark against the sand. Edward was thinking that they had known Ruth for ever, she hadn't any brothers or sisters and lived with her aunt just up the lane. He'd never thought of her as a girl — just someone who joined them in playing games. His thoughts ran on: funny how his parents had changed. They frowned a lot this year and were very serious, he'd caught snatches of their conversation together — it was always to do with the war. He kicked through the gentle surf, wasn't sure what he wanted to do next.

'What are you thinking about, Edward?' Ruth was at his side staring at him.

Edward poked at a piece of seaweed with his toes. 'Has your aunt altered? Mum and dad — they're not a lot of fun just now — they've got miserable.'

Ruth frowned. 'I think she gets a bit worried when she listens to the wireless.'

'Does she talk much about the war to you?'

'Not really, but I heard her talking to the milkman and he said it wouldn't last six months — he seemed quite certain.' Ruth couldn't remember her own parents, vaguely she recalled hearing her aunt saying her father had gone off somewhere soon after she was born, but no mention of her mother. So the boys had become her family, had been jolly good fun, but as she had grown older, Edward had become more and more important to her and William got in the way sometimes.

It was hot and the trees were hardly moving. 'Phew, I'm going to get some pop,' proclaimed William, pushing his feet into his sandals for the short journey across the shingle to the steps.

The sound of a car approaching quickly down the lane made the three look up. It bounced and jerked to a stop in the Hotel's driveway, raising dust which dispersed slowly.

'It's the Vicar,' observed Edward.

The driver stumbled out in great haste, half running with hands outstretched to shorten the distance to the side door on which they heard him pound and call out. The Rev. Ilett was usually a calm orderly man who spoke and walked with measured assurance and confidence.

'Golly, what's the matter?' blurted William.

'It's not Sunday is it?,' Edward asked Ruth anxiously, they went to church occasionally, sometimes played truant. They continued to stare hotelwards, and the car stood small and black, its door hanging open.

Suddenly the boys parents — Mr. and Mrs. Dorner appeared hurrying towards the wall overlooking the beach, followed closely by the Vicar. They were shouting and waving with extravagant gestures at the children. Edward reached the steps ahead of the others.

His father's urgent and anxious voice reached him. 'Come up all of you now — now as fast as you can. We've got to go. Hurry — come on hurry!' And Mrs. Dorner gathered air with her arms frantically as she leaned far out over the wall at them. Three pairs of young legs accelerated their owners up the steps. They found fear on the fair face of Mrs. Dorner, intense anxiety on her husband's, and only a little less on the Vicar's.

'We've got to go — leave the house now,' panted Mr. Dorner. 'Run inside boys, get a coat, put shoes on — anything you can carry, then jump into the car, I'll get it out now. Get a move on. Don't ask questions — do it.'

The boys raced off, pursued by their mother. 'Just get clothes — warm ones.' 'What do we want coats for? It's too hot. What are we . . . ?' Their voices faded away inside.

Mr. Dorner clutched at Ruth. 'Where's Mrs. Le Ney — your aunt — d' you know? Quickly Ruth. The Vicar says she's not at home. Where is she?'

Ruth stared into Mr. Dorner's face and then at the Vicar. 'I think she's gone into town shopping, but I'm not sure.' Her rapidly rising anxiety was plain.

'It's all right, Ruth, nothing to worry about. I just wanted to know, that's all. I — I have something important to tell her.' His hand on her shoulder was reassuring, but his worried eyes were not. He then ran off in the direction of the garage at the side of the house.

Ruth did not understand. Where were they going? What was happening?

Mr. Dorner flung the garage doors open, then disappeared inside. She heard the engine start and the car appeared. Watched as he jumped out, leaving the engine running, and hurried inside calling urgently for his family to be quick.

Ruth looked at the Reverend Ilett. Everything had happened so quickly. The adult faces and their expressions.

The Vicar took her hand. 'I think it might be better if I drove you home. Your aunt may have returned. It is really a matter for her to decide what to do.' He straightened and looked away from the questions evolving in the young features. 'It's to do with the war Ruth, I'm sorry.'

Below them the sea murmured gently and the bright leaves stirred in that lovely place.

Edward peered into his wardrobe. Couldn't think. Pictures on the wall. Bag on the end of his bed, comics on the floor. He heard his mother calling. What was William taking? How long were they going for? Where? His binoculars — a present for his birthday, stuffed them into his pocket. 'Coming,' he shouted.

In the hall his father, shirt-sleeved, had a case in his hand, and a black box under the other arm. Their mother was dropping food into a bag, and on a chair a pile of clothes topped by her hat. She looked hot and agitated and kept repeating, 'Oh dear, oh dear.'

Outside Edward turned to see his father with his arm around their mother's shoulder. 'We'll be all right, I'll lock up. You get in the car with the children.'

'I'm going ahead with Ruth,' the Vicar said, 'better I think if I see whether her aunt is home.' He looked at the group around him. 'Before we separate, please,' and raised his hand. 'The blessing of God Almighty . . . '

Ruth opened her eyes, the boys looked funny. William had his long overcoat on, sandalled and bare legged while Edward wore his school cap, carried a raincoat and a small suitcase, and had knee-length stockings on.

The Vicar shook hands with Mr. and Mrs. Dorner. 'Good luck. I'll try and keep an eye on things for you. Don't know how things will go, of course.' He motioned at his car. 'Get in Ruth, Mr.

and Mrs. Dorner are following us.' He leaned out of the window, looked back at the others. 'Make sure you get the boat — it's the last one.'

Reaching the lane the engine stalled and Ruth looking back, was surprised to see Mr. Dorner pushing something between the rocks halfway down the steps to the beach.

The Vicar stabbed at the starter button and then they were climbing quickly, and Ruth in the heat and gloom of the car, hoped that her aunt would be waiting for her. So many questions to ask. There was her house — solid, comforting, the narrow stream running nearby. She alighted hastily.

'Remember, Ruth,' the Vicar said, 'wait until your aunt returns if she is not in.'

He drove off quickly, and Ruth raced up the path, to find both the front and back doors locked. A chair stood on the small rear lawn with a magazine on it. Oh, where had she gone? Then Ruth remembered her aunt saying something about seeing her friend, Mrs. De Marre. She saw the Dorner family car coming very fast up the lane. It stopped and she gasped through the open window. 'She's not in, but I think she may be at her friends. The Vicar said to wait, but I'd rather find her. It's Elder Place.'

'We'll drop you, it's on our way,' said Mr. Dorner.

She scrambled into the car and they set off, the wheels spinning. Ruth's gaze rested on Mrs. Dorner, seeing her yellow hat, the large handbag clutched to her cardigan, beneath the fawn coat. She must be very hot.

'You can come with us if you don't see your aunt.

She can, can't she Dad?' said William, speaking at his father's back.

'Why? Where are you going? You're not leaving, are you?' She was becoming very anxious. It was turning into a very strange day.

'The last boat for England is leaving in about half an hour or less. I'm taking Mrs. Dorner and the boys away to England.' The strain in his voice was clearly evident and he spoke in the tone of a man caught up in something he knew was happening, but couldn't believe that it was.

'But I want to see you again.' It was all very dreadful.

'You will, Ruth, don't worry. We'll be back soon. It could blow over in weeks.' He glanced her a smile which was gone almost before it had begun.

Edward felt awful. It was like going back to school after the holidays, only ten times worse. Riding in the car and not going back home. They never did that, they always went home again.

The car was lurching and bumping about, they were going much faster than usual, and it was very hot all squeezed in together.

'What about the car, Dad?' asked William.

'I'll leave it near the terminal buildings. Perhaps someone will look after it for us.'

'My aunt will look after it for you, Mr. Dorner, but I don't want you all to go.' Ruth was unhappy now. What a horrible day.

'Do you think we're doing the right thing, John?' said Mrs. Dorner in a small voice.

Her husband gave an almost imperceptible shake of his head. 'I think so — I'm not sure. We'll be all right, don't worry,' but his tone was flat, and Margaret Dorner turned a worried tense face against the window.

They were now nearing the bottom of the Grange and Mr. Dorner stopped the car again. 'I think it's as far as we can take you, Ruth, I'm sorry we haven't time . . . if you get out now.' His fingers were busy tapping and curling on the wheel. Then he plunged a hand into his pocket. 'Take this, and if you don't find your aunt, get a bus back home or call into the Police Station. You'll be all right.'

Ruth looked at the money in her hand. 'Oh thanks, Mr. Dorner.' It all seemed so unreal. She leaned into the car. 'Bye Mrs. Dorner, bye Edward — William. I will see you again?' More speech was impossible. The boys just looked at her helplessly. Then she turned and ran, her young heart heavy. Would she ever see them again? Glanced back, hand up to wave, but they had gone.

The entrance and jetty to White Rock were busy, lorries loaded with tomatoes, people carrying cases, belongings. A short line of cars, and Edward saw they were empty — abandoned. The odd taxi hastening away. A hurrying stream of islanders, making for the ferry which was beginning to breathe darkly and heavily through its funnel in preparation for departure.

William heard it first through the open window of the car. A dull thumping sound. His father thought it sounded like the Castle Cornet guns, but doubted whether they still continued the ceremony. In any case it was after midday and the guns were usually fired at that time.

Mr. Dorner halted the car behind the others on the jetty road; it was impossible to take it further. 'Will all passengers please alight here,' he joked but his smile was strained as he handed his wife down and kept hold of her hand. On summer days gone by they had strolled on the walk above and leaned over to watch the water and gaze across to Herm. Was he doing the right thing for his family? The alternative? His wife and two sons under an occupying army. It had been rumoured for some time now that they would come. He patted the car's bonnet, then hurried his family to join the throng.

'Edward! William!' The high-pitched cry came from behind them. Ruth's dodging, darting figure caught up with them. 'I decided to come with you to see you off. I can go home later, I'll be all right. Auntie will be home then,' she panted and gasped. 'Thought I might be too late.'

Mr. Dorner looked very concerned for her and undecided. 'I hope your aunt doesn't mind, Ruth,' and he turned to lead the way, with Ruth clinging onto Edward.

'Come with us Ruthie,' urged William.

'She can't, not without Mrs. Le Ney, William,' said his father.

Ruth glanced at his worried and upset face. 'I'll look after your house for you whilst you're away, Mr. Dorner.'

'Thanks Ruth, you're a good girl. May not be long. You must turn back now.' But she was reluctant to leave them.

Halfway to the boat. Men on the deck, moving ropes. The gangway coming into sight on the other side. The pressure of people around them.

A new sound came with the intermittent thumping noise. Aircraft — several, dark and low over the bay. Edward tugged his binoculars from his pocket trying to focus and carried along on the end of Ruth's hand. An image held for a second — the swastika showed clearly on the plane's side. German! Objects fell from the plane.

'They're bombing the harbour!' the cry went up.

People stumbled in the desperate race, lay sprawled against the ground clinging to belongings. The noise was deafening. Bombs, screams, shouted names.

They were running frantically, William losing his footing — dragged along on his toes. Edward could feel his mother's arms over his shoulder from behind. His father shepherding the others — human shields. Too late — no stopping now. His mother was praying, his father urging them on. 'Keep going — nearly there. Together — keep together,' his parent yelled. A hundred yards to go.

A blast behind them. Edward was knocked to the ground. His hands were free, jerked from the others. Feet scrambling over him. A different sound — sharp, mechanical, precise. Terrible screams. He looked up and forward. Ruth ahead — upright. 'Ruth!' he shrieked, 'get down.' He flung himself upon her, over her, covering her, hiding his face in her hair. Something hit his ankle — a sharp pain.

He dared to glance up. Was that William in front? He scrambled to his feet, dragging Ruth with him, nearly falling again in the panic to reach the boat and swept along again. 'William! William! Here we're here.' Hands joining tightly. His parents must be ahead. Bags and cases littered their path, smoke enveloping them, and bodies pushing the three on.

No time to talk, arms locked in each others. Edward glanced up at the ferry, larger now, its smoke joining that from the harbour. Frantic exhortations from the gangplank to hurry. The bottleneck at its foot. Difficult to see, their faces shoved against the coats in front.

'Go on Ruth, get on with William,' he urged. His foot reached the gangway — felt it move with the boat. Above — the high sides — the only shelter between them and the harbour. His parents must be on board. He fell in his haste and felt the pain in his leg again. Hands pushed them inside to join those crouched beneath the windows, lying on the decks or just sitting fearfully upon such baggage as they had managed to bring aboard.

The three bent together under some steps off a passageway, frightened and confused.

Ruth recovered enough to shout her distress. 'I want to get off — she won't know where I am — I want to go home.' Lurching to her feet she ran towards the deck opening and the gangway, but the tide of people pressing inwards forced her back with a real risk of being trampled. She regained shelter again to huddle close to the brothers and crying despairingly.

The boat swayed and Edward heard the doors clang. It was all so horrible. He must look for his parents. They were somewhere on the boat he was sure. People were calling out for relatives and friends and the lights kept flickering. A vibration began through the floor. Someone shouted that they were moving.

About an hour later conditions had settled down on board, and leaving William and Ruth together, Edward searched every face and place that he could find, but Mr. and Mrs. Dorner were not to be found. Heavy-hearted and near to tears he rejoined the others. He told William that they may be on board somewhere that he had not yet looked. But his young mind, bruised as it was, told him that they would have come seeking William and himself if they had been aboard the ferry.

Ruth sat knees to her chin staring at the floor, hands in pockets. Yes! that was it — she was asleep. Soon she would hear her aunt's voice, look at her bedroom ceiling or see the sky above Moulin Huet. Something hard touched her fingers in her dress pocket. She knew what it was before it came into view. But her mind did not want to accept the truth. The Ormer shell she had picked up from the beach after their game that morning! A few grains of sand adhered to the inside. So few hours ago. The nightmare was real! Along with Edward and William she had left her island home and was heading for the unknown. Her aunt would worry — would not know where she was and she, Ruth, couldn't tell her. Had her aunt reached home before the planes came? She pressed her head against her knees again in anguished helplessness, sick of body and heart.

However, later she had recovered sufficiently to speculate with the boys on what had happened to their parents. 'I think they were separated from us in the rush. They'll know you've got on here all right — be back home now, it's quick by car. They'll be all right,' she said reassuringly.

'And mum and dad will be able to tell your aunt that you're here with us. She won't worry then — well, not as much anyway,' William offered helpfully.

Ruth's face had brightened, 'be able to come to our house, keep each other company'.

'And,' put in Edward 'keep the hotel going. It won't get rotten and fall down or something.'

They were given a drink — tea — and it had a funny taste. That plus the confined space and motion of the boat made Edward sick again. For the rest of his life he was to remember the taste of stewed tea.

Then someone came round taking names and Ruth, looking up from her corner, declared desperately, 'I didn't really mean to come on the boat, I just came to see my friends off. I'd like to go home again.'

The older eyes looked into the younger. 'I'm sorry m'dear, but we can't do that for you. We'd all like to go back, but I'm afraid there's a war on.' The mouth gave a quick optimistic smile. 'But maybe not for long eh?' Ruth's fair head sank back against the bulkhead.

'You haven't seen a Mr. and Mrs. Dorner have you' the boy's pale face questioned with an eager anxiety. 'Our mum and dad — William's and mine. The planes came — we were separated, I can't find them — I've looked.'

'Mr and Mrs. Dorner eh? I'll remember. Keep an ear open for 'em. Don't worry son.' The eyes swept them. 'All together are you?' They nodded, then dozed off fitfully, each covered by a portion of William's winter coat.

Several hours later they disembarked in a more orderly fashion than they had gone aboard. With many others they waited in a large hall, the lights were on and the windows were covered in dark blue. People with papers and clothing came and went, and Ruth acquired a brown coat to cover her dress. They found out that they were in England, in Weymouth.

The back of Edward's heel hurt, made him limp. He wished his father and mother were there — they'd always been there. Heard his father. 'Stand up Edward, don't slouch.' His mother saying to William, 'Crabs are for the beach, not for the bedroom.' Hopelessly he gazed at the people with papers in their hands. Nobody had seen his parents, but other children had theirs, small family knots. It made him sad.

Ruth looked at the outline of the boat at the quayside, which had brought them. How long before she could board it or its sister to return to the island which she had left so unwillingly? If only that gangway was touching White Rock harbour wall in St. Peter Port.

Later a train rushed them through the night. Huddled together on the floor of the corridor, occasionally seeing their reflections in the windows flying over a strange land. Aware of the hiss and puff of steam and swaying carriage. Of the legs and voices that came and went, the sound of the wheels over the rails, taking them even further from their homes. Then, exhausted, sleep brought its curtain down between each young person and their memories of that calamitous day.

The cobbled forecourt of the station glistened in the rain of mid-morning in Daleford. Ruth, Edward and William stood waiting with others for a bus to take them to accommodation in the town. They looked about them, at the dark hill towering behind the station, touched by thick clouds. Ahead a street ascending steeply with stone buildings either side.

They gazed at one another, cold, very anxious and uncertain of what lay ahead for them. Evacuees — they were to hear the term many times in the future.

Ruth wondered if the blue, the yellow, the peaceful scene of the island bay the previous morning had been real. And the Ormer shell remained clasped in her hand to tell her that, indeed, it had.

2

Their first home on foreign soil — a large grim mill type building of the kind they had seen on the way from the station. Edward, William and Ruth together with others sat in a great hall for meals, and upstairs two floors had been turned into dormitories for the new arrivals, one for the women and another for the men. Edward and William shared a narrow hard bed, and Ruth, for the first time since leaving Guernsey, passed the night out of sight of the boys.

In the morning the three with most of the other evacuees were in the grounds behind the railings surrounding the building. It was preferable to being inside that depressing place. People on the pavement outside looked at them in curiosity, and a man and a woman pointed at Ruth. 'We'll take the girl.'

'No!' Edward sprang forward. 'No! She's not going. Ruth stays with us — we're all together.' He looked anxiously at the man with a list in his hand. 'We want to go together, Ruth mustn't go by herself.'

The man went away and a discussion followed with another official at the door of the building behind them. Then he returned. 'For the time being you children are going to stay here.'

A small victory, leaving them staring somewhat cheered into the street. At least they were being allowed to stay together. But for how long?

That night, despite the circumstances in which Ruth found herself she had to giggle at Edward and William attired in huge and ill-fitting pyjamas as they hesitantly entered the female dormitory.

'Sorry Ruth that we have to be in that other room', said Edward, 'but we'll see you in the morning.'

Ruth wanted someone to cuddle her. If only it could be Edward. 'I'm all right, it's my fault for being here anyway.' Admiration shone brightly blue as she gazed at him. 'You were very brave on the pier, Edward. You saved me — I'm sure you did — you lay over me — I remember.'

'I think I fell over you — I was rushing.'

'No,' she said definitely, 'you covered me, stopped things hitting me.'

She seemed to like him lying on her — she was funny that way. 'Come on William,' urged Edward turning to go.

William followed slowly looking back at the occasional glimpse of corsets and other female attire. 'Night Ruthie,' he called as he finally managed to take his eyes away from the adult flesh.

The following day Edward was taken to the local infirmary for an examination of his right foot. It hurt quite a lot as it had done ever since that dash to the boat when he had felt something hit the back of his ankle. Edward told the doctor what had happened in those desperate minutes trying to reach the ferry. There was some doubt as to the outcome of the treatment and he was told he might be left with a limp.

'It was a bullet,' hc explained later with an air of

importance to a suitably impressed William.

'Gosh,' exclaimed his brother, 'that was a real war then.'

How real was to come home to him in the following months when the problem of the ankle faded under the thought of just how long the war and their miserable situation would last.

A week afterwards they were visited by an official of the local education department. 'We've got a school here in Daleford for you to attend,' he announced. 'You'll understand that we must keep up with your education. No one knows how long you're going to be in England, so we must see to it that that part of your life is not neglected.'

School! They'd forgotten about it.

'You'll live at the school,' the official added.

Edward and William stared at him, neither had expected that. 'A boarding school,' exclaimed Edward.

'An orphanage — the pupils live in.'

'Orphanage!' William's gasp was only a split second behind Edward's. 'But we're not orphans — our parents live in Guernsey. They were not able to get here with us — they're still there,' he blurted earnestly.

The official observed the look on the young face. 'Yes, yes of course, I don't doubt that they are. But you see for the time being we have to look on you as being orph . . . ' He corrected himself, 'without your parents for the time being. It's a very fine school.' He was sorry for them but these were difficult times for everyone; it could go on for years. 'You'll have good food, uniforms, everything you need.'

'And we'll be together, William and myself?' asked Edward anxiously.

'Well you may get separated by class sometimes, but otherwise . . . ' he shrugged.

The eyes of the older boy were clinging to his, deadly serious. 'Can Ruth come with us? We're all together you see.'

'Ruth? Oh yes, the girl,' and he frowned. 'No, I don't think so, Although there's a section for the girls, there isn't a vacancy. Perhaps at a future date, but I can't promise.'

'But Ruthie's our friend,' protested William. 'She's always been our friend. We have to look after her until we go back home. Mrs. Le Ney would be mad if we didn't.'

The official looked at his watch and stood up. He must be firm. 'Now I can't say any more about the matter. You'll be called for tomorrow. It's not far away and I'll be coming to see you from time to time. Goodbye boys,' he smiled cheerfully and hurried away.

Ruth was upset when they told her. Wondered where she would be sent.

'He did say there was a girl's part. P'raps there'll be a place for you soon. We told him we all wanted to be together,' said Edward encouragingly. She'd been a good sport coming to see them off like that on the White Rock pier — just jolly bad luck.

'Don't cry Ruthie.' William patted her shoulder. 'Our school's not far away — he said so.'

'I know,' exclaimed Edward, 'as soon as we get there we'll tell the head about you, and you want to be with us.'

'That's a good idea Edward but,' her forehead wrinkled. 'I don't think they'll take any notice. I'll be all right,' she sighed.

'We'll come and see you Ruthie. We can meet and play like we used to do.' Then William's eyes strayed past her into the woman's dormitory, but no one was to be seen in any state of undress.

Ruth waved them off the next day then cried into her bed, feeling very lonely. Later she wrote a letter to her aunt informing her of all that happened and would she pass a message on to Mr. and Mrs. Dorner that the boys were well and going to a school called an orphanage which was a bit silly. It was only for a while until they all came home again. She was all right and hoped to join them soon at this school. The town of Daleford was full of hills and clouds and no sea. She apologised for the fact that she had got on the boat by mistake — she couldn't avoid it — it had been awful. Hoped that her aunt wouldn't be cross, she would return as soon as possible. Having sealed the letter and addressed it Ruth began to feel more cheerful.

The man in charge did not have the heart to tell Ruth that her letter would not be posted — that the Channel Islands were occupied. Being a kindly and compassionate man he told her to keep on writing to her aunt and that he would post each one. Of course, he informed her gently, it may be a long time before she received a reply because all the boats and planes had been withdrawn. Ruth seemed to understand. Sadly, he watched her leave. So young and such a nicely brought up little girl, with eyes that were almost violet.

The boy's new school was a large Victorian building with a dome-like centre having several clock faces. The school, which went by the name of St. Justs, was known locally as Justs. From its highest windows, some in their dormitory, they could see the distant moors and the huge valley with its toy-like railway in the bottom. A dense wood flourished on the side nearest to the school.

Daleford lay nearby, its mill chimneys like headless stalks towering over a dark garden, and the ever-present layer of smoke hanging inside the crater of hills which surrounded the town.

For meals they sat at long tables in a very large room with a piano in one corner. The passages and corridors were of stone, sombre and numerous with marble statues of former benefactors and heads of the school looking down from their pedestals. An imposing place, at first forbidding and awe-inspiring to Edward and William, and quite unlike their early places of learning in Guernsey. They were clothed, fed and issued with rough-textured rugby jerseys in the school colours of blue and yellow. William took to the game much more easily than Edward whose ankle injury, though healing, made him unable to run quickly.

But the one saving grace in their eyes was the swimming pool — the most modern aspect of the whole building. In it they could close their eyes and swim and imagine they were in the waters of Moulin Huet or Fermain.

Both lessons and pupils were strange at first to Edward and William. Their sudden uprooting from home and becoming strangers — foreigners in some eyes — made their ability to learn and adjust to the new life at Justs slower than it would otherwise have been.

All schools have bullies and Justs was no exception, Grestland being one of them. He had come across William rearranging things in his locker. One of William's possessions was a teddy bear which he had snatched up before the family's dash to the harbour — a mascot, and he'd had it since a small child. Grestland's jeers and those of his friends had been cruel and hurtful. Taunted, William reacted by lashing out at his tormentor. But he was no match for the bigger boy.

Edward came to William's defence and forced Grestland away. The bully turned on Edward who held his own for a while, but the injury to his foot made him less nimble, and unable to avoid every blow. The fight was stopped when a master appeared on the scene, and Edward was left with a sore and puffy face.

However, the matter did not end there because a few days later when Edward went for a swim in the early evening, he found Grestland there already in the water with one of his cronies. He stood up pushing the hair from his face, and Edward had seen enough to know that Grestland was a poor performer in water.

A truculent light sprang into the others eyes on seeing Edward. 'Look who's come for a swim — the little orphan from Guernsey. Have you got a teddy bear as well?' he sneered mimicking Edward's accent.

Edward walked down the few steps into the pool,

feeling sickened that Grestland should be there, but he had stood up for William and if at all possible that was going to be the end of the matter.

Grestland meant otherwise and pushed Edward on the chest who then fell backwards to sit in the water. That was a bad mistake.

The insults, the bruising still on his face and the attack on William fuelled Edward into a human torpedo intent on sinking Grestland. In a second he was underneath Grestland, had him by his legs and pulling him into the deeper end. Then he let go and Grestland came up gasping and looking around wildly for Edward. Again his legs went from under him and he thrashed about as Edward repeated the attack. Edward was in his element. How many times had he swum in the waters of Moulin Huet and Fermain around the rocks, developing the ability to hold his breath for long periods. His foot did not hurt in the pool, and Grestland's height and weight meant nothing now. Grestland tried to reach the shallow end, his efforts weakening fast, his arms slapping the water. Holding him Edward then swam to the steps where he dragged Grestland out and left him semi-conscious. And William and Edward were never bullied again.

Ruth had to wait another fortnight before she was moved elsewhere. It had been a lonely miserable time without the boys, but she kept hoping that perhaps a place would be found for her at the same school. To her dismay it was not to be. She was taken one Saturday morning — a grey drizzly day, and one which matched her spirits, to meet the Lowton family with whom she was going to live.

The Lowton family lived in a terraced house near town and consisted of Mr. Lowton, a thin balding man with eyes magnified by his spectacles, and his wife Janet, also lean, sallow and dark-haired, with an upper body which she held permanently bent forwards from the waist, giving her the perfect position for conversing with small children. Mr. Lowton it appeared had some disability which stopped him from serving in the armed forces. Instead he worked in engineering. They had one daughter Jean who was about Ruth's age, trim, neat-figured with sharp features and darting brown eyes under a copper canopy of hair. She went to a school in town which Ruth herself joined the following week.

It became quite obvious within a very short time of going to stay with the Lowtons that Jean resented the intrusion of Ruth into her family. Her memory was retentive, and everything that Ruth said in the course of conversation with her new family was immediately public knowledge at the school: one topic being that she still wrote letters home.

'Don't you know there's a war on?' some jeered.

Yes she did! Oh yes she did! Better than any of them. However, there were some with whom she was quite popular who liked her difference, and felt sorry for her at the predicament she found herself in.

The school itself was next to the main road, had a large playground and a covered cloister-like area beneath a section of the school for rainy days. Sometimes Ruth would sit on the damp bench, a lonely figure, and stare at the enclosing hills.

Once she went to the pictures with Jean and her father. During it the news showed a picture of the Channel Islands and the commentator's voice saying that German troops now occupied them. Ruth cried quietly in the darkness of the cinema and afterwards in her room. She prayed that her aunt and Mr. and Mrs. Dorner were all right.

Edward and William came to see her occasionally after she had written to them informing them where she was living. She always felt better for their visits, but parting always made her wish fervently that she could soon be transferred to be with them.

During the next week two incidents involving members of the Lowton family convinced Ruth that she would be much happier elsewhere, even if it was not to be with Edward and William.

Mr. Lowton was an air raid warden, and if the siren went during the night he went along the street knocking on doors and warning people. Ruth used to hear the drone of planes and then they would all troop down into the cellar and sit getting colder and colder until the all clear wailed again. Mr. Lowton appeared to feel very important in his uniform and helmet.

It was during one of these alerts that Ruth was startled by a dull thudding sound and a vibration that shook her bed as she sat on the edge of it. She heard voices and her door opened, and the dim light from the landing showed Mr. Lowton just inside her doorway.

'Are the planes about again, Mr. Lowton?' she asked.

He didn't answer at once but came to the bedside

and sat down beside her. 'Just one I think. You're not frightened are you Ruth? You mustn't be,' and his arm passed across her shoulders. 'I'll see you're all right.' His hand had tightened on Ruth's elbow, pulling her against him. 'I can make you happy here, Ruth, if you'll let me. You could be very happy here. I like you — we all like you.' His hand had moved to the top of her hip, his thumb in the crease of her thigh. His voice was very peculiar and Ruth was uneasy — it was all very strange suddenly.

'I like you very much. Let me carry you,' and his other hand had gone searching under her knee. 'I'll look after you.'

Ruth felt herself being lifted but Mr. Lowton did not stand up. Instead he rested her on his lap, his breath fanning her cheek.

'Think of me as your friend — your best friend.' His voice had become very hoarse. 'I'll be your daddy, you're a lovely girl.' One hand was cupping her cheek, her head being turned towards his face, and the light from the doorway caught his glasses, accentuating the feverish look behind them. To Ruth it was another bad dream like many others she'd had.

'You're not my daddy,' she cried out. 'Let me go, I want my aunt. Please let me go.' She struggled violently and slipped from his grasp to the floor, then dashed out and down the stairs, confused and frightened, not by the threat of bombers, but the one posed by Mr. Lowton and his desires.

The little fool, he thought, perhaps he'd been a bit hasty. Hoped she'd keep her mouth shut. She was well developed for her age, and walked like a young gazelle.

One day Ruth arrived at the Lowton house from school and as usual went straight up to her bedroom to deposit her school bag, have a wash and then join the family for tea downstairs. To her surprise Jean was just coming out of Ruth's room. She had something in her hand, and disappeared into her parent's bedroom. Ruth, looking after her saw her place something on the dressing table, then leave closing the door behind her.

'Jean, what have you taken from my room?'

'You'll see,' and off she went downstairs, glancing back when she reached the bottom and then disappearing from sight.

Ruth went quickly into her room, already guessing what had been taken. The Ormer shell had gone from its place by her bedside. Why had Jean taken it to her parent's bedroom? Just another stupid prank to annoy and irritate her? Glancing down the stairs Ruth saw there was no one about. If she could just slip into the bedroom and take the shell from its place on the Lowton's dressing table. Oh! how glad she would be to move elsewhere — some place where she could be friends with everyone.

She tiptoed towards the door, feeling awful, and pushed it open. The shell lay upwards, catching the light from the landing and showing up sharply against the dark wood on which it lay. With a gasp of relief Ruth picked it up and pushed it into her school bag and then turned to leave.

'What are you doing in our bedroom, Ruth?' Mr.

Lowton's voice made her jump. He was standing at the top of the stairs watching her.

'I — I've just been for my shell. It was in your room Mr. Lowton.'

'What on earth is a shell doing there? Who put it there?'

'Jean did.'

'I did not. She's lying again, Dad.' Jean's face appeared from behind her father as she craned from around the banister at the top of the stairs.

'I want to know, Ruth. What are you doing in our bedroom?' His tone had become angry.

Ruth shook her head in frustration and some fear. Oh what had happened to her world? If only she could wake up to find her aunt telling her she was late for school. Anything to break out of this alien world she found herself in.

'I'm telling the truth, Mr. Lowton. Please believe me. I only went in to get my shell. Look, I have it here. I've just put it into my bag,' and she brought it out, letting it lie in her hand.

'She always keeps it in there, Dad. She hasn't been in for that.'

Mr. Lowton advanced towards Ruth. 'Now, just what have you been doing in there?' Stood looking down on her. 'I can't understand it. We take you into our house, make you welcome and you repay us by sneaking about where you shouldn't be. You're becoming a bad influence. I'll have a word with the authorities.'

Ruth glimpsed again Jean's smirking features and realised that she had planned everything, had gone to tell her father, knowing that Ruth would attempt to retrieve the shell.

Father and daughter went downstairs, Mr. Lowton's voice fading. 'One thing I cannot stand is thieving . . . ' And there went a man who not so long before would have taken Ruth's young virginity from her without a second's remorse.

Two days later the morning recess at school found Ruth sitting in the gloom of the playground shelter. During the lesson earlier she had realised suddenly that it was her aunt's birthday and she couldn't see her to wish her many happy returns. She sighed, hunched and looking out on the noisy groups of children. She brought the Ormer shell which she now carried everywhere out of her pocket, a link with home and a reminder that she had indeed lived in happier days.

Suddenly she became aware of someone in front of her, the object snatched from her fingers, and Jean racing away with it around the playground, to twist in the centre of her friends and jeer. 'Look what I've got — Ruth Le Ney's shell — silly old shell. She takes it to bed with her. I've seen her and she talks to it. She's loony.' The others laughed with her.

Ruth ran after her. 'Please give it back to me, Jean, give it to me please. It means a lot to me — I've saved it.' She tried to snatch it back but Jean evaded her and darted away.

'It's only an old shell, why are you so bothered about it?'

'It's all I've got to remind me of home. Give it to me. It's only a shell — it's not worth anything.'

Jean moved towards the railings bordering the

playground and separating the latter from the main road. With a malicious look at Ruth she said, 'Oh well, if it's not worth anything I'm going to chuck it away — only a shell,' and she raised her arm to throw it into the road.

'No! — don't!' The words jerked from Ruth pleadingly.

But Jean was enjoying herself. 'If you want it come and get it,' she teased. 'I'm going to wait for a car. Your stupid shell will be smashed to smithereens.'

'No!' cried Ruth desperately and started towards her, hand outstretched, and Jean waited until Ruth was almost up to her then dashed away, only to collide heavily with another girl. Off balance, she staggered and Ruth, running hard unable to stop, knocked her against the railings. The shell dropped to the ground and Ruth swooped upon it, in utter relief that it was hers again.

Jean lay face twisted with pain and holding her arm. Someone fetched a teacher.

'It was Ruth Le Ney,' said Jean, her face screwed up as they led her away. 'She pushed me into the railings, Sir, I think my arm's broken. She did it on purpose.'

Ruth looked on aghast, unable to believe her ears. As a result of the incident she paid a visit the next day to the headmaster's study. With the headmaster was another man whom she recognised as Mr. Page who had interviewed Edward and William before they had been transferred to St. Justs. Mr. Bernett, the head, was an elderly well-meaning man with a distinct list to the right when walking, the result of years of carrying weighty educational tomes under his right arm. He had spoken only briefly to Ruth when he had welcomed her to the school. Ruth gave her version of what had occurred, and both men listened attentively.

Then Mr. Bernett said, 'You know that Jean's arm is broken, Ruth?'

She looked at them in dismay, fearing the worst.

'Well we believe it was not your fault. I understand that you were trying to retrieve something she had taken from you.'

Ruth sighed in relief. 'Yes Sir, I bumped into her and she fell.'

The head nodded. 'Yes, yes, there were witnesses. But what was it that she had taken from you?'

Ruth told them but did not say that she had the shell in her pocket; they may confiscate it. Mr. Bernett looked a little nonplussed at the importance she attached to the object.

'We know it must be very different for you, Ruth here, and also very difficult, but perhaps things will change for the better — for all of us.' He studied the young fair face with the frank summer-blue eyes. A damned shame for her, swept up on the tide of war and deposited on a foreign shore. He indicated his colleague. 'Mr. Page here would like to talk to you.'

'Are you happy where you are now living Ruth?' enquired Mr. Page.

Ruth hesitated. How could she be happy anywhere but home? Jean didn't like her — never had from the first day. And Mr. Lowton that night . . . His hands on her body. It had been a miserable time, lonely, sharing a home with strangers, then air raid drill to the shelters at school in those horrid gas masks, and lost in her attempt to catch up on her lessons.

'Just say yes or no.' The adult face in front of her had become sterner.

Ruth shook her head and whispered.

'And you definitely did not go into the Lowton's bedroom to steal anything?'

The eyes opposite told him the truth before the lips. 'Oh no! No I did not. Jean had hidden my shell in the bedroom. I just wanted it back, that's all.'

Mr. Page believed her. He'd been to see the Lowtons. Mr. Lowton had complained — a proper little Hitler. A uniform on and his self-importance came out. He nodded. 'All right Ruth,' then glanced at the headmaster. 'Well now, in view of what you've told us and what we know ourselves, we think it would be better for all concerned if you were transferred somewhere else.' He saw the instant apprehension his words had caused. 'Don't worry, it's obvious that you're not happy with the Lowtons, and perhaps a change of school also would help, though,' — he threw a smile at the headmaster, 'this is as fine a school as you would wish for. However,' Mr. Page went on 'there is now a vacancy at St. Justs and we have decided to place you there.'

Ruth could hardly keep still. 'You mean where Edward and William are, Sir?'

He smiled and nodded, gratified to see the happy response on the young face opposite. 'Yes, but you must settle down there and apply yourself to your lessons. You will live in of course.'

She would not mind that, just to be near Edward

and William again. 'D'you think,' she asked the adult figures across the table with a hopeful earnestness, 'that we'll be able to go home soon — Edward, William and myself?'

The headmaster and Mr. Page were both men who could lie if it was in a good cause, and the good cause stood innocently before them. A glance of collusion between them, and the head answered with a seriousness befitting the question. 'Yes, I do really believe that the way things are going it should not be too long before you can all go home to that lovely island of yours. From what I hear our forces are doing well.'

It was a different spirited girl that left them shortly afterwards, and as Mr. Page watched her leave the thought came that Ruth Le Ney could grow into quite a beauty. Apple and cream complexion, fair and lissom bodied, but very young for her age. He hoped that life did not hurt her too much, and shook his head pondering on the fact that the shell appeared to mean such a lot to her, but people clung to strange things sometimes for comfort.

3

As the spring and summer of another year came again, Ruth, Edward and William waited anxiously and expectantly for news of the liberation of their island. Some of the masters had radios and would from time to time inform them on how things were going in the war. Newspapers that came into school were eagerly scanned, but to the three exiles repatriation seemed a long way off. But the one even more important topic when the three met concerned their loved ones whom they had left behind. What were they doing? How were they faring under the rule of occupation by enemy forces? Each would try to guess what their relative would be doing at that precise moment. It was a way of keeping in touch; they didn't seem so far away.

'Aunt May will be making jam, or knitting or seeing Mrs. De Marre, and growing tomatoes,' Ruth guessed.

'Our mum,' said William, 'will be baking. I'd say some gauche. I like it when she puts in more raisins.'

'Dad will be painting the house ready for when the visitors start coming again,' Edward was sure. And they all agreed that was a nice thought.

'Wouldn't they be surprised to see us at this big school and all together,' said Ruth. What a lot they would have to tell them when they were back home.

A week later there was high excitement — a message from Ruth's Aunt May, via the Red Cross.

The message read, 'Overjoyed to hear from you. I'm well. We are coping. All love, Aunt May.' Ruth recalled that when she had first arrived at the school, the headmistress had promised to try and get word to Mrs. Le Ney through the organisation.

After the excitement the boys showed some disappointment and perplexity.

'They can only put so many words,' explained Ruth. 'Aunt May couldn't get a message from your parents on it.' She gazed at the brothers, felt sorry for them. She'd had a message addressed to her, they had not. Tried to cheer them up. 'Look, Aunty May's put 'we are coping.' She's meant to include your mum and dad. That's how she's done it. The three gazed with both fascination and fear at the message with the German authority stamp upon it.

'Well,' said William, 'at least Ruthie's aunt got a message out.' His face had brightened.

'Yes, mum and dad will probably send the next one,' said Edward hopefully but unlike his brother his frown remained.

Time went by and still there was no news of the war coming to an end. For Ruth, Edward and William the school was home and the focal point of their lives. William, while not the quickest in the classroom, was turning into a fine young sportsman, playing rugby for the school junior team, enjoyed a game of fives, and was quite good at tennis. He appeared to be taking to his new life easily and was well liked in his class. He was also becoming popular with the girls, and on occasions when the sexes met he was never short of their company. He was growing taller, almost Edward's height, auburn haired with grey-blue eyes which were becoming more roguish by the month and a smile that could flash on and off like a lamp. If there was a fashion in the limited sartorial scope of the school, William would attempt it, be it a scarf worn a certain fashion, tie tied differently, or a blazer slung an alternative way.

Edward, on the other hand, made steady progress with school work but was handicapped by the ankle injury he sustained in the bombing of the harbour. He could not run very well, so that ball games were difficult for him, but he continued with his beloved swimming and was as happy as could be in the circumstances. At times though he was lost in thoughts about Guernsey and everything he had left behind.

Sometimes in the better weather Ruth would play tennis with Edward on the courts which were sheltered by shrubbery and trees from the main building. Edward was slow around the court, but Ruth was happy just to be with him. He remained as he had always been, her favourite of the brothers. She felt awful if she saw him talking to other girls. Hadn't she known him so very much longer than they? A childhood bond between them as they had grown up. At the school dance Edward took her rather awkwardly around the floor once, the music stopped and the announcement was made that the dance was now an 'excuse me.' The music recommenced and she and Edward began dancing again. Then a pat came on her shoulder, and a girl from her form claimed Edward. Ruth hesitated.

'Come on Ruth, move over, it's an excuse me, didn't you know?'

William going by joined in, 'Ruthie, share him — give the others a chance. You can't hang on to him for ever,' and off they drifted laughing.

Ruth sat out watching Edward and the girl continue with the dance, the serpent of jealousy already beginning to stir itself within her young mind. She was thankful when after that particular quickstep Edward left his partner to join her again. He had always a slightly protective air in his relationship with her and would not leave her to sit by herself.

The boys liked her she thought, but she knew she had the reputation of being a bit 'proper' — rather stand-offish, as one form-mate had remarked. Ruth did not care — just waiting for the day when she, Edward and William would go back to Guernsey, carry on life where they had left off. She and Edward would get married. This was just an interlude, but sometimes Ruth deluded herself into not realising what a long interlude it was becoming. Too long in fact for them to slip back into their former life. They had changed — all three — and were continuing to do so.

That night after the dance she lingered with Edward a while. He was quiet, being no chatterbox, but she didn't mind. William was not to be seen and she presumed he had also left for bed, or more likely was in a corridor with some girl. Ruth was tired and after parting from Edward was soon in bed, the other girls drifting in shortly afterwards. Amongst them was Wanda, the girl William had danced with mostly. She seemed to take a long time to get ready for bed and seemed nervous about something. Then after Matron had done her rounds, all the lights with the exception of a dim one at the dormitory entrance, were extinguished. For a while there was talk about the evening which meant about the boys, then the room fell silent.

Now that she was in bed Ruth found it difficult to sleep. She slammed her pillow several times and lay this way and that, but then surrendered to the fact that sleep would come when it wished and not before. Some of the tunes played for the dance came into her mind. Some day she must play them on the piano — Stardust, Deep Purple and Glen Miller melodies.

Ruth's bed was sixth on the right hand side from the doorway. Beyond her pillow the rows of beds with the curves and outlines of her form-mates. Her eyes closed. Some time later she awakened. How long she had slept she had no idea. Aware of movement from Wanda's bed, the girl who had monopolised William for most of the evening. The movement was regular and the bedclothes seemed to stand high from the mattress, a strange horizontal to-ing and fro-ing of white in the semi-darkness. Perhaps Wanda was having a nightmare — she seemed to be breathing heavily. As Ruth watched, the continuous motion of the clothes stopped and the tent-like erection subsided. Wanda's coverings were flatter but odd in their outline. Ruth sighed and sat up. Two of them couldn't sleep. She decided to go to the bathroom, and if Wanda was awake, commiserate with her.

Making for the dormitory door Ruth approached Wanda's bed. The soles of two feet projected upwards from beneath the clothes at the bottom of the bed, agitated feet scrabbling for a hold as if climbing a slippery hill. Ruth paused, bent forward towards the pillow, and said in just above a whisper, 'Wanda, it's Ruth, I can't sleep either.'

The shocked face of Wanda suddenly shot up from somewhere below the edge of the sheet. All movement had ceased abruptly and the bedclothes had settled into an untidy rather thick mass running down the centre of the bed.

Ruth's face became suddenly no less shocked. A darker head was visible by the side of Wanda's. A boy's head! The head turned and Ruth recognised the face. It was William!

'Don't say anything Ruthie — don't tell please,' he pleaded, looking up at her from the shelter of the sheet. 'If I'm found out I'm for the high jump.'

Ruth turned away, bathroom forgotten, towards her own bed. 'No — I — I won't, William but you shouldn't be in here.'

'Thanks Ruthie.'

She was aware out of the corner of her eye of his figure disappearing through the door, shoes in hand. Embarrassed and annoyed she lay thinking, even more awake. That idiot William. If he had been caught by staff he would have been expelled from the school she was sure. And Edward would have been mad with William. He always tried to make sure that William was all right, very much the older brother even if only by a year. As for Wanda, she was stupid and boy mad. Certainly expulsion would have been her fate also.

In some ways she didn't fully understand the discovery altered her relationship with William. Always he had been the younger brother, but he had been just that, Edward's younger brother — young William who always called her Ruthie. Now he was a youth, had been in bed with a girl, and young William didn't seem to fit him any more. But supposing it had been Edward instead of William in that bed. Ruth felt sick at the thought. Edward was quieter, and trying she knew to make the best of his education there. When they were alone he used to tell her of his ideas for when he returned to Guernsey and the hotel. He would draw sketches of alterations to the rooms and how he would discuss them with his father. He thought he would quite like going into the hotel and holiday business. Perhaps he could work for his parents — help them.

It always cheered her to talk with Edward on such topics, and gave her renewed hope that it wouldn't be long before peace was declared. Then perhaps marriage, and she would be at his side to help with his plans. How wonderful it would be.

A few days later she saw William. He was watching her playing a netball game and afterwards he spoke to her. He seemed rather anxious. 'Ruthie, you haven't said anything to Edward about the other night, have you?'

'No, it's your affair, but you're stupid, William. If you'd been found out.' She shook her head admonishingly. 'They're pretty strict on that sort of thing. We've got to be careful, William. We don't want to be separated again. Anyway Wanda's boy struck.'

William nodded then said nonchalantly, 'Well I've finished with her.' He seemed quite unconcerned about the incident and flashed a smile. 'But thanks again, Ruthie, I'll do the same for you some time,' and he turned to go.

'How are you doing with your lessons?' she asked after him.

He half turned and made a grimace and shrugged. 'Oh they're a bore, Ruthie, I get fed up with them, I'll be glad when I leave school.'

'But what will you do?'

'Oh I'll find something,' and off he went, leaving Ruth rather troubled. She herself had not found the academic side of the school easy, but she had stuck at it and was relieved at being told that she could stay on at the school to take further examinations in music. Her fear had been that she would have to find work in Daleford.

But William would have to leave school when he was sixteen if the war went on, and she knew Edward liked to have him around. 'Mum and dad will be mad if I didn't look after him,' he had said often. Poor Edward she thought, always having to keep an eye on someone. She remembered vividly his body shielding hers on the quayside from the bombs. Now that she was older and looking back, she realised his action had been a very brave one. And nearly four years had passed since then. She would be seventeen in a few days and the boys always made sure that she had a card and a small present from the pocket money they were allowed, and she did the same for them, getting the school cook to make a cake for each when it was their birthday. Her feelings for Edward had not altered. He was the one boy in her life, and her heart twisted in anguish if he even spent a short time in the company of another girl.

Ruth had her photograph taken on her birthday, and together with the boys had tea in the town and saw a film. The news beforehand showed the progress of the war, with British bombers striking back at the enemy homeland. The desert victory earlier had also signalled better things to come, and the three returned to the school more optimistic than they had been for a long time.

She now had her own small room and in its privacy one day she compared the school photograph of herself soon after her arrival with the one taken on her seventeenth birthday. The earlier with its anxious and tense face, sitting cross-legged with a lot of strangers, the future unknown and forbidding. The recent one showed a young lady with a smile which, whilst not wholly free of apprehension, signified that its owner had come to terms with some of that unknown and was better able to face the near future.

June 1944 came and the whole school buzzed with the news of the invasion of occupied Europe by allied forces. Anyone with a radio was immediately in great demand, and staff passed on the latest news to the classrooms. The head made a special announcement to the whole school and declared a half day off for everyone

In high excitement Edward, William and Ruth

discussed the matter. Was it possible that in a short time they would be back in Guernsey? A bottle of home made elderberry wine — a by-product of Ruth's taking of a cookery course — was shared between them and they got slightly drunk.

'I'll make another bottle to drink the night before we go home,' she promised.

They hugged each other, and Edward responded to her by giving her a kiss and holding her around the shoulders as he said, 'You've been great Ruth. It was bad luck that you got caught up in this but you've stuck it out with us. We couldn't have managed without you.' Then he sat down, obviously surprised at his loquacity and spontaneous championing of her.

For Ruth it was an afternoon of as near happiness as was possible in the circumstances. The possibility of the island being reclaimed and the feel of Edward's lips on hers, albeit momentarily, and his arm around her created this emotion. The elderberry wine had been good, very good, and under its influence she was certain that she and Edward had an understanding. It was unspoken of course, but it was there she was sure — had always been.

Later she played a selection of tunes from the musical shows and the boys sang to them, and William's voice cracked once. Edward's had broken some time before, but had not yet settled to the light baritone it was to become. In the end they all lost the ability to say anything of consequence and Ruth laughed so much that she couldn't concentrate on finding the right keys.

But then the school settled into a routine again, and the weeks went by with no more news regarding the possibility of the Channel Islands being liberated soon.

It was about this time that a new teacher — a woman in her late twenties — arrived at the school to teach natural history and biology amongst other things. Her duties involved teaching the boys as well as the girls in those subjects and she was the first woman to be employed in the boy's section.

William from his desk looked at Mrs. Thurrocks with interest. She was talking about plants and illustrating one on the blackboard. He wasn't particularly interested in the subject, or for that matter any classroom subject in the school curriculum. He got through but only just, and had found it hard work. Edward was in the form above, was older, but he seemed to find the lessons easier than he, William did. Perhaps soon they could finish with all this and go home. His eyes followed the stretching of Mrs. Thurrocks dress over her buttocks and thighs as she drew upon the board, and then focused on the vee between the rounded part of her hips. When she sat down at her desk he could see the full long curve of the back of her left thigh as it lay across the other. William just raised his stare in time. She must have thought he was puzzling over the subject on the board.

'Something you don't understand, Dorner?'

William hesitated, rather caught off guard. If he told the truth, he didn't understand any of it.

Mrs. Thurrocks came and leaned over him at this side. 'It's William isn't it?'

'Yes, Miss.' Her shoulder was close to his face, and he could smell the perspiration from her armpit.

'It's the photosynthesis, that's the problem is it?'

He might as well agree and nodded. She had rather pale blue eyes he'd noticed, and they had a staring quality about them, and her mousy hair was tied by a black ribbon at the back. Her left hand rested on the desk, and he saw the gold ring. His mother had one like that — a wedding ring.

'Well, just memorise, William,' said Mrs. Thurrocks, 'what is on the board.' She looked down into his face. 'The plant has to feed like all of us have, William.' Her hand passed along his right shoulder with a slight but steady pressure then slid gently off his left, an exploratory gesture if he had realised it then.

In the next weeks he was to realise also that she was paying more attention to him than to the others in that particular class, spending more time in explanation and correction of his work. William did his best to concentrate on the subject, but his concentration lapsed within five minutes of Mrs. Thurrocks entering the classroom. He thought about her at night when he was in bed, and once he dreamed about her. He was on horseback riding through a wood. The horse was a mousy colour and moving easily and gently along. Suddenly it began to buck and rear and race along, William clinging on for dear life with legs and hands. Then the horse stopped abruptly and turned its head and he found himself looking into the mocking face of Mrs. Thurrocks as he sat upon her naked back.

The image of his dream was still strong in his mind when he took his place next day in the classroom. A kneeling Mrs. Thurrocks — on all fours. He could imagine . . . The chalk moved across the blackboard and William turned the pages of his notebook and began to sketch what he thought he saw. Almost without realising it over the last year he had developed a liking and ability for sketching — quick, urgent pen or pencil outlines of anything that took his fancy. And without doubt Mrs. Thurrocks had taken his youthful one.

'William.' Her voice made him start. She was standing at his shoulder looking down at the page of sketches. There was no time to flick the page over back to the notes on natural history. His face became furnace red in seconds, his body rigid with embarrassment.

'I don't think you've really come to grips with the subject this morning, William. I think it might be better if you stayed behind for extra tuition some time, don't you?'

He glanced sideways in the direction of her waist. 'Yes, Miss — I — I suppose so.'

'Well we'll have to arrange something then, won't we?' Her voice was just a little different from normal — rather husky. Her third finger rested momentarily on his sketch of a kneeling woman, and just below the one sitting cross-legged at the desk naked. 'Your diagrammatic work is quite good,' she threw over her shoulder as she moved away.

William sank inside himself in relief. She hadn't given him away. What an ass he would have appeared. After the lesson he made his way out quickly in the general rush to the door. She must think him a real idiot — a silly youth with a crush on his teacher, and drawing indecent pictures. She would know what he was thinking each time she took the class.

Occasionally the form would go into the nearby woods for a practical lesson, and on one such day the form made its way into the woods.

It was early September and very warm, with wasps doing their dance on the backs of large blackberries. William noticed that Mrs. Thurrocks was wearing a green and white thin short-sleeved dress with grey buttons down its front, which he liked. She had rather a large nose, and had a brown mole on her left cheek. She was not pretty like Ruth, William decided, but Ruthie was a friend more like a sister.

The class was a noisy party as it made its way slowly through the woods. About a third were interested in the subject. For the others including himself it was an afternoon away from the school. They halted near a clearing and Mrs. Thurrocks addressed them.

'Those of you taking natural history as a subject in your coming examinations had better pay attention because in the examination you'll be on your own. I shall not be there to give you the answers. Now take your note-books because for your homework next week I want a detailed diagram of the common fern and an essay on its life history and how it relates to its surroundings.'

There were groans from a few, including William. What on earth he was going to do in the examination he just did not know.

'You may split up into groups if that will help,' said Mrs. Thurrocks.

The form drifted apart, William knowing that some would find a quiet spot and share cigarettes or just lay about. About half a dozen remained with their form mistress, she leading them to a shaded spot overhung by trees and thick with ferns.

William held his notebook open but he wasn't listening. He was busy watching Mrs. Thurrocks. Once she turned and caught him staring. She didn't say anything, but carried on with the lesson. A few minutes later she announced a short break during which they could catch up on their notes 'and' — shooting a glance at him — 'for those who have not made any so far, whilst I see how the others are getting on.'

William saw the wasp as it settled on her neck. Mrs. Thurrocks gave a startled cry and knocked it off, then backed away as it flew straight towards her again. She staggered and would have fallen had not William caught her round the shoulders and waist just before she hit the ground. For a second he held her and brought her upright, her full weight in his grasp. Not Mrs. Thurrocks the teacher, but a woman frightened for the moment and looking up at him wide-eyed. She felt like a warm pliable cushion in his arms. He caught a glimpse of her thigh as her dress rucked up above one knee. He didn't want to let her go, keeping hold until she was upright again, his fingers letting go of her arms only at the very last moment.

'Thank you, Dorner.' Her hands fluttered over her

dress, straightening it. 'They're such vicious things, I don't like them.' She didn't look at him and soon afterwards the class made its way back to the school, a medium-sized woman accompanied by gangling uniformed youths.

William followed, unable to take his eyes off her movements, remembering the all too brief pleasure of holding her. Not like Wanda — different — a full grown woman. He'd held a full grown woman for the first time. She had stumbled into his arms, no one else's, and he watched her hips and remembered his dream.

For the next few days he was plagued by the tangle of a young man's emotions. The touch of Mrs. Thurrocks had set the fire going. Morose one day, another filled with the hope that something would occur to propel Mrs. Thurrocks into his arms again. He snapped at Edward and was quiet with Ruth.

'Don't worry William,' Edward had consoled him. 'Things are going well in Europe. It won't be long before it's all over.'

But he couldn't tell Edward that that wasn't the cause of his moods. Of course he couldn't wait to get back to Guernsey, but his immediate concern was in the shape of his natural history teacher.

The following week as he was filing out with the rest of the class Mrs. Thurrocks called to him, 'Dorner, just a moment. I want to arrange some extra tuition for you regarding your practical work.'

The voices and footsteps faded away in the corridor outside. Mrs. Thurrocks remained seated at her desk playing with a pen in her fingers, letting its point bounce up and down on to the blotter above her books. She did not look at him and seemed hesitant to speak. He noticed the brown slide to keep her hair back over her left ear.

'Now William,' she began, 'I believe I mentioned, er, some more practical study for you,' her pen point dropped again, 'field work.' Her left hand fingered her forehead, hiding part of her face from him. 'I think I can spare some time — er next Saturday — the afternoon, perhaps an hour.' She paused. 'I do think that — well — it could be for your benefit.' Suddenly she glanced up at him, then away. 'But of course it's your day off.' She laughed, a short rather desperate sound. 'I don't suppose you'd care to do natural history then — out of school hours sort of thing.'

William tried to shake and nod his head simultaneously. 'Yes — no, I don't mind at all. I — I know it's my weakest subject. I wouldn't be doing anything special anyway.' The words fell out of his mouth. He was going to be alone with her, even if it was only to poke about in the undergrowth for some rotten plants. An excitement flooded through him, controlled him, masking his earlier surprise at how different she sounded and behaved when not actually teaching the form.

Mrs. Thurrocks continued to look at her desk top, the backs of her fingers moving restlessly across her lips. She spoke jerkily through them, 'Oh — oh well then, that's fine, William. Of course I cannot be seen alone with you near the school.' Her expression became anxious. 'It will be out of hours and no one must know about it. You mustn't say anything to anyone.'

'I won't — I certainly won't, Mrs. Thurrocks.'

'You see I — I haven't the time to spare for everyone.'

'It's very good of you Mrs. Thurrocks. Don't worry, I won't say a thing.' His pulse was reaching new speeds.

'So I shall meet you where class was held last week. There's a large rock nearby. Do you remember?'

Did he remember! He had held her momentarily and had relived the experience again and again in his imagination. He'd find it all right.

'About three o'clock then, I think an hour will be sufficient.' He had difficulty in catching her lowered voice. He paused, not sure whether she had finished with him.

'If I get there first, I'll look out for you, what I mean . . .'

Mrs. Thurrocks looked at him fully. 'You mean what shall I be wearing?' A gleam of humour suddenly appeared in the eyes of his teacher. 'What colour d'you like, William?'

New courage rushed him along and he blurted, 'I liked the green and white one you had on the other day, Miss.'

Her teeth showed between Mrs. Thurrocks' lips. 'The one with the buttons down the front?'

He nodded, finding it an effort to speak, remembering how he had wanted to undo them so much.

'All right. Now I must get on, William.'

In a daze William found the door, then glanced

back to see Mrs. Thurrocks with her head in her hands.

William's daze continued the remainder of the week. He would remember nothing of her lesson he was sure. Natural history — natural woman preferably. What his class mates would think if they knew!

He refused Edward's offer to accompany him and Ruth for tea and pictures in Daleford that coming Saturday, making the excuse that he was going to discuss the next rugby season with others of the team.

He knew Ruth wouldn't mind, she liked to have Edward to herself. Funny chap, Edward, he admired him, but William doubted whether Edward would have noticed Mrs. Thurrocks' body. He was too busy always planning what he was going to do back in Guernsey, and had great plans to help their father put the hotel more in the public eye, having read somewhere that the island after the war would see an upsurge in tourism.

On the following Saturday Mrs. Thurrocks filled William's mind as he made his way to their meeting place. There was no sign of her and he stood by the rock she had mentioned. It was a warm afternoon beneath the sullen clouds, and almost three o'clock by his watch — an article which William cherished — bought by Ruth and Edward for his last birthday. His heart was pounding, mouth dry, the excitement at waiting for her to appear brought with it a strange relief that she had not. He rested his notebook on the flat surface of the rock and stared between the branches of the trees, the high ferns and foliage making their venue well hidden.

Then he saw her making her way carefully down over the springy hillocks towards him. She was serious-faced and entered the tiny clearing slowly.

'Thought I was going to be late, just had a few things to do,' she said shortly. A quick thin smile appeared and she took a step towards him, giving a sweeping glance around her. He saw that she was wearing a fawn raincoat open to reveal the green and white dress with a white belt around her waist.

William was pleased. It gave him a peculiar feeling that she should have done that for him.

'I see you've got your notebook,' she observed, then hesitated. 'I think it might be as well if I went individually through the plants we studied here last week.' Her manner was uneasy, unsure.

For the next quarter of an hour Mrs. Thurrocks pulled and pushed aside the undergrowth to reveal the objects of the private lesson. A succession of things came from her hands to his as she expounded and explained. Sometimes she stumbled over her words and didn't look him in the face very often.

William noticed her hands — small, podgy, with a ring on the left hand. He noticed other things as he stood by awkwardly. The shape and contours of her body as she leaned this way and that, and once knelt down and stretched to reach something. Again he was reminded of his dream. How could he concentrate and make notes? He did his best but he knew it was rubbish, his intellect dimmed by the presence of Mrs. Thurrocks, but he was careful to make a show of interest in what she was saying, bringing his eyes quickly to her face when on the rare occasions she looked directly at him.

He was greatly relieved when she said, 'I think we'll have a rest for a few minutes, William.' She had been different, irritable and brusque with him, and if he had not just understood immediately, frowning and biting her lip. He began to wish that he had not come. He had done so only because of her. She had been much nicer to him in the classroom. He felt awkward and stood watching as she took the raincoat off, saw the rise of her breasts as she shrugged it off.

Mrs. Thurrocks dropped her raincoat on the grass, smoothed the material and then sat down upon it, and leaned back upon her hands. 'Come and sit down, William.' It was the voice of a teacher to a rather difficult pupil.

William lowered himself to sit on the ground at the very edge of the garment, noticing the shallow valley her dress made over her thighs, and the swell of flesh below her belt.

'I believe you had to leave the Channel Islands very quickly, William.' Her statement surprised him.

'Er, yes, we had to — very quickly.' It seemed so long ago.

'And your brother — isn't he in the sixth?'

'Yes, Edward.' He felt he ought to say something more. 'And Ruthie came with us.' Saw the slight frown. 'Ruth Le Ney — a friend of ours.'

'Oh yes, I know her.'

William relaxed a little. It was better than making notes on bloody natural history, and over the next few minutes he told Mrs. Thurrocks briefly what had happened to them and how they had arrived in

England. When he had finished their eyes met and held for the first time that afternoon.

'It must have been very difficult for you, William. I'm not surprised you had a lot to catch up on.' Her voice had become softer. Suddenly she appeared to notice that he was not sharing the raincoat with her and touched it. 'Sit here, William, not on the grass. I don't want you to be stung by a wasp.'

William hitched himself on to the garment, conscious of her closeness.

'I did rather make a spectacle of myself last week, but I've always been frightened of wasps,' his companion confided. 'I was rather silly,' and she gave a short nervous laugh, a tense sound in the quiet of the glade. 'But I'm glad you were there to catch me.'

'Well, you might have hurt yourself.' The sudden change in her manner towards him was surprising.

She was silent a short while, then her next question caught him completely unawares. 'Why did you come here today, William?' Her voice was thin and husky like it had been when she had called him back after class and they had discussed extra tuition.

William pulled at a clump of grass, breaking off a few blades. What a strange afternoon it was becoming. 'Well, to brush up on my natural history, I suppose, Mrs. Thurrocks.'

'My name's Celia — call me Celia, William.' Her eyes were sidelong at him, and they had a peculiar light to them. 'You asked me to wear this dress — d'you like it?'

'Yes.' Things were happening to him. He didn't seem to have much control over his thoughts.

'And me — d'you like me?' She was now leaning on one elbow turned towards him. He wasn't aware of having seen her move.

William was confused. The swift change in her conversation, the sketches, his desires, the woman almost touching him. Reality and imagination were blending. He nodded and his voice was difficult to manipulate. 'Yes, I do.' Liked her body anyway; he'd thought about it enough.

'I've seen you staring at me, William.' Her tongue showed, moistening her lips.

William turned towards her, stretching out his legs. His body had grown — he couldn't help it. Mrs. Thurrocks had disappeared and in her place was a woman now half lying on her back — a woman called Celia. She was tugging at something on her left hand. It came off and she sighed deeply, a sound of resignation.

'Have you done any more sketches of me, William?' She didn't wait for his answer but continued in a breathless way. 'They were quite artistic and realistic. Did you know that?'

William didn't care. He mumbled something incoherent and incomprehensible, seeing the round of her breasts beneath the grey buttons and aware that she had raised her left knee, her forefoot toying with the ground. The dress slipped back, revealing her thigh. Her back was almost flat to the ground. As if drawn by a magnet William edged against her. Heard the sharp intake of breath. Her voice was almost inaudible.

'Now William here I am. You don't have to imagine any more. Touch me.'

His hand was already on the velvet flesh. Mrs. Thurrocks shuddered and whether by accident or design brushed the opening of his trousers as she raised her hands to let them lie palm upwards behind her head.

A fever held William. His hands wanted a thousand fingers to possess her at once. He was youthful, impatient and potent. The firm, shallow and closed valley between her thighs of a few minutes before had now become a wide, high, soft-sided gorge into which he fell eagerly. As in his dreams her breasts like the pommel of a saddle. He was clumsy and fumbling in his blind desire. She swallowed him, pain, surprise and pleasure showing above the clenched teeth. With each of his thrusts she gave a high-pitched cry.

What was left of William's intellect ticked over slowly. Mrs. Thurrocks — Celia — his teacher. Like a green and white moth pinned to the ground. She of the magnificent thighs and hips. Sat at the desk. Put chalk on the blackboard. Gave him homework. His passion increased, driving her in short violent movements over her raincoat until the ferns dangled over and stroked her throat and head.

Something caught his eye in her half closed right hand. It was a ring, she had worn it earlier. His mind went blank again under her urgent movements. But his ecstasy was all too brief and the ferns shook again in short spasms and then were still.

They sat apart silently, William feeling just as awkward now as he had done before he had made love to her. He glanced over at her, seeing the ring shining again on her finger. Why had she taken it off? She had also put on her raincoat and drawn it around her knees, her hands up to her face. A peculiar woman, he thought. Before she had made him feel king of the world. Now he felt miserable — cut off from her. He didn't know what to say, saw her shoulders moving and realised she was crying. Trying to understand he placed an arm across them. 'What's the matter Celia?' He found it hard to call her by her first name. In the aftermath of their passionate lovemaking she had reverted in his mind to Mrs. Thurrocks.

She did not answer or look up.

'Celia,' he tried again.

'Get away from me Dorner, don't touch me,' and she wriggled her upper body to shake him off. 'You wouldn't understand what's the matter,' said his companion fiercely into her hands. 'You're still a boy.'

William, shocked at the sudden change of manner towards him, gazed miserably out beyond the enclosing trees. 'What have I done?' then turned to look at her. 'I didn't mean to do that, just couldn't help myself. I'm very sorry.'

'No!' The sound was sharp in the quiet of the woods, 'there's nothing to be sorry about.'

William was at a loss. 'I just can't understand what . . . '

'Of course you cannot,' Mrs. Thurrocks snapped, raising wet eyes to him briefly, 'I don't expect you to.' She was hunched up, hair bedraggled and the limbs that had tortured William's brain into wild desire were now hidden in the folds of her raincoat.

It was all so unexpected. 'I don't want you to be

upset, Mrs. Thurrocks.' Her surname came out automatically.

'It's not your fault, William — it's mine,' she murmured angrily through tears, then gathered herself enough to go on. 'I'm ashamed, William — ashamed. I'm a married woman.' She thrust her hand in his direction. 'See! — the ring — my wedding ring.'

William remembered she had taken it off before they had made love. He hadn't thought of her as a married woman with a husband. Nobody in the school had ever seen him.

A sudden anxiety took William. He hoped she wouldn't say anything about that afternoon. 'Your husband — is he in Daleford, Mrs. Thurrocks?'

The latter looked at him from between her fingers and gave a bitter laugh. 'Don't worry, William, he's a long way away — captured early in the war — he's in a prison camp.' She sat upright, dabbed her eyes and pushed at her hair and sighed. 'We were married just before he left for overseas.' The handkerchief moved to her nose and she looked at William over its folds. 'I've been weak, very weak. I just couldn't fight it any longer.' Her eyes had softened. 'Don't worry, William, if it hadn't been you it might have been someone else.' Then to William's surprise she leaned nearer to him and brought his head down to hers and kissed him full on the lips. Then tenderly she murmured, 'But I'm glad it was you, William, and it was better than natural history wasn't it?' To which William had to agree entirely.

Straightening her clothes she stood up facing him

with red and suddenly worried eyes. 'William, no one must know about this. If Harry found out it would kill him, and I should lose my job.'

William was sure he wouldn't tell. It had been an emotional, confusing afternoon, but an experience that he would not forget as long as he lived.

'We must not meet again, William. It's not right and I've never done anything like this before.' She finished fastening her raincoat. 'And I'm at least ten years older than you are.'

William's spirits dropped. 'Couldn't we just come for a walk?' he suggested without much conviction.

'William, that's rather naïve of you,' and Mrs. Thurrock's voice had just a little of the classroom about it. She shook her head firmly. 'You'll find other girls — you're very attractive. I'm sorry.' Reaching up she placed a kiss upon his cheek and added, 'I'm a married woman. I must not forget that — ever.' Then with a squeeze of his arm she left him and he gazed after her until she disappeared from sight.

He followed her about five minutes later, despondent and drained, but not before he had glanced back and seen again where Mrs. Thurrock's heels had grooved furrows in the autumn earth.

But Mrs. Celia Thurrocks did forget that she was a married woman several times during the following weeks, always outside and away from her home.

As a result William's marks for natural history and other subjects taught by her continued to improve by the month. He also continued to sketch quite proficiently — his drawings becoming extremely erotic. And Celia sat at her desk and moved in front of the blackboard, glowing with the knowledge that she was the model. And for future outside lessons the class, whether they realised it or not, never revisited the quiet place with its ferns and rock.

No one in William's form, least of all his teacher of French — Mr. Heslop, would say that William had a good knowledge of that language.

'You really must get down to the subject this term, Dorner. The examination will be coming up early next year and much more effort is required if you're going to get anywhere near the required standard.' Mr. Heslop was a bachelor of about forty — small, dark-haired, a man who knew his subject but lacked the essential ability to control the class, he had also an unusual hobby which kept him outdoors during his free time when he was not teaching.

William was to find out exactly what it was.

One Sunday he, Edward and Ruth went for a walk. It was a pleasant day, mellow, and perhaps one of the last warm and sunny days before the weather turned for the worse as it did usually very early in that northern clime. Ruth had borrowed a camera from one of her friends, and William took a photograph of her and Edward together. Later, on the way back through the woods, Ruth said why didn't they stop for a while and rest, but what she actually meant, William knew, was to prolong her time with Edward for as long as possible. He left them together and continued slowly upwards. They would catch up with him later. Something moving to his right above a mossy bank caught his eye. It was a man, and William stared as the figure moved stealthily towards some bushes, creeping on hands and knees. He was almost in full view to William and the latter could hardly believe his eyes. It was Mr. Heslop, his French master. What on earth was he doing crawling about in the woods?

William saw something pale beyond the foliage, and edged his way until he was close enough to be able to see what his French teacher was so interested in. It was a couple, bare from their waists down. He was shocked at the look of Mr. Heslop's face. The staring eyes, the tongue showing, the features transfixed and quite unlike the person he presented to his class. A peeping tom! William had seen him often in the vicinity of the woods. Now he knew why.

Then William remembered the camera he was carrying. He still had it after taking a shot of Ruth and Edward earlier. On the spur of the moment he took a picture of Mr. Heslop with the couple in view. Then he stole away feeling guilty of committing the same crime as his teacher.

William did not mention his discovery to Ruth and Edward, but as soon as they were back in school he made straight for the chemistry laboratory to get the photographs developed. It was one particular shot that William was interested in seeing, and his science teacher would have been very surprised to see the care and application that William applied to the task.

Ruth and Edward, particularly Ruth, were pleased at the photographs showing them together. But then so was William with his which remained hidden until one day the following week. He had had a bad week academically speaking. Mr. Heslop, particularly, had been insistent that more revision was required. So William had, rather to his French master's surprise, asked to see him to discuss the matter.

William made his way to Mr. Heslop's study, realising that he had not made the progress at the school that he should have. Most lessons had been difficult for him, apart from his art work, about which some of the staff had been scathing.

'No prospects in art, Dorner. Learn something with a little more substance to it. Art will not get you far. You ought to be preparing for a proper job when you leave here.'

William's mind returned quickly to the present, his fingers touching the photograph in his pocket. Drastic measures were called to aid him in what was left of his time at Justs. He sat facing Mr. Heslop nervously. The latter looked quite normal and sat as usual with one shoulder leaning in front of the other as if he had edged through life. William, perhaps unkindly, thought it more likely to have been from his stealthy sorties amongst the bushes.

'Now Dorner, I believe you've come to see me about the miserable state of your French.' His tone was sympathetic; he wasn't a hard man.

'Yes — yes I have. I really could do with some help.'

Mr. Heslop looked pleased. 'That's encouraging. It's the first step on the ladder when you seek help — shows you want to make progress.' He gazed pleasantly at William from behind his glasses. 'You see Dorner, language can be beautiful and French is no exception. There's beauty in everything.'

William wondered if that included a couple making love in the woods.

Mr. Heslop continued. 'You know Dorner, the French language should come easily to you, born in the Channel Islands.'

'I suppose so Sir.' Guernsey and his parents seemed a long way away, and also a long time ago. He hoped they were all right.

Mr. Heslop was studying him. 'You don't seem sure, Dorner. Would you yourself like to suggest how I can help you? Perhaps we can further fire your new enthusiasm in that way.'

William had known it wasn't going to be easy, but now the moment had come it was almost impossible for him to say that which he had decided on — almost. But then he thought of Edward's scholastic career so far. Not brilliant but streets ahead of his own effort. And Ruthie, although she was older by two years, she had made her mark in music, and she was also quite good in some other subjects. He must have something to show for his time at school. This could be his last year there, and if the war did not end soon he would have to find work in Daleford. He didn't want any menial job — it must be well paid. Fleeting courage came with that spur.

'Sir, I know I'm not going to learn enough in time to get me through — it's hopeless — I know it. I — I just wondered if there was some way my marks could be higher — sort of make things look better for me.'

'The only way you're going to get higher marks,

Dorner, is when your work is of a higher standard. That must be obvious.' Mr. Heslop's tone was matter of fact and dismissive.

'I have some sketches, Sir. You'd like them — I can draw.'

'Sketches Dorner, What d'you mean?' Mr. Heslop frowned.

'Women, girls, in poses. I've quite a lot. You wouldn't want some, would you Sir?'

Despite the other's expression he pushed on. 'Just a few more marks would make all the difference Sir.' He felt a fool and knew he was behaving like one.

Mr. Heslop stared at him with a half smile of disbelief. 'This must be a joke, Dorner. There must be surely another reason for your visit.'

William shook his head. 'I thought,' he shrugged hopelessly, 'just an exchange; no one would know.'

'Well, it's original Dorner, I'll say that for you. But you didn't really think that I would give you marks you are not entitled to in exchange for some adolescent drawings?' He stood up. 'I won't report this to the head, Dorner. I have no doubt he wouldn't believe me if I did. I should not wish to be made out to be as big an idiot as you have made yourself with this preposterous suggestion. Spend your time revising, that will get you further than trying to cheat. No, Dorner, my integrity is absolute.'

William stood up also — a school youth who looked like an adult and towered over Mr. Heslop. He was desperate and played his second and last card. 'Isn't it a kind of cheating to watch couples in the woods, Sir?'

A flash of fury appeared behind the spectacles. 'You'd better leave Dorner. I don't have to . . . '

'I saw you in the woods,' interrupted William, 'on Sunday last, Sir. You were watching a couple and you were on your hands and knees, Sir.'

'Dorner, if you leave now this conversation will go no further. I shall consider that you are ill and excuse you on those grounds.' His voice was calm and level but his hand was supporting him against the back of his armchair.

'I have a photograph, Sir — of you. It was you, Sir,' persisted William steadily.

'A photograph!' The eyes glinted and widened in shock.

'Yes Sir, it developed well — it's very clear.' He was beginning to relax. Things might go his way, although Heslop wasn't a bad old stick. In fact he rather respected him as a teacher.

'You have the photograph?' Mr. Heslop's tone suggested that he knew the answer.

William nodded and withdrew it from his pocket and held it shoulder high.

'All right, put it away.' The master waved a hand rapidly in front of his face and turned to sit down quite heavily, then leaned forward, hands clasped, staring into the fireplace.

'It was only a favour I wanted Sir. A few marks wouldn't have made any difference to you or anyone else, and when I leave just a good report — that's all Sir.'

Mr. Heslop removed his spectacles and plucked the bridge of his nose, then replaced them. 'I must say, Dorner, that you show remarkable resourcefulness. Blackmail now together with your other accomplishment — drawing and photography. Quite obviously the arts are your strong points.' He motioned with his hand. 'You'd better sit down again because perhaps what I'm going to tell you now may shock you as much as that photograph has shocked me.'

What was he on about? Why couldn't they just make the arrangement for the marking to be better and leave it at that? Impatiently William waited.

'You see Dorner, I too have a picture — of you.'

Alarm ran through William, his mind immediately going to his meetings in the wood with Mrs. Thurrocks.

A smile touched the edges of the other's mouth. 'You don't have to worry, Dorner. My picture, you will be relieved to know, is a mental one — stored in the memory.' He stretched a finger in William's direction. 'But just as vivid and clear as yours is of me.'

Some little satisfaction showed as he continued, 'I, like yourself was just passing through the woods one Saturday afternoon when I stumbled, almost literally on this couple.' He paused and glanced away. 'I must confess that I stayed and watched.'

William's colour was rising in embarrassment and with it a fear that Mrs. Thurrocks had been recognised. How close had Mr. Heslop been? Thank God that he hadn't had a camera.

Mr. Heslop was breathing more quickly and his eyes held a collector's delight at some discovery. 'I must say, Dorner, that it was quite a spectacle — rampant primitive lovemaking.' His eyes strayed in recollection again. 'And your lady partner was absolutely abandoned — the row she made it's a wonder you didn't draw a larger audience.' He glanced at William sharply. 'A girl from the school is she?'

William subsided inwardly in relief. Old Heslop hadn't recognised Mrs. Thurrocks. 'No, actually I met her in town,' he lied, 'coming out of the pictures one day.'

His teacher studied him for a moment, then laughed shortly and somewhat bitterly. 'Strange isn't it Dorner, you have everything I could have wished for — youth, vigour, the ability to love a woman easily. Yet to you at this moment the world is a cruel place, and all for the sake of a few extra marks in French.' His hand moved at William. 'I would exchange my lot for yours immediately.'

William murmured his sympathy.

'No, Dorner, we have each seen the other as we really are. My concern is that I have shown my weakness. I suppose I was bound to be found out sometime. Yours could be called a weakness, but a rather enviable kind I should have thought. However,' he rose to his feet, 'you must now leave, Dorner. It has been interesting to say the least.' He must have observed the question in the youth's eyes and nodded as he spoke. 'Yes, Dorner, something will be done.'

William reached the door with rising spirits.

'Dorner.'

'Yes, Sir.'

'You know, I can't help thinking that a combination of your talents would make the learning of French superfluous.' William looked nonplussed as the older man went on, 'I was thinking on the lines of an art gallery and a part time gigolo.'

William wasn't quite sure about the latter's meaning and just gave a polite laugh and a heartfelt 'Thank you very much, Sir,' then stepped into the corridor.

Mr. Heslop stood in the doorway of his study. 'William — it is William, I believe.'

The youth turned back. 'Yes that's right, Mr. Heslop.'

'Er — I was thinking, you did mention some sketches. I think perhaps a couple of the less erotic ones would look well on my walls.'

William grinned. 'Specially for you, Sir.'

And so French was added to the small but nevertheless important list of subjects showing a distinct rise in the number of marks being given. The headmaster was very pleased, and Mr. Heslop basked in his praise for his tenacity and conscientiousness in imparting his knowledge to William. And Mrs. Thurrocks also received her share for her part in her pupil's improvement.

William slept easily at night now. He had cheated, but in doing so had caused others to benefit in some way.

And during that Autumn, the cry of what might have been a stoat or a weasel came from the wood in the late afternoon at the weekends. In reality it was Mrs. Thurrocks who continued to take off her wedding ring in the company of her young lover.

4

On Christmas Eve Ruth and the brothers attended a party at Scarton Manor near Daleford — the home of Redvers Scarton, his wife Winifred, and Elaine their daughter.

Mr. Scarton was a governor of the school and each Christmas invited some of the members of the upper forms to his home, and that year the three had been invited to attend.

A bouncing, rattling old motor coach with a blacked-out interior took them, driven by an elderly man called Thomas. He was broad of speech and the racket from the engine so great that everyone had difficulty in understanding everything he said. But all were happy at the prospect of spending Christmas Eve away from school.

They entered the grounds and along a drive flanked by tall trees to come to stop in front of a large house, its rooftops outlined occasionally by the fitful moonlight. Inside big flames within a high fireplace bounced their welcome off the dark wood of the walls and galleries, and thick curtains kept the light away from chance enemy aircraft. In a corner of the great hall stood a Christmas tree with a lighted candle clipped to each and every branch, and nearby was a grand piano although music was coming from a gramophone.

The three were introduced to the Scartons — Redvers Scarton, a tall raw-boned man with an accent not quite as broad as his employee Thomas. His wife Winifred, a petite very pale fair-haired person who appeared to float everywhere on account of her small and very quickly taken steps, rather like a ballet dancer. A woman very anxious to see that her young guests enjoyed themselves. Miss Elaine Scarton, their daughter, was dressed in cherry red which contrasted strongly with her creamy face and nearly black hair. She had bold darting eyes constantly on the move over the males present in the company.

It was a cheerful, colourful gathering with friends and relatives of the Scartons joining the guests from the school. Occasionally the elderly man who had brought them would be seen fuelling the fire with logs and coal, and white-aproned figures kept the tables full of Christmas fare. The war did not seem to have touched Scarton Manor and its inmates.

There was dancing and Edward took Ruth, or rather Ruth took him. He knew his dancing had not improved much. 'You must dance with someone else, Ruth,' he said. 'It must be hard work trundling me about.'

'Course not, silly,' she laughed happily, 'I don't mind — I'm with you. I don't really care about the dance, we're together.'

Actually he was darned hot, but Ruth was enjoying herself and it pleased him as she hadn't had much to smile about during the last few years. Yet she'd become a very pretty girl. He hadn't taken much notice until recently — almost grown-up she was.

Later someone else took her for a dance, and

Edward quite pleased to cool off, sat comfortably in a high-backed chair sipping at a glass of home-made wine. A happy scene, he thought, something else to remember and recall to his parents when he and William returned to Guernsey.

'Are they looking after you, lad?' The voice of Mr. Scarton broke into his thoughts.

'Yes Sir, they are, thank you. I was just sitting this one out. Ruth and William are busy.' He could see William talking to a couple of girls, whilst Ruth was now one of a small group by the Christmas tree.

Mr. Scarton sat down nearby. 'Doesn't look as if it's going to be a white Christmas, I've just looked out. It's turning colder — may be a heavy frost, but nothing more.' He studied Edward a moment. 'You won't get much snow where you come from.'

'No,' Edward replied. 'I think we once had about half an inch, and it was gone in a day.'

'I suppose you can't wait to get back eh?'

He couldn't — he was desperate to return. 'There's so much I want to do at home. It's frustrating, and each day I hope will be the last of the war.'

His host nodded sympathetically. 'With a bit of bloody luck I think this will be the last wartime Christmas — won't go on much longer,' he stated confidently. 'Can't have been easy for you — er . . . '

'Edward,' he supplied.

'Aye, Edward. I'd forgotten just for the moment.'

Edward on first meeting Redvers Scarton had thought he had a rather cruel hard face with narrow eyes, but when he smiled his eyes opened showing plenty of brown and warmth.

'Once called in to St. Peter Port — just overnight mind you,' his companion went on. 'I think we'd been to France — liked what I saw of it. Wouldn't have minded returning there. Stayed in Old Government House. Anyway, you'll soon be back. I can't see it lasting, Edward, not with the amount of bloody metal we're turning out.'

Edward looked puzzled. 'Metal?'

'Tanks, lad. My company builds 'em, and by jove we should swamp Jerry now.'

Edward was surprised, it felt rather strange to be talking to a man who made tanks, or at least his company did. Other people had jobs making furniture, confectionery, household goods, all kinds of things. His host made tanks for war!

Mr. Scarton glanced at Edward's nearly empty glass. 'Like something stronger than that stuff?' Then, not waiting for his guest's answer, he opened a cupboard nearby and poured another drink. 'There, try that. I'll bet there isn't another bottle of that in Daleford. A Scottish associate gave it to me — a favour given, favour received you might say. The best whisky in Scotland. Ever had whisky before?'

'No, no I haven't,' and he gazed down at the contents of his glass.

'Get it supped then, Edward, it won't do you any good keeping it in there,' and he watched as Edward took a sip. 'Go on, get some down.'

Edward did his best not to choke — the taste was dreadful. He thought his throat was being torn open as the liquid ran down.

'Now what d'you think of that?' His host's

expectant gaze was full on him.

Edward decided to say what Mr. Scarton obviously wanted to hear, and cleared his throat. 'Jolly good, thank you — very kind of you.'

'You'll remember your first whisky then?'

Edward was in no doubt that he would. Actually it wasn't too bad once the liquid had got further down.

'Drink up then,' ordered the older man, 'more if you want some.' Edward raised his glass. 'A very happy Christmas, Sir.' He had to drink it so he might as well look pleasant.

Redvers Scarton appeared pleased. 'Thanks lad, and to you and your family,' and tipped his glass. 'A drop of good stuff,' he said appreciatively afterwards.

It wasn't bad at all, decided Edward. He was warm, comfortable and uplifted in spirits by his host's confidence in forecasting an end to the war in Europe that coming year.

'And what's your father do, Edward?'

'He's an hotelier. He and my mother run the Ormer Hotel.' Edward paused. 'Well, they did. It will be closed now because of the occupation.' His eyes slid away reflectively. 'Actually, I don't know what's happening, we don't hear much,' and shrugged. 'It all seems so long ago now.' He was finding it easy now to talk to the man opposite, and went on to tell him briefly what had happened when they had had to leave so quickly.

Mr. Scarton gazed and listened intently until Edward had finished. 'By jove,' he said shaking his head in wonder and admiration, 'you've had something to put up with. I just hope it all goes well for you from now on — I do. I like the sound of your hotel — the what hotel?'

Edward told him again and his host seemed impressed. 'You know Edward, after it's all over we'll have to come and stay there.'

'That would be great, Sir. I want to go into the business if I can, and we could repay you for your kindness tonight inviting us here.'

Redvers Scarton looked strangely embarrassed. 'Nothing, lad,' he said bluffly. 'You must come up again some time in the new year. Now I'd better go and supervise a few things, otherwise they'll wonder where the hell I am,' and off his tall figure went to be swallowed up amongst the other guests.

During the evening Ruth played the piano, hesitantly at first then with more confidence as she went on. Lovely melodies from the latest shows in London — romantic sounds from Novello and Coward. She was glad of the buzz of conversation and laughter around; any mistakes were not so evident. Mrs. Scarton had found out she had taken lessons and had implored her to play. Over the top of the piano she could see Edward sitting by himself: he looked contented enough. A slight irritation came. At least he could have come and stood by her side. Guests moved in front of the piano and she lost sight of him.

'So you've been roped into playing?' Elaine Scarton stood looking down on her.

Ruth smiled round. 'Yes, your mother insisted. She wouldn't believe me when I told her that I've never played at a function like this before.'

'Well mercifully then half of them won't hear you,' said Elaine rather ungraciously. Her eyes drifted over Ruth dismissively. 'Have you taken lessons?'

'Oh, yes, one of my subjects at St. Just's. I'm not really very good yet. I need a lot of practice.'

'Oh, you mean the Orphanage.' The tone was slightly disparaging. 'They teach music there do they?'

Ruth stopped playing and turned to look at Elaine. 'I think it's a good school,' she said defensively. 'It's done well for us and I shall always remember it.' She would with some affection, sadness and a little bitterness. Some of her youthful years had been spent there instead of at home. 'I believe you play don't you, Elaine?'

'Yes,' her eyes were glancing about the room, 'classical — mostly.'

'And where did you learn? Did you have private lessons?'

'Yes, at Sunlands.'

'Sunlands?' Ruth had never heard of it.

'It's a finishing school — the best — up in the Dales. I'm on my last term there.'

So that was where she got her slightly unusual accent, a mixture of correct English and a northern harshness. 'And what are you going to do afterwards? Will you work in your father's factory?'

'Work in Daddy's what!' Elaine exclaimed indignantly. 'I should think not. I haven't made up my mind, but it will definitely not be there. In fact I don't think I'll bother working, there's much more interesting things to do.' She was busy peering between the heads in front of the piano.

'And I think I've seen one.'

Ruth watched her threading her way across the room. A spoilt brat, she thought, home now with her parents and no doubt unaware of the misery in the world during the last four years. From what she had seen of Miss Elaine Scarton it appeared that her main occupation was with the opposite sex. Ruth began to play again, thinking that perhaps she was assessing Elaine too harshly, too quickly. She herself was obsessed with one of them. Where was he? Looking over the piano top she saw him, exactly where he had been when she had seen him last. Only this time Elaine was sitting close by him, taking animatedly while looking up into his face. The melody faded away under Ruth's fingers. Someone else could take a turn; they were not listening anyway. A more important matter — namely Edward Dorner — demanded her immediate attention.

Just as she was making her way over to them they stood up, smiling at something said between them.

'There Edward, I've finished my stint at the piano,' and her heart warmed to him once more. Dark-suited, the slow smile in the flushed face, handsome in the Christmas lighting.

'It sounded marvellous, Ruth. You've done very well to learn to play like that. I wouldn't have the patience,' and Edward's look lingered a little longer than usual on her. She'd saved hard for that blue dress and had mentioned that it hadn't fitted her, but had been busy with needle and cotton to alter it. He thought she looked well, blue eyes blooming at him, and he wondered why she was holding her hands tightly together in front of her. Certainly she was quite pretty, but she was Ruth. He turned to Elaine, dark and striking, something reaching out to him from her, uninhibited in her manner. A totally different sensation running through him, and he did not — could not hide it.

'I was just telling Edward that we have that in common — we both play the piano,' said Elaine.

That was a lie, thought Ruth. The way they had looked and the smiles had had nothing to do with pianos.

Someone had put on a record. Elaine's hand reached out and found Edward's easily. 'Your brother and I are going to dance. He says he can't. I want to find out.'

Her brother! 'No Elaine, Edward is not my brother.'

'Oh I thought he was. Sorry and all that.'

'No, I'm not,' put in Edward, just standing there. He was beginning to enjoy himself and shrugged. 'We've just known each other a long time.'

'Yes, yes we have,' said Ruth quickly — too quickly — then added, 'since we were very young actually.'

A wicked gleam was growing in Elaine's gaze at Ruth.

'We go back a long time, don't we, Ruth?' Edward's smile and tone were affable, nothing more.

Ruth was uncomfortable, awkward under Elaine's mocking gaze. Edward was more than a friend. He was — he was. 'We — we have an understanding, I suppose,' she finished lamely. And in her heart a stifled voice said that it was untrue. She regretted the words as soon as they left her — childish and gauche. She looked at Edward for help. Damn you Edward, say so please! Oh why didn't he? After all those years. They did have an understanding — they did. Please Edward, she willed him, say so. The darkened lights masked her own quickly rising colour. She wanted to hide. And Edward just stood there.

'Oh, then you won't mind if I take your Edward,' and Ruth winced at the emphasised 'your'. 'I may bring him back.'

Edward gave her a fatuous smile as, linked by their hands, he followed Elaine.

Ruth hid her wretched emotions behind a piece of Christmas cake. What a simple idiot she must have appeared to Elaine. Simple and childlike. Even her choice of words — an understanding — how old-fashioned it must have sounded. She must also have embarrassed Edward. He wouldn't want to show his feelings too much, not being a demonstrative person. Ruth remembered the approval in his eyes when they had danced together earlier. Perhaps she had behaved too possessively and comforted herself with the thought that it would not be Christmas Eve every day and Elaine would be a memory by the morning.

However, Edward seemed to be enjoying himself, laughing down into the closely upturned features of Elaine as he danced stiffly with her. Perhaps that would put her off, hoped Ruth. Elaine knew nothing about their former lives, of the bond that existed between them after the incident that had caused his lameness.

For a while she was drawn into conversation with other guests, her cheerful exterior belying the unease her straying eyes revealed when she could no longer see Edward or Elaine. Of William there was no sign. If only she had William's temperament. It was more than likely he was under the mistletoe with some girl, and uncaring of anyone else.

Then near midnight someone suggested carol singing and Ruth was again pressed into playing for them.

'Where's Elaine?' said a voice, and Ruth, anxious-eyed, could not see Edward either. But a minute later they came into the hall, Edward still on the end of Elaine's hand.

'They were under the mistletoe,' announced the finder.

Ruth watched them miserably and tried to ignore what she had heard. A kiss under the mistletoe — what was that? It didn't mean anything so why was she making herself so unhappy? She played for the singing, and no doubt if anyone noticed the lack of vitality in her fingers it was put down to her inexperience with that particular instrument.

Edward looked flushed and rather unsteady and Elaine's stare was mocking Ruth across the piano.

Then it was Christmas Day and presents piled below the tree were distributed to the guests, and not long afterwards the trio left, tumbling into the old coach again with the others from the school. It was cold in the vehicle and Ruth sat huddled into her coat. She was quiet and distant in her manner on the way back, eliciting anxious enquiries from

Edward and William, but she brushed them aside saying she was just tired.

'You were great on the piano, Ruthie,' enthused William. 'You can certainly play the thing.'

'Yes, you earned your supper tonight,' said Edward. 'Not surprised you're tired, you must have played an hour or two.' He sighed. 'I'm a bit tired now, but I must say I've enjoyed the evening.'

'So have I,' agreed William lolling back in his seat. 'Best Christmas Eve for a long time.'

Of course they'd enjoyed themselves, she thought irritably. Edward like a child in the hands of Elaine Scarton, and William, well he didn't seem to worry about anything or anybody.

'Never mind Ruth, you'll soon be home and tucked up in bed,' Edward said comfortingly.

She wished it could have been in his bed, the two of them together, he saying he loved her and had done all his life.

Edward settled back contentedly. 'Nice old boy, Mr. Scarton — we talked together — gave me a whisky. First time I've had any and my throat felt as if it were going to catch fire.' He turned to Ruth. 'He told me to visit them sometime in the new year. Nice of him wasn't it?'

Ruth nodded in the dimness of the coach, another prick from jealousy's knife hurting her. Elaine might be there and prayed that she would be away at her finishing school if and when Edward went up to the hall again. Perhaps he would have forgotten in the morning about the invitation. He was more loquacious than usual; it must be the drink he'd had.

The object of her thoughts spoke again. 'You know, going up there to that house has given me some ideas for the hotel when I get back. One or two features I saw at the hall could be used at home — corner seats, large fireplaces, alcoves. Then maybe winter holidays in Guernsey. I don't mean just the odd day or two but proper holidays with the accent on comfort and cosiness, perhaps entertainment — music. I can just imagine it now. I think I could make a go of it, but I'll have to discuss it with Dad first.'

He sounded so enthusiastic. If only he were like that towards her, but Ruth consoled herself with the thought that at least he wasn't waxing enthusiastically over Elaine. Better his dreams of Guernsey than dreams of her.

Before they parted company on their return to the school they arranged to meet later that day although they had no plans. Some of the teaching staff had gone home for the Christmas holidays, as had some of the pupils, so the place would be very quiet.

Edward gave her a peck on the cheek, and patted her shoulder in brotherly fashion as he wished her happy Christmas and good night. 'You looked nice tonight Ruth, very nice.'

The compliment was better than nothing but it wasn't enough. He hadn't said what she wanted to hear — he never did. She gazed hopelessly after them, Edward leaning more than perhaps he realised upon William as they disappeared from view. And from somewhere in the valley below came the sounds of the Salvation Army playing carols. Each Christmas night for the last four years she had heard them. They always sounded the same — never changed. Like Edward's feelings and attitude towards her. The brotherly pat had said it all — again.

Christmas morning came and volunteers were asked to form a choir to sing carols in the local hospital grounds. Ruth, Edward and William having nothing else to do joined the party. Edward had a bit of a head from the night before, and insisted that it had nothing to do with the whisky among other liquids that he had imbibed at Scarton Manor. It was a bright crisp day and led by the local vicar they gave a creditable rendering of all the well known carols. Afterwards and as it was continuing fine the choir sang outside various private houses.

At many places they were invited in and drinks offered — some being home-made concoctions, and always plenty of ginger wine. There were also a variety of Christmas cakes, some made with real fruit, but nobody in the choir was impolite enough to question where the fruit had come from in such straitened times.

The money collected from the carol singing was going to be divided between the hospital fund and the Red Cross organisation. Ruth remembered the very early days after their scrambled arrival when she had written letters home thinking they would reach Guernsey in the normal fashion. Now she realised the good work of the Red Cross and the tortuous difficult path that the messages took that were entrusted to it.

When the choir eventually finished their tour it was noticeable that even the vicar wobbled unsteadily away from the last door.

'It has been more of a success than I had dared hope.' His voice felt rather thick. Had the choir noticed? Excused himself, by saying he had a sore throat coming on. People had shown great generosity and not all of it monetary. Taking the choir back to the vicarage for tea seemed a good idea in the circumstances. There would be safety in numbers when surrounded by members of the carol party. His wife would perhaps not notice his hands against the chair, or that he was not conversing at close quarters with her.

Later, addressing his congregation, he gave thanks for the efforts of the carol singers which had brought in a significant sum of money. He hoped their songs had comforted and cheered those they had visited in these hard and difficult times. He thanked the pupils from St. Justs amongst whom were those who had sought sanctuary in England, and wished them a speedy return very soon to their own homes across the water. Privately in his own prayers that night he asked that whatever it was that was troubling the young lady in the trio from Guernsey, would be resolved quickly. An uneasy spirit was quite plain beneath the open countenance.

Another year made its entrance, and hopes were high between Ruth, Edward and William that nineteen forty-five was going to see the end of the war. The allies were pushing steadily on deep into enemy territory, and it should be over in the near future. As usual the talk between them was all about when they would be able to return. The Channel

Islands had not yet been freed, the all-out attack being concentrated in Europe itself. But then the unthinkable happened — a breakthrough by the enemy, stifling the quickly risen dreams and hopes of the three. The considered opinion of the older staff at the school was that it was a last gasp effort of a dying army, but nobody could be sure.

Then bad news of a more personal nature assailed Ruth. She was told that now she was eighteen she would have to leave St. Justs and find work. It was a shock and turned her nearly as grey and cold as the February day. Looking across the valley from the school windows she saw the curving mass of white broken by the black-sided stone walls, and merging into the darker grey of the moors. She had never thought about having to leave, but of course the war was still on and the boys were still being called up for service at eighteen.

Edward and William were stunned. 'They can't do it. You're a member of the school until we get back,' Edward said in angry dismay.

'They can't break into your studies like that, Ruthie,' said William. 'Don't worry, it's all a mistake. The idiots have lost their heads.'

But they could do it, they had not lost their heads and it was not a mistake. The war was dragging on and the effort still demanded was a total one. And for the second time since leaving Guernsey she was separated from Edward and William. Her new home was a hostel for girls in part of what used to be a cotton mill just outside Daleford.

The hostel seemed a horrible place after what had become to her the cosy confines of school life. It held girls of all types — some away from home like herself, others with no home but the hostel. Rough, crude, good and bad ones, some of strictly limited educational and mental abilities. The talk was usually about men, some picking up servicemen home on leave, meeting them in local dance halls and public houses. Coarse talk on their conquests was bandied about and Ruth cringed before the broadside of such obscene crudity. She had dreams of her own about Edward but in comparison with their ideas her love was pure.

'What's yours like, Leney?' They pronounced her name as one word. 'Where are you hiding him?'

When she told them he was still at school, they laughed and called her a baby snatcher. But mostly, to her great relief, they left her alone. She was unhappy but realised that she had been lucky to stay at the school as long as she had.

If the hostel had been a shock, a worse one followed when she was sent to work at an engineering firm situated on the other side of Daleford. The Daleford Machine Tool Company it was called and it was a subsidiary of the Scarton Manufacturing Company. To Ruth's great surprise she found that it was the same Scarton — Redvers Scarton of Scarton Manor — where she, Edward and William had spent the previous Christmas Eve. At the Daleford Machine Tool Company Ruth was taught to use a lathe. It was a nightmare of shift work, being hardly awake in the mornings and so tired she could barely trudge to catch the evening bus. Once she missed it. Snow had fallen during the day and the slush had hardened into treacherous tiny mountains over which she stumbled into the darkness. She was reprimanded by the foreman and warned about her timekeeping, and each day she prayed for the day when she could leave. The factory was cold, the floor damp and she felt unwell quite often.

There was another hazard which she also found out about very soon after going to work there. The searching, feeling, touching hands of the men on the shop floor. They were mostly older men — too old for conscription and some with a disability, although Ruth found out that their disability did not stop them from acting offensively and rudely towards her. Their hands would slide about her as they passed or pretended to stumble and lean against her. Also she was frightened when she left work in case someone was lying in wait for her. She complained but was told that she was working with men and so she would have to put up with a bit of horse play, as they called it.

If it hadn't been for the fact that she met Edward and William occasionally she felt that she could not have carried on, and once she was so upset that she broke down and wept in front of them. Edward wanted to confront Mr. Scarton with what Ruth was having to endure, but Ruth desisted. 'I'll stick it out. You may get into trouble.' The truth of the matter was that she did not want Edward anywhere near Scarton Manor or Redvers Scarton, because where he was, so might Elaine be.

Edward agreed reluctantly but insisted that he meet her after her day shift and escort her back to the hostel gates. When she was on night shift he would come to the hostel and ride with her to the factory. He was now in his eighteenth year and one of the older boys in the school and was allowed that freedom. His action was a further diamond on the ring of love in her heart for him, and when she thanked him he just brushed it aside with a rather embarrassed laugh. 'I have to look after you, Ruth, I feel responsible for you.'

Oh God, if only he would feel something else for her. He may do, but he never showed it. He was kindness itself to her, caring and protective, but no word of love or look came from him.

But one day he looked worried. 'D'you realise Ruth, when I'm eighteen I shall have to join up. I just hope the war finishes before then, otherwise I won't be able to keep an eye on you. I could be sent anywhere.'

Ruth sighed. Having an eye kept on her was perhaps better than no attention at all. His mentioning of joining up shocked her as it had never occurred to her that Edward would have to go, but the years had passed and he was nearly at the age of conscription. She had assumed that the dreadful affair would have been over by now. Each night she prayed into her pillow that it would be very soon.

Ruth was to suffer one more indignity, and it happened when she was working on the day shift. The rumour was that old man Scarton, the boss, was to pay a visit. Ruth hoped that if he did he would not recognise her. Perhaps he would just look into that part of the factory and pass on quickly elsewhere. After all, she was only one amongst many people employed there, but on the other hand there were fewer women and she was one of the youngest.

About half past two the word spread that he was in the building. Someone had seen his Daimler outside the main office. Ruth bent over her machine, regretting the fact that she was near to and facing the main entry into the workshop.

She was conscious of the door opening, a group coming in. Mr. Scarton's voice and the work manager's, glimpsed the foreman, and a woman partly hidden behind them. Ruth began to set her lathe, the footsteps getting closer, the voices louder. There was a pause as the group clustered around a machine, talking to the operator. Then movement down the aisle to take them past her. Ruth stole a glance, thinking they were gone, and looked straight into the face of Redvers Scarton. She saw him hesitate momentarily, frowning, the light of recognition come and go as he tried to put a name to her face, before he and the party moved on, with the exception of one person.

Ruth was aware of a figure on the edge of her vision and turned to find Elaine Scarton regarding her with an insolent amusement. The last person that she would have had to see her. Mortified she wished that she was anywhere but there. Ruth knew what a sight she must look, having an ill-fitting dirty overall, flat shoes, thick stockings, and a scarf hiding her hair, with the ends sticking up like rabbits' ears. She felt scruffy and knew she looked it. At her worst in front of Elaine who was clean, perfumed, with shining black perfectly groomed hair atop a green thick winter coat and a white scarf hung carelessly round her neck.

'It's Ruth, isn't it? You came to my party at Christmas?'

'Yes, I did — er, hello Elaine.' It was awful.

'Rather a change from the school isn't it? You were doing something in music.'

'Yes, I had to leave. I was eighteen — had to come here.'

'I suppose you told them you knew Daddy.'

'No, I didn't. I was told to come here — I didn't know where I was being sent.' She resented the other's remark and squirmed under the up and down gaze of Elaine. 'It will be your turn soon, Elaine,' Ruth enjoyed reminding her. She was about the same age.

'If you think I attended Sunlands to end up doing this . . . .' She gestured contemptuously and grandly about her. 'No, Daddy knows some people — somebody in administration. I wouldn't mind that.' She glanced around, wrinkling her nose, then eyed Ruth again. 'I must say you look dreadful in that outfit, but still you're one of his workers aren't you.'

Ruth tried to stifle her mounting anger. 'I thought you were still at Sunlands.'

'Oh, I thought I'd like a few days at home. I wasn't doing anything special today, so when Daddy asked me to come along I thought it would be a change.'

A change! Ruth half turned away to her machine. She must carry on working, guessing that Elaine's father and escort would soon be returning. Wanted Elaine to go.

'How's Edward?'

Her question surprised Ruth and she glanced sideways sharply. 'Edward? Oh he's well — very well. I see him quite often,' she added defensively and irritated by Elaine's familiar use of his name.

'I must ask Daddy to invite him up again.'

Again! Ruth's heart jerked. The only time he had been up to the hall as far as she knew was when he accompanied William and herself the last Christmas. Had he been since?

'He seemed to fit in very well don't you think? Daddy liked him.'

But obviously she, Ruth, did not fit in with Elaine's plans for Edward. Aloud Ruth said as calmly as she could manage, 'It was very kind of your parents to invite us — we liked them very much,' and saw the flash of annoyance as her emphasis on them. Ruth wanted her gone. The day had been grey enough but now everything was depressing.

Elaine's father and party were approaching again and Redvers Scarton nodded at Ruth and murmured, 'Afternoon,' as he passed by. 'Coming Elaine?'

'Yes, Daddy, just having a word with one of your workers,' and her eyes dropped over Ruth from head to toe again, then she glanced around the workshop, crinkling her face in distaste. 'I shouldn't have thought that Edward would have wanted you here.' She stared straight at Ruth with a vicious little smile and shrugged. 'But perhaps he doesn't care.' Pulling her coat together she threw the ends of her scarf over her shoulder. 'What odd thing did you call it — an understanding?' The smile grew more cruel.

'Are you sure you have one, because I doubt it?'

Miserably Ruth started after her. Edward did care about her — she knew he did. Had he gone up to the Manor by himself? Or was Elaine just trying to make trouble between them? She had stirred up doubt and despair in Ruth's mind, and the latter that night felt her spirits were at rock bottom, knowing that Elaine was a threat to their relationship. Edward could get hurt if he became entangled with Elaine. Instinctively Ruth knew what the other's nature was — a new face — a novelty, and when that appeal wore off . . . .Edward was serious — too serious to see the trap. He was not a William. William was happy-go-lucky; he wouldn't have been hurt.

For a day or two she was upset after the encounter with Elaine, but then one morning in February — a wonderful rare blue-skied frosty one, she took a walk in the valley near the hostel instead of going to bed after her night shift. It had seemed too nice to hide herself away in sleep. The walk did her a lot of good, clearing her head and thoughts. The trees and foliage were still, inattentive, waiting in suspended animation for spring to touch them again. It was peaceful and calm and the smoke drifted upwards from cottages nearby. Passing one she saw an elderly man in his garden.

He nodded, 'Mornin' miss.'

'Good morning,' she returned. 'Isn't it lovely — such a change.'

'Aye it is.' He thumbed his waistcoat further on to his shoulder. 'Have you heard the news on the wireless this morn' yet?'

Ruth had been long enough in the district to understand the broad accent. 'No, I haven't heard any news today.'

'Aye well, Jerry's falling back. Our forces are pressing on t' Berlin.'

'Oh, that's wonderful, marvellous!' She could have kissed him. Excitement replaced her new-found calm of mind. Was this going to be the year when the war would be over and she and the boys could return home? The old man watched with some surprise as she waved and turned to retrace her walk, but this time with quick, eager, optimistic steps.

That night even going to work had lost its dread, buoyed up as she was with the news of that morning. And one aspect of Redvers Scarton's visit to the factory along with his daughter proved an advantage to Ruth. There was a new respect shown to her. It had been noted that Mr. Scarton had acknowledged Ruth, and that his daughter had had quite a long conversation with her. And Ruth let it be known that she had been invited to Scarton Manor as a guest once. Indeed there was a change in the workshop towards her. She knew the Scartons.

News of a different kind reached her via Edward. William had inexplicably failed in his school certificate examination. His class marks in certain subjects had been extraordinarily good, and in two reports at the term's end were glowing tributes to his attitude towards his work. And yet in the examination room he had failed miserably in those particular subjects. But of course, a certain lady and gentleman of the staff were not surprised. They had done their best for him, but could not be present in the examination room with him and write the papers. Now the prospects of life and work away from the school came nearer for William. At the end of the next term he would have to leave. It was something that William had overlooked during the flush of the too easily attained accolades for his form work, the day of reckoning in the examination room.

Ruth bent over her bench as music came from the loudspeaker on the walls, her foot tapping in time to the dance melody. Suddenly the music stopped and an announcement was made. 'We are interrupting this programme to give the news that the Allies have entered Berlin. Fighting is still going on, but the end of the third Reich is imminent. We shall keep you informed as further news comes in.'

The music restarted amid cheers from the workers, and Ruth could have danced on the lathe, so suddenly light-hearted did she feel. Soon — soon their nightmare would be over. She wondered if Edward and William had heard the good news.

They had, and on her day off the three took a bus ride to a wooded beauty spot with tall trees and a meandering stream. The path was narrow and Edward and Ruth walked side by side, William bringing up the rear. It was Spring and the daffodils nodded and bent inwards either side like anxious and approving attendants waiting on the bride. Ruth hoped and uttered her thousandth prayer that it would be so in the not too distant future and that she would be the bride on Edward's arm.

William's sigh from behind them brought her

back to earth. Despite the encouraging news from the war front, William was not his usual confident carefree self.

'Don't worry, William,' she said over her shoulder, guessing the reason for the sigh. 'We shall be going back home soon. You'll find work in Guernsey. I think it will be over before you have to work here.'

William's face brightened somewhat at this. 'You think so? I hope so.' He grimaced. 'I can't bear the thought of going to work in this dump.'

'Oh, it's not such a bad place, William. After all we might easily have got somewhere worse,' pointed out Edward. He knew that he could afford to be charitable towards Daleford now that there was a chance they would soon be leaving it, and added, 'At least we've been safe here.'

'Oh, yes,' agreed William, 'there's that about the place,' but his tone suggested that that was all there was to be said for the town. He looked up through the lowering trees glumly. 'It's starting to rain — it never seems to do anything else in Daleford, that or snow.'

Ruth smiled at him. 'Cheer up William. When you're on the boat you'll forget all about Daleford.' The very fact that she could now talk about the journey to Guernsey seriously made her tingle with excitement. A year ago it was just a dream which used to keep their spirits from crumbling completely.

Then came the day of victory in Europe, complete victory by the Allies over the enemy. Elated throats tight with emotion over the wireless. Edward and William arriving breathless at the factory, and Edward hugging Ruth and lifting her off the floor in joy at the news. 'It's over — it's over, Ruth,' he kept repeating.

And William, his examination results confined to the past, kissed her and shouted, 'Guernsey, here we come.'

The headmaster declared a day's holiday at the school to mark the victory. In the town everybody was congregating and singing. Groups danced to accordion music, streets held makeshift parties and lights were shone all the following night through. People got drunk and there were speeches and more speeches. The Palais glide was performed across the main street and people climbed lamp posts. Service men on leave were late back to barracks or ships — it didn't matter now. Flags flew from everywhere, and Ruth, Edward and William decided that Daleford was not such a bad place after all.

But when their excitement and relief had subsided enough for them to think rationally, the fact remained that the islands were not yet freed. How much longer? They scanned the newspapers each and every day and listened to the news. Their impatience showed in everything, with Ruth unable to concentrate properly at work, and Edward and William now idling their time away at the school, unable to settle again into what was left of their life at St. Justs. Edward was full of his plans for the hotel. William's academic career was in ruins, he admitting that it had never really risen above that state. Also the fleshy attractions of Mrs. Thurrocks had begun to fade.

Ruth continued working at Scartons; there was

nothing else she could do. The war in the Pacific was not yet over and arms were still needed for the Forces serving out there. Her hard-earned money was being put away, some of which would help to pay for the return journey to Guernsey. What she would do once there, she had no idea. Perhaps she could obtain a post as a teacher of young children and give piano lessons. But that was all in the future — the very near future she hoped fervently — one with Edward, remembering how he had hugged and squeezed her on victory day. If only he would do that more often.

After five long years the day came. Wireless and newspapers telling and showing the liberation of the islands. The three went to the pictures specially to see the newsreels — views of the forts and gun emplacements, and they recognised certain places — the town church, Vazon bay, Castle Cornet and High Street. Brief shots but enough to make Ruth cry, Edward gruff voiced and to put his arm around her comfortingly.

They held a party at the school to celebrate, and to Ruth and Edward's surprise Mrs. Thurrocks and Mr. Heslop put in an appearance. William seemed to know them socially quite well. Mrs. Thurrocks looked at times rather sad, whilst the French master and William were to be heard in profound and earnest discussion on photography and art.

Much later, in the small hours of the morning, another no less serious discussion took place between the three in Edward's study, all about setting a date for their return to Guernsey. It was decided that Edward would find out the times of the trains and boat, and from which port they would be sailing.

When they met again he looked serious. 'It's going to be very expensive — I don't see how we're going to do it. I've saved a little from the pocket money I've had, but it won't be enough to get us all back.' He hadn't really given much thought to the expense of returning; it had always seemed so far in the future. 'I could write home and borrow some,' he suggested.

'Yes, that's a good idea,' agreed Ruth, 'but I thought we had arranged not to let them know just when we were coming. It was going to be a surprise.'

Edward had forgotten about that for the moment. He couldn't wait to see their faces. It was like a dream; at long last they were going home. And now when they were free to do so they were short of the money.

William hadn't any — not even enough for his bus fare to the station. 'It just seems to have gone — my money didn't last.' He seemed irritated that they should have expected him to have saved some.

Ruth sighed. She hadn't expected him to have any. 'Look, there's no need to worry, I've saved some from my wages. I think we shall have enough.'

'No, you've worked for that, it's yours Ruth.' Edward looked determined. 'I'll get a job for a couple of weeks — anything. It isn't going to make any difference after five years.'

Edward the protector. Her eyes softened in their gaze at him. Apart from loving him, she owed him possibly her life, and was reminded of that each time she saw him walk with the limp. Her head moved equally determinedly. 'No Edward, it's what I've saved the money for. Let's go as soon as possible.' Thereupon she opened the old toffee tin in which she had kept her savings. In the bottom of the tin lay the Ormer shell — a piece of the island which had given her strength to carry on. She had treasured it all those dark years and it was returning with her.

The brothers watched anxiously as she counted the money into her lap. To their dismay there was not sufficient even when adding Edward's savings.

'You must go Ruth,' Edward said. 'We'll just have to ask our parents to pay for our fare over. It won't be a surprise but it can't be helped.'

'Yes it can Edward — we can do it, look.' She held up the money, 'I've enough for two of us to go. William is still a pupil here, so he could stay for another week at least. They won't ask him to leave. And you are the elder,' she pointed out.

'Well I don't want to stay here any longer than I have to,' and William gazed at them grumpily. 'Surely there's some way we can all go.'

'I wish there was but I've only got enough money to pay for two. You cannot get three tickets if you only have money for two.' William was annoying her with his rather selfish attitude, but the truth was that if one of the brothers was to accompany her, she preferred it to be Edward.

'Let William and I toss up,' suggested Edward, 'that would be fair. I mean he is the younger, and I wouldn't want mum and dad to think I'd just cleared off and left him.'

William bristled slightly. 'Oh, I'd be all right. When all is said and done I'm only a year younger,' he countered quickly. He knew what it was. Ruthie was sweet on Edward. Anyway, he could always pass the time by stirring old Thurrocks again. Trouble was, every time he mentioned home she became upset.

Ruth tossed the coin, praying that it would fall in Edward's favour. William, thinking of Mrs. Thurrocks' body, called tails and lost, and Ruth breathed a sigh of happy relief.

William took his losing in good part. 'When will you leave?'

'There's a boat out of Weymouth at one o'clock in the afternoon on Saturday. We'd have to catch the train on Friday to get us down in time.' He saw the lingering disappointment on his brother's face. 'Don't worry, Dad will send the money on — just a week that's all. In fact,' he added cheeringly, 'I might even come across and meet you in Weymouth.'

'I'll book the tickets then,' said Ruth. 'It could be the night train.' Whatever it was didn't matter. She and Edward were going home together.

5

The boat train drew in alongside the quay at Weymouth, and the Channel Islands ferry rose high out of the water above it. Two faces gazed at the vessel, each bearing the same question. Was this the same one that brought them over? That day so long ago when there had been no wish or time to know its name.

A leisurely walk up the gangway carrying their small amount of luggage and they were aboard. They descended the stairs into the passenger area, and after finding their seats returned to the deck and leaned over the side watching the small boats navigating the inner harbour. The sun shone, the breeze was gentle and the ferry moved quietly at her ropes.

As the ship edged away slowly from the quayside, Ruth sought Edward's hand. 'Are we really going back? Is it real?'

Edward nodded, looking into her face. 'Yes, it is. I've waited a long time for this Ruth — we both have. It must have been terrible for you, when you had to come with us. You deserve a medal the way you've put up with everything.' His arm went around her shoulders. 'They'll never believe it when we tell them everything that's happened to us.'

Ruth leaned heavily against him and sighed with happiness. 'Do you think Edward that we shall have changed much to them? I mean we're five years older now.'

Her companion smiled comfortingly. 'Not really, we're just bigger and grown up, and mostly the same, but they'll certainly be surprised and I can't wait to see them.'

'And me, won't it be marvellous! I wonder if they've altered much?'

Edward frowned. 'A little, I suppose, but when you get to a certain age you don't change very much — well, not until you're very old.' His images of his mother and father were from those frantic moments when he had seen them last.

'What d'you think they're doing now?' Ruth turned her back to the ship's rail.

'My guess is that Dad will be painting and getting things ready for the start of the next season. It's not so long since the war finished. Or he could be working outside — arranging his tables in the tea garden or something.'

'Aunt May could be in the greenhouse. She used to like to grow her own tomatoes,' mused Ruth. 'Either that or she'll be knitting, or she could be writing asking why I haven't let her know when I'm coming.'

'Yes, mine could be doing the same. Mum will be telling Dad to find out what those boys are doing not returning immediately. She won't understand. I don't think she's ever been out of Guernsey.' He gazed at Ruth in mock alarm. 'Just supposing they don't recognise us — what shall we do?'

Ruth laughed, realising that she had not done that very often over the last few years. 'Of course they'll recognise us, silly.'

This must be one of the happiest days of her life, going home with Edward by her side. A seagull settled on the rail nearby — a sharp eye gazing at them knowingly. Did it see love and happiness ahead for them?

Later she noticed the small alcove beneath the steps. Was that where the three of them had huddled together, frightened and confused after their desperate scramble aboard? Her face must have expressed the memory of that time because Edward suddenly enquired, 'What's the matter — seasick already?'

Recovering quickly she told him and Edward, holding her reassuringly, said confidently, 'It's all over now Ruth. We'll start our life again. Let's not think of the unhappy times — they've gone.'

Behind them in the distance the fading shores of England. Away from the likes of Elaine Scarton and her greed for conquests.

Edward's expression had become troubled. 'D'you think William will be all right on his own?'

'Of course he will I'm sure. It's only going to be another week before he joins us. After all he is seventeen now and he's at the school — he has bed and board.'

Edward looked doubtful. 'I'm just wondering what Mum and Dad will say when they find out I've left him over there.'

'Look Edward,' and there was that in her tone which made him glance sharply at her, 'you can't be responsible for William every minute of the day. Just tell them the truth, you hadn't the money. Anyway you are escorting me home. I'd rather you than William, and Aunt May will be very pleased you did.' She tugged at his arm. 'Come on, let's go and have something to eat — I'm starving.'

It was a peaceful smooth crossing and by about half past five they were watching from the deck as Herm Island slid by — Shell beach a strip of yellow gold in the late afternoon sunshine, and the darker bulk of Sark behind. Then they were turning gradually for the boat to point itself at St. Peter Port. To their left was Castle Cornet just as it had always looked, and beyond it the green headland overlooking Havelet bay.

Edward picked out the town church and its clock, and he felt proud at the compliments being made by other passengers on their first glimpse of the island.

'Look Ruth, look! I can see the buses lined up on the Esplanade.' Excitedly he turned to direct her gaze along his arm and found her crying quietly.

'I — I'm sorry, Edward — I'm an idiot but I can't help it. It's been such a long time. I've thought so much about home. Now I'm here . . . ' Ruth covered her nose and most of her face with her handkerchief.

'Sorry Ruth,' and he hugged her briefly. 'I just got carried away — it's beautiful isn't it?'

She sniffled, nodding. Would he ever be as enthusiastic over her? Would their association always consist of brief and comforting hugs?

Edward gathered their bags and then they made their way to the deck below to stand with other passengers waiting in front of the large doors from which they would disembark. The faces on the quayside were getting nearer. Smiles and waves to those on deck. Ruth saw a taxi, some cars, and the gangway being craned over the quayside. The gentle bump as the ship's side touched port, and the sharp shouts of the dockers. Doors were being opened and the noise of the gangway being made fast. Then the air and light of Guernsey touched Ruth and Edward as they were channelled forward.

Edward placed her in front of him and Ruth began the short descent to the quayside. She had a strange feeling inside her. They had scrambled up that gangway frightened children: now she and Edward were returning as young adults.

'Shall we take a taxi or a bus?' said Edward as his foot touched the native soil.

'A taxi,' replied Ruth firmly. 'Let's go home in style. I have enough I think. If we haven't, Aunt May will pay.'

They looked for an empty one, but even in that short time those that had been waiting for the boat were already taken and moving off.

'It won't be long before they're back,' said Ruth. Around them was the friendly bustling activity of a ship newly arrived in port. Greetings and embraces, snatches of animated conversation.

Edward knew that their greetings were still to come — he was impatient now. 'Why don't we start walking Ruth? By the time we get to the clock, a taxi should be returning and we can pick it up from there.'

They set off from the quayside into the White Rock jetty road. On the raised walk above it people were strolling and others leaning over the jetty wall in the evening sunshine. They passed a few parked cars and Edward remembered vividly how his father had abandoned their car that day and then they had made a dash for the boat. He wondered if his father had managed to get it back to the house? Or had it been too badly damaged in the air raid? The road surface was good — had no doubt been repaired by the occupying forces for their own use. Edward's eyes searched it. They had reached about the spot, he guessed, where the family had been when the bombing began. It gave him a strange sensation to be striding freely and unafraid over that particular part of the road. But there was nothing visible to tell of the awful fear and confusion during that terrible and unforgettable time.

Ruth had not forgotten either, being forcibly reminded of it by the limp of the young man at her side.

They had almost reached the small building with the clock at the Esplanade end of White Rock, when they saw a taxi coming from St. Julians Avenue. Edward stopped it, instructed the driver, 'Moulin Huet Road, La Maison Verde.' How strange and yet how good it felt to be asking for an island address.

'Down by the Bella Luce, isn't it?'

Nice, he thought, to hear the local accent — never taken any notice of it before. Of course he'd been a boy then, and he supposed things like that would not have been important.

'You see Ruth,' he smiled at her, 'I haven't forgotten the name of your house.'

In the shadows of the taxi she looked lovingly at him. The green house, so named her Aunt had said, because of the amount of ivy and moss upon its walls, and shrubbery around it. Whatever the reason it was wonderful and she was returning to it — her home after five years away. Familiar streets and houses passed by. Nothing seemed to have changed much apart from an air of neglect and shabbiness about some of the properties after the occupation. They left-forked at the top of the Grange, the other road going she knew to the west coast. Passed Saumerez Park where the summer country shows were held with floats and castles and horses. Sometimes as a change from Moulin Huet, she had when a child gone to Vazon and Cobo with their flat open beaches where you could run and run without having to avoid rocks.

She saw they had reached the Bella Luce Hotel, the narrow lane beyond sombre under the arching trees. Her heart began to thump beneath her dress. Not long now. 'Come in with me, Edward, just for a moment — say hello to Aunt May.' Wanted him to share that moment with her. Her throat was already tightening — knew she would make a fool of herself. Five years out of one's life was a long time, and she hoped that her aunt would have forgiven her for the stupid way in which she had been caught up that day at the harbour in the general pandemonium.

Edward hesitated a fraction. 'All right Ruth, just for a minute. I'd better come in just in case she doesn't recognise you. I can tell her who you are,' and they laughed in happy anticipation together.

Ruth glimpsed the house. The taxi was slowing, its interior darkened by the branches above. She was glad; her emotions were beginning to get the better of her. Her eyes were wet when she turned to Edward. 'Thanks Edward so much for looking after me away from home, and for saving me. Sorry about the leg,' and she brought his head down and kissed him on the lips — a kiss of love but without passion.

Edward cleared his throat, gripped her hand. 'I — well I couldn't do anything else could I? Just wish I could have done more. Hated you having to work like that.'

She touched his face. 'It's all over now.'

The taxi had stopped. Ruth's hands trembled as she searched her purse and paid the driver. The car turned in the lane and Edward picked up their luggage as it sped off.

'I think she'll be in the back having tea,' said Ruth.

'Look, if you don't mind Ruth, I won't come in, I'd rather get down home first.' He handed her her case. 'You don't mind do you?'

She smiled understandingly, had guessed he might change his mind. 'Of course not.' He was excited at the prospect of seeing his parents again, just as she was her aunt. 'Anyway I may come down later, but she'll want to know everything.'

'Righto, see you at our place,' and Edward hurried away down the lane. His people would want to know everything too. Five years to unravel and talk about, and they too must have a lot to tell him. The occupation — it couldn't have been easy. He wondered if his father had managed to get his car back from White Rock that day, and wondered if people with cars had been allowed to use them.

Perhaps only if they were engaged on important work.

The stream by the side of the lane murmured and kept him company as he began to half run, but as usual hampered by his ankle. Hoped they would not mind William not being with him. He and his father must get together over his — Edward's — new plans. No doubt it would be a shock to his father to have a grown up son returned and interested in the business and full of new ideas. First thing his mother would say, 'Have you been getting enough to eat, Edward?'

He glimpsed the Peastacks and the bay in the gold evening sun. He passed a couple with a child making their way slowly up the lane and in his happiness he smiled and waved at them. He was lucky — lived there at Moulin Huet — his beach. Some of its rocks came into view and he forgot his disability in his eagerness. Saw his home partly in the shadows, the headland ground dark behind it. He stopped momentarily at the drive entrance. Patches of concrete showed through the moss and overgrown grass. No lights — no one. Something about the roof — probably storm damage or something like that. His father was having it repaired. Of course, and the neglected drive would be seen to later. Yes, that was it. Oh, but now he was back he would be able to help and soon get the place looking smart again. Obviously his parents would not have had the money to spend on repairs during the occupation, so they couldn't open yet for the season. No guests — no money coming in. He should have realised.

Short-breathed he ran along the drive to the side door. Gripped the dirty knob and pushed it open, calling out as he did so, 'Mum, Dad, I'm back — hello — I'm back. Where are you?' Hurried from the gloom of the passage into the kitchen, talking as he went. 'I didn't let you know I was coming — I wanted to surprise you.' When his voice faded it was very quiet. He turned right towards the sitting room — the room the family used during the summer. There was a smell about the place. The door was open — the room empty, dust and plaster covering the floor. Empty beer bottles and papers lying on the bare boards. A red swastika stared at him from above the fireplace. Uncomprehendingly he stood in shock, then stumbled out and climbed the stairs, shouting, pulling himself up by the filthy banister rail.

'It's Edward, I've come back. Where are you?' Their bedroom, a hallowed and forbidden place when he had grown older, had been a place of sanctuary when he was a little child. A place where bad dreams were caressed away, their bed a place of privilege when he had been ill. Now it contained only one familiar item, a wardrobe stuck in a corner, and the last of the sun's rays entering through a large hole in the roof above. On the mantelpiece above the fire grate was a dirty card with foreign printing on it. His own room was the same — empty. The once cosy lived-in bedroom from where he had snatched the few things to take with him that day when the family had fled the house. Now it was a darkening, empty brooding place. A terrible feeling was clutching at his senses. His voice echoed amongst the rooms downstairs. He noticed things he had not done before. The kitchen had wires standing out from the walls, an old chair leaned against the sink — no other furniture. But the mirror was still on its hook in the passage leading to the guests' dining room. The same mirror in which Matilde, the maid, had bent her knees to pat and arrange her hair before entering the dining room. It had always been just a little low set. And the dining room — in season a hub of chatter and clink of cutlery and glass, of brown faces and smiles — now empty as the other rooms, and only the long heavy curtains either side of the window overlooking the terrace and sea remained to reassure Edward that this was indeed the place that had once been home to him.

He blundered outside again into the twilight. The garage was empty. A rag fluttered from a cross member and an old oil can lay on its side on the floor. Of the tea garden nothing remained. The tables had gone and only a flat area of waist-high weeds gave an indication of where it had once been. He rushed round to the front terrace. A thick concrete observation post with slits in its walls faced out to sea on what had been his mother's carefully tended rockery garden, while of the terrace itself half of it had been taken by a square building with small windows and the door long gone.

He returned inside, calling out again, but there was no conviction or strength to the sound. The mirror mocked him with its dark reflection, and the murmur of the sea came through the broken window. A desperate dread filled him. Half his brain was working telling him something he couldn't accept. The nightmarish thought never allowed in those five years to be dwelt upon in case it was a fact. The Red Cross messages — never mentioning or coming from his parents. The messages from Ruth's aunt via the Red Cross had never included them by name. She had thought his parents were in England — that they were all together. Outside again he descended the steps to the beach, his heart rebelling ferociously. No! they had moved out. Obviously the Germans had taken over the house in view of its key position overlooking the bay. That was it, of course. They were now perhaps at that very moment leaving their new home to come and find him. Ruth's aunt would know where they had gone, and would by now have got in touch to inform them that he was back again. His mind embraced and clung to the idea. But the lifeless, dark, broken hulk that had once been his home — the Ormer House Hotel — overlooked him and the beach with sightless merciless eyes. And Edward knew. In the darkness amongst the rocks where he had spent to much of his earlier life, he fell to his knees, his face to the sand.

Ruth found him, her own tears unseen by him as she gently touched him. It was awful to see him like that. 'Edward, dear Edward. It's me, Ruth.' What could she say? The shock had been tremendous, even to her, but she had had to come and find him to try and share the burden of the bereavement.

Gasps of utter misery against the sand shook Edward's body and she knelt by him, arm about his shoulders. There, after how long she was not aware, he lifted his upper body and they knelt side by side in the darkness.

'Is it true?' he uttered at last through his fingers, and her own increased their pressure as she brought his head down to her breast. It was answer enough. And her own tears fell to the sand alongside his. She had only found out for sure when after the first joyful reunion with her aunt, the latter had asked with a strange look on her face whether Mr. and Mrs. Dorner had returned with them. The facts were that those killed on the pier had not been identified properly, and it was thought perhaps the whole family had managed to get on to the boat. The general opinion was that the parents had not and had perished in the attack. A ceremony had been performed for the dead, but nobody until now had been quite sure.

Edward took a deep breath and stood up, and Ruth helped to support him. 'I'm sorry, Edward, so sorry.'

A shudder ran through him. 'I was going to help them, Ruth. I wanted to do something for them — could have talked to them now. I knew them only when I was a young boy. Oh, if only they hadn't decided to leave.' Remorse, regret were in his shaking weakening voice. A hand covered his face. 'You're sure? There couldn't be a mistake?'

All the compassion that Ruth felt was in her gentle soft reply. 'No, Edward dearest, not now, but they were together. They did what they thought was best at the time.' She felt him shiver. 'Come home, Edward, with me. My aunt and I will look after you. Don't stay here, you're cold. Please.'

He turned away from her, freeing his arm. 'No, not yet, I cannot face anybody. I'll just go back to the house for now,' and his bowed shadowy figure began to move away in the direction of the steps.

Ruth followed. 'No, don't go, Edward. Please come with me. You'll feel better. Don't go in there by yourself.'

'It's my home, Ruth,' he said simply.

Ruth was frightened that he might do something to himself in the state he was in — under the shock he had just received. 'Let me come with you, Edward, then we'll go up to my house.'

'No, Ruth. I'll come up later. Just now I must go back in there again.' His voice was firmer, determined.

'Well all right,' she agreed reluctantly, 'but I'll come for you in half an hour.'

In the darkness he turned to her. 'No, I don't want you to, Ruth. I shall come up later, but I'm not sure just when.' Even in his distraught state his innate politeness showed. 'I'm grateful to you and your aunt for the offer. Thank her. I'll be all right. I just want to be by myself.' He was adamant.

'Don't stay long will you?' she said anxiously after him, but he did not reply.

Ruth walked hesitantly away along the drive, remembering how five years before she and Edward's family had stood with the vicar while he blessed them before the ill-fated dash to freedom. From behind her came the sound of a door closing.

In the darkness of the ruined family home, Edward, still in shock, could not come to terms with his loss, and slipped back through the years. He was a small boy again, lost in the darkness and calling for his parents, his voice echoing upwards to fade into the night beyond the broken roof.

When several hours later he had not appeared, Ruth, accompanied by her aunt, returned hurriedly to what had once been the Dorner family home. They found Edward slumped against the stair rails three steps from the bottom, exhausted and quiet. Between them Ruth and her aunt managed to get him into the car and took him back to La Maison Verde, where with the help of a large amount of her aunt's whisky and a warm bed, Edward became oblivious to the anguish and misery that had overtaken him so suddenly after his long wished return to his native Guernsey.

For two days he lived in a twilight of disbelief, but then he realised that he could pretend no longer. His parents were dead, killed as he and they raced for the shelter of the last boat. They had been dead five years, but nobody had been sure enough to say for certain until he and Ruth returned. People had been interred in St. Mark's cemetery but identification had been difficult.

Ruth never left his side, but felt an outsider before his withdrawn manner. Her aunt saw the change that five years had wrought in him, thinking that he had grown into a fine young man but overtaken by the tragedy. She had been overwhelmed with joy at receiving Ruth home again, and was still finding it difficult to adjust to having a young adult woman return in place of a young girl who had suddenly disappeared so many years before. What had been a happy reunion was overshadowed by what had happened to Edward and William's parents.

On the third day after their return Edward set off for town alone. Ruth had wanted to accompany him but once more it seemed that he preferred his own company. She was uneasy about him going. His expression had been a distant one, still coming to terms with his loss. She was desperately sorry for him but as always her first thoughts were about their relationship, and his keeping her at arms' length hurt her. She loved him and wanted to comfort him and offer solace when he needed it most. On the other hand, she consoled herself, it was only natural that the agony of mind that had engulfed him would leave little room for other consideration. Perhaps hers was a selfish attitude, but if you loved someone so much then it was forgivable.

Edward walked down High Street in a daze. He wasn't sure why he'd come into town, but he'd had to get out of doors away from Moulin Huet. Memories were too strong near his old home. But it proved the same in town. Families — some with children at hand out for the day, and he remembered his father taking William and himself to the pictures with interval ice creams and pop. Going fishing in the rowing boat. Sometimes his mother would join them for a trip to Herm, and once to Sark to picnic. Regret flooded his being. Now when he was old enough and articulate he could not show them his gratitude. They must have worked hard to give him and William a good home and upbringing. It was too late — five years too late. He leaned against the support of a shop window, bowed his head in utter lonely misery. He was very tired and his appetite had been almost non-existent since his return to the island.

His forehead touched the cool window. Through it his eyes registered articles of furniture, paintings and pottery. Not knowing what to do next he continued to gaze almost unseeingly into the window — almost. A table occupied pride of place in the window. Dark wooded, oblong and to seat perhaps four to six persons around it. It had been well used with cracks and cuts at its edges, and scratches on its flat surface which it wore honourably as befitted a strongly constituted elderly piece of furniture. One end was in line with Edward's dull and disinterested gaze. A small rectangular indentation of the wood enclosed two letters carved near its edge. They were quite distinct and they were enough to penetrate Edward's tired and still confused mind. The initials were E.D. Someone had carved the initials on the table edge — E.D. Those were his own! His eyes focused more sharply, so did his brain, and he bent to take a closer look. There was no mistake. Mentally he shrugged. A coincidence, someone else with the same initials. But his gaze continued to wander over the table. It was familiar — very familiar. In fact it looked just like the family table which had stood in their sitting room at the hotel. What was it doing in a shop window in High Street?

He edged inside the shop to get a closer look. There was no doubt about it — it was the Dorner family table around which ever since he could remember they had gathered for meals! The memory flashed back. One rainy Sunday lunchtime.

He had been bored and nearabouts five years of age. One of those days when his books, toys held no interest and the weather stopped him from playing on the beach. One object had held his interest however — a penknife given only a week before his birthday. The penknife had been new, sharp, and under cover of his hand he had cut his initials into the wood. A cuff round the ear and a half day in his room had been his reward for his artistry. William in his youthful way had admired the work, but was quickly put off from emulating his elder brother by threats of how many days he would spend upstairs, if he repeated the desecration of the dining table.

Edward stood fully in the window, directly behind the carving. He had sat there always opposite his father who sat at the other end. His eyes fell on the place where his mother used to sit and William opposite. The birthdays, the parties, the laughter and arguments that had taken place around that piece of his home. His mother rubbing hard to get the heat marks out of its polished top. And here it was on view in the shop front and priced at ten pounds.

A man came from the rear of the shop. 'Don't stand in the window; you may break some of the valuable porcelain. There's nothing there I'm sure for you,' and he gazed disdainfully and irritably at Edward's — it must be admitted — scruffy-looking dark-cheeked figure. Motioned him out.

Edward took no notice. 'This is our table — you've got our table.'

The man looked blank then frowned heavily. 'You mean it was sold to us and now you want it back. Is that it?' His tone was barely tolerant.

'No, it's ours. That's our table — it's always been ours, and what's more we didn't sell it to you. It was taken — it must have been, because it was in our house.'

The other glanced round at the half dozen or so people in the shop, then narrow-eyed back to Edward. 'What house? Where?' His manner was impatient, offhand. 'Look if you want to buy anything do so. If you don't I must ask you to leave now.'

'Ormer House Hotel — Moulin Huet. I'm Edward Dorner. This table was taken from there — it belongs to my parents.' Edward was angry. Past and present were becoming blurred again. The table should be at home. 'It belongs to my parents, Mr. and Mrs. Dorner — they have the hotel there.'

'Never heard of it,' the shopkeeper retorted brusquely. 'Now listen to me,' and his finger jutted out at Edward, 'I want you out of this shop pronto. That's my table — I paid for it. If you want it you pay me for it. Don't come in here trying to work something on me. If you're not out in a minute I'm ringing for the police.'

Edward's own finger stretched, pointing at the carved initials in the woodwork of the table. 'Those are my initials. I carved them when I was five. You or someone has stolen that table from our house.' With one swift movement he knocked the card bearing the price to the floor. Edward's world had collapsed and he couldn't cope with or understand this latest incident.

'Have you ten pounds?'

'No, it's ours. I'm not paying for it when it belongs to us.'

'Get out.'

'I will not, not until you get someone to return it to our house.'

The man grabbed Edward's arms. 'Come on you silly sod, you must be drunk or mad.'

Edward turned on him savagely, freeing his arm and then shoving the other away violently. The latter staggered in the confined space, to overbalance over a coffee table, then to crash into a cabinet full of delicately worked figures, knocking it to the floor and smashing its glass and most of the contents.

Edward in his miserable confusion of mind tried to move the table towards the door, but it was impossible without moving a lot of other articles. So he remained there, hands covering the carving that once before had brought him trouble. If only now he could hear his parents' chastising tones. He had not realised it then, but there had been idyllic times, in contrast to the hell into which he had stepped the last few days.

People were pressing with curiosity into the shop, a crowd gathering outside, and someone was telephoning. The jokes about lifelike dummies went unheeded as he continued to stand grimly over the table. The crowd was enjoying the free show, and the manager, not daring to risk the breaking of any more of his stock, tried to persuade Edward to surrender his position in the window. But Edward remained defiant. Then the police came and quietly but firmly managed to get him out.

'Your table is it, Sir?' the sergeant queried

pleasantly. He was puzzled. The young man didn't appear to have been drinking and there was a certainty about him regarding the ownership of the piece of furniture.

'It was stolen — it's our table from our house.'

'Stolen? You must be careful Sir. Have you proof?'

'No.' Edward shook his head helplessly. 'But I don't need it. That was our dining table and someone has taken it.'

'There has been a war, Sir. When did you last see it?'

It was difficult to concentrate. 'Oh, about five years ago.'

'Well now, it could have been anywhere in that time. Where do you live Sir?'

'The Ormer House Hotel.'

The other frowned heavily. 'Ormer House Hotel? Where's that?' and Edward told him. 'But Sir, that place has been empty for years.' He saw the anguish appear on the younger man's features.

'I didn't know. I returned only — yesterday I think it was.'

'Ah,' and the policeman's eyes slid away in understanding. 'I see Sir, so it's all been a surprise to you, hasn't it?' He put his notebook away. 'Look, the best thing we can do is for you to come to the station, give us some more details and we'll get something sorted out.' He glanced at the mess surrounding them. 'Of course, there's the matter of the damage.'

Behind him the owner was going on about thousands of pounds of breakages, but the sergeant said something aside to him, and then led Edward out of the shop and into the waiting police car.

'You'll see that he doesn't sell the table to anyone else please?' Edward pleaded desperately.

'I think we can arrange that, Sir.' He felt damned sorry for him. There had been the occupying forces, taking what they wanted, but there had been looters and thieves amongst those who had stayed behind.

The States dealt leniently with Edward. It was felt that there was a proportion of blame on both sides. The manager had grabbed Edward first, but the latter was at fault for being in the window and refusing to leave. They were sympathetic but warned him and it was deemed that he had suffered enough. They could well understand his feelings on seeing the article in the shop window. As regards reparation for the damage, he had no money — couldn't be fined — and he had no work, having so recently returned to the island.

He was found work on a farm in St. Saviours parish for a month and had to live in. His sleeping quarters were a prefabricated building near the main house. It was hard work, an early rise, feeding the pigs, cleaning out and generally doing the rough work about the place. But Edward stuck it. He was being paid his first wages and plans were forming in his mind for the future — the not too distant future. More importantly perhaps he did not have much time to dwell on the tragedy which had so altered his life, nor did he dare trust himself to think about it. Each day he was going to phone William and explain, but did not.

Some three weeks later he paid the ten pounds required for the family table, after Mrs. Le Ney,

Ruth's aunt, said he could store it at her house. It was a sad bitter occasion, but with it came a small satisfaction and a link with the home he had once known. He also wrote a letter to William after agonising for days over whether he should tell him that their parents were dead. He could not bring himself to do that and instead told him that things were not quite as straightforward as he had hoped, and would William stay put for another week or so until arrangements could be made to bring him over. He decided that for the time being it would be better for William to remain where he was.

Ruth procured a bicycle and rode over each day to see Edward at the farm. On his half day off sometimes they would go for walks or sit on the beach, but nowhere near to Moulin Huet. Edward could not face a return there yet. One day they were sitting against the sea wall at Vazon. The tide was well out and people were dotted along its wide expanse. It was warm, a rustle of breeze from offshore, and the water matched the sky in its summer blue. To their right, the empty fort, a reminder of the enemy now recently gone.

Ruth saw Edward's sad grey distant eyes. Was it six years since they and William had sat on another beach as children in what seemed now another world? She tucked her arm through his. 'Have you thought about what you may do now, Edward?'

He continued to look out to sea as he spoke with a sigh. 'Not really. I've thought of one or two things but oh, I don't know . . . .' He shrugged. 'The plans I had have all gone. I know this though, I'm not staying at this job much longer.'

Ruth knew he was unhappy at the farm, but guessed that he would feel the same at the present time wherever he was. It had been a dreadful shock for him and for her. 'What will you do about the house?' she asked gently, then wondered if she should have broached the subject.

'The house?' Edward turned his head slowly to look at her.

'Yes, I mean your old house — Ormer House.'

He gazed out to sea again, the lock of hair fluttering against his forehead, and Ruth saw his hands tightly locked together. 'What can I do? It's a ruin.'

'Perhaps you could get compensation from the States,' Ruth suggested.

'I don't know Ruth. I doubt it somehow.' His tone was lifeless, drained, and his face under the newly attained tan was haggard.

'I'll ask my aunt — she may know. If not, what about a solicitor? They would certainly tell you.' Impulsively she kissed him on the cheek. 'Come on, let's go down to the water.'

The sea had no master, Ruth thought. You paid homage to it. Tugged at its damp skirts and it listened like a parent while you confessed your sorrows and joys. Edward's arm rested easily on her shoulder as they went, and Ruth was content for the time being with that.

One afternoon Edward found himself in an upstairs room overlooking the Pollet, part of the offices of Defues, Defues and Haggard. Mr. Haggard, the senior partner, rose from behind his desk to shake hands — elderly, short, spare, large-nosed and bald. 'So you are Edward Dorner. Very sorry to hear about what happened — dreadful business. I did see your father occasionally, mainly over minor things to do with the hotel. Sit down please.'

Edward sat on a plain leather chair in front of the huge desk cum table. 'I came,' he began, 'to find out about my parents' house at Moulin Huet.' The memory came back strongly and he struggled with his emotions, but after a few moments he went on, 'Is there anything I can do? I'm not sure about anything now.'

'Have you seen the property?' asked Mr. Haggard. The stark look of anguish on the young man's face opposite affirmed this. 'Yes, of course you will have,' he said hurriedly.

Outside in the street it sounded busy. Life went on. Edward knew he must pull himself together.

Mr. Haggard did not sit down, but stood at his desk, the fingers of his right hand gently tapping its top and staring doubtfully down at Edward. 'The problem is that no will has been found. Your father did not place one with us and none of my colleagues know anything about one. However, the estate could be sold and the proceeds shared between yourself and your brother. We can prove your identities so there should be no problem there.'

'I don't think I'd like it sold,' said Edward quickly. William had also mentioned selling.

'Oh! you have some plans for it in the future?' The senior partner sat down, studied him in some surprise.

Vitality showed in Edward's listless eyes. 'Yes, I have. I want to restore our house, make it a successful hotel again. I can — I know I can. All the time I was away I thought of it and how to help Dad to modernise it . . . ' He stopped, looked away into the sky above the roof tops outside. When his gaze returned to the older man there was a resolve as well as sadness in his features, a new firmness to his voice. 'Now all I can think of is to do it myself. I want to do it for them, in my parents' memory, to make the place come alive as it used to be.' His shoulders dropped. 'But it will have to wait. I have no money and only a tuppenny job . . . ' He paused as a worrying thought presented itself. 'Can anyone else come and take over the house before I'm ready to do so?'

Mr. Haggard's reply was reassuring. 'Oh no, you and William will inherit the property. Of course, tramps, vagrants etc. can get in and unfortunately it will deteriorate further unless repairs are done to the property. And holidaymakers they could be interested in the remnants of the occupation — the gun emplacements and lookout which as you know were put up in the grounds of the house.' He thought for a moment then asked, 'Are you likely to see William in the near future?'

'No. As a matter of fact William is still in England.' Edward gave a weary smile. 'We had no money — not enough anyway — so Ruth who had worked during the last year in England had saved enough for she and I to return. I've written to William and hope to bring him over very soon.'

'When he does return ask him to pop in and see

me. How has he taken the news of your parents' passing?'

Edward looked extremely anxious. 'I'm afraid he doesn't know yet. I just couldn't tell him in the letter, so I'm waiting until I see him again.' He was dreading breaking the news to William.

'He's got to know sometime, but I do understand your reluctance, Edward,' said Mr. Haggard.

The solicitor stirred in his chair, half rose. 'Well, there we are young Edward. I do hope something good will come out of all this. You've taken on an unenviable task in some respects, but you are young and have time to see your ambition fulfilled.' He stood up fully.

It occurred to Edward that not once during the meeting with Mr. Haggard had the latter actually stepped past his desk. Even when he went to the window to glance out, he had kept within a line bounded by the front of it. Edward thought it might be that for him to have crossed that imaginary line would have placed Mr. Haggard in the land of the poverty-stricken and troubled. It was a safer, more secure world behind the desk.

When his client had gone Mr. Haggard stood looking down into the street. Where on earth was a youth of eighteen going to get enough money to restore a ruin like the former Ormer House Hotel?

Edward joined the throng in the street deep in thought. He was not poverty-stricken, being the owner, or part owner, of a property — such as it was. He tried to clear his mind for the task ahead. It was his burning ambition now more than ever to restore the family home. The question was, where was the money to come from? Edward decided not to return immediately to Ruth and her aunt and acquaint them with what had happened at the solicitor's. Instead he made straight for Moulin Huet and another look at the object of his problem. He had not visited it since that nightmare evening when he and Ruth had returned to the island.

It was mid afternoon when he arrived. A couple of yachts rode the gentle waves in the bay. The beach was busy, people sun-bathing, wading and swimming. A few children splashing in and out with shrieks of laughter, and some more serious examining the pools by the many rocks. In years gone by he, William and Ruth had played like that. He walked around the outside of the house but did not go in. Seeing it in the clear daylight did not ease the pain or make the house less of a ruin. Sitting on the wall which had been the rockery garden boundary he gazed sadly as some children clambered about the remains of the gun emplacement.

He turned his back when he could no longer bear to look at it any more, but sat hunched, staring out to sea over the happy people below. Somewhere in his subconscious the first strands of a plan were forming. The blue horizon kept his attention whilst his mind strove ever harder to add and develop the idea. Would it work? It would have to — a gamble. And how many years would it take? It would mean leaving again. And William? He could return to Guernsey and stay if he wished. What his plans would be when he, like Edward, had got over the first overwhelming numbing shock of their bereavement, only he would be able to sort out. For himself nothing else mattered. He must obtain enough money to be able to restore the house. Daring not to let his glance linger on the ruin, and trying to keep his emotions in check, he hurried away up the lane, glad of the shade and shadow under the arching trees to hide the anguish still so easily aroused in his heart.

Ruth watched as Edward got off the bus and walked towards her, her pulse taking flight at his slim upright figure, the dark auburn lock of hair untidily above his right eyebrow. And his limp not as pronounced as it used to be. She had been rather surprised when he had telephoned to ask her to meet him in the early evening. But happiness for her was where Edward was and she had looked forward to seeing him again eagerly.

He kissed her on the cheek. 'Thanks for coming, Ruth. I just had to talk to you.' His features were serious under the tan. 'I hope I didn't stop you from going somewhere else.'

'Of course not. I wasn't doing anything special.' Only that when she was in his company.

He surveyed her for a few seconds in the quick, rather shy way he had. Despite his problems he realised that Ruth had grown into a woman, and a stunner too. Lucky the chap she falls for, he thought. White dress, blue band round her hair matching the belt round her waist. Her eyes were the colour of a flower he'd seen on the cliff top. She would always listen, always loyal and uncomplaining. He took her arm. 'Shall we walk towards Fermain? Take the cliff path?'

'That'll be lovely, Edward,' she agreed readily. It was a beautiful evening — warm, and the sun having done its balancing act above St. Peter Port had dropped away to the other side of the island. She wondered what he wanted to talk to her about, had seen a compliment to her in his eyes. Dare she think further than that? Had he at last felt for her what she had always felt for him — love?

They climbed the steps to the path, the sea on their left, sombre coppices and foliage inland, and the occasional seat well placed for the views. Young couples passed by, some of whom looked in love, Ruth noticed. Did she and Edward look in love? After a few minutes they reached a clearing giving a full view over the water and the cliff falling steeply away below. They stopped and stood looking out. Ruth, concentrating her gaze, thought she could just make out the dark coastline of Jersey. At that moment they might have been the only people in the world. Still holding on to his arm she looked at her companion. There was a tension about him; she had felt it as they had walked along. His lips were tight together and he looked preoccupied. Was he having trouble putting into words what he now felt for her? Was that why he had asked her to meet him? Her breathing was shallow, she felt light-hearted and just a little tipsy without having had a drink — a glorious feeling. She let go of his arm and ran off along the path, glancing back at him as she did so, then halted, smiling happily like a child at play.

Edward, looking very surprised, hurried after her. 'Hey! Come back Ruth. Where are you going? What's come over you?'

She let him get to within a few yards of her, then darted away again as he quickened his pace. There was a half smile, a glad softening of the lines of worry to his features. 'What's got into you, Ruth? Ruth, you little devil, I want to tell you something.'

Ruth dodged off the path into the gloom of the undergrowth. She saw him stop and look around. Called out, 'I'm here Edward,' and leapt away again like a young deer. She was a child again playing hide and seek amongst the trees and rocks of their childhood. Sweethearts from that childhood. Heard his footsteps behind her. Turning, she waited. He was laughing, his cares forgotten, intent on catching her. Not since they were children had she seen him like that. This way and that to avoid his lunges, allowing him to get close then off again. He would never be fast enough to catch her, handicapped by his limp.

'Wait till I catch you.' He was just behind her.

She turned from the shelter of a bush. 'Do it first then,' but then stumbled backwards over a raised tree root to sprawl on to her back.

Edward was on her in seconds, forcing her to a bed of past autumn's leaves. He gazed down at her flushed face, his eyes bright and eager with the chase. 'What the hell's wrong with you?' he gasped down at her. He was enjoying his capture, her woman's curves straining beneath him, her hair spread like a halo around her face.

'Let me up you oaf,' she gasped, pretending to be angry, and struggled.

'Oaf, is it?' he exclaimed, seating himself more firmly than ever on her.

She submitted and went limp. 'I'm just happy that's all.' Did he realise why?

His face had lowered towards hers, the smile fading. A moment later her lips were imprisoned by his and her hands were tight upon his head to hold him there. He stretched upon her violently, and the twilight made a patchwork through the branches above them as Edward's body made love.

It was dark as Edward stirred by her side and leaned over her. 'I didn't mean to — I . . . '

Ruth's fingertips touched his lips. 'It's all right, my love,' she whispered, her being bursting with joy. He loved her! He did! She caressed his cheek, wanting to stay forever with him in that calm warm dark cocoon.

But then Edward rose and stood against a trunk of a tree nearby. Ruth could make out the white of his shirt and the blur of his face in the little light there was from the deep purple of the sky beyond the trees. And as always came the constant murmur of the sea below.

She couldn't contain herself any longer, must help him if he was having difficulty in voicing his feelings for her. 'Edward,' her voice was throaty, thin, 'you had something you wanted to talk to me about.' Waited with an eager expectancy, propped on an elbow and looking up towards him.

Edward half turned towards her. 'I'm going back to England as soon as I can raise enough money.'

'Going back!' The utterance was a mixture of disbelief, hurt and shock, her face suddenly taut, the wonderful dream gone from her eyes.

His voice came to her, reckless yet determined.

'There's no work here for me, not the kind I want.' His speech became hurried, vehement. 'I want money — lots of it — to help me to restore the house. I couldn't live here with it as it is — a blasted ruin. But if I work hard over there, it may not take me too long. I've got great plans for the house, Ruth.'

Ruth buried her face in the leaves. What a fool she'd been again. He had no plans for her — just the house. That's all he had wanted to talk about — about leaving. Her voice was a listless monotone. 'Surely you could stay and find work here, give yourself a chance to do well here.'

He stood looking down on her. 'I've thought of nothing else. I've made enquiries, but I know I'll do better on the mainland.'

She looked up at him, the heartache in her eyes. He couldn't see it. 'But whereabouts? Have you got work to go to?' It was all so awful. Just when she thought their lives were to be closely intertwined forever. Oh, damn the house. Why couldn't he sell what was left of it and buy another and settle down?

'I'm returning to Daleford,' he said simply.

'Daleford!' she gasped incredulously.

'Yes Ruth, Daleford.' Suddenly he had dropped to his knees at her side, a tense enthusiasm driving some of the strain from his more visible features. 'You remember one Christmas when we were invited up to that big house — Scarton Manor. Well, Mr. Scarton — he seemed to like me and he said if I ever needed work to let him know. So I'm going to see him.'

Ruth's blood ran cold. Did she remember? When

she had worked in his factory. She remembered also his daughter Elaine. No doubt she would still be around, and Edward would be her target immediately. Ruth despaired. 'When are you going?' she asked dully, miserably.

'I don't know. I need money to get there.'

The irony of the situation bit deep into her heart. For years they had planned and she had saved to return to Guernsey. Now all Edward wanted to do was to leave. She put her head into her hands, knowing she would lose him if he went back to Daleford.

Edward mistook the gesture. 'Don't worry, Ruth, I'll find a way. Just have to work a little longer until I've enough to get me over.'

She wanted to cry but could not. The anticlimax to her long-held hope had drained her. She would give him no help — not a penny.

Suddenly a raging anger took her, born of all the years of hope, disappointment and excuses she had made for Edward. What a bloody naïve empty-headed spineless creature she had been. He didn't love her, never had. Even during their passion of minutes before he had not mentioned one word of love. She had acted like a child and he had taken advantage of it. No! she had encouraged him, thinking that . . . Oh God, it was all so different. Ruth sobbed in her bitter anguish of heart.

He bent over. 'Ruth, what's the matter? I'm sorry I . . . .' He was concerned, but it didn't matter now.

She sprang to her feet, making him stagger backwards. 'Get away from me, Edward Dorner,' she flung at him brokenly. 'I had a dream, damn you. I thought you loved me — I thought you were going to ask me. Didn't you realise. I've loved you all these years. You never knew did you — never cared. Even when I was young, I loved you. I thought when you were older it would be different but it isn't, and you're not. Damn your bloody house. You think more of it than me. Well have it and live with it. Go and live in the damn ruin.' She turned and blundered away towards the path and ran stumbling along it, hearing him calling after her. But she did not look back. Heaven had turned to hell. His voice came again receding behind her. She had been flying towards heaven earlier, feet dancing over the ground. Now misery and shame was the force that drove her away.

Edward stopped and breathless watched her light-clothed figure disappearing into the darkness. His mind was in a turmoil. He had never quarrelled with Ruth before. She had seemed happy, and had astounded him by her sudden bout of coquettishness, her teasing of him. Her behaviour had aroused him, but nothing had been further from his mind when he had asked her to accompany him on the walk. She had been like a young deer of the forest and he had lost control of himself he admitted. Ruth had become a woman — no longer a leggy young girl. He had made love to her, had not meant to do, but she had encouraged him. The fact was he had been taken unawares by the strength of her feelings for him. He had had no idea, and yet . . . .Memories returned — things she'd said or done. And she'd never forgotten the fact that he had shielded her on the White Rock. Actually he'd just done it on the spur of the moment, and whether he had actually saved her life he doubted, but she seemed to think that he had. Then the much more recent memory of her submitting to him willingly. Words of love had come from her, and he could still feel the pressure of her arms around him as if she would never let him go — ever. Afterwards he had been shocked at the vehemence with which she had reacted when he had told her he was thinking of returning to the mainland. She had also displayed jealousy — a jealousy of his former home.

The next day he paid a visit to the cemetery where his parents had been buried. He'd been putting it off, but the feeling had persisted that he must go, even if it was for the first and only time. It was drizzling when he arrived and he wandered between the headstones looking for the names. Some graves were newly dug awaiting those to come and a few were just mounds with no sign of who was buried there. It occurred to Edward that it would save time if he found the vicar and enquired from him. Entering the church he found it busier than he had expected. Flowers were being arranged near the altar steps by two women and organ music came from somewhere near the roof. An elderly man in a cassock was busy arranging white cards and books near the last pew. He looked up as Edward approached.

'I'm looking for the vicar. Could I have a word with him please?'

'I think he's rather busy just now; we have a wedding soon. Could I help you? I'm the verger.'

Edward supposed he could. 'I'm looking for the

grave of my parents, Mr. and Mrs. Dorner. We had the Ormer House Hotel at Moulin Huet. They died at the beginning of the occupation. I'm Edward Dorner, their eldest son.'

The older man faced him. 'Edward Dorner! I'd have never recognised you; you've altered eh?' Pointed across the aisle. 'I saw you baptised here in that very font,' then his gnarled but strong hand gripped Edward's. 'I used to see you occasionally in the choir when you were older.'

Edward remembered. He hadn't lasted very long as he and a friend could never stop giggling when they caught sight of someone in the congregation they thought looked rather funny. Neither had their voices helped to keep them in the choir; they had been utterly dispensable. Edward had not minded in the least telling his parents that the choir was overmanned or words to that effect. He had much preferred to go down to the beach on summer evenings.

'How long have you been back in the island?'

'About three weeks.'

'I thought it would be one of you when I saw that business about the furniture in the paper.'

'Oh yes — the table.'

The other nodded sympathetically. 'There was a lot of it — thieving. Terrible thing when they can't keep their hands off other people's property. Expect it from Jerry, but not from your own, eh?' He glanced away momentarily. 'Sorry about your people, Edward. I know where they are but I'll get the vicar first. I think he has something for you.'

Edward was puzzled and wondered what it could

be as he gazed down the aisle after the verger. A depression came. His mother and father had been married he knew in that church. Had walked down that same aisle. Waiting at the rear of the church Edward felt a mood of defiance come over him. Why should the God of all things take good people like his parents away? Had it always to be done so cruelly?

The Reverend Ilett with his verger following was approaching quickly and Edward recognised him, thinner, greying but the same person who had come to warn the family of the impending occupation of the island. He grasped Edward's hand. 'Welcome back, Edward. You've grown since I saw you last. Is your brother with you?'

'No, it could be next week,' replied Edward. Could be, but he wasn't sure about anything just then.

'Oh well, perhaps we shall see you both quite often in the future.'

Edward glanced at the morning-coated men coming in, and the verger going to meet them.

'They are the ushers arriving. I have a wedding in a few minutes,' explained the vicar. 'Sorry I have to rush,' and he placed a hand on Edward's shoulder. 'A bad business about your people — er . . . .' He glanced in the verger's direction but he was busy. 'You wanted to see the grave, I understand.'

Edward nodded. He was aware the vicar was on edge, anxious to perform the ceremony he was being paid for. All he, Edward, wanted to see was the grave, that was all.

'Yes, well come this way then,' and the Rev. Ilett

smiled and nodded his way quickly past the guests beginning to come into the entrance. Edward followed the hurrying figure whose surplice and vestments billowed out in the breeze, the heavy drizzle wetting his face.

The vicar stopped at the rear of the cemetery near the boundary wall, in front of an overgrown slightly raised mound and gestured towards it. 'Perhaps now we can do something about it,' he murmured apologetically, and already beginning to edge away. 'You will excuse me, Edward.'

Suddenly the latter remembered. 'Mr. Briellard said you had something for me.'

'Yes — yes of course — I have, nearly forgot, I'm sorry,' and he dug hastily below his surplice and brought out an envelope and thrust it into Edward's hand. 'They belonged to your parents I believe. They were found.'

Edward stared down at the small lightweight parcel. When he glanced up the vicar was just disappearing round the corner of the church. The package was sealed, and whatever it contained was loose inside. Breaking it open Edward let the contents slide into the palm of his hand. Three rings lay there. A man's gold with a shield and initials set upon it, and two ladies' rings — one of plain gold and the other with a cluster of sapphire and diamonds in the shape of a heart. The initials J.D. were on the larger gold one — his father's. He guessed the others were his mother's before he looked on the inside of the small gold one, her wedding ring. He wasn't quite sure if he'd seen the other one before. When you were young you did not take much notice of things like that. His fingers enclosed them protectively, and as he leaned against the cemetery wall, the rain ran down his forehead to join the moisture in his eyes.

From the church came the sound of the wedding march as the bride entered. How long he remained there he did not know, but when he left the grounds he had made his mind up about what he had to do next. Firstly he made his way into town, wet and bedraggled but determined. There he found a pawnbroker's and handed over his late parent's rings in exchange for a sum of money which, whilst not all that he had expected, would with what he had saved up be enough to enable him to carry out his plans. Before leaving the pawnbroker Edward told him with a great intensity of feeling that he would be returning to claim the rings again, and at great pains to ensure that they would be kept safely until such times. Then he made his way to the shipping office and booked a ticket for the next morning's boat to Weymouth. Afterwards he returned to the church to find the wedding ceremony over and the verger brushing the confetti to the sides of the path. That person looked up in some surprise to see Edward so soon again and in such a dishevelled state.

Edward then gave Mr. Briellard some of the money he had obtained, and arranged for a headstone to be placed on the grave and for it to be kept tidy. He wasn't sure when he would be coming again. There were things he had to do — was going to be very busy.

Mr. Briellard assured him that his directions

would be carried out and that Edward had not to worry, he would be pleased to do that service for him. They shook hands and Edward departed leaving the verger looking after him anxiously, not liking the look on the young man's face with its tense and feverish light in the eyes. If he wasn't careful he'd be having a breakdown — needed some rest — mental as well as physical.

Edward felt a relief now that he had accomplished the tasks that he had set himself. He had found the grave, paid for a headstone, and obtained his ticket to England. But there remained one more no less difficult, and that was to write a letter to Ruth. He had not seen or heard from her since their quarrel on the cliff walk, and he was sad that he had upset her so much. They had been through a great deal together. Now he was going away, perhaps for a long time, and wouldn't see her again.

Doubts crept in. Should he leave? But then his resolve became unwavering again when he thought of his ambition regarding the property. Already he had found out that life was a hard adversary, and to survive well he must meet it head on — force what he wanted out of it. Miserably he sealed the letter. He would be in England by the time she received it. The last thing he wished to do to Ruth was cause her more hurt.

Edward gazed over the wake of the ferry, St. Peter Port dwindling in the distance. To come, the unenviable task of acquainting William with the terrible news, and in the mist beyond the unforeseeable future.

6

Ruth's fingers traced the ink of his words for the umpteenth time. He was sorry — had misunderstood — would be back someday. The quicker he made his money the sooner he would be able to return to Guernsey and restore the house. She threw the letter away from her. Damn the house! Not once had he mentioned that he loved her or even cared for her. The nearest he had got was that he would miss her. Just as he would a view or a dog. What a fool she had been. Given herself, the culmination of her thoughts and feelings for him over the years. And afterwards all he could think of was making money in Daleford and dreaming about that pile of ruins that had once been the Ormer Hotel.

William was bored and somewhat annoyed at being left behind in Daleford. Surely there was some way they could get him over. But of course Ruthie had to have Edward all to herself. They'd be swanning up and down Guernsey now, enjoying themselves whilst he stagnated. What was the hold up? He couldn't even spend time with Mrs. Thurrocks. She had now been reunited with her husband, and indeed had been quite cool and distant the last time they had met. Her eyes held a light which they had never shown for him, and he had noticed her pushing of the wedding ring tightly against the back of her finger.

Out for a stroll one day he entered a leafy avenue of fine detached houses and bungalows. Expensive cars squatted in the drive and wealth hung quite clearly beyond the enclosing fences and high walls. The sound of lawn mowers and distant voices came and occasionally he glimpsed someone through the trees. One dwelling was well separated from the others and the lawns were not so tidily kept, the trees and shrubbery having a more natural look about them; a cosier landscape, William thought. There was a terrace the full width of the house front and steps down into the garden area. A woman sat reading on the terrace, whilst another stretched from a step ladder towards the overgrown hedge bordering the garden. His glance was caught by the precarious position of the woman, and also by the tightness of her dress across her hips and breasts as she strained to reach the overgrown branches with the clippers she held. A bush momentarily cut short his sight of her. Suddenly there was a cry and a clattering sound of the steps. William flung the gate open and rushed over to her as she began to sit up grasping her ankle.

She looked up in surprise at his figure standing over her. No less surprised was her companion who had hurried to the other's side.

'I was passing,' he said, 'heard you fall — can I help?'

She nodded with a twisted but grateful smile. William put out his hand to help her up together with the aid of the other woman, but she got no further than halfway, then sank backwards unable to put any pressure on the injured foot. William putting his hands under her armpits, began to left her upright. She was heavy, being of plump proportions, and his hands touched the warm fullness of the sides of her breasts. Never in his young life had he touched a person whose flesh felt as soft as hers did. Even Mrs. Thurrocks' had not — they had always been taut and demanding, and Amanda's had still some youthful firmness about them. While her companion went for a chair William supported her. He wished that it would be a long time coming, so warm and pliant was the body close to his.

When the chair came she sat down with a sigh of relief. 'I knew that would happen one of these days. Lucky a strong young man was passing, wasn't it, Helena?'

'I don't know what we would have done without you,' said Helena — thinner, darker and older. 'And we don't even know your name.'

'William — William Dorner.'

'Well, William, I was just about to make a cup of tea. Would you care to join us? I think you deserve one after your good deed.'

He agreed readily. It would while away the time, he wasn't going anywhere special.

'Make yourself comfortable, I shall not be long. Are you all right, Adeline?'

'Yes, I haven't hurt it as much as I thought. In fact I think I can manage to get up to the seat.'

Helped by William she gained the terrace and they sat down together. She was small, plump and fair with heavy eyelids so that when she looked down or was silent she appeared to be almost asleep. For a few minutes they conversed in short bursts

— about the weather, the garden and her ankle which William noticed was attached to a shapely calf. He thought she seemed rather shy, giving little smiles then looking away. He found it difficult to guess her age. When you were in your eighteenth year many people appeared quite old. She was certainly older than Mrs. Thurrocks — quite a lot older he thought.

Then the tea appeared. It was very pleasant sitting there, the moors in the distance and the valley deep between. He was halfway through his second biscuit when the older woman exclaimed, 'How remiss of us. Here we are and we haven't introduced ourselves to you, William.' She gestured towards her companion. 'This is my stepsister — Miss Steck — and I am Mrs. Prind. And you must forgive me I've just forgotten your last name — Torner wasn't it?'

'No, Dorner.'

'I don't think that's a local name is it?'

'No, I come from the Channel Islands.'

'Oh, I've been to Jersey once when Mr. Prind was alive.'

'Actually I come from Guernsey.'

'And are you on holiday?' The shutters of Miss Steck's eyelids pulled upwards to reveal a gaze of pale blue.

'No.' He wouldn't have called it that. 'I've been here about six years. I'm waiting to go back, my brother's over there now, he's sending for me anytime soon.' William briefly explained how and why he and the others had come to Daleford.

'Oh! you poor boy!' exclaimed Mrs. Prind,

'separated for all those years from your parents.'

At that moment a wasp chose to hover over the biscuits and Mrs. Prind calmly folded a magazine from the table and took a swipe at it, whilst Miss Steck leaned far back and sideways on the seat in some alarm so that her head touched William's upper arm. Almost immediately she pushed herself upright and laid a small fingered hand on the limb in a gesture of apology followed by a murmured one. William was surprised at the feel of her fingers. For a fraction of a second they had been explorative, measuring — he was certain. 'Helena is quite brave with wasps. I'm terrified of them I must admit. They seem to come straight for me.'

'Well, not that time dear, the biscuits attracted it.'

William thought that any wasp with any liking for human flesh would have picked Miss Steck's pink and plump variety in preference to the rather hard, wrinkled and dark type of her stepsister. Order restored the latter asked, 'And where are you living now, William?'

'I'm still up at the school.'

'That can't be very pleasant. I should think that you've seen enough of the place without having to spend any more time there.'

William shrugged slightly. 'I've got used to it, it's the only home I've had for six years.'

'You were only young then when you had to leave Guernsey,' stated Mrs. Prind with a sympathetic understanding.

'Yes, I was only eleven I think — yes eleven.'

'And eighteen next,' she observed, smiling.

'You're a fine young man for your age, William.'

Miss Steck glanced at him from half-open eyes set in that rather flat face.

He felt a peculiar feeling when she did that, just as he had earlier when she had touched his arm. He smiled, not knowing just what to say, then took a sip of tea to hide the fact, his eyes again taking in the house and its surrounds. His hosts must be quite wealthy, he decided. When he had finished his drink should he continue his walk or go back to the school? 'Would you like me to finish off the hedge for you before I go?'

'That would be an enormous help William, but you must not detain yourself on our account, must he Adeline?'

'No, of course not, but it would be such a help. I know I shall not be able to do any more today.'

William rose. 'It'll not take me long — finish it in no time.' Picking the steps from where they had fallen he placed them by the hedge, and clambered up. Once he glanced at the terrace to find that Mrs. Prind had disappeared and Miss Steck watching him from the seat. Ten minutes later the work was done, the hedge pruned, levelled and neat.

'I'm sure you must be hot. Come and sit down again,' and she patted the woodwork. 'Helena is bringing you a glass of lemonade. You're very strong but, of course, you're very young also.'

Mrs. Prind appeared with lemonade and cakes.

'See Helena, William has finished it already.'

'That's marvellous. Unfortunately gardens get larger as one becomes older.'

William wasn't quite sure what she meant but eyed the cakes with interest. The short burst of energy had made him hungry.

A few minutes later he thanked them and prepared to leave, but then Mrs. Prind asked if he would assist her to get Miss Steck inside. Between them they helped her into the house and on to a settee where she reclined with the injured foot raised.

'Thank you again for your help, William. You came along just at the right time.'

'Yes, and you must come and see us again,' said Miss Steck looking up at him. 'Then you can see how my foot is progressing,' and the eyelids drooped a little as she spoke.

'If you'd like me to I'll come and cut the lawn for you tomorrow. I'm doing nothing and I'm not actually at school now — taking lessons I mean, so I'm free.'

Miss Steck's obvious pleasure brought life to her still and rather expressionless features.

'Of course we shall pay you, William.' Mrs. Prind waved a finger to and fro with small quick movements at his rising refusal. Digging into a handbag she brought out a note which she placed into his hand. 'That's for today, we're very grateful.'

William accepted the money thankfully. It was the first money he had ever earned for actually doing some work. He left the two ladies soon afterwards, Mrs. Prind closing the door on him and Miss Steck staring after him from the couch — an old face atop a younger body.

William returned to the Poplars and the stepsisters the day after and on a number of those that followed. They welcomed him, fed him, and paid him handsomely for any work he did. Miss Steck watched him almost constantly. It did not matter in what part of the house or garden he happened to be, he was aware of her surveillance. Sometimes he would catch a glimpse of her at a bedroom window, or just beyond the curtains in one of the rooms downstairs. Occasionally he would glance up from the task he was engaged in and find her observing him from another part of the garden. It could be rather disconcerting at times.

Two weeks after Ruth and Edward's departure for Guernsey he received a puzzling letter from Edward asking him to stay in Daleford a while longer as there were things to be sorted out. What did he mean? William decided that if word did not come for him to return in the next week he would telephone home from school and find out what the hold-up was. Out of contact with his home for so long he had forgotten that full communication would now be established again between the island and the outside world. Even so he looked anxiously for a letter, a telegram or a phone call each day. Just getting the place ready after five years of occupation could be a lengthy process, but he wondered why Edward had contacted him and not his parents. Surely seeing both their sons again after all that time would be of more importance to them than taking in holiday makers.

His tidying of the garden was almost completed, another day would do it. He had enjoyed his visits to the Poplars and the days had passed more quickly than they would otherwise have done. Now all he wanted was a message to take him home. But other jobs about the stepsister's house seemed to present themselves. A hinge on a door here, a spot of paint there, something to be moved, and light bulbs which mysteriously developed a very short life, needed renewing.

On the Thursday of that week William was as usual having tea with the two ladies before returning to the school. Miss Steck had just passed him a second cup, when he caught the urgent look she gave her stepsister.

Mrs. Prind patted her lips with the back of her forefinger. 'Ah yes, William, Miss Steck and I have been discussing something. You have been very good and kind to us — helping us such a lot, and we wondered whether you would care to spend a weekend here with us.' She flashed a quick rather nervous smile. 'Of course we shouldn't expect you to work or anything like that,' she shrugged slightly, 'just a change we thought — didn't we Adeline.'

William was aware that Miss Steck was staring at him intently over her cup which was halfway to her lips.

'Yes, we did, change for you,' and the cup remained in mid-air.

Why not? William didn't hesitate but thanked them for their invitation, and it was arranged that the coming Friday afternoon he would join them for the weekend. Back at school he remembered the feeling in his lower abdomen when Miss Steck had stared at him.

When he arrived for the weekend he found his room had a glorious vista over the woods and valley, and another angle of view of the chimney-like octagonal erection with an ornate top and balcony soaring hundreds of feet into the sky.

That first night he slept well in the soft confines of his new bed. From it he could see the night's canopy over the valley, and in his imagination he heard the murmur of the sea and was home again.

The following day was cool but fine, and William decided that a length of fencing could do with a dash of paint.

'Oh, but you're not here to work, we said,' Mrs. Prind protested.

'I don't mind at all — I quite like it.'

It took him most of the day and he finished by repainting the house name on its wooden block attached to the wall near the front door. Then he decided to have a shower. Unlike the school communal ones with their garden-like sprinklers and tepid water, the one in his bedroom was chromed and yellow tiled with a plastic curtain. The hot was very hot and the cold afterwards invigorating. Turning the supply off he squeezed his hair of remaining water. Was there a towel beyond the curtains? Thought he'd noticed one. Pulling them aside he stepped into the bedroom.

Miss Steck stood just inside its door. For a fraction they stared at each other, William in startled surprise, the other with something entirely different, the eyes wide open and fixed intently on his body. A towel was tight in her hands. She blinked quickly then thrust it towards him.

'I wondered whether there was a clean one for you. I didn't realise you were just getting out — I was going to leave it for you — sorry.'

'Quite all right — er — thank you Miss Steck.' The towel had imprints of her hands where they had clenched it, and he wondered how long she had been standing there. Glancing down at his body he saw that he had grown large, erect, and like the tower beyond the window, but he couldn't help it, hoped he had not offended her. He was young, strong, the hot water perhaps. If he had known she was there he would have groped through the curtains for one of the towels hanging from the rail next to the shower. Perhaps she'd never seen a naked man before and in full erection too. They'd called him 'horse' at school.

On his way downstairs he noticed there was no key in the bedroom door. If there was no key he could not lock it, but he felt reluctant about asking for one as it made it appear that he did not trust his hosts.

He saw very little of Miss Steck that evening, and on the one occasion she spoke to him, she did so from behind those very heavy lids and not directly to him. By mid-evening she had disappeared and Mrs. Prind informed him that her stepsister was having an early night.

'You mustn't mind, William, she doesn't mean anything by it, but Adeline has led a more sheltered life than I, and sometimes she can be perhaps a trifle shy.'

He didn't think the early night of a woman more than twice his age was because of shyness.

'Have you both lived here very long?'

Mrs. Prind took off her spectacles before

answering. It was a gesture that she did often. 'Myself about twenty-five years,' and her eyes held memories as they strayed from his to the fire. 'It was our second home for my husband and I. We moved in not long after we were married. We were very happy here.'

William spoke without thinking. 'And Mr. Prind, is he . . . ?'

'I'm afraid Mr. Prind died several years ago.'

'Oh, I'm sorry — I didn't mean to . . . '

'It's all right, William,' but she smiled sadly. 'In this world there are arrivals and departures. Vincent's departure was just very sudden that's all. I was lonely — very lonely at first. We had no children, although at one stage we were going to adopt, but we were over age by then. So Adeline came to live with me. She also was lonely as she had never married and had stayed at home until our father died.' She smiled brightly. 'Luckily we get on well together but if we tire of each other's company occasionally there's plenty of space here.' She slid her spectacles on to her nose again and picked up her magazine, flicked the pages then slid them off again and regarded William with a sudden anxiety. 'I do hope you're not bored here. It can't be much fun for a young man.'

He denied that vigorously. 'It's marvellous just to get away from the school, very kind of you to ask me.'

Mrs. Prind smiled with pleasure and settled back to read.

It was a bit boring, he thought, then he remembered the incident in his bedroom and the look on Miss Steck's face — but not without its surprises.

William found bed very pleasant. He was relaxed and warm — too warm, so he threw the clothes aside. The day had been still and close, perhaps the last one of the autumn. Daleford wasn't a bad place after all he decided, seeming quite pleasant now that he was on the verge of returning to Guernsey. The Island would seem strange now to his older eyes. What on earth he would do when he got there he did not know, but he had to admit that he had no particular ambition apart from obtaining pots of money. Not like Edward who thought of nothing but the hotel. Too much like bloody hard work it seemed to him. A football pools win would be just the job — if only he could find a system. William drifted off . . . .

Sometime later he awoke, the night air cool on his skin. He half turned towards the window, his hand feeling for the clothes he had thrown off earlier. Moonlight bathed the side of the bed and Miss Steck stood near its foot looking down on him. A gown hung loose from her shoulders. Apart from that she was unclothed. Her breasts protruded beyond its edges and the dark triangle of her lower body was clearly visible.

William, startled, pushed himself up on his hand.

Miss Steck moved nearer, her gown sliding from her. 'William.' It was a hoarse whisper, a plea, and he knew her eyes were like they had been before — wide and staring.

Fully awake now William gazed in stupefied fascination as the bed dipped under the weight of a rounded knee and heavy thigh. She bent forward and the moon turned her curves to white marble. Her words came thickly. 'You came for me, William — you did didn't you? You were sent to me — I knew it the first time you came.' Her nipples brushed the young hairs on his chest. 'Say you did — I know you did. Just for me — Oh William!' The room seemed to be full of Miss Steck and her moans and William's night dissolved into one of smothering flesh.

Nearer the dawn William, shocked and tired, realised it was not a dream, and Miss Steck's pale blue eyes held the look of a schoolgirl during the following day. She had been fearful before she had left his room, frightened that he would leave immediately and she would never see him again, and also that he would divulge her behaviour to her stepsister. But William kept silent over breakfast.

All that day Miss Adeline Steck went about with a secret little smile and towards evening her eyes strayed to the clock many times. She appeared again at his bedside, but this time William was better prepared. When he thought about it she was old enough to be his mother. Not that he had much time to think as his night visitor's rampant spinster flesh moved loose-mouthed over him, and her very ordinary face merging into the darkness.

Much later and before leaving him her fear showed again. 'You'll be staying tomorrow night, my William. Helena will not mind. You can stay here all the time — come and live here,' and her hands were busy even then, touching, measuring, nearly forty years of frustration and repression finding its insatiable outlet.

William towered over her. 'I'll be going home soon Adeline. I cannot stay.' He shrugged. 'Perhaps a couple more days. I'm ringing home today.'

She was silent, the heavy lids on a level with his upper waist.

'I'll come and see you before I go.' If she lived in Guernsey she'd be worth visiting now and again, he thought.

'Another month would not make any difference would it?'

'I've got to go home Adeline. My home is in Guernsey and my family.'

Her lips were pouting against his navel. 'But I've only just found you. All my life I've seen others with men. You love me — you said.'

He had — in bed. Then it had been easier to say he did.

'Come back after you've been home,' she urged him.

'Yes, I could — yes.' It was also easier to agree rather than to argue.

'And you will come back?' Her head had lowered, her voice was fading, she was getting to him again.

'Yes,' he nodded above her.

'You promise. You see I love you — never loved a man before — such a man.' Her words were slurred.

William made an effort. 'Helena will be getting up soon.' There was no lock on the door.

'Just once more,' and her teeth caught him.

It was Mrs. Prind over breakfast who suggested leaving his things with them until he found out just how much longer he was going to be in Daleford.

He was welcome to stay on at the Poplars.

Later Mrs. Prind accompanied him to the gate. 'I must say William that having you here has worked wonders for Adeline.' William glanced at her sharply but she was not looking at him. 'She's been happier, more interested in things — different altogether. Of course we lead such a quiet life here, and I suppose she gets tired of my company sometimes.' She smiled at him. 'But we have enjoyed yours, William, you've been very kind.'

He shrugged her remarks off. 'It was nothing. I've enjoyed my stay — a change from being up at St. Justs.'

Yes, it was true, certain aspects of his stay had been extremely enjoyable, a very pleasant interlude; but he was impatient to be away now and telephone home.

After leaving Mrs. Prind he wondered if she guessed what had been happening between himself and her stepsister. Perhaps not, but he couldn't be sure. It struck him that women seemed to like him. He never had any difficulty, and felt confident with them, maybe that was the reason. Poor Adeline, she'd have to make the most of the next night or two, he wasn't likely to be around Daleford much longer.

He rang exchange and waited eagerly for the number.

'I'm sorry caller, no number obtainable — hotel unknown.'

'The Ormer Hotel — Moulin Huet?'

'No, I'm sorry.'

Perhaps they had renamed it? Then he thought of

Ruth — she would know.

A few minutes later and he was through. 'Ruthie, it's me — William. What's going on? How much longer am I going to be here? What is Edward doing? I've been trying to ring them at home, but the operator doesn't have the number. Have they changed the name?'

There was silence. 'Ruthie.'

'Yes — hello William. I'm not sure, I . . . '

What was the matter with her? Sounded very quiet, flat-voiced, a thousand miles away. 'Have you seen mum and dad? Are they still at the hotel?' Six years were a long time, he thought. 'Ruthie.'

'Yes.'

'Oh.' There must be interference on the line. 'I was saying . . . '

'N-no, I haven't seen them.'

'Well, what about Edward?' William was becoming irritated. They'd just left him over there to his own devices, they were not bothering about him at all. He heard Ruth's sigh.

'Edward's on his way to you and — ' there was a break in the despondent voice.

'To Daleford?'

'Yes.'

'But why?' He couldn't understand, she didn't sound right. The whole thing was puzzling — a mess. 'Has Edward been staying with mum and dad then?' Perhaps they'd given the business up — had never started again after the war.

Another silence. 'No — no he hasn't.'

Something was wrong. 'You and Edward all right?'

'No, we quarrelled. He's decided to leave Guernsey.' The voice was near to collapse.

So that was it! Bloody love! It caused more misery in the world than anything else. 'But I thought he planned to stay and help run the business. He was so keen.'

'He did but . . . ' Her speech faded.

'Ruthie, what's the matter?' He attempted to cheer her up. 'Look, don't worry, he'll be back, there's nothing over here for him. You'll get together again.'

The small weak voice came. 'He has something to tell you.'

'Oh, what about?' What could be so important to make him return to Daleford?

'I can't tell you — I mustn't.'

'But could someone at home tell me, I mean . . . ? Mum and Dad are not ill are they?' That would explain everything. 'Ruthie' she kept going off — 'where are they then, in hospital?'

'Ed — Edward will tell you.'

'Ruthie, why can't you tell me if you know? Have they had an accident or something?' It was bloody stupid Edward coming back to tell him something which she could inform him of over the 'phone.

'No — well — Oh William I can't tell you. It's between you and Edward.' Irritation had strengthened her voice momentarily.

Hell! Why was everything so mixed up? He tried again firmly. 'Now look Ruthie, you must tell me, I want to know. I'm not living at the school just now, so I may not see Edward right away.'

Ruth's utterance when she replied was so quiet

that he had to strain to catch the sound. 'They're not here, William, your parents. I'm sorry.'

'How d'you mean?' The receiver felt heavy in his hand.

'They — they passed away six years ago . . . '

He wanted to sit, made a sound into the mouthpiece. And her voice continued to come, echoing thinly from it. 'They died the same day we came away. Sorry William . . . William.'

The headmaster found him bowed in a chair. Managed to find out what the dreadful news had been. Gave William a very large whisky — and another. Later, against the wishes and advice of the other, he staggered out into the world which a short time before had been beautiful and exciting, holding golden hopes. Now he trod deep into sodden autumn leaves whilst the wind swirled amongst the branches above — directionless, just as his mind was.

Many hours later he found himself back at the Poplars. But the William standing on the doorstep was very different from the one who had left that morning. Dirty, unkempt, with the youthful and vibrant light gone from his eyes. To their credit Mrs. Prind and Miss Steck coped with the stranger who had appeared out of the darkness. They got him to bed, trying to decipher his mumblings and waited on him anxiously until morning when with the daylight the reason for his plight fell from his now sober lips. Love can be selfish and Miss Steck was glad that he was returned to her, and for the next day or so both she and her stepsister were busier and more fully occupied than for many years past.

The result was that some twenty-four hours later William, staring through the bedroom window in deep depression, was forced to accept the fact that in the light of his parents decease, he faced a much more uncertain future. And try as he did, he found it hard to visualise his mother and father — they had during the last few years become rather shadowy figures in his memory.

His thoughts passed on to the property they would have left. There was that to be divided between him and Edward. Was there also any money to come?

A few days later Edward arrived and William was surprised how much thinner he looked in the face. Mrs. Prind made him a meal while Miss Steck, although receiving him civilly, viewed him with some suspicion. William was hers and she was going to do everything to keep him at the Poplars. Afterwards they were allowed to be alone to talk privately.

'Sorry you had to hear the bad news from Ruth,' Edward said.

'It would have been just the same coming from you.'

William looked pale and washed out, and he remembered his own feelings during that first awful time. 'They were killed on White Rock behind us — they wouldn't know anything.' Both were silent for a few moments, reflecting in their own ways.

'Where are you staying?' asked William.

'I'm in a flat. D'you remember some houses we visited when we went carol singing? Well, there was one vacant there — I remembered them saying something about turning them into flats after the war.'

Was it only last Christmas? They had been full of hope and excited about their futures in Guernsey. Edward looked around at William's comfortable surroundings. 'How long have you been here?'

'I'm not sure, on and off, about three weeks,' and briefly he acquainted Edward with how he had come to know the stepsisters, but did not mention that one of them was his mistress. Edward would have had a fit — he was a bit straightlaced.

'What will you do now, William?'

William shrugged. 'I just don't know. I may go back to Guernsey. In fact I will, but it depends on what I find there as to whether I'll stay. Is there much work?'

'Not a lot at present. I worked on a farm.'

'Oh blow that for a game,' exclaimed his brother. 'I want something different to that.'

Edward produced a piece of paper. 'This is the name of the solicitors acting for us. They want you to call in. There's some money for you.'

'Oh.' Sudden interest livened the dull eyes. 'D'you know how much?'

'No I don't, but he said that it was held in trust for you until you're twenty-one.'

'Oh hell, that's another three years.'

A ghost of a smile appeared on Edward's lips. 'Well you might spend it if you got it now.'

'What about our house — the hotel?'

'It's a ruin — an absolute ruin.' Edward shook his head at the memory. 'The Germans used it. The roof's off and everything.' He made an angry gesture with his hand, 'and squatters have been in.'

'So it's not worth much?'

'Not in its present state, it isn't.'

'What about us selling it as it is?' suggested William.

'No, I don't want to do that. I want to make enough money to restore it and turn it into a hotel again.'

'But where are you going to get enough to do that?'

'I'm going to work for it, William. I'll get it, don't you worry. I don't know how yet, but I will.' The fierce determination made his brother stare at him. It seemed that their former home was the only thing that Edward cared about. He — William — could think of things more interesting to slog his life out for, 'Ruthie said you'd quarrelled.'

Edward shifted in his chair. 'Oh, just a misunderstanding. She wasn't too pleased about me coming back here. I'd no idea she was so fond of me.'

Poor old Ruthie! thought William. Edward wouldn't have known if she'd carried a billboard in front of her with 'I love you' written on it.

'When are you going back to Guernsey?' Edward enquired. It was obvious he didn't want to talk about his relationship with Ruth.

'Towards the weekend, I think. I'll see what happens.'

'Have you got enough to get you there?'

William nodded with a return of his easy confident smile — the first since the bad news. 'I get paid for the work I do here. They're quite generous.' A cynical humour continued inside him. It was mostly night-work — he didn't do much around the house now.

Edward left soon afterwards after asking William to telephone him before his departure for Guernsey. He was relieved that his brother had managed to find such comfortable lodgings. In fact he thought that it seemed to suit him very well, although he thought William's choice of companions a trifle peculiar — a middle-aged widow and a rather plain-faced spinster.

When Edward had gone William thought about their conversation, or rather that part of it concerning the family house in the island. His brother had expressed his wish and ambition to rebuild it and turn it into a successful hotel again. Not once had he asked what he — William — thought should be done about the property. It seemed a better idea to sell at the highest possible figure and share it. But Edward had said nothing about equal shares, only about the money held in trust until he became of age. His brother had a lot of cheek suggesting that he, William, would spend it all quickly if the money became his immediately. Had he also been left some? He had not said so, and yet it appeared very strange that one and not the other should benefit in that way. That was the first thing he would do on arrival in Guernsey — make straight for the solicitor's office. After all Edward was only a year older and that did not give him the right to do what he wanted with the property. Neither he nor Edward had much money and they were not likely to earn and save enough for grandiose schemes like the restoration of a ruined hotel. Far better to make money from the property now. Edward's idea was crazy. Why work when you could enjoy the proceeds of a sale? The building and the land must be quite valuable. It was situated in a glorious part of the island.

A few days later William left the Poplars bound for Guernsey after promising the occupants, Miss Steck in particular, that he would be back in a week or two. If prospects were better over there, then he would be just a memory for the two ladies. On the train down country he fingered the money Adeline had given to him so that he would be certain of having enough to return. It would come in very useful towards the purchase of a car should he stay on in the island.

However, William did not find prospects any better. The idea of starting small and working his way up steadily did not appeal to him. Nor did his visit to Mr. Haggard the solicitor provide him with any optimism regarding the property. Matters had not been settled as yet and no will had been found but Edward was likely, being the elder son, to come into ownership of it, but nothing was certain. However, the money held in trust was some small consolation. At least he could be sure of that. Pity he couldn't have it now — would have come in handy — but old Haggard would not entertain such a notion and had been shocked by William's suggestion.

He visited the ruin, his previous life there now

having an aura of unreality. It was a pile of stones he gazed at — uninhabitable, defaced, and on closer inspection William did not deviate from his earlier thoughts after talking to Edward, that the project would swallow huge amounts of money. Edward's scheme was idiotic. He called on Ruth and found her tense and bitter, and changed from the bright hopeful open girl he had known. Her trouble, he knew, was Edward.

Why on earth she did not face up to the fact that Edward saw her just as the girl next door and nothing more, puzzled William. She was wasting her time and life. It wasn't as if he were in love with anyone else. Ruthie's rival was a house, or more truthfully a broken unsightly wreck.

William saw the island with new and older eyes; the cutting winds when the seasons were drawing on, the rock-strewn beach of Moulin Huet, uncomfortable and fairly inaccessible. The talk of Jersey being the island of the future. It seemed small now after the wide open spaces of Daleford and its surroundings. And the sea, with its ceaseless comings and goings he found irritating and boring. The only good thing to come out of his visit was a certain knowledge that he would gain financially when he came of age.

He returned to Daleford and the Poplars and into the arms of its welcoming duo — or rather into the more than welcoming arms of Miss Adeline Steck. William came to realise in the weeks that followed that the Poplars was now his home, and again, not for the first time, he realised that he had fallen like the proverbial cat — on to his feet.

The household ran on in an easy tranquil way, Adeline reclaiming the lover she had craved for, Mrs. Prind found a son late in life. As for William, he had acquired a new mother figure in his mistress.

7

Edward made his way to the Scarton factory, partly remembering its location through calling for Ruth when she had worked there. But on reaching the site he hardly recognised it as the wartime works he had known.

A huge glass-fronted building in blue and white, with gleaming cars inside, and a large forecourt with more cars — second-hand ones, row upon row. A smaller-windowed building that appeared to house offices adjoined the side of the showroom, and a blue and white flag with the Scarton name on it fluttered from its roof in the October wind. Behind the main showroom Edward discerned what he guessed were the old wartime factory sheds in which components for tanks had been made and in which Ruth had worked.

He mounted the steps into the offices. A sliding window to his right was marked 'Enquiries'. Inside a girl sat at a typewriter and she rose when she saw him, pulling the window aside.

'Could I speak to Mr. Scarton please?' Edward asked.

'Can you tell me your business, Sir? Are you a rep? Mr. Ironside deals with those.'

'No, I'm not. I'm Edward Dorner. I just wondered whether Mr. Scarton had a vacancy — a job. I'm looking for one.'

The girl pointed across the corridor to another

door. 'I think you'd best see Mr. Ironside first. I think he's in. Just knock on that door.' She leaned into the opening, tapping a pencil between upper and lower teeth as she added, 'Dunno whether they want anybody or not.'

Edward knocked and a voice called out for him to enter.

'Yes?' The speaker's hand let the beaker rest on the desk, his other paused over papers in front of him. Horn-rimmed spectacles stared from the top of the dark suit, and Edward thought the other was viewing him as a car, appraising him — seeing his weaknesses, his better points.

'I wondered if you had a vacancy in the firm. I'm looking for work.'

'What — as a salesman you mean?' His manner decreed that he thought the model before him was quite ordinary.

'Yes, well I mean anything you have. I'll try it.'

'Any experience?'

'No, I — I'm afraid not.'

'I don't think there's anything here for you sonny. These are upmarket cars. Got to know what you're doing.'

Edward raised his shoulders slightly. 'What about cleaning them — anything?' He was desperate to begin, to earn. The dream was a long way away, he must get started.

The other shook his head. 'Not that I know of,' and raised the beaker to his lips, gulped its contents and then said, 'What made you come here?'

'Mr. Scarton told me once that . . . .' He was not allowed to finish.

'You know him?' The voice and the face across the desk were visibly surprised.

Edward saw the opening and charged for it. 'Yes, I spent Christmas Eve with the family. If ever I wanted work I must see him.' Had he actually said that? Edward wasn't quite sure now, but it wasn't a moment to be timid or absolutely truthful.

Mr. Ironside gave him a more respectful look then stood up. 'Wait here a moment. What did you say your name was?'

'Dorner — Edward Dorner.'

The other was soon back. 'Yes, all right, he'll see you, and it's not Mr. Scarton now, it's Sir Redvers Scarton — don't forget.'

'I'll remember, thank you Mr. Ironside.' The latter stared after him, a trifle bemused. The old boy did remember him, only just but . . . .That model had more horses under the bonnet than he had expected.

'Come in — come in.' Sir Redvers stood in front of his desk as Edward hesitated respectfully in the doorway.

'Good morning, Sir.'

Sir Redvers came forward, a frown giving way to some recognition of his visitor. 'Christmas did you say?'

'Yes Sir. I was at St. Justs school and you invited us up one Christmas Eve. We were from the Channel Islands.'

'Blow me — of course I remember, yes. Didn't your sister play the piano for us?'

Edward smiled. 'A friend Sir, Ruth Le Ney — she played.'

Sir Redvers' hand came out to shake Edward's. 'Of course, a good time in the middle of a bad one eh?' and he laughed good-humouredly. 'Anyway, sit yourself down — Edward isn't it?'

'Yes, Sir Redvers.'

'Forget the Sir Redvers. Mr. Scarton will do between us. For services to the war effort,' he explained, and looked surprisingly coy for a moment, and perhaps seeking approval which he received instantly.

'Marvellous, Sir, very pleased. Without your armaments the war couldn't have been won.'

'Mine was only one of lots of firms, Edward, just lucky. Mind you I've worked hard for it.' He paused to survey his visitor a moment. 'Right now, young Edward, would you take a drink? If I remember you took whisky last time. I must say I enjoyed myself that night and you young folks certainly seemed to do.'

Edward observed that being knighted had not altered his northern speech. 'Very kind of you Sir — er — Mr. Scarton.'

'You'd rather have tea or coffee perhaps?'

'A coffee please.' The whisky had been at a buoyant optimistic happy time.

Sir Redvers ordered through the intercom then turned to Edward again. 'Now tell me what you've been doing recently. I thought you'd have stayed in that lovely island of yours. What made you come back here?'

Thereupon Edward described what he had found on his return, and his subsequent decision to find work in Daleford. He thought it best not to mention his desire to live again as soon as possible in Guernsey. It could be years before he was financially strong enough to realise his ambition. Or perhaps never . . . A different world altogether now, and ambition being all that was left for himself.

The coffee arrived and over the rim of his cup Edward saw the large picture of Scarton Manor directly behind Sir Redvers. One like that of the new Hotel Ormer would one day hang on his wall, he vowed to himself.

Sir Redvers had seen the direction of his gaze. 'You like the picture do you? Had it commissioned specially — a good job.' He leaned back in his chair, hands in pockets. 'Are you ambitious, Edward lad?'

The question was unexpected but he was quick to answer. 'Yes very Mr. Scarton.'

The older man nodded. 'Right then, I suppose you were surprised to see the new direction of attack I've taken — in business I mean.'

Edward knew what he meant. 'Oh the cars. Yes I was I suppose; thought I'd come to the wrong place at first.'

Sir Redvers leaned his forearms upon the desk, the fierce light of business drive in his eyes. 'That's where the future lies, Edward — in cars. The public's hungry for 'em. They'll take anything at present. The factories are gearing up for new models. It's a big challenge, Edward.' He rose from his seat, beckoned Edward over to the window, enthusiasm making his speech quicken. 'See all that space in front of the cars. Going to be even larger showrooms there — going for the quality stuff now. We're going to expand with showrooms all over the country.' He turned back into the room. 'I made one lot of bloody money, now I'm going to make another lot with this.' There was hard determination and pride in his voice. Seated at his desk again he waved Edward to sit opposite. 'Now, coming in with us?'

The swiftness of Sir Redvers' decision surprised Edward momentarily.

'You want the job don't you?' said the former, four square and bluntly.

Edward lost no time. 'I certainly do. Thank you very much Sir.'

'D'you know anything about cars?'

'No, I don't, but I like them and my father had one.'

'D'you drive?'

Edward shook his head, feeling inadequate.

'Well you've hardly had the time to learn,' his companion excused him, 'and in any case you're not likely to have to drive one yet. I'll see you get the chance though.'

Edward could hardly believe his luck — the long shot had come off. He was astonished how swiftly things had come about. 'Very kind of you, Sir.' It was easier to address him in that fashion rather than Mister.

Sir Redvers brushed his thanks aside gruffly but not unkindly. 'I know you — you've had a rough passage Edward and you came to me for a job. I'm giving you one, but you start at the bottom. See how you get on. I expect one hundred per cent effort. I don't stand any slacking,' and he gazed aggressively over the desk into Edward's face.

'No, of course not. I understand — I'll work hard for you,' replied the latter simply.

'When can you start?'

Edward had made up his mind to begin as he meant to carry on. 'Now, if you want me to,' and he saw the glint of satisfaction in the eyes opposite.

'That's what I like to see — keenness. By the way, have you lodgings?'

'Yes thanks, I've found a place where we once sang carols outside. They now have flats.'

Sir Redvers nodded. 'Good,' and looked at his watch. 'Have you eaten yet?'

'I had breakfast earlier. I hadn't thought about . . .'

'Well it's getting on for twelve now,' interrupted Sir Redvers. 'Get yourself over to the canteen — round the corner by the showroom. Tell them I've sent you — fix you up with some dinner. Then report to Mr. Ironside, he'll start you off.'

Edward was grateful and very thankful and said so. First step was accomplished.

Sir Redvers put out his hand. 'Good luck Edward. I don't think I'll be wrong about you.' He motioned with his hand to the picture behind him. 'I saw you eyeing the picture. Well, stick with me, work hard — no nonsense, and one day you can look at something similar and say — that's mine — through my efforts.'

Afterwards Edward thought how strange that Sir Redvers should pick a house as the spur to his — Edward's — goal. The very object that engaged most of his waking hours!

For the next few months Edward washed cars,

hosed them down, cleaned their insides and occasionally was allowed to polish the newer models standing warm and dry behind the showroom windows. As the year drew on the work became colder and wetter, it being mostly outside. But he began to have an understanding of the different cars that were brought in — the names of the different marques, prices, weaknesses and strengths. He also gained some knowledge of under bonnet affairs. Sir Redvers employed mechanics, but on occasions Edward would be allowed to help out. Changing wheels, batteries, it all became familiar to him, and the raw winds made his hands so cold he could hardly use them. Sometimes he wondered whether he had not been too hasty at taking the first job he could find, reminding himself occasionally that he had passed his school examinations, and had had a good education and should have gone in for one of the professions. Against that he realised that such a course of study was unpaid. At last he was earning — not very much, but it was a regular sum of money coming in. And money was what Edward wanted. Now and again he had been aware of his employer's figure at the window of his office. Had he not said 'work hard and I'll see you're all right', or words to that effect?

Edward's flat was simply a place to sit for an hour and dream, then to bed and early to work again in the morning. By the time he arrived home and had made himself a meal the day had almost gone. At times he was sunk in bitterness. What was he doing alone in a dreary room in front of a small gas fire? By rights he should have been at home — in

Guernsey — his head full of plans for the coming season in the hotel, and enjoying the company of his parents, and they his: the family together. But it could never be.

One day as he was drying off a car he had just washed he saw Sir Redvers' Rolls Royce pass and stop outside the offices. A woman was driving and as she got out Edward thought he recognised her as being Elaine Scarton. A few minutes later she reappeared accompanied by her father and together they drove away. In the short time that she had been visible Edward had noticed her well-dressed appearance and dark hair. She did not seem to have altered much and he wondered what she did now. Nothing, he guessed. She wouldn't need to work.

One morning in mid December he was called into Sir Redvers' office. 'I suppose you're wondering what I've called you in here for.' Not waiting for a reply he pointed to the chair on Edward's side of the desk. 'Sit down, you're not in the headmaster's study now.'

Edward gave a mental sigh of relief. His employer did not sound in too bad a mood. It was one thing being a guest has he had been of Sir Redvers that Christmas, but quite a different matter to be employed by that same person.

'I've been keeping an eye on you Edward these last months, and you haven't let me down.' Nodding in time to his words he continued, 'You've put your back into it — pleased with your effort, lad.' He straightened and still seated leaned a good half way across the desk. 'How d'you feel about coming inside?'

Edward must have looked a trifle perplexed. 'I mean into the showroom — the one for the seconds, try your hand at selling them. Sorry can't let you loose on the new stuff yet — that'll come.' Pausing he then shot the question, 'Think you can do it?'

Edward didn't hesitate. The next rung up the ladder was his. 'Yes I can — will do, and thanks for the opportunity, Sir Redvers.' He deserved it he knew, having worked damn hard and would continue to do so. It was a means to an end.

'Right — start January first next. There'll be an increasc in your wages. I expect results but I like to reward,' and Edward murmured his thanks again. Sir Redvers' regard became softer — less business-like. 'You'll be a long way from home next week, Edward.'

Edward knew he was referring to Christmas. 'Yes, but Daleford is my home now, Sir.'

The older man nodded. 'Yes, I s'pose it is, but look, don't get lonely. If you fancy a walk or a ride and a bit of company at the end of it, come and visit us — you know where we are — Scarton Manor. I'm sure you could manage a whisky and a piece of Christmas cake with cheese.'

Edward could hardly believe his ears. It was turning out to be quite a day. It was then left at that, after he had again offered his thanks, spirits suddenly lifted. But he did not close Sir Redvers' office door before glancing once more at the picture of Scarton Manor hanging on the wall, and transposed upon it was now a new and impressive freshly painted image of the Ormer Hotel.

The following Friday was the occasion of the

firm's buffet dance to be held in the Palace Hall in Daleford. Edward had heard of this coming event and had decided as a relative newcomer not to attend. He wasn't a good dancer and would be a wallflower for the evening. However he was persuaded to go by some of his colleagues from the firm, and thinking that it would be preferable to sitting in his flat alone. He wondered what William would be doing over Christmas. He had seen him twice since coming to work at Scartons. When he acquainted his brother with the nature of his work, William grimaced in mock horror.

'Washing cars! Hell fire, Edward. Is that the best you can do? Not much of a future in that.'

Edward hadn't prolonged that aspect of their conversation. Looking at William he decided that in some way his brother was doing very well without having to seek employment. He wore good clothes, rustled money in a wallet and had acquired the air of a leisured gentleman.

The Palace Hall's foyer and stage were bedecked with flowers and the large local band beat out a dance rhythm that had the sprung floor shaking under the dancers' feet. On either side of the stage was the blue and white emblem of the Scarton company. Coloured lights revolving from the ceiling shaded the women's dresses as they passed around the ballroom. Edward was glad that he had a suit to wear. One of his first purchases it had been advertised, worn once, and his size. It was light grey, in contrast to his dark hair and serious face.

He stood near the door surveying the scene. His work acquaintances had vanished, some to the bar, others on to the floor with girlfriends or wives. Upstairs in the balcony more people were watching and taking refreshments. Ruth would have liked the occasion — the thought surprising him — he had not been thinking of her beforehand. Actually he would have liked her at his side — someone he knew well, feeling somewhat out of things. Deciding to get a drink he found the bar was packed. Perhaps they were all like himself, getting courage from the bottle before setting foot on the dance floor. Idly he glanced sideways. Sir Redvers, evening-suited, stood nearby, his face in profile as he blew smoke from his cigar away from the couple he was in conversation with. Edward recognised Lady Scarton as one. He did not wish his employer to see him particularly. Sir Redvers had not mentioned the dance to him and may think that he was seeking his company.

Having obtained his drink Edward turned away from the bar hoping to find some place where he would be unobserved until he returned to the ballroom again. A group of young women were immediately in front of him chatting amongst themselves. Hesitating he waited for a space to appear through which he could edge his way. Just then one of the girls glanced up. It was Elaine Scarton dressed in a yellow long ballgown with a purple sash. Wide-eyed she stared at him and he smiled at her. 'Hello Elaine.' He might have known she would be present.

Elaine's face dissolved into delighted surprise as she detached herself from the group. 'Edward — Edward Dorner, what are you doing here in England? I thought you were tucked away back in

Guernsey.' If she saw the flash of brief pain in his eyes she did not comment upon it. Her dark eyes roved over his face. 'I do not believe it. Come on — tell. How d'you come to be here tonight?' She was all attention, her gaze capturing his.

He wanted a few seconds to think, his grief was private and locked away. 'Would you like a drink?' She was not holding one.

She gave a quick shake of her dark head, glanced beyond Edward. 'Tony's getting them. Doesn't matter — he can get me another later — or you can.' Her smile was sensual, inviting. She reached for his wrist. 'What on earth are you doing in a dump like Daleford? Did you come back for me?' Her eyes were bold, faintly mocking.

Edward was conscious of her nearness, her bare shoulders, the swinging emerald earrings. 'I had to come back, there was no work over there.'

'But how long have you been here?'

'About three months — just over.'

'And what are you doing for work?'

Edward hesitated a fraction. She'd get to know anyway. 'As a matter of fact I'm working for your father — his company.'

Elaine's eyes were wide, her nose wrinkling a little. 'You're what!' she exclaimed. 'Never, it's not true.'

He nodded, smiling into her eyes. 'It is. You remember last Christmas when we came up to the house for the evening. Well, your father and I were talking together and he said that if ever I wanted a job, to see him.' Edward shrugged, 'So here I am.'

'Just wait till I see Daddy — the sly old fogey. He

never said a thing about it to me.'

'I think perhaps he wanted to see if I would fit in, be good enough.'

'How super,' enthused Elaine. 'But I haven't seen you at the works.'

'I've seen you,' stated Edward. 'You picked your father up one day from the office. I saw you then.'

'Why on earth didn't you show yourself?'

'The fact is I work for your father. I didn't think he'd be very pleased if I were seen chatting to you in working hours.'

Elaine snorted. 'Of course he wouldn't have minded — he's an old softie really.'

Edward from his side of the fence did not think that was an apt description of Sir Redvers' working character. 'Anyway I didn't want to risk it,' and he glanced in her father's direction to see that he was still occupied conversing. 'From January he's going to allow me to sell cars, so I must have passed the first test.'

'I'm sure you have,' and the lights from the bar glinted in her dark eyes, 'with me too.'

Edward wasn't sure what to say to that, but her words and their tone made him feel confident — ready to flirt with her. 'What about your friend, Elaine? I think he's got your drink.'

'Oh Tony,' and she waved a dismissive hand. 'It's all right, he only brought me. I'm not tied to him you know.'

'Then let me get you one,' said Edward. It was hard lines on the other chap but . . . The evening was turning out better than he'd anticipated. Elaine followed him and they stood at the bar together, her shoulder close against his.

'To Christmas,' toasted Elaine as their glasses touched. A fleeting sadness enveloped Edward but he forced it away. He dare not dwell on the past. 'Where is your girlfriend — the fair-haired one? She was with you when you came up to the manor. Her name was Rhonda — or something like . . . '

'Ruth,' supplied Edward. 'Oh she's decided to stay in Guernsey. She didn't fancy coming back here.'

Elaine raised her already arched eyebrows. 'Hm — I'm surprised. She seemed very sweet on you, and she was jealous of me that night. I noticed her attention was always on you.'

Edward laughed shortly. 'Oh, I hadn't realised. Ruth's just a friend really, grown up together you know.' He didn't want to talk about her, but wondered what she was doing and hoped she was all right. She'd been very upset that night on the cliff path.

Elaine sipped from her glass then regarded him over it, eyes gleaming. 'Then I hope we're going to see a lot more of each other, Edward.' She made a face. 'Look — I'm going to call you Eddie. Edward seems a bit stuffy — formal. D'you mind?'

'No, of course not if you want to.' He did mind but she'd call him that anyway, he guessed. Being called Eddie reminded him of William's use of Ruthie, instead of Ruth. Strangely enough Elaine and William had something in common, a rather careless over-riding attitude, he thought.

'You look very smart, Eddie, more like one of the board than an employee.' Her gaze had been roving over him. Perhaps one day the former may be true and he would be one.

Her glass was empty. 'Another drink?'

She pondered a moment then put her glass down with a deliberate gesture. 'No, Eddie, I want to dance. Take me for one,' she demanded, and putting her arm through his she urged him toward the door, turning to wave gaily at her friends as she went.

'I'm not much of a dancer, Elaine,' protested Edward as they walked on to the floor, dodging the whirling couples as they did so. It was a quickstep and she leaned back away from him, her lower body and thighs pressed hard against him. It was deliberate and intoxicating. She was light on her feet and made him appear a much better dancer than he really was. But once he trod on her foot and her face crumpled in sudden pain, and an impatient anger flashed, so quickly that he wondered whether it had been there at all. Edward was rather surprised, mumbled his apologies and they carried on.

Later they sat in the balcony having refreshments and watching the circling heads below. She leaned against him as far as the arm rest between them would allow. 'You must come up to the house this Christmas, Eddie.'

'Thanks, I'd like that, Elaine,' and decided not to tell her that her father had also invited him. It would be an excuse to visit Scarton Manor twice and would pass the Christmas period more pleasantly.

'I don't know whether daddy is going to invite the band and singers again on Christmas Eve.' Her gaze swept upward to him. 'I hope not then we can be together undisturbed,' then added, 'the place is big enough anyway.' Her fingers rested just behind his knee.

Edward had just begun to cool down after the dance. Now her nearness and words were sending the blood coursing faster through him. 'What about your friends, Elaine? Don't you want to see them again?' After all she'd just left them flat. Not that he was complaining. He wanted to be with her for the remainder of the dance. The drink, the music, this attractive girl wanting his company, had combined to make the whole evening now first rate as far as he was concerned.

'No, I do not. Why do you say that? I'd rather be with you.' Her voice was petulant, suddenly irritable. 'Don't you want me?'

Her perfume came to him — expensive no doubt — as he bent nearer to her. 'Any man in the room would give anything for your company tonight, Elaine.'

The words came out of him easily, surprising him — quite unlike his usual small talk. Her lips were upturned, very close and his own touched them. Elaine drew away quickly but not before she had suddenly nipped his lower lip. 'That was a very complimentary and gallant thing to say Eddie,' she murmured.

Edward's mood had become such that he felt that he could have made any amount of compliments like that. A warning voice sounded. She was Sir Redvers' daughter, he just an employee. But he wasn't doing any harm, just wanting to throw off thoughts of the past for a while if possible. That night it was being made easy for him to do that.

'Look, they're letting the balloons go. Come on, let's go down. Quickly, Eddie, get me some, as many as you can — it's midnight.'

Edward stumbled between the seats to the aisle. Up the steps but not fast enough for Elaine.

'Oh, come on Eddie, they'll have all gone by the time we get down. Can't you hurry?' She was pushing him in her eagerness.

Edward couldn't — his leg wouldn't allow him to. However there were still some wafting down to the upward-stretched hands of the men trying to capture the biggest armful for their ladies. Bursting balloons were all over the dance floor and he managed to scoop three survivors into his arms and thrust them at Elaine.

'More, Eddie,' she urged, then one burst, and she gave a shriek. 'Oh Eddie, I've only two — I want more, Eddie — get me more,' and Edward scrambled and lurched at her command once again into the jolly throng to catch some for her. Then it was the last waltz and in the more shadowy parts of the ballroom Elaine moulded herself to his body, he curling his fingers into the dip of her spine; they seemed to fit there quite naturally. Once he caught her lips and she responded urgently, tightening her arms around him. He was relieved when she whispered that her father and mother had left earlier.

Edward stood in the foyer as people streamed out, not quite sure what was going to happen next. Elaine had left him saying she was going for her coat. She seemed a long time but he was prepared to wait. Suddenly she appeared and he made towards her, but she kept straight on through the doors.

'Goodnight, Eddie, see you some time.'

Edward followed. 'But Elaine, I . . . ' He saw the Rolls Royce against the pavement and watched her enter. Sir Redvers was not driving. It looked more like Thomas the chauffeur-cum-handyman who worked at the manor.

She waved to him and then was eased quietly away.

Edward stood looking after the car, feeling confused and let down. He saw some of her friends leaving with their escorts and nodding in his direction, and passing some remarks amongst themselves. Feeling rather foolish he began to make his way home, with a spring wound up inside him, and unable to understand why she had gone off like that. Her looks — the message he thought they had meant to convey. Her body against his, her lips, the things she had said — the inference behind them. Had she not said that he must go up that coming Christmas to the Manor? Yet all she had said as she swept past was that she would see him some time.

He fell into bed still wondering. What had he expected her to do? She could at least have given him a lift home. He fell asleep in a state of anti-climax and captivated by her bold dark beauty and access to wealth.

At work the day after saw Edward receiving sly glances and remarks from his colleagues. Some curious, others envious, and the warnings. 'Dancing with the boss's daughter — we saw you — lucky devil, how d'you do it? Moving up in the world are we? 'She's a tease, that's the rumour. Give you the come on and then — hey presto, you're out before you're in. Don't know what's hit you. Just when you think you've got a bull's eye.'

Mr. Ironside's remark was of a less personal nature. 'Dorner, if you want to be still employed here after Christmas my advice is to not let Sir Redvers see you with his daughter. Oh, I know you've met the old man socially, but my guess is that he'll be saving her for someone in a similar money bracket to himself. Don't want to lose you so soon.'

To both sets of advice Edward agreed in public. Privately he resented Mr. Ironside's assessment of his chances with Elaine, and also of his future financial prospects. It was just another goading arrow which made him even more determined to succeed. Of Elaine's peculiar whims he had had a taste, but come the light of that day and he had shrugged off the disappointment and annoyance he felt in the early hours of the morning. After all, she had left her friends and spent the remainder of the evening with him. Also he had to admit that she had made quite an impression on him, much more so than when they had met before up at the Manor, and it demanded a great effort to keep his mind on his work. There had been a fall of snow overnight and he spent some of the day clearing it from the rows of parked second-hand cars. It was cheerless work and cold but he took comfort from the fact that he would be spending more time on the sales side come the new year.

Two days later he received an invitation from Elaine to spend Christmas Eve with her and a few friends at Scarton Manor. Edward was pleased and excited at the prospect. She wanted to see him again, and he was certainly looking forward to seeing her.

The evening of December the twenty-fourth was cold, windy and black and Edward arrived by taxi. Late model cars stood outside — paint and chrome gleaming under electric lanterns, the ground yellowed below windows through half-drawn curtains. Elaine introduced him to the others present. Some he recognised from the night of the dance, others were strangers to him, and he guessed that there would be about three dozen people there.

There had been a fire blazing in the reception hall and another, hugely cheerful and roaring, warmed the large main room. Edward noticed bottles already empty and the guests in jovial mood. He had a drink then danced with Elaine and afterwards they sat close together on a sumptuous enfolding settee in a shadowy corner.

'My people are out for the evening,' and her eyes reflected the dancing flames. Edward was glad. He could relax with her knowing that Sir Redvers wouldn't be looking over their shoulders.

'I didn't know that Daddy had also invited you up during Christmas.'

'Oh, he just said that if I was not doing anything I had to call in sometime, but I'm glad you invited me — I wasn't too keen on coming without a proper invitation,' smiled Edward.

Elaine leaned even closer, so that the satiny swell of bosom pushed against his lapel. 'Actually I think he's taken to you, and that's something — he doesn't take to everybody. I think he would have liked to have had a son; I think now more than ever to help him in the business.' Her forehead wrinkled. 'I think he was rather stupid to go into business again. He'd no need to — he's rich.' Edward had no doubts about the truth of Elaine's latter statement. It was also a pleasant relief to hear that her father liked him.

He found her eager lips for a time then she drew away. 'You're different, Eddie, and that's what I like about you. Mavis and Babs think your accent's a knockout — so do I.'

Edward's hands rose from her waist to the rounded softness above — her breasts in the stunning red dress, but only just in he had observed. He wasn't experienced in caressing young women or any woman for that matter. His lips sought hers again and he was lost for a while. But not for long because somewhat to his surprise she said, 'Would you like something to eat Eddie? I'm famished.'

He muttered something in agreement and sat there feeling just a little put out that she should have disturbed his very very pleasant interlude there on the couch — would rather stay where he was. She seemed a restless, unsettled woman. He gazed after her, at the hips swinging sinuously from side to side in the vivid smooth garment.

Someone was playing the piano and he remembered when Ruth had sat at that piano and played. Ruth — at least you knew where you were with Ruth. Edward smiled wryly to himself. At least he thought he had done until that time of their walk along the cliff path. Then she had shocked him with the strength of her feelings for him. What was she doing at that precise moment? He peered beyond the guests working their way around the table to see who was playing, but they were hidden. Slinking back on to the couch he thought that perhaps the last three months had all been a dream. It was Ruth playing the piano and they would go back to school later with William, excited and expectant at the prospect of going back to Guernsey again and into the arms of their respective families.

'There Eddie, pie and sausage rolls. Eddie . . . ' Her voice banished his thoughts, and he took the plate, continuing to stare up at her.

'Did I come alone tonight in a taxi?' Her answer held the key.

Elaine regarded him in astonishment. 'If you can't remember how you came Eddie, then you've been putting the drink away quicker than I thought.' She plumped down beside him. 'Of course you came alone Eddie. I saw you get out of the taxi.'

So the nightmare had been real and had passed on, but its memory was vivid in his mind. He laughed shortly, mirthlessly, to cover up his momentary illusion. 'It's all right, I only wanted to know whether you take notice of your guests when they arrive.' It sounded ridiculous he knew, but she would think him even more ridiculous if he had revealed the real reason for his asking.

Later in the evening the persistent rhythmic beat of Latin American music came from the radiogram. Elaine gripped Edward's hand. 'I want to conga, Eddie. I must — just listen.' Edward was not at all keen, being comfortable and until then very close to Elaine, but she was on her feet and insistent. She pulled him along in a hurry to join the file of dancers, swaying and snaking between the furniture and then to the hall passed the red flickering fire there, and in and out of other rooms.

Having been persuaded to join the dance Edward found himself enjoying the sensation through his partner's abandoned movements of her hips, and the swell of her lower body as his fingers interlocked to keep hold of her. Other feminine hands were round his body; he didn't know whose. It was exciting, things were hazy and he was hot. Someone shouted to turn the sound up. And the conga became ragged as the column stumbled up the wide staircase on to the gallery.

It was getting shorter too as some guests fell out to rest on the stairs whilst others detached themselves discreetly and vanished through the nearest bedroom door.

Elaine suddenly did the same, letting go of the person in front and veering with Edward clinging on towards the door at the end of the corridor just off the gallery. Fumbling with the door, she opened it and fell on to the bed inside with Edward half standing, half lying over her. She squirmed under him to look up at the ceiling and blowing out her cheeks, her hands falling palms up at the sides of her head.

Edward, panting from his exertions, gazed down on her supine form, taken aback somewhat by her sudden collapse and submission beneath him on the bed. His mouth descended on hers and she further surprised him with her instant reaction, her body pressing upwards in short urgent movements. He enjoyed her breasts, releasing them from their containing fabric feverishly. He'd never done that before with any woman and his hands fluttered, touching like butterflies. The gleam of her eyes from beneath their nearly closed lids were disconcerting, as if she were watching him. His hand moved downwards to the hem of her dress, plucked at it. Her voice came strongly. 'No! Eddie, no!' and she struggled against him. 'They'll wonder where we are.' Pushing him away she sat up. 'We'd better go down.'

Edward straightened reluctantly, half drunk with the alcohol and also from the brief sexual encounter with his hostess, now busy straightening her dress and hair with impatient fingers. She gave him a quick smile. 'Sorry, Eddie, but it doesn't look good if I'm not around. It's my party — I must show myself.' She patted his face. 'Some other time, darling.'

Edward followed her silently downstairs. A couple were shuffling close together to the now slow music, and two more were deep in each other's arms in dark corners. Others were still drifting round the table, hungry after their exertions.

'I could do with a coffee,' said Elaine and went over to join them, whilst Edward sank into the more welcoming depths of the Scarton Manor furniture. She returned almost immediately, frowning and sighing heavily. 'None left. I'll get Phyllis to bring some more,' and she disappeared in the direction of the kitchen. He felt irritated, frustrated. A strange girl Elaine. Blowing so warm one minute, cooling quickly the next. Remembered the rumours about her. A tease was one and so far in their acquaintance that would adequately describe her behaviour. But he liked her, found her exhilarating and exciting, but completely spoilt.

The object of his thoughts stood above him, frowning in annoyance. 'Guess what, Eddie? Phyllis has taken herself off — gone home.'

Time hadn't meant anything since his arrival, but Edward was surprised when he saw the clock — it was nearly twelve. 'Well, I suppose it is late, and Christmas Eve. Perhaps she has a family, wants to be with them.' Even as he spoke the dagger of his own fashioning struck agonisingly. That night he too should have been in the shelter of his own.

'Daddy pays her a good enough wage. She shouldn't have gone so early,' Elaine complained irritably. 'She's always saying how she likes to see young people enjoying themselves, and then she goes and leaves us in the lurch.'

'What age is this Phyllis?'

Elaine raised elegant but disintcrested shoulders. 'Oh, I don't know — getting on — she came with the place.'

Edward remembered the person vaguely from his last visit — grey-haired, aproned and elderly. 'Is her husband the man who called for you after the works dance?'

'Yes, that's Thomas,' and her tone suggested that any more attention focused on the elderly employees would be unwelcome.

Edward sat sipping at his coffee in front of the fire, Elaine curled up against him. The flames leapt and crackled and took his imagination with them.

This is how it would be some day when he had his own place — the new Ormer Hotel. Secure, rich, successful, the sea outside and the building restored; perhaps his hand resting fingers spread as it did now on the curving thigh of a woman. They kissed, his lips following hers even when she had drawn away. The Christmas cards lined up on the broad mantelpiece brought him into the present again. Cards to the Scarton family, amongst themselves and from relatives. Sobering thoughts penetrated the haze of alcohol and excitement of Elaine's company, bringing a sudden despondency. Where were his cards — family cards? Where was his mantelpiece above a comforting warming fire? He had sent a card to Ruth, but so far had not had one in reply. William had sent one after receiving his.

Elaine's mocking voice came at his ear. 'My God, we are serious aren't we? It is Christmas Eve you know, Eddie. Who were you thinking of — little Ruth?'

Irritation edged his reply. 'No, I wasn't, nothing like that at all.' It was private. He wasn't going to divulge those thoughts to Elaine.

'She seemed stuck on you before, Eddie.'

'Oh, Ruth's always been a bit like that. We've just grown up together.'

From outside came the sound of carol singers. He stood up hoping to dispel the mantle of altered mood that had so swiftly settled upon him. 'Come on Elaine, let's have a look. They deserve to be listened to.' Then someone suggested inviting them in. Edward remembered his own attempts with Ruth and William at carol singing a year ago, and how glad they had been to be taken in for warmth and refreshments.

The vicar of the local church of St. Michael and St. Mark's headed his choir into the cheerful atmosphere of Scarton Manor, but he was at once apologetic and somewhat embarrassed when he entered the great room, the latter emotion because of the abandoned postures and complete lack of attention by some guests lost in each other's arms. Others, it was quite clear, had difficulty in judging the size of the choir as they stared at the new arrivals over their drinks.

'I must apologise for coming,' he said, 'at what is obviously an inopportune time, and again for the quite small choir I could muster tonight. It is a temptation I suppose on a cold night to stay at home. However . . . ' The vicar gave another quick glance around, 'perhaps it may be better if we get on our way again.' But he and his choir were persuaded to sing, and afterwards stood politely refreshing themselves from the table with their backs discreetly to the others.

Afterwards as they were leaving the vicar said to Elaine, 'I'm sorry I didn't have the chance to speak to your parents. However I may see them later, but please give them my regards and wish them a happy Christmas.' Then lowering his voice he went on, 'You know I do hope we haven't intruded tonight. I had no idea . . . ' And all the while the members of the choir kept casting envious and longing glances towards the room they had just left.

Outside, the vicar felt that he had lost a little of his enthusiasm for carol singing that night, and shook his head: young people of today! He had to admit though that one of the young ladies had revealed a fine pair of legs. No doubt they and their owner would be in bed, and quite probably joined by someone else's, long after he himself had risen for the early Christmas Day service. He remembered the Dorner boy, grown suddenly into a young man. There had been a gravity beyond his years about him. The vicar turned his attention to his charges. 'All right boys, not too much noise. Save it for the service in the morning. Keep together.'

Edward watched their torches and lanterns swinging and fading into the distance. He had a sadness and decided to take his leave also, having enjoyed himself immensely, but now he wanted to be away.

Elaine was not pleased. 'Where are you going? It's Christmas Day now, you might as well stay on for breakfast.' Her beautiful dark eyes were sullen and incomprehending.

'I don't think your father would be pleased if I were still here at breakfast time.'

'I invited you — not daddy.' She gestured at the others still in view. 'They'll be here for a long time yet.'

Silently Edward agreed with her. They looked incapable of standing up, never mind going anywhere. 'But they don't work for him Elaine — I do.'

She smacked her lips irritably. 'I think you're frightened of him, Eddie.'

He smiled. 'Perhaps I am, or I might have reason to be if I stayed on.'

The irritation faded from the face opposite. She slid her arm round his neck and he could feel her breasts pressing against his shirt front. 'Oh,' she breathed, 'and why?'

He was close to losing himself in her eyes, and his own were not focusing too well. 'You're very lovely Elaine, and if I stay I may not behave myself.'

Elaine leaned away in mocking amusement. 'You think that by leaving you're going to protect my honour, is that it? You silly boy, Eddie. What a quaint old thing you are.' She clung close again. 'Anyway that didn't seem a consideration to you earlier when you had me on the bed. You'd have had my honour gone in quick time.'

Edward remembered. It seemed a long time ago. Should have gone easy with the drink. Making a strong effort he said, 'I'll call a taxi. Where's your telephone?'

'A taxi? What do you want a taxi for?'

'Well I came in one, so I'll go back in one,' he replied simply.

'Like hell you will, Eddie. Thomas will take you.'

'Thomas?'

'Yes, our chauffeur-handyman.' Irritability was present in her tone again.

'Oh yes, but at this time of the night? He'll be in bed.'

'He'll get up and take you.'

'I can't have him doing that. I'll take a taxi, no need to disturb him, and anyway he's an old man.'

'He's our chauffeur — it's what he's there for.'

'No, Elaine. I appreciate it and thanks, but I'd rather not,' he said determinedly.

'I'll take you then,' she pouted with equal determination. 'Daddy's got the Rolls but there's the Daimler.'

'Look Elaine you're not going to leave your guests because of me.'

Elaine sighed in exasperation. 'Oh, go to hell then Eddie.'

'Can we meet tomorrow then?'

'I don't know,' she frowned looking up at him crossly from beneath lowered lids. 'I may tell Daddy after all that you tried to ravage me in the bedroom.'

Edward gave a tired smile. 'Well I suppose that's true, but I didn't get far though.'

She hit him quite hard on the face in mock anger. 'You . . .'

He caught her and crushed her to him, stopping whatever she meant to say. Her teeth caught his lip, but then suddenly she pulled away from him. 'There's the phone over there — call me tomorrow.'

Edward was surprised by her sudden acquiescence to his leaving. What a changeable, quicksilver creature she was.

In the taxi home he thought he had done the right thing in leaving when he did. If her father had returned and found him the worse for drink it wouldn't have done much for his chances of fulfilling his present ambitions with the Scarton family nor the ones he had for the future.

In the coming weeks he was to see a lot of Elaine Scarton. It was certain that she liked him a great deal. They dined out, went to shows and made occasional visits to the cinema. But it was a costly time for Edward. He hadn't a car of his own so she would call for him in the Rolls, and an expensive car meant more often than not an expensive place to eat in. If often took much or most of his earnings for one week. Sir Redvers' daughter was used to the good things of life and she expected to be to able to continue in that way when she was in his company. It was only afterwards that Edward counted the cost. Whilst he was with her it mattered little — a glimpse of the riches that some day he would acquire to enable him to fulfil his secret ambition in Guernsey.

There was however one other factor, and that was his growing infatuation with Elaine Scarton. When he was with her all things seemed attainable except, ironically enough, herself, as yet. She was stimulating, good to be seen with, giving him the will to see ahead to what might be achieved if he remained sensible and did not do anything to upset her father. Elaine certainly did a lot to help him gain respect. The attention of waiters, shop assistants, the openings the mention of her name gave, and he found himself slotting in quite easily into his new role of Elaine's escort.

Two things of note occurred early in the new year. On the first day of his new appointment as junior salesman, Sir Redvers took him to the line of second-hand cars and stopped at the oldest and cheapest one on show. 'Now Edward, see this car — not exactly the best we have or the most modern,' to which Edward agreed and wondered what his employer was leading to. 'Right then. When a prospective buyer comes along and he shows an interest in this car, even the slightest interest, I want you to convince that customer that this vehicle is the very best in the world.' His finger pointed at Edward's person, moving in short jabs to emphasise his words. 'If you believe it, he will — never forget that Edward. Follow that maxim and you'll never look back. Understand?' His regard of the younger man was almost a glare, but Edward had become used to the two Sir Redvers — the keen rock hard man of business, and the off-duty one, pleasant and affable.

'I'll do that — I understand, Sir Redvers.' The time may come he hoped when perhaps it would be Redvers, but whenever he met him at the Manor in the company of Elaine, 'Sir' was sufficient. And he had already decided from day one that he would follow wholeheartedly whatever guidance her father gave, being eager for success and the financial rewards that it could bring.

A fortnight after beginning his new role of salesman Edward was inspecting the line of cars and making sure they were presented as well as possible. It was one of those clear blue-skied winter days with the low sun reminding everyone that Spring was the next quarter to come. A taxi drew up outside the main showroom and three people got out. Edward was surprised to see that one was William, the others being the two ladies with whom he was living. Watching, he saw William lead the way into the showroom, and Mr. Ironside coming from his office to meet them. Edward, curious, followed but entered by the door at the opposite end.

The group stood talking for a few minutes then Mr. Ironside ushered them slowly along the line of models and also in Edward's direction. The latter knew he couldn't interfere — he wasn't allowed to sell from the main showroom yet — but perhaps he would get a chance to speak to William. The latter looked smart in a white trench coat with Miss Steck by his side and Mrs. Prind looking somewhat bemused behind them. Were William's companions going to buy one of the cars? If so, the lucky devil, thought Edward. They were all good quality, radiators gleaming and their insides smelling of leather and polished wood. Black, maroon, dark green and pearl grey amongst the colours. There was also a convertible — an Alvis in dark blue and grey, with a three-position hood. This was Edward's favourite and a constant reminder that if he worked hard enough, listened and learned, then some day that machine could stand outside the new Ormer Hotel.

The group were only a car away from him now. Edward wondered if William had seen him. Surely he would not ignore him. The party was just turning from the last in the line to retrace and inspect the others again. 'Morning William,' he said quietly.

His brother half turned, hesitated slightly before speaking. 'Oh, morning Edward — I didn't just see you — wasn't expecting you to be here.' He shot a glance at his lady companions. 'We're just thinking of buying a car,' and Edward noted the 'we'. 'Miss Steck thought I might be able to help her choose one.' Edward also noted the mention of Miss Steck and not her companion Mrs. Prind. Obviously it was the younger woman who held the purse on this occasion.

The group began to retrace their steps, slowly, Mr. Ironside throwing a puzzled look over his shoulder in Edward's direction. The latter stayed where he was but within earshot. William stopped at the Alvis convertible — it had obviously caught his fancy — with Mr. Ironside explaining the positioning and workings of the hood to his prospective customers. Edward watched in envy. To be able to drive that, even if it wasn't yours. But then he heard Mrs. Prind remark, 'Don't you think, Adeline, that it may be a little draughty in this climate?' It was obvious that William did not agree with that observation, and it was equally obvious that Miss Steck had until that moment thought of pleasing only one person. But she did hesitate and Mr. Ironside — good salesman as he was — stepped straight in with the alternative — the maroon car next to it — another Alvis, but a saloon one with a sunshine roof which he pointed out to them and demonstrated.

Edward observed William trailing reluctant fingers across the bonnet of the convertible as he followed the two ladies. He couldn't help feeling relieved that Mrs. Prind had suggested that the convertible would be unsuitable, and that William was not going to get the chance to drive it. They sat in the saloon, William in the driving seat, with Miss Steck by his side and Mrs. Prind trying out the rear compartment. The stepsisters appeared quite taken with the car and both settled comfortably into their respective places. As for William, he looked for all the world as if he were the prospective purchaser, peering at and trying this and that whilst Mr.

Ironside answered his questions most politely and respectfully.

'What d'you think William?' asked the younger woman. 'I think it would do us very well, but you being a man will know about these things.' She regarded him with little short of adoration.

William's glance went back to the open car alongside, but Mrs. Prind again reminded her stepsister of the British climate and said they ought to be sensible about the matter. Whereupon Miss Steck replied, 'Yes, perhaps you're right, Helena,' and quite forgetting about the times she spent naked at all hours of the night with the young man at her side. She patted his arm saying, 'But this is very nice, isn't it William, and very substantial.' Mr. Ironside then suggested he gave them a trial run, and with William relegated to the rear seat alongside Mrs. Prind, they set off after Edward had slid the glass doors of the showroom aside for them. Watching them disappear up the road he wished William well but doubted whether his brother had any ambition apart from attaining an easy lifestyle. Certainly he seemed to be doing very well without actually working.

Turning back into the showroom he stood at the bonnet of the convertible, staring down at its graceful lines. Some day one like that could be his, but he knew he was going to have to work hard for it, or anything else he desired.

Within a quarter of an hour Mr. Ironside, alone and looking pleased, drew up alongside the showroom. 'Right Dorner, they're taking it — lunching at the Royal. You're picking them up at two-thirty, but before that I want you to get down to the tax office.' He turned on his heel and went into his office, and by the time Edward had reached him he was handing him documents. 'Take the Morris over there. Two-thirty at the Royal, and I'll have the Alvis ready for when you get back.'

It was a peculiar sensation being chauffeur to William and his companions, Edward found. William sat in front, the ladies behind.

'We've decided on the Alvis saloon, Edward,' announced his brother, and Edward again noted his use of the plural.

'It's a very fine car, William,' and he couldn't quite keep the note of envy out of his voice. He couldn't afford any car yet, although he reminded himself that he did ride around occasionally in Sir Redvers' Rolls Royce with Elaine.

'We're very pleased with it,' came Miss Steck's voice from the rear. 'It rides very well. I'm sure we're going to enjoy getting about in it. William said that it was quite easy to drive, didn't you William?' and Edward saw his brother turn and flash a confident smile at the two women.

'I hadn't realised that you worked at Scartons, Edward,' said Mrs. Prind. 'William said that you worked at a garage, but didn't mention which one.'

Did he care, wondered Edward? 'Well, I had to find work and this came along so I took it,' said Edward lightly, thinking that William had known all along where he had worked.

'You must come for tea Edward some time, mustn't he Adeline?' said Mrs. Prind. 'It will be a change for you.'

'Yes, that's right, yes — yes, I suppose it would.' Miss Steck's voice did not hold a great deal of encouragement and Edward guessed why. He remembered mentioning to the stepsisters his ambition to return to Guernsey. Daleford was a stepping stone to that end. But Adeline Steck viewed anything that connected William to that foreign place as a threat to her affair with him. Therefore the less Edward saw of him the better.

Five minutes later the transaction had been completed and the trio drove away, seen off by Mr. Ironside at close quarters and by Edward at a distance. William looked, and no doubt felt, very superior at the wheel, with Miss Steck, his benefactor, by his side in front and beaming contentedly at him, while Mrs. Prind occupied the rear, clutching her large handbag and wearing an expression of bemused pleasure. It was after all her stepsister's second acquisition in the last few months.

Watching them leave Edward wondered if Mrs. Prind knew about her stepsister and his brother. Surely she must know that one of the beds each night remained empty until dawn. Perhaps it was a case of anything to keep Miss Adeline happy. The latter must be very well off he thought. That car was an expensive one, and from what he had heard price had not been a consideration. How long would it be before William was out in the vehicle by himself? Lucky him! Edward returned to his line of cars doubting that he was going to get a customer for one of his as well-heeled as the one who had just been driven away by William.

8

Edward became a frequent visitor to Scarton Manor at both Sir Redvers invitation and also his daughter's. On the last occasion, having escorted Elaine home after a visit to the theatre, he had remained for refreshments before returning to his flat. Both Lady Scarton and Elaine were out of the room for the moment. He and Sir Redvers were ensconced in a smaller lounge, cosy with the firelight, enriching further the red velvet curtains drawn across the windows. It was warm and Edward was comfortable in the armchair at one side of the fireplace. Sir Redvers sat opposite, cigar in mouth, brandy in hand. He puffed out a strand of smoke and regarded Edward as he did so, then spoke in a quiet confidential voice — quiet for him at least, but his voice still carried strongly. 'Nice girl our Elaine, eh Edward? How d'you get on with her? Seems to me you get on all right.'

There was only one answer to the first question, and Edward was not slow to reply. 'She's a very beautiful girl, Sir, and a lively personality.' It wasn't hard for him to say — he meant it, then added, 'I like her company very much indeed.'

Sir Redvers eyes gleamed, having heard what he wanted to hear. 'Aye, that's what I thought, Edward,' and drew on his cigar, then stabbed with it in characteristic fashion to punctuate his words. 'I'd say Elaine was rather fond of you — not really for me to say anything of course, but I know my own daughter.' He glanced at Edward's empty hands. 'D'you want a brandy with your coffee?' His guest's polite refusal brought a look of approval from him. 'Just as well to be sensible, keep a clear head for the morning's business eh?' He shifted nearer. 'And talking of that Edward, expansion is going to be the name of the game — expansion, that's what it's all about. I've bought some land in the midlands. Building's going ahead very soon. That'll be the tenth we've put on the map.' He gave a single sideways shake of his head. 'Yes, that's the name of the game — expansion. The time's coming when we'll move south until we cover the country.' Then, not waiting for Edward's contribution, he went on, 'Later I may go into heavy stuff — lorries, vans, that sort of thing. Businesses need them you know.' He stood up, back to the fire. 'The romance of business: get a smell of it and it sticks with you for ever. It's exciting, Edward. Dammit, I don't need the money but it's building an empire again, something different. Mind you,' and a crafty wary look appeared, 'I'm not decrying money. You can do damn all without it in this world. I'd rather be sodding well comfortable if I'm going to be miserable.'

Edward agreed, expressing his keen interest and smiling inwardly at Sir Redvers' straightforward broad-spoken delivery, but also accepting fully the truth of his words. He'd already had a taste in his young life of having almost nothing. Now possibly he owned a ruin but couldn't do anything with it, though some day he would, but how long was some day going to be?

Sir Redvers was speaking again. 'I could go on cruises, but I'd be bloody sick — I usually am. My wife seemed to enjoy them, but to tell you the truth they're not my type of people that we meet. Divorced women and prancing men, and I'm not one for sitting round a swimming pool either. No, give me business. It stops you from going stagnant.'

Business for business's sake. Edward wasn't sure about that, but certainly his host's enthusiasm and confidence was infectious. The older man stared down on him. 'So you're going to stay with me are you? Going all the way?'

Edward realised what he meant. 'Oh yes I am — of course, Sir. I want to be successful, that's for certain,' he said with great conviction.

Sir Redvers nodded in satisfaction. 'I think you're ambitious, Edward. That's good. Hard work — there's no other way. Stay with me and if you've got opinions or ideas let's have 'em. It'll be to your benefit and the company's.' He flicked his ash into fire then regarded Edward again. 'Off the record I'm quite pleased with your progress. You've applied yourself, got stuck in. I like that.'

Edward thanked him. 'You gave me the chance, Sir. I was grateful for the opportunity and I've tried to do my best.'

'If you hadn't you'd have been out in quick time.' The tone was stern but the eyes held a kindly glint.

Later, as Edward got ready for bed, he thought that he had made quite a good start to the year. Sir Redvers seemed to like him and was pleased with his work so far. Elaine also liked him, he knew, but for her father to say so was even more pleasing. His daughter was spoilt, headstrong and impulsive but for Edward she was part of his life now. When he was with her he drowned in her dark wayward eyes. As regards the Scarton organisation he was surprised how large it was. He had no idea they had so many sales outlets until his conversation with his employer.

February came with heavy snow in the district turning the stone walls of the countryside into dark long slices of Christmas cake with a top of icing. Buses became stuck in drifts, snow ploughs were out and gangs of diggers were employed, and Edward went to work in the dark and returned to his flat in the dark. At times he wished that he was back in Guernsey. Snow and conditions obtaining in Daleford just then were unheard of there. Frosts yes, and perhaps even a sprinkling of snow, but nothing of the severity he was experiencing now. Trade slowed but there were jobs to be done such as helping to prepare the cars for when the weather improved and the sales increased with the Spring. Occasionally he was allowed to assist Mr. Ironside in the sale of new ones. It was however still his responsibility for the secondhands outside, but now he had aid from a youth taken on recently in keeping them clean.

There was in the out-districts still a light covering of snow when the Spring month arrived and also a bitter raw wind. As he shrugged his overcoat off on arrival at work, one of the office girls approached him.

'Oh Mr. Dorner, a lady called at the office

yesterday just after you left, wanting to see you. I said you wouldn't be back until this morning.'

Edward was surprised. 'What did she want to see me about?'

'She didn't say.'

'What was she like?'

'Oh, youngish, fair, a bit stout — difficult to say as she was well wrapped up. Seemed very tired, walked slowly — a bit heavy sort of.'

'And she didn't say anything? I mean about what she wanted to see me for?'

'No. I gave her a cup of tea and then she left. She was cold when she came and worried about something I'd say.'

Edward was mystified. Apart from Elaine and the woman who rented his flat to him he did not know any other. It wasn't Elaine, that was for certain, and his landlady certainly did not fill the description at all. What about Miss Steck? She was plump, fair, but certainly not a young woman. For most of the day his work occupied his mind but on occasions he found himself wondering who the caller might have been. Perhaps the person would return and, if the matter was important would get in touch again.

That evening Edward climbed the stairs to his flat as usual. It wasn't much but it was welcoming at the end of his working day, though sometimes there he seemed a long way from the fulfilment of his dreams. Pushing the door open he saw the light was on, but had no time to be surprised about that for he had a visitor. Facing him from the one easy chair he possessed was Ruth Le Ney! She had risen albeit slowly by the time he'd managed to gasp her name.

'Ruth! What on earth are you doing here?' He moved into the room.

'Oh Edward, how good to see you,' and her arms went around his neck in a tight embrace. Edward felt her tears on his cheek. He didn't understand. Ruth was the last person he had expected to see. Suddenly he knew she had been the caller at work — the description fitted her. 'H — how are you Ruth?' It had been all anger and bitterness last time he had seen her. 'You called at work yesterday, didn't you?' He could hardly believe she was standing there.

Ruth moved back slightly from him so that she could face him, but left her hands around his shoulders. 'Yes it was me, but I had your address, so I thought I'd come here instead. Your landlady let me in. Oh Edward, how I've longed to see you again.' The hood pushed back revealed the joy in the violet eyes at their reunion and also the weariness present.

Edward's hands resting on her waist became aware of the thickness of her body beneath the voluminous coat. 'Why have you come over, Ruth?'

'You're not pleased to see me?' And the light in the eyes was fading.

'It's always very nice to see you, Ruth, you know that, but . . . '

'Only very nice?'

'Oh, you know what I mean Ruth.' He was tired and he seemed to have developed the habit of saying the wrong things in her company. 'When did you arrive in Daleford?'

'Two days ago.'

'But where are you staying?'

Ruth fluttered a hand impatiently. 'Oh it doesn't matter, I found somewhere,' and a wry smile appeared. 'I did live in Daleford for a while you remember.' Her fingers touched his cheek and Edward felt their chill.

'I'll light the fire, Ruth. The landlady should have done it for you.'

'I kept my coat on — I'm all right.'

She looked pale he thought. After he had put a match to the fire she sat down, and he was surprised again at her bulk. 'I'll make a drink for us,' he said, glancing at her as she sat leaning toward the fire, her coat pulled around her, and the firelight showing between the strands of her hair turning it red gold.

He sat opposite her, still astonished that she should be there at all — the last person he had expected to see on that winter's evening. 'How is your aunt?' he asked, feeling strangely ill at ease for someone who had lain in passion with her not so very long ago.

'She was all right the last time I saw her,' she replied, then saw his surprise. 'I haven't lived at home for the last three months. Like you I have my own place — a flat.' Suddenly Ruth gazed at him fully. 'I didn't want her to find out. I couldn't have stood it — the explanations and everything. I had to come to you.'

Edward stared back at her blankly. 'How d'you mean, Ruth?'

Her words tumbled out eagerly. 'Our baby, Edward — our baby, that's why I've come. I wanted to be near you. I'm expecting our baby, Edward.

There's no one else, you know that. Oh Edward, I didn't know what to do. I didn't want to stay at home.' She searched his face anxiously. 'You remember, Edward, last September? You do don't you?'

Yes, he remembered — the recent past catching up very quickly with him — very quickly. The brief totally unexpected pleasure of her body that day near Fermain. It had been dimmed by his involvement with work and Elaine. Elaine! She didn't have any problems like this. No wonder he had been unable to think of a stout young fair-haired person. She had conceived very quickly. His brain regained the function of speech. 'Are you sure?' knowing he didn't have to ask — had only to look at her, but he wanted time. 'What about your aunt?'

'She doesn't know. I haven't seen her very often with having my own flat. I just said that I was going to join you and William again.' A semblance of a smile came. 'I am of age now. I can make my own decisions.'

Edward glanced between the now open edges of her coat, seeing her swollen body. The months mounted up in his mind. In two more she could give birth. He swore inwardly. Just when he was beginning to see his way, things getting better, the last thing he wanted was trouble like this. He was sorry for her. It had happened quickly — not even an affair. Just a sudden invitation which his youthfulness could not ignore. He'd never thought of doing that with her ever. Worry, concerns for her and himself and the shock of her news took hold of him. His fingers patted his forehead in frustration and rising anger. 'And what can I do Ruth about it?'

Her eyes held her soul, her voice an ill-suppressed plea. 'Would you marry me Edward? We'd be happy I know. I love you. The baby would be ours and we could go back to Guernsey. I could work later — we'd manage. I do love you, Edward. I'm sorry I said the wrong things last time. I was mad. I thought you . . . '

Ruth recoiled in her chair as he rose quickly, his emotions boiling over. 'That I loved you,' he finished roughly. 'Well I don't Ruth. It's just a plot isn't it, to get me involved? Give you a baby and then it's plain sailing — I have to marry you. Well I'm not going to do. You can go back to Guernsey and have it there. I want no part of it. I'll send money but I've nothing else to offer. Oh God, why did you have to come, Ruth?'

Even as he spoke he was hating himself, seeing the misery, complete and utter misery on her face. Was he actually saying that? He had wanted to, but now he wished he hadn't. That look would haunt him.

'You won't marry me,' she stated in a low monotone, and her regard drifting away from him. She stood up clumsily, her eyes reverting to him again — eyes once filled with warm vitality, now clouded and empty. 'And you don't love me.' She had reached the door before he moved.

'Where are you going?'

Ruth did not look at him but opened the door. 'What d'you care?'

He touched her arm. She rounded on him, her

eyes burning a violet fire. 'Get away from me.'

'But where are you staying?'

'That is my affair. We'll do without you,' and he noticed the inclusion of the unborn child.

She began to hurry awkwardly down the stairs and Edward followed. 'You just can't walk the streets Ruth in your condition.'

'A condition you care nothing about,' she retorted breathlessly. 'I travelled by myself to see you and I'm sure I can find my way in Daleford — this hell place,' she added half choking as she reached the bottom of the stairs.

He followed her down the path, the bitter wind striking them viciously. 'I'll take you back,' he shouted, but she took no notice and started to disappear into the night. He dashed after her and caught her up, held her in a strong grip. 'Come back you idiot. Ruth, I do care. I'll drive you.' He was allowed to use one of the firm's cars — it stood at the kerb. 'You're not going anywhere by yourself tonight. Now get in,' he said harshly.

She got in reluctantly and slumped into the seat, staring ahead silently, after giving him the briefest of directions. It was a poor district of apartments and terraced houses which had seen better days.

He turned on her. 'Why the hell Ruth didn't you tell me? I could have found something better.'

She turned to him bleak-faced in the street lights. 'I thought it would only be for one or two days, and that you and I . . . ' She broke off. 'Now I know different. Leave me alone, I can manage.' Anxiously and miserably he stared after her until her bulky figure was lost to sight behind the half glassed door.

He did not sleep much that night. Ruth, the slim fair-haired flower-eyed girl next door, a sunny natural playmate of earlier years, the loyal friend at school. The things they and William had gone through together — their hopes, fears and joys. Now she was a woman and had been for some time. That friend of the sands and picnics of another world had changed — carrying his baby and misshapen by it, demanding his love which he did not feel for her. Being very fond of her, his heart ached to see her in her present unhappy state, and doing the decent thing and marrying her would solve nothing. He had his plans and they did not include marriage to Ruth Le Ney. But it was all a dreadful business, and he fell into a fitful sleep later agonising over what was to be done.

Over the next two months Edward was a frequent visitor to Ruth's bedsit. She had long since run out of money so he paid the rent and collected food each week for her. He recognised that he was responsible for her condition, and also felt responsible for her to a great extent whilst she was in Daleford and until she had had the baby. He hoped then that he could persuade her to have it adopted, and then for her to return to Guernsey with no one any the wiser. But when he came to discuss that particular problem with her she was adamant about wanting to keep the child. Several times she asked him to reconsider her offer of marriage, but he refused as gently as he could, being embarrassed and sorry to see the extent to which she had lost her pride.

He did however obtain from her a grudging

promise that she would return to Guernsey with the child as soon as she was able to travel. At least that was something, and his responsibility would end there. But each time he left her alone he was uneasy, their meetings full of long silences, her moods alternating between depression and a brooding accusation as she sat hunched and heavy.

A few days before the birth was expected Edward managed to get Ruth into a small nursing home on the outskirts of the town. It was going to cost him most of the savings he had painstakingly built up since he had begun working at Scartons although, as he had found out, Elaine was not an inexpensive person to know.

He went to see Ruth the day after the birth. He found her flushed, entranced with her new arrival, and for the first time in many weeks she smiled when she saw him.

'Look Edward! It's a boy. We've got a boy. What shall we call him?'

Again the 'we' was not lost to him. Would there always be this tie between them forever? He bent over the bed, into the wizened face of the child and touched the tiny fingers.

He shrugged. 'Oh anything you like — you choose a name.' He wanted to be away to resume his new life. Elaine, he thought, must have been puzzled, wondering as to why their more extravagant outings had come to an end during the last few weeks. She had remarked once rather crossly that he was always tired and losing interest in her. He had made the excuse that he was working hard for her father. At first he had been surprised at her petulant outbursts when things did not go her way, but he had become used to them, and he was still captivated by her.

'Frederick — that's what I'll call him.' Ruth's voice brought him to his present surroundings. Edward remembered that she'd had an uncle Frederick — had always liked him.

'Frederick Edward Dorner — that sounds very impressive,' and she looked up at him hopefully and he could see the longing in her eyes and the sadness behind. 'Shall we . . . ?'

He frowned irritably, making an impatient gesture of his hands, palms outwards. 'No I don't think so Ruth.' It was as if they were married. 'Call it Frederick if you wish but I do not want it to have my surname.' She could call it by her family name of Le Ney, but he wanted no part of it. Her idea must have been that when he saw the baby he would talk about marriage.

He left Ruth with her head turned away from him to the wall, her erstwhile enthusiastic hands limp upon the bed, and the child unheeded. Depression was heavy on him on the way home. He'd hurt her again savagely, the very last thing he would have wished to do. When she was back in Guernsey he would feel great relief. If Elaine found out his chances of progress romantically and in business would disappear overnight, of that he was sure. The excuse that it had been a five minute affair before he became involved with Elaine would not help him, and if it became known that he had a son . . . Edward shuddered. He had made no mention of his problem to his brother, being sure that as far as William knew, Ruth was home in Guernsey.

A week later and Ruth was ready to return to the island, having stayed in her bed sit after her return from the nursing home. Edward got the parting over as quickly as possible after seeing that she had sufficient money and her tickets. She was going by air. It was quicker and easier, the taxi coming to take her and the child the following morning.

Over the next few weeks Edward threw himself with all his energy into consolidating his position at Scartons. Now the worry of Ruth and the child was gone he felt freer and more content than for a long time. He liked his work dealing with cars, driving the different makes and more importantly helping to sell them. Then in the early summer of that year Sir Redvers promoted him to area manager for the Northern part of the organisation, and this involved travelling to other branches. An increase in his salary went with the more responsible position and Edward felt that at last good fortune was beginning to turn his way.

He was also, when his work allowed, spending a lot of time at Scarton Manor, almost every weekend when he was free, staying over until Monday morning. The invitations were almost always from Elaine, and occasionally from Sir Redvers and Lady Scarton. Sometimes he attended house and tennis parties; at other times there would be just the family and himself, and during this time he became even more fascinated by Elaine. He was swept along in her company, by her lifestyle, the dark eyes forever promising. There was no doubt also that she was intrigued by him, his manners and speech — his difference, introducing him as her Channel Islander.

If there was a warning in her attitude towards a new possession, Edward chose to ignore it. At that time even if he had stopped to consider, he would have felt that he had no choice. Her lissom limbs on the tennis court beneath the white skirt, the provocative poses she adopted sometimes when seated opposite him tempted Edward often, but after the lesson of Ruth and the trouble that had ensued, he tried hard not to repeat that mistake. He went cold at the thought of that happening to Elaine. His job would go that was certain, Sir Redvers not being the sort of man to countenance any impropriety with his pride and joy of a daughter outside of marriage.

They were not even engaged. Before the shock appearance of Ruth he had decided to ask Elaine to marry him, but he had been worried by the fact that at the time he was only a second string car salesman. Now of course with his promotion and higher salary he felt that he could approach both Elaine and her father more confidently. One other thing hastened his decision to ask for her hand. There were other young fellows from local families with better paid jobs than his showing interest in her, and whose parents knew the Scartons. She teased them, flirted with them and danced with them, but still preferred Edward's company as far as he knew. But he did not want to leave the matter to chance.

The next weekend he decided that he would propose to Elaine, but when he met her she was in a restless mood — edgy, swirling her skirt as she made short backward and forward steps in the smaller lounge in her home. 'Take me somewhere different tonight Eddie — I feel like a change — a gamble.' Perching impatiently on the arm of his chair she exclaimed suddenly, 'Hallfield House! I want to go there — haven't been for a while.'

Hallfield House, a very expensive place he'd heard, with dancing, cabaret by stars appearing at the theatres nearby — and gambling. He was uneasy about going there but he couldn't refuse, nor did he wish to. It was definitely a place to go if you had money. If not you steered clear.

'Book a table, Eddie sweetie, and I'll put some glad rags on.' She avoided his grasp and swayed out, leaving him wondering whether the atmosphere of Hallfield House would induce her to say 'yes' to his proposal.

Hallfield House was a cosy sixteenth century mullioned-windowed place with log fires burning even on that summer evening, and full of elegant women and dinner-jacketed escorts. Edward was sorry he hadn't got an evening suit and determined to buy one at the first opportunity. If he married Elaine he was going to need one, and also plenty of money if the prices on the menu were anything to go by. Nevertheless by the time the meal was over he was feeling relaxed and proud to be accompanying Elaine, who drew more than her share of admiring glances from other male diners. She was as usual splendidly vivacious, her eyes roving to catch those glances, perfectly groomed and wearing expensive jewellery of her own. Edward had not been able so far to present her with anything equally costly. A piano was being played and he decided to ask her — now was the time.

He reached across oblivious to his knocking over his glass as he did so. She was just opening her bag and he knew what for — a cigarette. He didn't like her to smoke, had never said anything, but it made her look hard. 'Elaine, I want to marry you — let's get married soon.'

Her hand stayed partly hidden as she looked up at him. 'Well — well, darling Eddie, you've taken the plunge at last.' Surprise, faint mockery and delight were present in those glittering dark eyes. 'Ask me again. I want to hear it again properly. I wasn't paying attention before.'

She hadn't refused him, but trust Elaine to make him work for it first. It was like a fever — he caught it each time he was with her. 'You're driving me mad, Elaine. Marry me please.'

'Oh Eddie darling — yes, yes, I will,' and she leaned across the table, pouted her lips and he stretched eagerly to cover them with his own, then sat back, his mind like the flame atop the candle burning between them. He beckoned a waiter.

'Champagne Eddie, let's celebrate with champagne, not that stuff,' and she indicated their near empty wine bottle.

'Yes why not? Let's.'

'Any particular sort Sir?' and the waiter hovered.

'Oh — er — bring the best.' Edward was becoming reckless in his joy. 'This young lady has just consented to marry me,' and smiled loosely up at the man.

The other's eyes slid to Elaine and back. 'Congratulations Sir, Madam. The best — certainly Sir,' and away he went.

Later they went into a room where roulette was being played, and Elaine gambled, Edward beside her in a haze of well-being and happiness. Afterwards they danced and then returned to the gambling again.

Elaine's excited voice in his ear. 'Eddie, give me another fiver. This time I'm going to be lucky — I know it.' Whether she was or not Edward laughed and clung to her waist in a state of heaven, and reaching for his wallet at frequent intervals. Then they retreated to their table and finished off the champagne, Elaine's laughter getting a little shriller by each glass, her dancing a little less elegant. They swayed together on the floor.

'Eddie, little darling, I want you to ask Daddy. You've got to ask for my hand you know.'

He murmured his acquiescence into her neck. The way he felt just then he would have asked anybody for anything.

'I want to play roulette again. I feel lucky, Eddie.'

'Now — again?' He was comfortable against her — Sir Redvers Scarton's only daughter, and going to marry her. He had a feeling that she had not been all that lucky so far at the spinning wheel, but it was all very vague — a marvellous dream-like evening.

Elaine called the numbers and he watched the coloured balls bouncing around, and he felt as if he were going round with them. From her gasps and cries he thought she won some and lost some.

Seated on his knee sometime after midnight she enthused, 'A great evening, Eddie. I like to have a good fling occasionally.'

He could see where the curve of her breasts

disappeared into the dress, and his lips touched the spot momentarily. Just as he was withdrawing she pulled his head hard against her, forcing his face into the same place. He could smell her flesh, the perfume, and feel her heart. Then suddenly she released him. 'I want to leave now, Eddie,' she demanded. 'Settle the bill and let's go,' and slipped from his lap, vanishing towards the cloakroom. God! He thought, she was like a jack in the box, and just as he was enjoying himself.

The bill appeared at his elbow, the figure on it clearing his brain quicker than a deluge of cold water. He focused his vision as keenly as he could, but the total remained the same. Fifty pounds, seventeen shillings and fourpence. The fourpence was a nonsense — as the whole thing was. He went through his wallet — it was very thin. The nightmare sobered him almost completely. He hadn't enough left — unable to pay, and realised that a lot of it had gone on the gaming tables. What an idiot! And on a night when he had proposed to her — Sir Redvers Scarton's daughter — been accepted, and couldn't pay the bloody bill.

The head waiter brought the manager discreetly. The gentleman had a problem?

Yes, he certainly had. Unfortunately he'd gambled quite a lot and hadn't realised how much and now he found himself short. How dreadful it was. 'We were celebrating, Elaine — er — Miss Scarton said she would marry me. I'm afraid I got carried away. I will pay you certainly — as soon as possible,' Edward assured him desperately. He blundered on, clutching at her name to help himself. 'My fiancée is

Miss Elaine Scarton, daughter of Sir Redvers Scarton. He would vouch for me.'

Immediately there was a lightening of the atmosphere. 'Oh, Sir Redvers, Sir. He's well known here. Yes, well I'm sure something can be arranged. Would you mind signing an I.O.U.?'

It was all he could do. His relief was immense, and it had all been done without too much fuss, and he was grateful for that. He'd pay it back some way. He thanked them and joined Elaine waiting rather impatiently in the hall.

'Couldn't you pay the bill or something, Eddie?'

He managed not to betray himself, brushed it aside. 'They were just busy — didn't bring it right away — forgotten I think.'

Greatly relieved he sank into the driving seat of the Daimler. Elaine had refused to be driven in his old firm's car. Sir Redvers must not find out that his prospective son in law had run up a bill which he could not settle while escorting his daughter. It would not do his chances much good either in the firm or when he came to ask for his daughter's hand in marriage. It seemed to him at times that one member of the Scarton family gave him money, whilst another member helped him to spend it.

The clock on the dashboard said one-thirty, not the time of the night to ask his employer to give his consent. A pity, thought Edward. Perhaps two hours earlier and he would have risked it. Instead he told a drowsy Elaine at his shoulder that he would be up to see her father the following Friday evening. He drove the car into the garage next to the Rolls, then embraced her and she responded passionately, but when his embrace became something else she pushed herself away from him. 'No! No Eddie. I'm tired now. I'll make it up to you later.'

Rather disgruntled but not saying anything he saw her inside and then drove off in his cold old car. He was mad about her, but short of marrying her he'd be a hundred years old before he managed to get to sleep with her. In any case fatigue had affected him also. Nevertheless before he turned in a return of the elation he had experienced earlier occurred. What a night! Elaine agreeing to marry him, the awful embarrassment over the bill. How she'd enjoyed her gambling session, but hell fire, she was extravagant and expensive.

His salary at the end of the week would enable him to pay off the debt but he vowed that never again would he be put in the position of having to do that again. It was a week of strain, Edward being on tenterhooks. Should Hallfield House contact him at work regarding the money Sir Redvers may get to hear of the incident, and he hoped fervently that Hallfield House would give him until the weekend to cancel the outstanding amount.

On the Friday evening he was due at Scarton Manor to ask Elaine's father for permission to marry her, and as that day drew near Edward became progressively more nervous and doubtful about the outcome of his visit. He was the area manager for the firm, but he was a non-native of the district, a southerner, a foreigner who had popped up from nowhere so to speak and who had begged more or less of Sir Redvers for a job. Also he had no parents to refer to and his background had been changed completely. Sir Redvers was a Yorkshireman with scant regard for anyone outside the county, and it was more than likely that he would want a suitor for his daughter who came from another equally successful country family. What's more, Edward knew that he himself was in a poor state financially. Ruth's stay in Daleford and the fees at the nursing home had taken nearly all he had saved, and last Saturday's gambling fling by Elaine had just about finished off his remaining pecuniary assets. As a prospective son-in-law he must appear very fifth rate he decided, which was all very chastening, and by the time he was on his way to Scarton Manor he had almost abandoned his hopes of marrying Elaine. Perhaps he would not even mention the matter, just spend the evening there, enjoying himself in her company.

But several nudges from Edward's subconscious tenacity kept a small hope flickering. After all he was a fairly frequent visitor, and Sir Redvers seemed to like him well enough, and more importantly Elaine wanted to marry him, and as Edward had found out, that which Miss Elaine Scarton wanted she usually got. One more plus in Edward's favour was the fact that Sir Redvers and Lady Scarton must be aware of his feelings towards their daughter and hers towards him, yet nothing had been said or done to stop the relationship from developing. And so on arrival, his spirits, whilst not soaring, were well above the doubtful gloom surrounding him when he had set out for Scarton Manor.

'Daddy's in the small lounge,' Elaine informed him, breaking away after their third kiss and adding with a gleam, 'Best of luck, Eddie.'

'Does he know what I've come to see him about?'

'He has an idea.'

Making his way to the rear of the house he met Lady Scarton.

'Good evening Edward,' and her blue eyes were perky, busy over him, then lingering as if taking notice of him properly for the first time. 'Have you seen Elaine?'

'Yes, I'm just going to have a word with Sir Redvers now.'

She nodded with a pre-knowledge, and then observed, 'You look very smart Edward.'

Hoping that may help him in the next few minutes he replied, 'Thanks. Perhaps it's the sunshine. It always makes a person feel and look better.' It was true he had done his best to present himself in the best possible light, having a slight tan and wearing his best grey suit.

'I suppose it does, but one gets so little of it I'm afraid in Daleford,' she remarked as she left him.

Edward knocked and pushed the lounge door open. Sir Redvers was standing on the terrace to one side of the open French windows. Turning, he beckoned him. 'Come out and look at this.'

Edward joined him to look out over the lawns and trees on that still and warm summer's evening. He noticed the near straight lines of the new-mown lawn. It was like a small park, lacking he thought in only one thing — the seat at its end.

'Did you ever see anything as peaceful as that, Edward?' said Elaine's father pointing his unlit cigar at it. 'We don't get many good days but when we do you can't beat 'em!' He glanced at his young companion, adding, 'In England's green and pleasant land eh?'

'It is beautiful Sir, and you've a lovely garden,' which was the truth. Came the song of a bird and the fluttering of a butterfly having a late evening.

'Could be yours some day, Edward. These things have all got to be worked for.' He turned his back on the view and moved inside. 'Drink?'

Why not? It would loosen him up a bit, being somewhat taut. He had a small straight whisky.

Sir Redvers sat down with his back to the windows. 'How's Edward then?'

Meeting him socially Edward felt as if he were not employed by him, that they had not met for some time. The fact that they saw each other occasionally during the working week seemed irrelevant. 'Oh, fairly well Sir, thanks. And you?'

Elaine's father put down his glass. 'That's better,' he uttered appreciatively, then in reply to Edward's enquiry, 'Not so bad, Edward, for an old man.'

Edward had got used to that also. Even from his youthful position Sir Redvers would not qualify as being old. He could not see the other's features clearly, the latter having his back to the light, but felt that he was being regarded keenly.

'Well now, Edward, Elaine said you wanted to ask me something.'

This was it, thought Edward, and for some reason wished he were standing to talk. He leaned forward earnestly, elbows on knees, both hands round his glass. 'I — I wondered, Sir, if you would give me permission to marry Elaine.' It was out — he had said it — there was no retracting now. 'I think a great deal of her . . . ' He stopped. It would help if he could see the older man's expression.

Sir Redvers picked up his drink but did not put it to his lips. 'You think a great deal of her do you? Is that all?' The words were said gently enough but there was an abrasive quality too.

Edward knew of his omission, hastened to rectify it. 'Oh no — I — I love her very much.'

'That's better, lad. The man that marries my daughter has to do.' His tone became sympathetic. 'I know what you mean — I've gone through it.'

He sipped at his drink then picked up his still smouldering cigar and puffed once then asked, 'Now Edward, what are your prospects? After all, as you can see, she's been used to the best all her life. She's hardly likely to take to a tuppenny-halfpenny existence is she?'

His question caught Edward by total surprise. He worked for the man after all. He must know if anybody did what his prospects were. But he realised swiftly that he was under close examination, and what he said next would have a very serious bearing on whether he married Elaine and joined the Scarton family and all it meant in terms of finance and influence for the future. He remembered the picture of that very house he was in on Sir Redvers' office wall and his employer's words, 'If you want it enough and work hard, you'll get it.'

'I'll try and copy you, Sir, do my best for the firm, work hard and provide Elaine with everything she's been used to. I owe you a lot, Sir Redvers, and I'm going to make sure that I repay that debt by making her happy. I'm sure I can.'

The older man was silent a moment before speaking. 'You don't owe me that much, Edward. You've worked hard, come on well. You know as well as I do if you hadn't you'd have been out.'

Yes, he was sure he would have been. Nevertheless, the man opposite had given him the chance, and in a number of ways he'd shown kindness in his brusque forthright way. As regards the object of his visit that evening, he felt relieved that he hadn't been turned down yet. He must present himself in the best possible way. Was he such a pauper? Hadn't he got assets of his own? The hotel, or rather its ruins — it was more or less his, he liked to think. In the effort of trying to do well at Scartons and his courtship of Elaine, his old home had been pushed to the rear of his mind. The whisky oiled his tongue.

'I forgot to mention, Sir, when you asked me about my prospects that I was left hotel property in Guernsey.'

Sir Redvers straightened in his chair. 'Were you by jove?' he exclaimed, and Edward then told him briefly about it, feeling a quick return of anguish at the reawakened memories.

His host was impressed and very interested. 'So you're a man of property, Edward — well I'll be blowed.'

Edward shook his head. 'It's a ruin really, but it's in a first class position and the land is no doubt very valuable.'

'No doubt, no doubt,' agreed Elaine's father. 'Just needs money spending on it,' and he paused looking thoughtful. 'Well, we'll have to see about it sometime — sounds a good proposition.' He rose, indicating the other's glass, 'Another, Edward?'

Why not? Things were going well. After handing Edward his refilled glass Sir Redvers remained standing, back to the empty fireplace and gazing out through the French windows into the early dusk. He spoke reflectively while continuing to look outwards. 'You know, Edward, a man can be lucky in lots of different ways. I've been lucky in business, made money and have what it can buy, but I never had a son,' and regret was in tone and expression. 'Don't get me wrong though, I've as fine a daughter as any man could wish for, and I don't need to tell you that,' he said proudly. 'The bloody apple of my eye and don't you forget it young man, but a son's a different thing altogether. We haven't had one, and we're past the time now to raise one.' He sipped from his glass then stared down at Edward. 'Fact is that I've come to look on you more as a son than an employee. You'd have just been about the age if I'd had one of my own.' A glint came in the glance. 'You're a bloody southerner, but not one from this country — you're tarred with a different brush altogether,' and he smiled, taking away any offence Edward may have felt over his words.

Edward did not have any feeling of offence. Instead the hurdle he had come to surmount that evening was almost cleared. He had yet to land foursquare, but the ground was increasingly favourable.

'You've got presence, politeness and a nice personality — three 'pees' I call 'em, but they go a long way. Aye, and you'll be an asset to the organisation.' He finished off his drink quickly, placing the glass down with an air of finality on the mantelpiece. 'You say Elaine will have you?'

'Oh yes, Sir, she accepted me last week providing that you did also.' He was becoming used to the peculiar ways of Sir Redvers' speech.

'Right then, I'll tell you what I'm going to do. I'm going to accept your proposal for Elaine's hand. Get on and marry her,' and he thrust his hand out to clasp that of Edward as the latter sprang joyfully up from the chair.

'Thank you very much indeed, Sir. I'll look after her, don't you worry.'

Their hands fell apart. 'I'm sure you will, Edward lad. By the way, now you're going to be in the family don't keep calling me Sir Redvers or Sir when we're being social. Redvers is all you need here. At work it's a different matter. Call me as you've always called me. Remember here it's Redvers,' and he picked up the decanter. 'Now let's just celebrate with one more before we join the ladies. You know what they'll be like. It'll be wedding talk until the very day. You'll be sick of it, I'll tell you — I've been through it.' He laughed gruffly, patted Edward on the back heavily. 'To the Scartons and the Dorners.' Heady moments for Edward as he repeated the toast. 'Remind me Edward to have another chat about your property in Guernsey some time.'

He would — he most certainly would. The vision was drawing nearer. Scarton money to rebuild his family home and Elaine to be his partner in the venture. Life was beginning to smile on him.

The announcement of Sir Redvers Scarton's daughter's engagement was not a small paltry one line in the local paper. It was a large print potted biography of the family and carried several paragraphs on Edward himself. No date had yet been set for the wedding but it was likely to be early autumn. And not so very far away a pair of violet eyes under a fair head closed in shock on seeing the announcement, and later dampened the pillow with bitter tears.

9

Edward was swept along on the tide of preparation for the wedding by the Scarton women, September eleventh being chosen as the day. For him it was like being on the upper end of a spinning top — a whirl of two months of new faces, work commitments, rehearsals for the ceremony, choosing presents and deciding on furniture for their new home. Not that he decided on much; Elaine and her mother did most of that, but Edward did not mind. He was marrying into the Scarton family and he was mad about Elaine. Beyond that was the lure of advancement in the family business and the dream of the rebuilding of his old home in Guernsey with the help of his new-found ally — his father-in-law to be.

Elaine's parents had offered them part of the manor as their future home. It was large and had more than sufficient rooms for them to be comfortable and private. Money had been no object in the preparation and making ready for the bridal couple. Their quarters were to be at the rear of the house facing the gardens and the tennis court. Edward thought it would be delightful and was eager to begin married life. The honeymoon was to be spent in Majorca, this being Sir Redvers's personal present to the couple.

The matter of an engagement ring for Elaine was causing Edward some concern for the simple reason that he could not afford the sort that he would like to present to her. She was quite uncomprehending over the matter, surveying and inspecting samples in the jewellers that they always seemed to be passing. He made the excuse that they had not yet seen anything good enough but as soon as he saw anything suitable, he would buy it for her. Unfortunately he had made the mistake of giving himself only a week to find such a ring and Elaine was already becoming restless and reminding him in great expectation that she could hardly wait. Had he already got it? What colour of stones had it and how many? Edward knew he had been a fool playing the rich man without having the money. His mind went back to another time in the past when money had been raised quickly. The solution came again — his parents' rings, in particular his mother's ring. Why not give Elaine his most treasured possession? It was not new but it meant a lot to him and he was sure that she would value it all the more for that reason. Perhaps later he could give her another, new and more modern, when his finances had improved. He took the ring and cleaned it, saddened by the memories it evoked, but consoled by the fact that his parents — his mother particularly — would be overjoyed to know that it was going to be on his bride to be's finger. A tear fell and wet the stones — rubies and diamonds. He polished it away chastising himself for submitting to the sadness that overcame him on the very rare occasions.

Elaine received the ring rather strangely he thought, twisting it between her fingers and examining it closely before slipping it on to her finger. Then she put her hand this way and that, and he was hurt by the slight wrinkling of her nose that she could not or did not care to disguise.

'Don't you like it?' he asked anxiously.

'Oh yes,' but he knew that she didn't by her flat voice. 'But Eddie, you know I prefer emeralds to go with diamonds.' Her tone and manner were peevish and disappointed. Taking it off she brought it up close to his face. 'Look Eddie, there're some scratches — see.'

It flashed into his mind that perhaps they had been made in his mother's beloved terraced garden, or more likely when she had died on the jetty.

'It's second-hand, isn't it?' Elaine stared at him over the ring.

He nodded glumly. 'Yes, it belonged to my mother. I — I . . . ' What had he thought? That this modern, wealthy, want for nothing daughter of Sir Redvers Scarton would settle for someone else's ring. He should have known better. 'All right, Elaine. I'll buy you another.'

'I'll make this do for now, Eddie,' and she put it on her finger again. 'Actually it's quite nice.'

Quite nice! He sat in a chair feeling deflated whilst she telephoned someone called Mavis about bridesmaids and dresses, but he did not hear a mention of the ring.

The following week on one evening he had a visit from William. Edward was rather surprised. He had not seen his brother for some time, the latter appearing to have settled down to a life of comparative ease under the wings of Miss Steck and her stepsister. He looked well, sporting a blazer and cravat, and carrying gauntlets. Glancing out of the window Edward saw that he had arrived in the Alvis purchased from Scarton's. Edward smiled to himself, having wondered how long it would be before William began using the car for himself.

'I see you've been doing very well for yourself', his brother said. 'I saw the announcement in the local,' then glanced around the bed-sitter disparagingly. 'Won't be long before you can leave this lot behind. I don't know how you've stuck it here.'

Edward shrugged. 'I just had to take what I could get — no choice.'

William gazed at him in a grudging admiration. 'How did you manage to corner a rich little girl like that? I wouldn't have thought that she was your type at all.'

Edward remembered William had met her on that Christmas Eve when they had been invited up to the Manor from St. Just's. 'I just happened to work for her father that's all. We met — that was it. I must admit though William I'm staggered at my luck. I'm crazy about her.' A small warning voice told him not to say too much about his dealings with the family. Maybe it was a jealous voice, but he'd worked hard for whatever success had come his way, and he had not reminded the Scarton family too often that he had a brother.

'Have you got a house yet?'

'We're going to live at the Manor, in part of the house. It's very nice.'

'I'll bet it is. And are you staying in Daleford for the honeymoon?'

'No, we're flying to Majorca.'

'You lucky devil,' his brother exclaimed, 'you've really landed in a gold mine haven't you? My God, you've really got your feet under the table there.' His tone was envious and surprised. 'Marrying the boss's daughter, good job and bags of money,' he added eyeing Edward.

Edward poured another coffee for them, thinking that he'd worked damned hard to succeed in the business and also with Elaine. William could have got a job if he had wanted to, but William he knew was inclined to be just a little on the lazy side. In any case he'd done all right so far without actually being employed. His brother's obvious envy and surprise irritated Edward somewhat. 'Well, you're doing all right aren't you, driving around in an expensive car, living in a detached house — best part of town — and you don't have to turn out for work?' And to himself 'keeping Miss Steck happy'. As long as William did that he would not have a care. It must be rather strange he thought, pleasuring a woman half as old again every night, but obviously the benefits were worth it. It struck him then that of the three — William, Ruth and himself — only William had never had to work.

His brother's next enquiry caught him off balance. 'How's Ruth these days? Do you hear from her?'

Edward's look sharpened on William, he couldn't help it. Any mention of Ruth brought an immediate response in him. 'She's in Guernsey,' he replied hurriedly.

'Yes, I thought she would be,' and there was faint surprise in William's voice.

'Oh yes, she's all right — writes occasionally.'

William put his cup down. 'Never writes to me, but of course you always were her favourite. I'm surprised you two never got together. I should have thought she was more your sort than Elaine Scarton.'

'How d'you mean?'

'Well, of course I haven't seen your intended since that night up at the Manor at Christmas, but she struck me as rather a flighty piece of goods.'

Edward frowned at the flippant choice of words by his brother, and seeing this William added, 'No slight intended, Edward, just my impression that's all.' He shrugged slightly. 'Then again, we're all a bit older — we shall all have changed.'

'I think a great deal of her,' said Edward. 'She means a lot to me.'

'Yes, I'm sure she does.' Was there a slight note of cynicism and envy there again? Edward decided that he wasn't going to be offended by William. After all he didn't see him very often.

William crossed his hands over his knees, gazing directly at his brother. 'You know it's a funny thing, but I could have sworn I saw Ruth in Daleford the other day.'

'Couldn't be. I . . . ' The words jerked from Edward, stopped himself just in time. 'I mean I had a letter from her yesterday,' he lied hastily.

William was eyeing him thoughtfully. 'Oh I know it couldn't have been because this woman was carrying a baby. But I was so sure that I almost stopped the car, but it was too busy, a lot of traffic, and I had Adeline with me. If I'd stopped to speak to a young attractive woman, well . . . ' — he grimaced and raised his eyebrows — 'she'd have thrown me out and I'm not ready to leave yet. She's my bread and butter you might say.'

Edward was hardly listening. Could it have been Ruth that William had seen? Surely not. And carrying a child? Suppose it was? But it couldn't be. She was back in Guernsey.

His brother's voice intruded on his thoughts. 'Does Ruth know that you're getting married?'

Why did William keep on about Ruth? 'No, I'm sure she doesn't. She's hardly likely to see the Daleford news.'

'You're not going to invite her to the wedding?' William saw the expression on Edward's face. 'Well perhaps not, maybe not the thing to do, probably be upset.' He paused then went on, 'By the way I haven't had an invite to the wedding yet. Tell Elaine she just can't miss out her future brother-in-law.'

Edward had known this would happen, was bound to do. He couldn't announce his forthcoming marriage and expect William to show no interest. On the one hand, as his closest relation, he wished to invite him, but on the other he did not want him around the Scarton household too often afterwards. Edward smiled more affably than he felt. 'Oh, don't worry, you haven't been forgotten, William. It's just that we've been very busy, you know how it is.'

'Anyway you don't need to send an invitation to me as the best man surely?' pointed out William.

Edward stared at him. Best man! He knew there was something he had to arrange. Damn, he'd forgotten. There was no way out and in any case it would have looked strange asking someone else when his brother was available. 'No, of course not,' he agreed quickly. 'Matter of fact, I was going to call this week and see you.' He had a feeling that he did not sound convincing, and momentarily their eyes locked and Edward guessed that William realised the truth. Hurrying to mask the awkwardness he felt, his words came staccato fashion. 'St. Paul's Church — twelve noon — September eleventh. Car will call for you and we've got to be there first. Grey morning-suit, topper, but in any case I'll see you before then.' He was anxious that William should go, wanted time to think things over now that his brother was to become involved with the wedding.

William however did not look eager to leave and further surprised him with his sudden change of topic. 'This matter of our parent's house in Guernsey. I still think it would be a good idea to sell it and make some money.'

'We don't even know whether it's ours to sell,' pointed out Edward. 'No will has been found yet.'

All William wanted to do was to get his hands on the proceeds of the sale. He himself did not, although the money would be very welcome, but his plans for the building still remained in his mind for some day in the future.

'Well, what about the solicitors and courts? Don't they settle that kind of thing?' persisted William. 'After all, it's not doing a damn thing for anyone like it is. It's just a bloody ruin. I mean we can't wait forever until they've found a will, and perhaps there isn't one. People know we lived there so it shouldn't be hard to prove that we inherit it.'

His tone had become irritable.

The last thing Edward wanted just then was to quarrel with his brother. He had quite enough on his mind. 'Look, wait until after the wedding, and perhaps we can make inquiries in Guernsey, see what can be done.'

'All right, but I'm going to hold you to that. It's time something was done.' Then William's face relaxed into its usual ready smile. 'Anyway, let's enjoy the wedding first. I'm looking forward to it and seeing how the rich live, and that will include you soon.'

Then to Edward's relief he left shortly afterwards, but leaving the former with a vague feeling of unease at William's coming participation in the wedding ceremony.

For some time Edward sat thinking. He'd always thought of their former home in Guernsey in a proprietary way, but he had been jolted out of this assumption by what William had said. Until the will was found or the courts decided, he could not claim complete ownership, and remembered getting carried away in Sir Redvers presence, saying that he had property in Guernsey. He took comfort from the fact that it might be some time before Sir Redvers decided to have a look at it. William was impatient to turn the property into money and Edward guessed the reason for that. His brother wanted to spread his wings — getting bored with life at the Poplars. He was a kept man and until he had money of his own he would be dependent on Miss Adeline Steck for every penny.

Edward's thoughts passed on to Ruth and

William's assertion that he had seen her in Daleford. He was quite mistaken of course; she was in Guernsey, no doubt about that. He wondered if William had heard that Ruth had been over and had had a child. He hoped to heaven that Elaine never found out that a child of his had been born in Daleford. Of course his liaison with Ruth had been before his courtship of Elaine, and as long as Ruth and the child stayed in Guernsey there would be no risk of jeopardising his forthcoming marriage. What had she called the child? Frederick? He hadn't thought about it before, but how strange it felt to realise that he was father to a tiny boy in Guernsey.

September came and no chance to think of anything but the wedding. A frenzied time with Elaine changing her bridal gown once more, but finally everything was to her satisfaction. The reception afterwards was to be held at Scarton Manor, and if the weather was kind, outside as well as in. And Edward began to wonder if his prepared speech was as witty and original as it might have been.

The evening but one before the day of the wedding, he paid his last visit to the Manor as a bachelor, Lady Scarton being quite certain that it was unlucky to see the bride the day before the wedding. 'It's an old superstition, Edward, but I'm sure that it's correct.'

The other words of warning came from Sir Redvers over a drink together that same evening. 'I shan't see you again until church, Edward, so here's to you and Elaine. If you make as good a job of being a husband as you've done for the firm you'll please me damned well.' He put out his hand and Edward took it, and somewhat to his surprise the older man kept a grip on it and carried on forthrightly, 'When you're married Edward, I want no shenanikins — no laking about — you understand what I mean? I won't tolerate my little girl being hurt. You take her for better or worse, know what I mean lad?'

Lad did, after his initial surprise. 'I'll do anything to keep her happy, Redvers, I promise.' Couldn't her father see that he was mad about her? But the warning was there.

'That's all right then. Just thought I'd mention it.' His face lost its sternness, and the eyes which had bored into Edward's looked away. 'See you in church then, Edward.'

The morning of the wedding broke with a light drizzle, but by mid-morning a breeze had arisen giving tantalising glimpses of sun and blue sky between the hurrying clouds, and playing sculptor with the bridesmaids' dresses.

Inside the church Edward sat with William at his side, feeling rather chilly and waiting for his bride to appear. If only his parents had been there to see him married. The last church he had been in was St. Martins in Guernsey when he had been to enquire about their graves. His thoughts ran on. He wasn't too sure about churches. Perhaps it was their huge pillars, the cold stone, joy and grief over the years swirling up and around them in equal measure into their gloomy vast arches.

He glanced at his brother. Suddenly, in a short time William had become involved in this new life he was making for himself, but of course he realised that it was stupid to have thought that he could keep his only brother out of such an important occasion as this. The fact was that William now had a door — albeit a small one — into that new life, and also into the Scarton family, and it made Edward uneasy on his wedding day.

A sudden hum in the congregation behind, then the music began and Edward left the pew to await his bride. The rustling of dresses and steady steps and there she was, ravishing and dark-eyed beside him. A provocative look up at him from under her veil, then her glance of smiling acknowledgement across to William. No! Edward's mind shouted. It should be all his today — not a flicker of an eyelid for any other man. Just him! It was the first strike of jealousy. He recovered quickly. She was going to be his — all his very soon.

The service progressed and the ring was produced, and Edward was in a haze of nervous happiness, repeating after the vicar the words of the ceremony. Finally they were married, the gold on Elaine's finger next to her engagement ring — his mother's. He was glad to see that she was wearing it; it must have pleased her after all.

A baby's cry came from the back of the church and died away to a gurgle.

Afterwards in the vestry they signed the register, and William made Elaine smile at his murmured remarks as she bent to sign. Edward noticed and did not like it, but then the incident was forgotten in the preparation for the return walk down the aisle. They set off, Elaine on his right arm, towards the mass of faces accompanied by the rousing triumphant sound of the Wedding March swelling behind them. Edward proud but self-conscious, wishing the aisle was shorter in length. The colourful splendid hats of the women, and the faces underneath staring, eyeing and scrutinising as the couple passed, and then turning after them.

They had almost reached the end of the nave. Elaine, smiling and murmuring to well-wishers on her right, the sound of bells coming through the open doors, and the cool air fanning their faces. A glimpse of more people outside, bags and cartons of confetti at the ready. The last pew on Edward's left — a woman with a child in her arms — at the very end of it, only feet away. He glanced at her and into the face of Ruth! The eyes, accusing under the disguising hat locked with his; a second — but one which sent his mind staggering. He glanced backwards but the head did not turn. Ruth! It was Ruth! With the child, Frederick!

'Eddie.' Elaine's voice penetrated his tangled senses. They had stopped just inside the entrance. 'Are you feeling all right?'

His lips moved in a smile. 'Yes — yes of course I am. Just the excitement that's all, a little dizzy — nothing — it's gone.'

He was aware of Elaine giving him a funny look, and then they emerged into the overcast outside. Pats on the back, congratulations, laughter, showers of confetti, guests spilling from the church behind and surrounding them. Photographs in groups, then the two of them alone. The official wedding photographer arranging folds and creases, toppers and large hats bobbing and faces chatting.

'Are you cold, Edward?' someone asked.

He smiled vaguely, uttered something pertinent, and glanced around, but of Ruth there was no sign. Had it been Ruth? Of course it had — he was sure.

'Bear up, Edward. You haven't been drinking already have you?' It was William, his voice just a little too loud and jovial. Had he seen her?

Edward followed Elaine into the wedding car, confetti still on his head, and they set off for the family home and reception. Elaine was busy straightening and arranging her dress for which he was thankful. It gave him time to compose himself after the shock of seeing Ruth in the church like that, and with the boy Frederick. She had not been there when he and William had arrived for the ceremony, of that he was sure. Elaine, he guessed, had not seen Ruth. She had been on his right hand, away from her. In any case, Ruth's hat had shaded her face until the last moment when he had been almost alongside her. Damn her. What was she still doing in Daleford? She should have caught the plane the day after he had seen her last. Everything had been arranged. Why did she have to turn up now, at his wedding of all times? What did she think she would gain by it? He'd married the girl he wanted.

'For a man who's just married the girl of his dreams, Eddie darling, you're not showing much interest in her.' Elaine's petulant plaintive voice brought him quickly out of his thoughts.

He leaned over swiftly and kissed her, angry with Ruth and also himself for allowing the sight of her to upset him so much. 'You enchanting witch, it's because I can't believe you've married me,' and he saw the petulance fade quickly and her regard soften. 'My handsome Channel islander,' and she caressed his face. 'You looked quite shaky back there, Eddie. Did you have a bucker-up before you left home? William thought you must have had — or two maybe.'

To hell with William and what he thought, interfering already. He couldn't quite keep his annoyance hidden. 'No I did not. I had nothing; I didn't need it. Just dizzy for a moment, it was nothing.' He caught the eye of the chauffeur in the driving mirror. The man must think it strange, just married and the bridegroom set-faced, cross-looking. Edward knew that he must relax. After all it was his wedding day, the county wedding of the year.

The reception came and went with so many new faces, so many handshakes. Sir Redvers friends, business associates. Edward made his speech, stumbling here and there. Elaine, his Yorkshire rose, whom he would tend and care for as long as he lived. He hoped to become a naturalised Yorkshireman, and would never forget the people of Daleford, how much they had helped when he and the others like him had arrived in the town during the war, and he was thankful that he was deposited here, otherwise he would never have met his bride. It seemed to go down well with everyone, his father-in-law looking particularly pleased, and afterwards the latter congratulated him.

'Nice little speech, Edward lad. You've got a nice

approach. Liked what you said about Elaine. The sky's the limit in the business for you, I think.'

Edward thought that he had made a good start. Elaine had once said that Redvers admired his different, more refined speech and his manners. If you married a man's daughter and he also employed you and liked you on both counts — business and personally — then you were not doing too badly. He just hoped it would continue in that fashion.

They honeymooned in that wondrous Spanish island, a place of sun, rocky coves and inlets, of rising cliffs and headlands. It reminded Edward very much of his birthplace — a Mediterranean Guernsey. It brought memories of his early years on the sands near his home. He adored that warm island — a fitting place for his adoration of the woman he had just married. She was sophisticated, glossy and provocative, lounging around the pool or hotel gardens in affected poses, appearing to enjoy the effect she had on the waiters, as they hovered around with drinks. She displayed her finest dresses on and around the hotel dance floor, and the occasional night club they visited. And Edward was quite content to stand alongside the woman who evoked such admiration from other men, and he saw other, much stronger, emotions in their eyes.

But she was not a woman of the sea and its environs. Not even the beach held her interest for very long, and she hated getting wet, particularly her hair. Not for her the walk through the moderate surf, not even ankle deep, although she did wet her feet twice on rare excursions along a wide almost empty beach, but her manner was far from happy.

As Edward found out, she was at her best in the expensive shops surrounding the squares in the capital, spending, then squealing with delight afterwards at her purchase as she examined it once more in between sipping at her exotic cocktails. Edward went cold sometimes at the thought of what it would have cost him if his father-in-law had not paid for the holiday itself as his present to them.

A month into their married life and Edward's happiness and infatuation continued unabated. Waiting on his wife hand and foot, work prospering and feeling that he could tackle anything the company asked him to do. He counted himself a lucky man, and so it appeared did William who paid occasional visits to Scarton Manor. But always sooner or later during the visit the subject of their old home would crop up, William impatient to have something done about the property. But for Edward, newly wed and taken up with marriage and the family business, the matter had receded into the background of his life. He suggested to William that he should get in touch with the solicitors in St. Peter Port, and find out if a will had turned up yet. He was sure it had not because the firm would have been in contact with either himself or William before then, but at least it would keep William occupied doing something about it. Edward recognised that soon he may have to put the matter through the courts if a will was not found. Whether the court could force him to agree to sell the property and share the proceeds, he did not know. Obviously if the old building was sold the idea of his father-in-law's backing him with finance for its restoration would vanish.

Occasionally he would think of Ruth. She had never really been banished from his thoughts. Since that shock sighting of her in the church he had neither seen nor heard anything of her. What had she hoped to gain from being there? He wasn't going to leave Elaine and run off with her. Edward hoped that she was managing. He had felt sorry for her and had not meant to hurt her in any way, but she was a grown woman now and should have understood these things happened. Perhaps she had met someone else and was happier. He hoped so.

One evening Edward was sitting by himself in front of the fire reading one of the motoring journals. He liked to see what they thought about certain models coming on to the market, and thought it important to keep abreast of the latest trends.

Elaine had taken the car and had gone to visit one of her girl friends, taking the wedding photographs with her. The house was quiet although he knew that his in-laws were about in the other part of the building. Edward let the magazine rest on his knees, the subject of a conversation he'd had with Redvers that day coming into his mind. The latter had been talking about supermarkets. 'You know Edward, I think we ought to look into buying a bit of land here and there in the near future. Supermarkets are a big thing in America, and my feeling is we'll see 'em here before long. We ought to be ready. Shopping under one roof — big car park; we could be the first. Think it over, see what you think.'

Edward smiled to himself. Redvers was a live wire

— never missed anything. He himself had reservations about big shopping halls. The British public were used to the small shop with its personal service. Leaning forward he poked the fire into flames then stretched his legs towards the renewed heat.

Two distinct sounding knocks came at the French windows. Edward glanced towards them, startled. The curtains were undrawn and he saw a figure outside in the darkness. He stood up, surprised. Callers usually came to the main door at the front of the house. Pulling one of the doors open he looked into the face of Ruth! He stared at her, his mind struggling for a reason. It was seven-thirty on a Tuesday in late October, and yet Ruth Le Ney stood on the terrace outside his lounge. Her hair shone gold in the reflected light, her face framed by the high collar of her coat.

'Hello Edward.' There was a breathless anticipation in the voice.

Shocked — a movement of his head in disbelief came before words. 'What are you doing here? You can't come here, Ruth. Why the hell are you not in Guernsey?'

'I had to come to see you, Edward. I've got to talk to you, it's important.'

He waved a hand irritably. 'It can't be more important than the fact that you should stop following me and go home.' He continued to stare at her. 'When — when did you arrive?'

'I didn't. I live in Daleford. I never left.'

The question must have been obvious on his face for she went on, 'I stayed, found work and somewhere to live.' She glanced past him. 'I saw that you were alone.'

'Yes, Elaine's out and she may come back at any time.' What could he say if he was discovered with Ruth? 'Look Ruth, you can't do this. Please stop it. Go back to Guernsey. I'm a married man now. I'm married to Elaine. Do you understand?' His voice became harsher. 'Don't you understand?'

Ruth's eyes glowed darkly, and her words ladened with longing. 'Come with me, Edward. Come and live with us, your child and me. I love you Edward, always have. You loved me a little, you did — I know you did.' She held up something in her hand which glittered as it caught the light. 'Remember Edward, when we were young, that day on the beach. We played — that day before we had to leave. I saved it, I've always carried it. I was your girl friend then.'

Edward recognised the Ormer shell, knowing that she had kept it. 'But we're not children any more, Ruth. We change, grow up. I have a wife and a home now.'

'And where is she now?' riposted Ruth. 'Why isn't she here with you?' She came closer to him. 'You covered me with your body to save me that day, Edward. I've never forgotten. I know that we're not children any more, but neither do I forget that I gave birth to your child. Maybe you didn't love me then, but love would come — I know it would.' She was touching him with the length of her body, her voice a rapid whispering of persuasive pleading. 'Get a divorce, come with me, Edward. We'll manage. I'll work. Be a father to your child. Please, Edward.' Her fingers curled on to his shoulders.

Edward grabbed her hands, pulled them down and gripped them tightly. 'You must be crazy, Ruth. I'm not going to divorce Elaine to marry you. I love Elaine, that's why I married her. Can't you understand that?' He saw her flinch, but he didn't care. 'Now leave me alone. I don't want to see you again. Stop following me, go away and live your life and leave me to live mine — as I wish.' He let go of her hands. Something had been pricking into the flesh of his left one and he realised it was the shell she was still holding.

Ruth pressed it into his palm. 'Please Edward, hold it between us, say you love me,' and the wide violet eyes stared into his beseechingly.

'Then will you leave me alone and get out of my life?' It was stupid but if he got rid of her he would do it — say it.

Ruth stepped back. 'No I won't,' she flung at him fiercely. 'I love you — I'll always be somewhere near you.'

Edward was getting desperate, fearful of losing all that he had worked for. Ruth was out of her mind. Suddenly his restraint went and grabbing her arm he turned her roughly and pushed her away across the terrace. She stumbled and fell and he threw the shell after the sprawling form, seeing it hit her and bounce away into the darkness beyond the edge of the light from the room. 'Leave me alone,' he grated. 'I don't want to see you or that damned shell again,' and was aware of her scrabbling on her hands and knees to find it.

When she had found it she stood up clutching it, her hand close to her breast as if fearful of losing the object again. The body and coat blended into the gloom, leaving the face turned towards him and reflected in the dim light showing a dreadful hurt and misery. Then the features with their halo of fair hair vanished into the darkness.

Edward turned to go in then stopped. What had he done? Anguish in him, he ran after her calling her name, but the wind tossed it back at him contemptuously. He stood looking out from the terrace, sick at heart, his anger dying as quickly as it had arisen. He should have reasoned more with her calmly, been gentler with her, told her lies if it would have pleased her. Promised that he would come to her in Guernsey. It was idiocy but it might have made her return there. After all they had grown up together, and she had been a loyal friend — more like a sister. Perhaps that was the trouble, and he sighed hopelessly. If she'd been a stranger and they meeting for the first time as adults it might have been different. He remembered how she had worked to obtain money for them to return to the island. But loyalty and love could be taken to extreme limits. That far off day when they had dashed for the boat. Was it possible that even as a young girl, rather than lose him to some foreign place, she had deliberately chosen to go along with him, risk injury and an uncertain future? Could that have been? Now she was out there somewhere, upset and alone, and he not knowing where she had been staying. What a mess, and he swore. Life had been too good over the last few months — it had to change. He should have known when she appeared in church at his wedding. Something she had said once came back to him, that 'they had an understanding.' He shook his head miserably. What they had was a misunderstanding.

A voice from the room behind made him start visibly. 'I think you're right about these figures, Edward. They do . . . '

Edward turned quickly. Elaine's father was staring at him from the doorway. 'What the hell are you doing out there Edward? You'll get your death of cold,' and on the latter re-entering exclaimed, 'Bloody hell, you look as if you've seen a ghost. What's wrong lad?' he asked with an anxious scrutiny of his son-in-law.

Edward tried to get his mind in some sort of order. 'I — I thought I heard something or someone outside, but I couldn't see anything — maybe a cat or dog.' Avoiding the other's eyes he added, 'You're right, it is a bit chilly out there,' and he was glad to turn away and fasten the French windows. It gave him moments to collect himself.

'Where's Elaine?'

'She's gone to Mavis — took some of the wedding photographs.'

'Well, when she gets back have an early night. I can't have you falling by the wayside. You're my right hand man now you know.'

Edward poked the fire a little longer than was necessary, and managed a smile back over his shoulder. 'Oh, I'm all right, thanks.'

'You two all right? I mean you're hitting if off together?' The older man's gaze was direct.

'Oh yes, wonderfully well. Yes we're very happy.'

He was and meant it — had been until a few minutes ago.

Redvers seemed satisfied. 'Good — good.' Then to Edward's relief he tapped the papers in his hand. 'D'you know Edward, if these projected figures for next year come right, then we're set to make Scartons the largest retailers in the country,' then nodded with his words. 'Another half million in the bank eh Edward?' He glanced at the open magazine on the chair. 'That's why you've got on Edward. You're keen. That's what I like to see. Right, I'm off — see you tomorrow,' and the door closed behind him leaving Edward thinking that he would give that half million if it was his to resolve the problem of Ruth.

He sat staring into the fire. If Redvers had come in a minute earlier . . . His father-in-law's query regarding their relationship returned. Yes, he was happy in a knife edge sort of way. Elaine wasn't easy to live with, but he didn't mind so long as he was near her. She was a glittering star who even in marriage retained some of the quality of the heavenly ones — an unattainability, just out of reach in some way.

She was later home than he had expected. He made to help her with her coat.

'It's all right, I can manage,' and she smiled her thanks thinly, taking her hat and gloves off in jerky movements. 'I thought you'd have gone to bed.'

'No, your father came over — we talked.'

'About business I'll bet.' She didn't look at him.

'Where are the photographs? Have you brought them back?'

'Photos?' Just for a second the eyes were blank. 'Oh yes — of course, silly of me, I must have left them in the car.' She opened the door. 'I'm tired, I'm going straight up.'

In bed he reached for her buttocks, but she shrugged them away from his hand. 'Oh Eddie, you know how tired I am.'

'Oh, all right, sorry — yes I suppose you are.' He didn't stop to reason why. And even if he had seen the pine needles earlier which had adhered to her coat, it was quite possible that with his degree of infatuation he would not have questioned them.

The next day Edward heard that Thomas, the elderly chauffeur-handyman who lived in the lodge, had seen a woman in the grounds the day before, and Edward guessed that it had been Ruth. It was also about this time that he learned of the cottage that the family owned when he came across Redvers fuming at something in the local paper.

His father-in-law threw the paper down in disgust. 'Bloody fools — they never learn, the cheapest isn't always the best — very rarely is.'

Seeing Edward's puzzled expression he went on, 'You'll have heard about the new dam they're building up in the Lanford valley?' Edward had vaguely. 'Well. The idiots have accepted the tender of a firm I damn well know are cheapjacks. It won't last. In the long run it'll be dear. Had a few words with some of the local council not many days ago.' Redvers puffed out his cheeks contemptuously. 'Oh, they'd see the ratepayers got value for money. What the hell do they know about the job? There isn't a builder amongst the lot. All theory and desk work. I tell you Edward, it'll cost more — much more in the long run.' He raised a finger. 'Mind you Edward, I'm not against the dam at all. I think a drop of water enhances the countryside besides storing the damn stuff. Believe it or not lad, but in this district where we get such a lot of rain, we flaming well get short of water when we've had a fortnight's sunshine.' His features relaxed. 'Anyway, it'll be a grand walk round it from the cottage — blow all the cobwebs away. Should be finished by next spring.'

'Cottage? Which cottage is that?'

His father-in-law regarded him as if he were an idiot. 'Our cottage of course, the one in Landford Crags.' Stared at the younger man in surprise. 'Don't tell me you didn't know?'

Edward's expression gave his answer. 'Good God, I should have thought Elaine would have told you, taken you up there.' He gave a sly glance. 'When you were courting.'

It was a complete surprise to Edward. He knew the Landford Crags — a local beauty spot with a stream running down the valley. When they were at school he, Ruth and William had visited it on numerous occasions. He also recollected seeing something in the paper about a dam being built up there, and objections from some townspeople that it would spoil the beauty of the place. Personally he agreed with Redvers that a patch of water would help to further beautify its surroundings. The main fears that bus loads of trippers would frequent the spot and destroy the natural tranquillity of the area were unfounded, Edward thought. It wasn't very accessible — no proper roads, just two cart tracks on either side of the valley, and only serious ramblers would reach that part of the valley further up where he guessed the dam was being built.

Redvers' voice returned him to the present. 'You'll have to go up sometime and take a look. Get Elaine to show you around the cottage. You must spend some weekends there, just the thing — very relaxing. You'll come back refreshed, eh?' He laughed loudly, patted his son-in-law on the back. 'Ready for more triumphs with the Scarton company.'

Afterwards Edward mentioned the cottage to Elaine and about going up to see it.

'It's nothing, Eddie darling, just a shack really. I'd forgotten about it. Not the sort of place one would visit at this time of the year — damp and all that. I haven't been up for ages.'

She didn't seem keen on the idea, but Edward was curious and it would be somewhere to go apart from restaurants and nightclubs at the weekends. For once he persisted. He gave in to her on most occasions, and she agreed very reluctantly. He thought it a bit strange, but on the other hand she was not a country girl as such. The countryside was something to get through to reach more sophisticated venues.

The following Sunday they drove up to the cottage, Elaine silent apart from giving grudging directions as they approached it. They passed the old mill with its tiny dam. Teas used to be served there during the war, but it looked closed and shuttered now. He remembered running over the stepping stones to the other side of the stream, quite wide and rushing at that part, trying not to fall in, and loud laughter from the others when once he had done so. Now they were split up — anger, suspicions, worries replacing the laughter and camaraderie. The track grew a little steeper, the stream further below, and about two hundred yards ahead Edward spotted a building half way down their side of the valley. A rougher steeper track branched down towards it and he decided to park the car at the top. Elaine refused to accompany him saying that she was cold. He guessed that it was an excuse, but it puzzled him as to why she was so unenthusiastic.

Leaving her sitting staring impatiently ahead, he walked slowly down to the cottage. It appeared to be larger than he had expected, tucked away against the valley side, conifers and pines at its back and sides. A single-storey stone and wooden building. Reaching it he saw that it had a veranda running the length of its front with clear views across the valley from it. A gorgeous place — peaceful, in the middle of nature, and in the spring and summer Edward thought that it would be paradise. The curtains were drawn and he tried to look through the chinks between their edges, but it was impossible to see much of the interior. On the way up to the Crags he had asked Elaine if she had the key, but she had informed him that she had forgotten it. Perhaps it was one of those days when he couldn't do anything right for her; there had been a few of those recently. He retraced his steps back to the car and once they were on the return to Scarton Manor her attitude became easier towards him, he getting the feeling that she was relieved to be away from the vicinity of the cottage. Edward did not remark on this change in her, but wondered at it nevertheless.

10

In the following February Edward took Elaine to Guernsey, perhaps too early in the year for a warm holiday, but she was expecting their child and so excited was he that he could think of no other way to celebrate than to take her there. In any case he had always promised to show her his former home and the island. He was certain she would enjoy the change and the fact that he had booked them into one of the best hotels. They would walk on the cliff paths through hedged tunnels and glades of scent and flowers, with the sea ever present below. He couldn't wait to see her delight.

Edward was to be bitterly disappointed. February was not usually the month of warm sun and lazy walks. In his excitement at the prospect of taking her, his imagination had painted a perfect holiday. But Elaine was not impressed, the weather being drizzly with only occasional bouts of sun. On their first trip to the cliffs, one look at the soft muddy path and the damp branches either side had her face creased in distaste. It had been quite different that hot summer evening when he had been with Ruth on the path to Fermain, when he had lain in a quick passion in one of the dark green bowers.

They danced in the hotel in the evening, but even that seemed to bore her, and when they sat one out at the bar her fingers drummed, and her feet kicked air impatiently. Edward apologised for the weather, but pointed out that it was milder than Daleford at that time of the year. To him the place was beautiful. He would never tire of it, appreciating it now more than ever. He showed her the little chapel built of shells by monks, the forts and gun emplacements left by the enemy occupying forces, and also the underground hospital built by them. Victor Hugo's house in Hauteville she found cold and gloomy, but showed an inordinate amount of interest in the view from the writer's attic studio from where it was said he could see the house of his mistress. She even smiled when told by the guide that the said mistress visited the great man even when his wife was occupying the house.

For some reason Edward had not taken Elaine to see his old home soon after arriving in Guernsey. Perhaps at first he had wanted her to see and feel the delights of the island, and then with a flourish of pride point out the place, the thought of which had kept him going through those dark years of exile in Daleford. He did decide however on the last day of the holiday to show it to her, but felt disappointed that she had not requested him to do so before.

Always he pictured his birthplace at its best, as it once was, and as he would like it some day. But Elaine did not view it like that at all.

'A pile of old stones,' she exclaimed cruelly, hurtfully. 'I wouldn't live there if you paid me. God, it's depressing.' She didn't even want to peep inside. It belonged to a world she had never known, and he realised then that he had made a great mistake in bringing her.

Edward looked at the empty sands, the grey sea

echoing the clouds, the broken house, and he turned away dispirited, the fire gone from his ambition to give new life some day to the old Ormer Hotel.

Before they left the island he paid another visit to the solicitors to be told that the position regarding the property was just the same as it had been before. No will had been found, though he and William were obviously the beneficiaries, and would gain if the estate were sold. He was advised to reach an agreement with William whereby this could come about, the view being that the restoration was not worth contemplating because of the costs involved. It was also pointed out to Edward that if William should go to court it was quite likely that he would be granted an order for the dissolution of the estate.

On the return flight Edward stared dejectedly out of the window. Apart from the failure of the holiday itself the idea of someday living and working in a restored Ormer Hotel now seemed very unlikely. He might just as well tell William that he would agree and to set the wheels in motion, forget about the place and concentrate on his life and work in Daleford. But a few days in Daleford without the sound or smell of the sea served to revive Edward's dying hopes as regards the Guernsey property, and when he next saw William he told him the lie that the solicitors had advised waiting a few months longer. He was aware that his brother, through Elaine, would hear that a visit had been made to the solicitor's, and no doubt her poor impression of the property would not only strengthen William's argument, but would also have a bearing on whether

Redvers would put money into the project at some future date.

Used as he was to Elaine's vagaries of mood, Edward was yet surprised by the change in her on settling in again at Scarton Manor after the holiday. She appeared cheerful, was talkative and smiled with a regained vivacity that had been much missing during the fortnight before. A remarkable transformation for which he couldn't understand the reason. But so long as she was happy, that was all that mattered. Nevertheless he thought she could have tried a little harder to please him on their Guernsey holiday.

One day soon after his return, Thomas stopped him as he drove through the gates by the lodge. Edward smiled to himself. He saw the old man around the house quite often and had grown to like him very much. He was also a source of information of all kinds, not a gossip, but when necessary he could reveal an astounding range of knowledge of local goings on. If ever there was a brown man Thomas was he, favouring brown in almost everything. A brown battered hat atop a lighter brown outdoor creased face, pullover of the same shade and up to April a long brown overcoat which was doing its best to change the pattern and call itself black. A brown-jacketed potato of a man, but the eyes staring at Edward through the open window of the car were of the keenest blue, shrewd and penetrating in their gaze.

'Evenin' Mr. Edward.'

'Evening Thomas. Everything all right?' Edward had now progressed in the art of understanding

Thomas's very broad accent and could expect to understand almost all of what he said.

'Aye, I think so. Change to see the nights getting lighter,' and he came closer to the car so that his hat brim bent as it met the top of the window frame. There was no doubt that he had been eating pickled onions. 'Just wanted to tell you that a woman was enquiring after you when you were away — seen her in't grounds afore.'

'What did she look like?' He had no need to ask — he knew.

'Oh, fair haired — 'bout twenty five — a bonny-looking woman she was.' The eyes looking in had become even more attentive as their owner paused, and Edward knew that he must be careful over what he said, and tried to keep any knowledge out of his face.

'A mystery to me, Thomas,' he replied in disinterested fashion. 'Did she say what she wanted?' As if he didn't know.

'No, just asked if you were at home. She seemed to know you, and funny thing is I seem to have know'd her from somewhere, but blessed if I know where.'

Edward looked ahead through the screen. 'My landlady where I lived before had a daughter. Perhaps I was behind with the rent and she's come to collect it,' he joked.

Thomas's face remained exactly as it was. 'Aye, happen so Mr. Edward. Just thought I'd let you know.' Their eyes met again.

'Yes, and thanks Thomas. Let me know if you see her again.'

'Right Mr. Edward.' He was just about to take a step back when he bent forward again. 'Are you and the lady of the house settling down now at the Manor?' he asked rather quaintly.

'Yes, I think we are Thomas. We're very happy living here,' and sought to change the subject quickly. 'How's your wife?'

'Oh, the Missis is all right Mr. Edward. Blistered her hand on the stove this morn, but she's right now though.'

'Oh, sorry to hear that.' He was. She was a nice lady.

'I'll be getting on then,' and the body and face slid away as Edward moved off.

Edward drove slowly up the drive. He had lied to Thomas. They were not happy, for various reasons. As regards his own life he should have been happy. A lovely young wife, the very best of homes, a good job, and the car he was driving — the very latest Jaguar sports XK140 roadster. All should have added up to happiness beyond measure. But this latest sighting of Ruth by Thomas was worrying. Why, oh why couldn't she just go home and leave him alone?

He garaged the car but did not get out, but sat thinking, staring out along the bonnet in the half light. Elaine seemed to be going her own way more and more; out in the evenings, a note left here and there. Only occasionally did they dine together and then her conversation was limited. In bed his overtures were endured rather than welcomed, and he could feel the strain between them. He thought the world of her — the Elaine he had known for a short time. She had a cold when his lips and body wanted to love her, and her impatient disinterested voice telling him to hurry, filled him with misery. It took two to make a life of love and in their marriage only one was trying. Damned if he knew just how many bunches of flowers he had sent her. They made her superficially sweet for a day or so, then relations between them worsened again.

Edward sighed. Maybe he was partly to blame. In an effort to please her father even more at work, he had he knew put in a lot of hours when he should have been at home paying more attention to Elaine. Then of course Ruth's appearance had not helped. Always she was at the back of his mind, and he damned her for the trouble she had caused him. Nevertheless he worried about her welfare, being alone somewhere with the boy Frederick to care for.

There was also a new and growing problem which had become more acute since Elaine and he had returned to Guernsey — the presence of William at Scarton Manor. His visits were becoming more frequent and it was very noticeable to Edward that the few occasions when Elaine laughed or appeared happy in the house, were when William was present also.

A couple of times recently Redvers had asked him how he was settling down to married life. They had, he thought, just been bland enquiries — father-in-law to son-in-law — but if Redvers discovered that relations between them were not too good, it might affect his prospects within the firm. He remembered Redver's words to him before the marriage about wanting 'no shenaniking' after they were married.

Well, as far as he, Edward, was concerned there had been none on his part; he thought too much of Elaine. What about her? The very thought of her being untrue made him feel sick. No — she was headstrong, spoilt, opening up like a flower in the sun to new sights, sounds and companionship, but nothing more . . . .

In June of that year Elaine gave birth to a baby girl. It should have been a joyous occasion, and in a way it was for Edward — a love child, the result of their union. The truth was those bedtime unions had become increasingly rare. As for Elaine, the child had during the latter stages of her pregnancy been a burden to her, in the sense that her excursions away from Scarton Manor had become necessarily less and less frequent. Being confined to the house had done nothing to improve relationships between them. Edward was reminded of a dog he had once known, an animal far too energetic to be bothered with a litter. The sight of a ball was enough to unleash her excitement, bounding away from her basket, leaving the still suckling pups squirming in a confused heap behind her, and so it was with his wife, straining to be free of the encumbrances of child rearing — to be off with friends, going to parties and enjoying herself. Motherhood was definitely not her forte.

Edward gazed at the child thinking that it had his looks, although it was difficult to tell at such a young age, but convincing himself that it did anyway, its merry eyes and podgy hands trying their simple best to communicate. Redvers and his wife were happy, the former remarking often that he could see himself in the child. Edward was pleased, his father-in-law's deep interest in the child diverting any suspicions he may have had about the state of his daughter's marriage, for the time being at least. As for Lady Scarton she found herself being an almost full-time nanny which she did not appear to mind, Elaine feigning a succession of headaches, nausea attacks, yet just having enough strength to take the car for a drive — the change away from the house, she said, doing wonders for her complete recovery — by any standards a very long post natal one.

To the family Edward appeared in agreement, saying that it would do her good. In himself he was confused, hurt and miserable. The result was his concentration at work began to suffer. He could think of nothing else but the fact that Elaine and he were growing further and further apart. He dreaded the times when as part of his work he had to be elsewhere in the country. They did not have much to say to each other when he was home, but he felt worse when he was away from her.

One Wednesday some five weeks after the birth, Edward arrived home well into the evening. He was later than usual because a recent new model of car, examples of which were in the showrooms around the country, had been found to have a steering linkage defect and all were being modified on information from the factory. This had meant form filling, telephone calls and discussions with the men working on the vehicles. Redvers had told him to go home and that he would follow. But Edward just did not feel like going home immediately. He had to have a while to himself to think, to decide on what he could do to save his marriage For once he would keep Elaine waiting and wondering, she having done it often enough to him. He drove off the premises into a lovely evening — almost dusk, warm and still. He kept the hood of the roadster down, thinking that perhaps the air over him would calm his mind and help his thoughts.

He took each road as it came — driving automatically, searching in his mind for a solution to his problem. He was sad. The idea of going anywhere but straight home a few months ago would have been unthinkable. Elaine's arms round his neck, a welcome from those dark eyes. He had told himself how fortunate he was so many times.

Edward found that he was on the road which, if he kept to it, would lead him to the cottage at Landford Crags. It struck him then that he did not have a key, but decided that it didn't matter. He would sit in the car and rest awhile under the trees. It would be peaceful and quiet. He remembered reading that the dam was finished, also of seeing the picture of local councillors and the chairman of the construction company posing on the bridge across it.

It was only when he was nearing the rough track leading down to the cottage that he caught a glimpse of a car parked near the building. He was surprised and curious as to who could be there. He decided to find out. After all it belonged to the Scarton family and he was part of that family. Nearing the cottage he saw that it was Elaine's car, of that there was no doubt. He stood staring at it, puzzled. How could it be Elaine's? She would be at home now. Had someone borrowed it? Edward reached the veranda and stepped on to it. A voice came from inside — a woman's. It came again and he stopped exactly where he was, hand gripping white against the green of the veranda rail. Elaine's voice! It was — no mistaking it. Seemed to be coming from a room at the other end. Talking to someone freely in happy tones, laughter punctuating her words. What was she doing there? Who was she with? He took a stride but then a man's voice joined in. Instantly recognisable — William's! What were both doing together there? Edward's brain refused momentarily to find a reason. Far better to seek an excuse for them, less agonising. It refused to do that either, the knife of terrible truth already penetrating him.

He crept nearer — he couldn't help himself — drawn irresistibly towards the window which was open at its bottom, the edge of a lace curtain protruding through it. The words of the occupants became distinct.

'I'll have to go soon, darling Will.'

'No, plenty of time — early yet.'

'He'll be back — mooning about wondering where I am.'

'You told him you were going to the city for the day?'

'I didn't say anything. He was gone early this morning. I stayed asleep. He can play with the baby for a while. I've got you.'

The sound of a hand on flesh, then Elaine's voice. 'You're hurting me, you devil.'

'You like that, don't you?'

Edward heard her muffled reply. 'Yes — yes. Oh God, I don't want to go back. An hour or two isn't long enough, Will.'

'Just ten minutes, then I'll let you return to your husband.' William's voice was mocking, derisive and proprietary.

'Yes, back to earnest Edward. He makes me want to scream, he's so insufferably earnest. I just can't stand it. He fusses like a nanny, rolls over on his back if I'm nice to him. He adores me you know.' Her expression of distaste penetrated the gap below the window. 'I can't stand him any longer. What did I see in him? A novelty. I . . . ' Her voice was suddenly strangled, stifled. 'No, William, let me up.' Her breath shuddered from her. 'No more. Oh you devil — what have you got there? Will — Will . . . .' The sounds of their lovemaking followed, skewering Edward's tortured mind as he stumbled from the veranda.

Away up the lane blindly to the car, away from the calm and green of that valley, so at odds with the cauldron of desperate despairing emotions engulfing him. William, his brother, thrusting into Elaine — she so familiar and submitting. How long had the affair being going on? The car sped on taking him from that place of awful truth. He could have had a dozen accidents, but perhaps fate had decided that he had suffered enough for one day. Elaine's contemptuous words hammered into his brain, speared his heart. 'Earnest Edward — insufferably earnest Edward — earnest Edward — earnest Edward — can't stand him — can't stand him . . . '

The drive to Scarton Manor opened up before him, but he did not want to go in. Not his home now — it had become a fortress of torment. He had loved her, tried to make a home for them and she had laughed at him behind his back. Forcing himself to enter, he met his father-in-law.

'What the hell's wrong, Edward?'

Just sufficient control of his faculties for him to answer, 'Just had a near miss with the car — be all right in a minute,' and staggered past, leaving Redvers staring after him aghast.

Edward leaned against the fireplace. He had to think. A voice mocked him — why? What about? His marriage was in ruins, so think about what? Memories came — cruel ones. Her stories about going to her girl friends, shopping expeditions, coming home late. All those times she had been unfaithful, he was sure. Her moroseness on their holiday and her impatience to return to Daleford. Her sudden change of mood on her arrival home, restless to be under a man other than her husband. He, Edward, had been a novelty she had said. That was all — something new. A brilliant moth flitting from one candle to another, and obviously William's candle was more enticing than his. The humiliation his wife had poured on him, and his own bitter jealous coarseness made him squirm inside. His wife! He wanted to be sick. How many more? Was William the only one? She'd even left their child alone at times. His brain dwelt on the child momentarily, and he hurried to gaze down upon it, awake and gurgling in its cot. God — was it his? He couldn't be sure — couldn't be sure of anything now.

Edward stood facing the door, his heart as empty as the fireplace behind him, ready for the confrontation with Elaine that was to come. He felt ashamed. Why had he not stayed at the cottage and claimed that which was his — his wife? Put up a show — fought for her. Instead, the shock of discovery had made him want to flee from the place as fast as possible. He heard her steps and the door opened. She hesitated momentarily on seeing him, their eyes meeting, hers slipping away. She flung the cardigan she was carrying on to a chair. 'What are you standing there for Eddie?'

It was a peculiar thing for her to say, he thought. Something to mask her nerves, no doubt taken aback by the sight of him as she came through the doorway. 'I've a perfect right to stand in my home if I wish to.' His bitter rage was boiling beneath the surface, but his voice was almost without emotion. And he just continued to stare at her, seeing the yellow dress, the rather wide curving hips under it. It was like a play back of a film. Little mannerisms which he barely noticed before now told him of the lie she had been living, her body still damp from his brother's embraces.

Elaine shot him a glance, guarded, surprise in it, but ignored his remark, pushing her dark hair back with a two-handed motion, then positioning her belt buckle in the centre of her waist. 'It's a hellish hot evening, Eddie. The rush hour traffic gets worse . . . ' She picked up her cardigan, turned away. 'Think I'll have a shower — cool down.'

To flush the sexual sweat off her more likely, he

thought. 'Shopping expedition today was it? Didn't you buy anything?'

She stopped, hand on the door but not facing him, and he knew she was struggling to collect herself.

'Oh nothing much — nothing I really cared for.' Her tone was offhand, careless.

'What have you bought?' He was getting a savage sadistic enjoyment from making her struggle for excuses.

'Oh — er — ' She fluttered her hands. 'Just something and nothing.'

'Where is it? You didn't bring anything in with you.'

She gave a ragged nervous laugh. 'Oh they're in the car — forgotten to bring them.' She opened the door wider, was halfway through. 'I'll just look at Maxine.'

'Been to Bretfield have you?' His voice was strained now.

'Of course I've been to Bretfield,' she retorted irritably. 'Stop asking me silly questions, Eddie,' and she turned her back on him.

Edward's raging emotion erupted at this. 'Wait! You bloody tramp!' The force of his words pulled her round to face him, shock on her face. 'I'll tell you why you're hot. Not because of flaming shopping in Bretfield. No, a bit nearer than that — Landford Crags,' he grated. He strode across the room as he spoke and she recoiled, the nearest expression to fear he had ever seen on her face. 'Earnest Eddie am I? Insufferable Eddie. You can't stand me can you? The novelty's worn off, has it?'

Noticed the compressed thin lips, the selfish eyes searching for a way out.

'Look Eddie I've just come home. I don't know what y . . . .'

'Don't lie,' he interjected fiercely. 'I heard you say that not an hour ago. Your damn voice saying that about me — your husband to another man.'

He saw the expressions come and go leaving wide-eyed disbelief. 'I was there,' he followed up. 'I heard you. I wanted a quiet place to think. I went up, saw your car and I heard you.' Shook his head at the memory. 'Christ almighty Elaine, I loved you. I thought you were the greatest thing on this earth. Couldn't believe my luck. You meant everything to me. I wanted to spend my life making you happy.' Accusation and total misery stared out of his eyes at her. Oh, why couldn't it be a play they were rehearsing, and able to throw these unreal lines away instantly? But it was now, and real and happening. He gestured towards Maxine's room. 'Is that child ours? Can I believe it is? How many more have you taken to the cottage?' he flung at her. Twisting the knife inside himself he continued hoarsely, 'I'll bet he's not been the only one. No wonder you didn't mention the cottage to me. I might have spoilt everything for you.' Edward laughed, a terrible despairing hopeless sound. Life seemed to be draining away from him.

Suddenly Elaine's face registered hate, so completely that he was staggered by its intensity. 'All right, so I did meet someone today. I can't stand the sight of you any more, with your bloody limp and foreign ways. Hell! What did I see in you? Must have been mad. You've used me, you bloody hypocrite. All you're interested in is money. That's all you married me for.'

Edward's head and mouth moved in denial.

'You bore me sick. I want a man to make me feel alive. I've already got a perfectly good father. I don't want two. I want to enjoy myself, not stick at home. Where have I been? Where am I going? Well now you know and you can't stop me. The only joy I get with you is when I see the back of you.'

In dreadful misery Edward saw her pulling at her fingers, wrenching something off. She threw it at him viciously, missing him and hitting the wall behind him. The second object hit him full in the face, an instant stab of pain, then it fell to the floor at his feet. His mother's ring — the one he had given to Elaine on their engagement.

'Take your bloody mother's ring,' she shouted. 'You couldn't even buy me a new one. As far as I'm concerned I'm unmarried from now. You're out of my life.' Her dark eyes glittered like flint in contempt. 'What sort of man are you anyway? If you knew I was there with someone else, why didn't you do something about it?'

Edward was conscious of the blood running down his cheek as she continued her tirade. 'You think you're so bloody perfect, you pompous hypocrite. You think I don't know there's been a woman coming round here for weeks. You're no better than I am.'

'It's not true. I sent her away,' the words ejaculating from him.

'What — afterwards?'

'No — no — never — I didn't.'

'I damn well don't care,' Elaine screamed at him. 'You sod, get out of my life — I want no part in yours. I know this, if I stop with you any longer I'll be dead.'

The walls of the room shook as she slammed the door on him, but not before Edward had glimpsed Redvers standing beyond his daughter in the hall. For the first time since he had met the former he kept a door closed on him, knowing he couldn't face another member of the Scarton family just then. What Redvers had heard didn't matter now. It was over — everything was over. Marriage, work — everything.

He sat there in a void of mind, head in hands, for how long he didn't know. The spot on the carpet became larger as the blood dripped from between his palms. Later, much later, he picked up the rings from the floor, his emotions savaged again by the knowledge that she had worn them during her infidelity with William. And others? Metal and stones hot against another man's flesh in lust.

Alone in bed that night some sort of order returned to his mind. He had put Elaine on a pedestal, idolised her. Had spent a lot of time at work, which he had had to do to make a success and to prove himself to Redvers. To make money to satisfy her extravagant ways. She had liked to gamble. He had preferred his home, not being a bright lights person, but Elaine was — perpetually. Things had to be going on all the time. She had never been a relaxing person. After work he had been tired sometimes and it had felt good to be home and to rest, but obviously it was not what she had wanted. That she hated him had shattered Edward. The cruel jibe about his mother's ring. He hadn't been able at the time to afford a new one, and he realised now that Elaine had needed new things, new experiences, all the time. That meant new contacts, and new men. She had been right in one thing he knew. What sort of man had he been to leave her with another at the cottage without attempting to confront them? He'd failed her as a husband totally. But that it should have been William — his brother! The thought made him want to vomit. How could she? How could he? All too easily it seemed. Other thoughts tumbled from his brain. She'd want a divorce, that was certain. He would be out of the family, and that meant out of work. Redvers being what he was would never countenance having a man working for him who failed to make his daughter happy in marriage.

Strangely enough he found himself thinking about Ruth. How ironic, he finding himself in very much the same position as she had with him. Elaine wanted him out of her life, and he had done his utmost to do the same to Ruth. What a mess he was making of his own. He had been surprised that Elaine had known about a woman's visits to the Manor, although he didn't think that she knew Ruth had been the one. It had given her an excuse for her own affair, but in retrospect he thought she would have gone off with someone else in any case. Even when they had first started courting her eyes had been everywhere, calculating, seeking. When he could think about it with a degree of clarity and calm, he knew he had fallen through the trap door of infatuation into a hell of mind, forever uneasy and never at rest.

The next few days after the quarrel he was away on the firm's business, and glad to get away to think about his future while in the loneliness of his hotel rooms. She was filing for divorce on the grounds of his infidelity. He had laughed bitterly — would contest that lie and put his own version forward, but he would not try for reconciliation with her. There was no possibility of that, neither did he wish it now. What he would do when they were divorced he did not know. He had very little money put away. It had all gone on providing as scintillating a lifestyle as possible for Elaine. As regards their home it was part of the main house so it would revert back to its previous use, and couldn't be sold to provide money for either party. He would be the one to go — couldn't see any future in their living in separate rooms. As for his in-laws, Lady Scarton had not been a bad mother-in-law at all — an inoffensive woman under the shadow of her husband's forthright personality. As for the latter, Edward felt sorry that things had turned out as they had. Redvers had been good to him in the past, but how much he knew of the reason for the break-up of the marriage, Edward wasn't sure.

'Why the hell couldn't you and Elaine make a go of it?' he had asked. And Edward had stared at him helplessly, the question requiring a very lengthy answer.

'I gather Elaine says there's been another woman around. By Christ Edward, if there has I'll deal with you myself,' he threatened. 'I bloody well warned you over any shenanikins after you were married.'

Edward didn't care now, knowing there had not been any on his part, and he stated so forcibly, but recognising that he couldn't win. Elaine would not be blamed.

'Well, if you didn't have a woman on the side, what was the problem then?'

The eyes remained on Edward ruthlessly. Edward had seen the same look when Redvers had been near to settling a business deal. Edward hesitated. If he told the truth, it would no doubt hasten his departure from the firm, and he would like to stay as long as possible to give himself chance to reorganise his life. On the other hand, Elaine had lied, accused him, and the man opposite had brought her up to be spoilt, selfish, and with more money than had been good for her. Why should he spare his feelings? He was not likely to believe Edward's story anyway. Elaine naturally would not have admitted the adultery to her father.

'I went up to the cottage one day and found Elaine with another man,' he said simply.

Redvers surprised him by jumping up from his chair, exclaiming with an angry cynicism, 'Your buggering generation comes out of church already thinking about divorce.' It certainly wasn't the verbal reaction Edward had expected. 'And what in flaming hell is going to happen to the child?'

Edward didn't know. Perhaps Elaine would be given the custody of it. God! what a mess he was in. He had two children and had brought neither woman happiness.

Work dragged on uneasily for Edward, having for the time being lost his enthusiasm and the drive which had characterised his rise in the organisation up to recently. So many problems seemed to be pressing in on him that he found it difficult to concentrate. Redvers' attitude had altered subtly — if such a term could be applied to his father-in-law. The camaraderie of being one of the family was now missing from his relationship with him, and Edward now felt that he was regarded simply as an employee.

Of Elaine he saw very little. It was like living in separate flats. He knew she was in the house sometimes, but she avoided him. No meal was ever ready for him. He made his own often, though whenever she could Mildred, Thomas's wife, would see that a meal was taken to his room. She was a kind old soul and was plainly upset by the happenings between Elaine and himself. As she reminded him once, with a furtive backward glance at the door, 'Miss Elaine always were a wilful child, Mr. Edward,' and Edward felt he had allies in the elderly couple. But her apple pies and steak and kidney pudding did not do anything to mend the rift between himself and Elaine, his sadness and bitterness remaining. He wondered if she still went up to the cottage. Was William aware that he — Edward — knew of their meetings? Had Elaine told him? When Edward thought over the quarrel with Elaine he did not remember mentioning his brother's name, although he could have done in the white heat of his anger, but he had a feeling that he had not. But of all people, that it should have been

William — the wrecker of his marriage, and notably absent from the Manor these days. Or had he been just one amongst others? Edward couldn't bear to think about it, and forced his mind to focus on other things. His daughter, Maxime, helped him to retain some balance at that time, her small features, innocent and puckered, lighting up whenever he drew near. Elaine could not stop him from sometimes trundling the baby and pram around the grounds of the Manor. There was no knowing how long he would be able to continue doing that, or even to see the child.

The following week it rained steadily each day until Saturday — heavy saturating rain, a depressing downpour of unwanted water. Then the skies cleared, the sun shone and Edward's spirits rose a few degrees. In the afternoon he went into the garden and busied himself. It kept his mind off Elaine. There was a gardener retained by Redvers for the grounds of the house, but Edward since they were married had taken it upon himself to look after that part at the rear of the house. Having their own particular piece of garden made it seem more like their own home. He cleared a few weeds here and there, cut some of the hedge, straightened things up generally, then leaned on something quite often and turned his face to the sun.

From beyond the French doors he occasionally heard the burbling and cries of Maxime. Elaine had gone out — he tried not to think of where — and so had Redvers for a round of golf, the latter not asking Edward now to accompany him as he had on previous occasions. Lady Scarton was in he knew, having seen her not long before talking to Mildred, and then a few minutes ago he had heard her kitching and cooing to the baby. Edward made himself a cup of tea and sat on the terrace thinking, and the time passed. Later he roused himself to collect his garden tools and put them away. A breeze had sprung up and the evening was cooling quickly.

Ruth walked up to the house in the shadow of the trees lining the drive. Her pride was gone. She was tired, hopelessly in love, and just hoping that a miracle would occur to change Edward's heart towards her. Hurt to the depths of her being by his treatment of her the last time they had met, yet she clung to the idea that somehow, some way, he would at last see her as his true love. She knew she was a fool, an addle-headed blind fool, ripping her inner self to shreds on the armour of his attitude towards her. Once more — just once more. Another humiliation and she would take Frederick and live her life as best she could somewhere else, and concentrate on bringing the child up, and in doing so dim the memory of Edward and what he had meant to her. It had been desperately hard going out to work, looking after Frederick but always the dream of Edward and herself at the end of it all. A flame of hope still flickered within her, at the rumours of a rift between Edward and his wife. The rumours and other relevant information had been passed on by Mildred the cook. One day Ruth had met her returning to the Lodge and, unable to help herself, she had broken down and confessed the huge and seemingly insurmountable trouble to that kindly soul. Since then Mildred had become a sounding and listening post for Ruth. But as Mildred had said, 'If Thomas had to find out, he'd never forgive me — no, he would not.' Mildred, he'd say, you keep to your station. Thomas is very loyal and so am I Miss Ruth, but I must say Mr. Edward has not looked a happy man for a while. There's been a blazing row, Miss Elaine leaving him a lot — someone else in the background I've heard. Seems she's always up at the cottage — Landford Crags, and on a Saturday she goes out early evening and always by herself.' Then Mildred added with a meaningful gleam and glance from her elderly but expressive blue eyes, 'That is when she passes the Lodge.' But there was a very different expression in the older woman's face as she watched through the window as Ruth left. There had been trouble already in the Scarton family. More, she was certain, was on its way, and that young woman was heading for a breakdown if she wasn't careful. Mildred turned away shaking her head, and did not mention the matter to Thomas when he came home.

Ruth had seen Elaine in her car going down the drive an hour before. Was she meeting someone else, entertaining them at the cottage? Mildred seemed to think so. Nearing the house, Ruth seethed with a bitter anger. Elaine had taken Edward away from her. If it had not been for Elaine she and Edward would have been together now — in love. Instead she had had him and tossed him aside. A new thrill was obviously dazzling her. Ruth's anger turned on Edward. The idiot. Couldn't he have seen what she was like — a spoilt wanton bitch?

A few lights were on in the house, but the

entrance was in shadow as Ruth tried the door and found it open. This time she was sure that Edward would welcome her. He would realise that his love had been misplaced before and his arms would encompass her in welcoming love. Forgiveness would be his. How overjoyed he was going to be at seeing her. She would make him happy again. What plans they would fashion together. A sudden optimism flared in her exhausted mind. Why should she creep to her love's room? Ought to run and shout — emblazon their refound love on everyone's ears. How his face would light up when he saw her. She had no doubts now as she smiled to herself. No one would hurt Edward again. She clutched at the Ormer shell in her pocket. This time it would bring them together.

She reached a small inner hall, vaguely remembering it from the Christmas visit. A dim light above made it a shadowy private place. A thin strip of yellow came from beneath a door to her left. Suddenly the telephone rang close by — strident and shattering the dream she was making for herself, the noise filling her head. Must be stopped — stopped, otherwise it might bring a member of the Scarton family. She lifted the receiver. A man's voice poured from it loudly, agitatedly, words tumbling from him breathlessly without break — urgent and imploring. The receiver tumbled from Ruth's hand back on to its rest. Confused emotions cavorted in her as she stepped away from the instrument and the silence returned.

Edward heard the telephone as, with a cup of tea at his elbow, he struggled to make some sense of his life. The ringing stopped, then silence. He did not hear anyone answering although Lady Scarton was in and Redvers may have returned, yet there was no one talking. Leaving his chair he pulled the door open and looked into the hall. Ruth's face came out of the shadows, wrenching a sound of shock from him. 'God! Ruth! What the hell are you doing?' For the moment he couldn't pronounce anything else. There was a strange look on her face — he was to try and remember the expression later. 'What have you come here again for? Can't you understand I don't want you here.'

She came slowly towards him as if oblivious to his rejection. 'You'll be free now Edward. Come with me — I love you. Please don't send me away again. This is the last time, Edward my love. Let me make you happy — I can. Don't send me away — I couldn't live, Edward. Let's go now together.'

He stared at her in a turmoil of mind. If he were found with her he would be in effect condoning Elaine's affair with one of his own. Fiercely he whispered, 'Look Ruth, I'm sorry and I didn't mean to hurt you last time, but we've been through all this before. I can't come with you — you know I can't. Now please go and leave me. I've had enough trouble as it is, you must know that.'

He wanted to be raging mad with her, but her sudden appearance had nonplussed him and he couldn't deal with it properly. He was extremely tired and drained, but conscious of just how long they had known each other.

'Come with me to see Frederick.'

'No,' and immediately regretting his refusal. He

would have liked to have seen the boy, but he couldn't think straight. This wasn't the time or place to be discussing the child.

A terrible look of despair came to the face opposite. 'You don't love me, Edward — you really don't?' As the eyes slipped away from his he cursed himself for what he saw there. Elaine must have seen the same in his. He well knew the agony.

Footsteps beyond the hall. One last look at him as she slipped out of sight into his room.

Lady Scarton appeared. 'Oh, you've taken it Edward,' and regarded him enquiringly.

Edward forced his mind to work. 'Someone for Elaine.' A name came to him — 'Mavis'.

His mother-in-law gave a perplexed smile. 'Oh, and d'you know where Elaine's gone?'

Edward shook his head, but having a good idea, and he had a reckless desire to shout it aloud. 'Yes, she's up at the cottage playing mummies and daddies with another man.' Elaine's mother must know what was going on, he was sure.

'Redvers isn't back yet — he shouldn't be long.' Then putting her head forward she peered at him. 'Everything all right Edward?'

No! it damn well wasn't — everything was wrong. He smiled wanly and told part of the truth, 'I'm just very worried that's all, thanks.'

She nodded still observing him. 'Yes I suppose so. It's all rather dreadful isn't it?' then to his relief, after giving him another searching glance, she left without saying anything more.

Quickly he regained his room. Ruth must get off the premises at once. But Ruth had gone, the

French doors slightly open and the draught moving the curtains gently. Edward closed them and turned back into the room. Something caught his eye on the low table next to his chair. It shone dully, pearl-like. It was the Ormer shell which he had seen many times before. Treasured by Ruth since the day as youngsters they had left Guernsey. He knew that it had come to mean something much more than just a memento to her, she imbuing it with something which had never, for him anyway, been there in the first place. Now she had left it behind — a symbolic gesture that she had gone from his life finally. A great and utter loneliness swept over him as he slumped, head resting on hands, in one of which the shell still remained enclosed. Later he wondered briefly about the telephone call. Who had actually made it? Ruth had not said, yet she must have picked the phone up, and he, being so shocked to see her, had not thought to ask.

And Elaine did not return to Scarton Manor that night.

The sound penetrated the cottage like the rising wind, or a distant train. Elaine knelt up, her lover's body still clinging, stark awake now. She stretched, rubbed the window of its condensation. It was black — dense black — everything. No sky, no stars, no outlines of trees. A roaring — so loud. No time for thought, to cry out. The wall of water smashed through, flung her away, freezing her heated flesh in seconds, and the radiogram to which they had danced naked earlier followed along with the veranda and the late summer trees.

11

Elaine's body rested in the church from which she had been married not so very long before. Another one — a man's — had been found some way down the valley. The devastation had been immense when the dam walls had given way and the water had rushed down the valley. There ensued an outcry against the builders and all concerned in the construction. The council was accused of choosing the cheapest tender for the building of the dam, without first judging the quality of the firm given the job. It was all as Redvers Scarton had said, but he remained quiet on the subject. His daughter had gone — it was too late for her. To reporters he said that she often went up there to the cottage, being particularly keen on photography and the collecting and noting of wild flowers. She must have become, he informed them, so engrossed in her hobby that she had failed to return in time to avoid the catastrophe. It was a gallant attempt to save his daughter's reputation.

But Edward knew better and smiled twistedly. Her hobby had been collecting men, and he had been just one specimen.

Whilst the official enquiry got under way into the local disaster, Redvers Scarton began one of his own. His daughter was dead, and so was the person thought to have been with her that evening at the family cottage. It could not be proved that he had been there — anything else was rumour and conjecture. But Redvers was well aware that one person had a good idea of whether someone had been with her that night — his son-in-law. Their relationship had become very cool, and Edward was certain that it was only a matter of time before he became unemployed. He guessed that Redvers now blamed him in some measure for Elaine's absence from their home on numerous occasions during their marriage. Perhaps he had found out about Ruth's visits and drawn the wrong conclusion.

About a fortnight later Edward had visitors — the police, an older man in plain clothes and a youngish sergeant. They were sorry to bother him at such an unhappy time but they had their job to do.

Edward was surprised and somewhat nervous at their calling. His fortunes recently had been ill-starred and somehow when he regarded the two men of the law, he had a strange feeling that those fortunes were not going to improve very much, yet he couldn't understand why they should want to question him.

Did he know that his wife had gone up to the cottage?

No, he did not at the time.

Did he receive a call that evening about eight-thirty from the reservoir keeper?

No, he certainly did not. But as soon as he had denied it, something in his mind struggled for recognition — something he should have been aware of.

Was he sure? Their eyes were keen — fixed on him intently.

Of course he was sure, and again he had this strange feeling.

Had he been in all that evening?

Yes he had — done a bit of gardening that afternoon and finished before dusk, and stayed in his room the remainder of the evening.

Had he slipped out at all? Into the garden again perhaps? Or a stroll around it? Their manner was amiable, their tone something of around the fireside sort.

No, most definitely not. He had been tired and welcomed the chance to sit down and rest. What on earth were they asking all those questions for? What possible reason could they have? His mother-in-law, Lady Scarton, would bear him out on that he informed them. The junior of the two policemen was taking notes.

'Ah yes, Lady Scarton,' and the questioner pursed his lips then ran a finger down the bridge of his nose. 'Did you take a phone call during the evening, Sir?'

Edward was aware of an intensifying of the other's stare. He nodded. 'Yes I did.'

'About what time Sir?' and seeing Edward's hesitation urged him, 'roughly Sir.'

Edward tried to think. Days had passed since then. 'Oh, eight thirty to nine, but I really can't be sure. There was no reason why I should take note of the time.'

'Oh no, of course not Sir. Very difficult to remember these things afterwards.' His voice was apologetic. 'But you could remember though who the call was from, could you Sir?' His hand was covering his mouth, forefinger resting just below his nose — an easy relaxed pose, but the eyes looking at Edward were unwavering.

Edward recalled the incident quickly and clearly. Ruth had picked the phone up but had not said who the call had been from. He had lied to Lady Scarton who obviously thought he had taken the call. Why on earth he hadn't just said it had been a wrong number Heaven only knew. Instead he had guessed and told his mother-in-law that it had been a woman friend of Elaine's — Mavis. He'd heard the name often enough, and Elaine he had realised had used it often as an excuse to go out.

The note-taker had stopped, pen poised. They were waiting and he realised that he could not alter his story now — would have to stick to what he had said to Lady Scarton. Edward gave a slight shrug. 'It — it was from one of Elaine's friends — Mavis, I suppose she wanted to talk to Elaine.'

The policeman's regard remained fixed on him. 'You're sure you took no other call that night, Sir?'

'Yes, I'm sure.'

'Not one other?'

'No.' What the hell was the man going on about it for?

'Just the one from this girl called Mavis.'

Oh why, oh why had Ruth not said who the caller had been? 'Yes — I mean why should it have been so important that the call came from her?' He was perplexed and showed it.

The other shrugged, his face serious. 'Just one more query Sir and then we can leave it at that for now. It has been reported that a woman has been seen around the grounds several times, and asking for you Sir — seemed to know you. Was she of any importance to you Sir? Do you know this person?'

Ruth. Somehow or other the police had found out that she had visited him. Hell! Where was all this leading? 'No, I don't know of any woman coming to see me,' he lied. Ruth must be kept out of the matter — it had nothing to do with her at all.

The policeman fingered his chin. 'You see Mr. Dorner, you will forgive me if I put it more bluntly to you, there were rumours that you and Mrs. Dorner did not always shall we say, hit it off.'

Momentarily Edward's shoulders sagged. He couldn't help the movement nor the sad regret which appeared in his face. 'Yes, that's true. We had our differences, but there was no other woman during our marriage.' A trace of irritability showed as he added, 'You can believe me or not.'

'Just routine Sir. We have to ask these questions. Seems silly sometimes I suppose.' His answer was not enlightening and Edward felt uneasy after he and his companion had gone. Why had they been so insistent on the telephone call? His unease increased the more he thought about the conversation with them. He had a feeling that there was something he did not know about, but should. He was to find out very soon.

Two days later he was taken to the local police station and questioned again at length regarding the evening of the disaster, and the phone call in particular. He was shocked when advised to obtain the services of a lawyer. He knew it was no use appealing to Redvers to help in the matter — that person was in the opposite camp now. However one was found locally — a Mr. Denton — tall, pale, youthful-looking even with the fringe of beard he sported in a narrow half circle on mouth and cheeks, and not much older than Edward himself. But the eyes behind the spectacles were clear and keen. 'I don't think the prosecution have much of a case here,' he said cheerfully, opening his case and taking papers out.

Edward looked at him. He too had been cheerful, forward-looking and industrious a year or so ago, confident in the future. Now he was back where he had started and worse, facing some charge he knew nothing about. All they could talk about were telephone calls. They didn't seem to want to believe him. 'I'm sure they haven't,' he said testily, 'I haven't done anything wrong. Do you know what I'm supposed to have done?'

'Don't you?' He studied Edward for seconds. 'No, you don't do you? Well Mr. Dorner, they're trying to get you on a charge of manslaughter. Bloody ridiculous but there it is.'

Shock made it difficult for Edward to say anything sensible. 'But — manslaughter — I haven't killed anyone. Do you m . . . ?'

'Of course you haven't,' interjected the other, 'and they know that. Sir Redvers Scarton is behind them and he's after someone's head, no matter whose it is. He's lost his daughter and he wants someone to pay for it. You know him better than I do.'

Yes he did. 'No shenanikins,' he had been warned, 'or else'. Well he hadn't shenanikined or whatever, and yet he was facing a charge.

'It all hangs on that telephone call, but not to worry because,' Mr. Denton flung a hand sideways in a gesture of triumphant dismissal, 'I've met the person who took the call. She's admitted it, been to the police, and says she did nothing about the call because she said your wife was at the cottage with someone else. Also she and you have been friends since childhood, and if it hadn't been for Elaine Scarton you would have married her.' He gave his papers a thump. 'So you see that lets you out. They haven't a case against you to make sense in court. They'll probably quash the whole thing very soon.'

Edward heard what was being said, but as if from a distance, his mind in a turmoil. Ruth! It was Ruth who had come forward, had remained in Daleford. All along he had denied there being another woman — had told the truth. He had given everything to his marriage to Elaine, but now realised of course what a bitch she had been. However there had been no affair with Ruth since his marriage, and she must not be allowed to put the idca about that he had engaged in one with her. Now she had come to save him. Just like her — the bloody idiot. Why hadn't she gone home? Must have seen the case in the papers. His counsel's voice penetrated.

'So you see there's no need to worry at all, a clear case of jealousy. Her chance to get rid of your wife, and her admission will clear you without a doubt. A clean-cut case of the triangle again — jealous woman, the wife, and the husband in the middle.' He sat back in his chair in a movement of contented satisfaction, and a self-congratulatory professional's smile at the layman across the desk.

'That's not true.' Perversely and against himself Edward heard the words as if from someone else.

'What d'you mean?' The other's body had tensed, the smile fading.

'Just isn't true. This woman's lying. She didn't take the call — I did.'

The spectacles, white from the reflection of the office window, focused on him, the forehead creased deeply. 'What the blazes are you on about? You know this Le Ney woman don't you?'

'Oh yes, we were youngsters together, then I lost sight of her after that.' The lie came easily, surprisingly so.

His counsel leaned halfway across the desk. 'Listen Mr. Dorner, I don't think you realise, they're trying to get you for manslaughter or as near as matters — it's a serious charge. This woman's come forward. Let her take it if she wants to. To hell with being mister gallant. Cut out this romantic nonsense. She's guilty, so let her get on with it.' He was annoyed, quite annoyed.

'She was not the other woman. There wasn't one,' stated Edward simply. 'Never has been.'

'But you've been seeing her,' exploded the face opposite. 'Damn it, what are you trying to do? Get into prison?'

Did it matter now? The way he felt just then, it did not. He just wanted to rest quietly away from everything until his mind was settled and at peace. 'No, I haven't, not in the sense that you mean,' then added listlessly, 'people do that sort of thing to draw attention to themselves, a bit of limelight, saying they've done something when they haven't. You must have had cases like that before.'

'Look Dorner,' and in his anger the other forgot to give him the courtesy of title, 'the limelight you'll get is in court and several years in prison. Don't be a fool.'

Edward remained silent and Mr. Denton swallowed. 'Now listen to me Mr. Dorner, you engaged me as your defence counsel. How the hell can I defend you if you insist on pleading guilty?'

'I suppose I am guilty in a way,' reflected Edward quietly as if to himself. 'Must have done something wrong otherwise she wouldn't have gone off with others.'

All the pleasantries that may have been there at the start of the conversation had departed from Mr. Denton's face as thin-mouthed he glared at his client, then said, 'Well let me tell you something Mr. Dorner. If you want to ruin your life that's your affair, but you're not going to damn well ruin my record. I'm ambitious. I want to get to the top of my profession and quick. I haven't had a failure yet as a defence counsel,' he repeatedly stabbed a finger over the desk at Edward and went on vehemently, 'and I'm going to make bloody sure that your case isn't going to wreck that record. You are not guilty — understand.'

Out of the wreckage of his hopes and life a vestige of humour bubbled inwardly in Edward. He couldn't plead guilty because it would wreck his counsel's record! The other, taking Edward's silence to mean agreement, went on, 'I've spoken to this woman, Ruth, and she's quite prepared to stand up in court and admit that she's the one who should be in your place. She took that call — didn't pass the message on, and as a result any chance of your wife getting away from the cottage in time had gone. Now,' and a thin smile of relief showed, 'leave it to me and the charge will be dropped against you. This time next week you'll wonder what all the fuss was about.'

But the following week the charge was very much on and against Edward. He didn't wonder what all the fuss was about because he knew well enough. The police did not believe Ruth's statement, and although she tried to see him while he was awaiting trial, he would not talk to her, reiterating to his counsel and police that she had nothing to do with the matter.

His counsel was equally loath to have a blemish on his record and dug into the recent memories of staff at Scarton Manor. He received no help from Sir Redvers who had no doubt as to who was the guilty party, but Mr. Denton returned to his office well pleased with his findings and the statements obtained. A worried Mildred had not wished to reveal confidences passed to her from Ruth, but Thomas had said that it was better she did, so she listened to her husband as she had for the most of her life. However, it was a lodge divided — Thomas on the side of Edward, and Mildred always with the sad face of Ruth before her.

The trial opened, the prosecution's case being that Edward took the call from the reservoir keeper, knowing that his wife was at the cottage, and did nothing to warn her of the impending disaster, thus constituting a charge of manslaughter against him.

The keeper, a Mr. Nolan, was the first of the prosecution's witnesses to give evidence. That Saturday evening he was out taking his dog for a walk. On the way back a car passed him and recognised Mrs. Dorner as the driver and heading for the cottage, she being accompanied by a man whom he did not recognise. His lodge he said was on the opposite side of the valley to the Scartons' cottage, and he crossed the bridge at the eastern end of the structure on his way back to the lodge. Down the valley and on the other side he saw a light in the cottage and guessed that Mrs. Dorner and the person who had been accompanying her were inside. He had often seen the light on in the evening during the last year. He went on to say that he heard a grating cracking sound, and of gushing water. Running back towards the bridge he saw a break in the wall about a third of the way up, and that the wall was giving way, and water was already forcing its way out. He dashed back to the lodge and telephoned Scarton Manor, not able to find the cottage number. It was later that he found out that it was ex-directory.

At the point counsel reminded him that he was under oath. Did someone actually lift the receiver at Scarton Manor?

Yes he was certain, no doubt about it; he could hear them breathing. He wanted to warn the family of the break in the wall and he had already seen Mrs. Dorner going towards the cottage and afterwards had seen the light. He didn't ask who it was at the other end, but just kept repeating urgently his warning for them to get in touch with

Mrs. Dorner at the cottage. As near as he could remember the time was about seven to seven-thirty.

The next witness was Lady Scarton, obviously in great distress, and the judge expressing his sympathy of the loss of their daughter. Yes, she had heard the telephone ringing and when she reached it Edward Dorner, her son-in-law, was standing near it.

Had she seen anyone else — a woman?

'No, definitely not, he was alone.'

'Did he say who the call was from?'

'Yes, from a friend of Elaine's — a girl called Mavis.'

'Yet, it could not have been from that person could it?'

'No, it could not.'

'Will you please tell the court why, Lady Scarton.'

'Because Mrs. Beaver — Mavis — was at the time just out of operation and still unconscious in the Daleford General Hospital.'

Again Edward rued bitterly his choice of that person's name when his mother-in-law had enquired of him as to who had made the call. Why had he not said 'wrong number' and left it at that? So simple. Instead he had to pick one of Elaine's women friends. It was a lie and he had been incriminated by it. In the eyes of the jury he knew he was damned from the start. If he could lie about that then they would think he could lie about anything else. Looking at some of the faces in the court he saw well-known ones, from what had been his family by marriage. Eaten with them, drunk with them, laughed with them. Now they appeared as strangers to him again.

Sir Redvers was called next, telling the court of hearing his daughter and son-in-law quarrelling one evening. Of how Elaine had said that if she stayed any longer with the accused she would die.

Mildred's turn came and went — a short one but enough to add to the general evidence suggesting that Edward had indeed been in love with Ruth and had seized his opportunity that night to ignore the reservoir keeper's warning, knowing his wife was in extreme danger.

Edward's counsel did not call him to give evidence. 'I'm not having you up there saying you're guilty. I say you're not and I'm going to prove it.'

Edward watched aghast as Ruth entered the witness box. The sea and the fresh blue sky of Guernsey came with her. She appeared calm, relieved to be there even. Her face had thinned and she looked older, but she was determined and firm in her answering of the questions.

She admitted that she had loved the accused since childhood. They had grown up together and had fled their island together, had attended the same school in Daleford. Edward had met Elaine Scarton and had married her when all her life she had been hoping that it would be her that he married. She had indeed been to the house before and knew the layout, and admitted being seen several times in the grounds as well as calling at the lodge — but uninvited she added to Mildred's great relief. On that day in question she had decided to try for the last time to change Edward's mind and having seen Elaine Dorner go out, had entered the Manor and made straight to that part of the house occupied by

Edward. The telephone was in a small inner hall near to the Dorner's sitting room. Approaching his room the phone had rung. She had picked it up and had heard the frantic call by the reservoir keeper asking that Mrs. Dorner and her companion be telephoned instantly, and told to get out on to high ground immediately. She had put the receiver down and had deliberately kept silent about the message.

At this point Edward leapt to his feet. 'No, no, it's not true,' only to be warned about his conduct in court. It was true he knew, but in a way he was just as guilty. His love, or fascination with Elaine — whatever it had been — had turned to a bitter anger, wanting her to be hurt and punished for her betrayal of their wedding vows.

His counsel then addressed Ruth. 'Miss Le Ney, will you tell the court why you have come forward to volunteer your evidence?'

Edward saw her glance in his direction. 'I did not want him to be blamed for something that he did not do,' she said simply, her Guernsey voice sounding on those northern ears.

'Very praiseworthy Miss Le Ney, and I'm sure my client thinks so too.' He paused, then asked of her, 'You love this man Edward Dorner?'

'Yes, I do.'

'And you have done for a very long time?'

'Yes.'

'But he married another, when you thought he should have married you?'

Ruth nodded in agreement. 'He was unhappy.'

'Did he tell you so?'

'No he didn't, but I knew he was — later.'

'So when the opportunity presented itself to harm her — at the very least — you took it, knowing from the phone call by the reservoir keeper that there was a very real chance of Elaine Dorner being drowned if she was not warned immediately. Is that correct Miss Le Ney?'

'Yes it is Sir.' Ruth's head had bowed.

'Just one more question please Miss Le Ney. Isn't it also correct to say that at no time did Mr. Dorner entertain you or your idea of his leaving his wife on the occasions when you saw him after his marriage?'

'Yes it is Sir.'

'And that he told you to go back to Guernsey and leave him alone on those same occasions.'

'Yes, that is true also.' Her voice was thin and lifeless.

Edward gazed at her helplessly. What was she doing? Did she realise? Doing her best to get herself imprisoned. Their lives had intermingled ever since they were young children, but never had he expected to be vying with her for sentence in a public court room. And whether he loved her or not was a private affair. She had declared her love for him often enough, but doing it in public must be dreadfully embarrassing for her, and it angered him to hear her having to do so. Perhaps she herself did not care any more, having been hurt so many times before, but she must not be allowed to suffer on his account again. He must make certain that they believed he was responsible for taking that telephone call that night at Scarton Manor.

He had to wait though, the prosecuting counsel now addressing her. 'You say Miss Le Ney that you walked into Scarton Manor that evening without anyone seeing you?'

'Yes Sir.' She looked so tired, Edward thought, felt sorry for her and wanted to rush over and support her.

'You mean you walked up the long drive, passed the lodge, through the front door, which it seems was conveniently open, then found your way inside and were just abreast the telephone when it rang?' The prosecutor's voice and expression were charged with doubt.

'Yes.'

'Then what did you do?'

'I picked it up.'

'But why? You're in someone else's house, and when the phone rings you pick it up,' counsel stated sceptically. 'That seems a very strange thing to do. Were you expecting a call at that very moment?'

'No.'

'Then why on earth should you pick up the receiver?'

'Because I was on my way to see Edward. I thought that by stopping it ringing, whoever was in would think that it had been answered. I did not want anyone to see me going to Edward's room.'

'Very well Miss Le Ney. Now you have said you took the call from Mr. Nolan, the reservoir keeper. Will you please tell the court as near as possible what he said.'

'Well, he was very agitated and spoke very quickly and repeating himself. I think he said, 'Nolan — the reservoir keeper — lower wall broken — water coming through. Get message to cottage, seen Mrs.

Dorner going that way earlier, light is on, get message to her.' '

Prosecuting counsel gave a cynical half smile. 'That's a very good recollection Miss Le Ney, but of course it must be remembered that you came forward to confess your part after Mr. Nolan had already spoken to the press, so it would have been quite easy for you to have memorised his statement and then come forward.'

It hadn't been like that at all. Ruth looked at the faces beyond the wigs, and at Edward staring up at her with that awful anxiety. He was so alone now. She wasn't going to let him save her twice. He didn't love her and yet he was persisting in trying to protect her. The face under the wig was speaking again.

'May I remind you of Lady Scarton's evidence when she said that just before she reached the inner hall the telephone stopped ringing. Upon opening the door she found, not you Miss Le Ney but the accused, Edward Dorner, standing by the instrument. Now surely if you had taken that message you would have been present and Lady Scarton would have seen you. But she did not. Nor anyone else, only her son-in-law by the telephone. She accepted quite naturally, and I think correctly, that he had taken the call.'

'No.' The sound jerked from Ruth. 'I heard her coming and put the telephone down, then Edward came out from his room.'

Her questioner could not quite keep the triumphant satisfaction from his voice as he said, 'D'you mean to tell the court that whilst Mr. Nolan was shouting urgently and frantically a warning into your ear, you heard Lady Scarton coming?'

Oh! would he never stop his questioning? Couldn't he see that she was telling the truth? 'Well, just as I put it down I heard her.' She was making a horrible mess of it, she knew. It wasn't what she had meant to say at all. It sounded all wrong.

'And in that short time you were able to disappear from her sight and the accused take your place?' Then with a meaningful look at the jury the prosecuting counsel sat down with the air of a man well pleased with the work in hand.

Edward listened as his defence counsel put his case to the jury. He was described as a gallant man trying to defend his childhood friend; a mistaken and hopeless attempt to take the place of the guilty person. The look that Lady Scarton had seen on his client's face, a disturbed one, was only natural to a man suddenly confronted by a woman who had no right to be in the house — a woman ravaged by jealousy and spurned by the accused. He pointed out the old saying, 'Hell hath no fury like a woman scorned' . . . What an opportunity when she took that call to harm the woman who had become the wife of the man she herself had wanted, and by her own admission had always loved. Almost certainly, he went on, as a result of her action in not relating the message, Elaine Dorner died in that awful torrent of water that bore down upon the isolated cottage that evening. She had also admitted that she went to the Manor to try to persuade Edward Dorner to leave his wife. Why then did she not inform him immediately of the matter of life and death nature of the call so that he could warn his wife in seconds with a call to the cottage? The reason was clear now, and the jury must return a verdict of not guilty for his client Mr. Edward Dorner.

Afterwards Edward confronted Mr. Denton. 'You can't — I won't allow you, she's not guilty — I am.'

'She's as guilty as hell and you know it. That's why she volunteered and she's admitted it to me. I don't know who's the madder, you or her. Now listen, if you go on persisting you'll find yourself in prison for perjury in court. One of you is guilty and it's not going to be you. I'm not losing this case because you want to play the hero.'

Despite his counsel's apparent gross confidence, Edward noticed his anxious fiddling with his papers.

The prosecution summarised their case by pointing out that the accused had not been allowed by his counsel to be questioned. What had they to hide? The accused had admitted to being in all that evening and of hearing the all important ringing of the telephone at the time the reservoir keeper made his call. The call had been taken — of that there was not the slightest doubt — by someone. That someone, the prosecution believed, was Edward Dorner. They had the evidence of Lady Scarton who had arrived on the scene to find him standing by the telephone. There had been no one else — no Miss Le Ney. And what had the accused said when Lady Scarton inquired as to where the call came from? He had said from a friend of his wife's, a Miss Mavis Beaver, a woman who could not possibly have made the call because she was just coming round after an operation. The accused had lied deliberately. Why? Simply to stop help reaching his wife whom he knew was then in a perilous position at the cottage. Also his failure to report the true nature of the call resulted not only in the death of his wife but also of one other person. The fact that more lives were not lost is a miracle for which we must be thankful.

Edward glanced at the jury. They would think he was a monster.

And what, the prosecutor asked, what were they to make of the remarks by Elaine Dorner and overheard by her father Sir Redvers Scarton? She had said that if she stayed any longer in the house, she would die. Were they to think those were just the words used by a woman in a domestic tiff, or did they signify something much more serious — the real threat of an attempt on her life of which she had some knowledge was imminent?

Lastly, the question posed by Miss Le Ney and her putting herself forward as the guilty party. A woman in love, obsessed with the idea that the accused was hers by some divine right, and that even after the accused had been married some time she still would not accept the fact that he wanted nothing more to do with her. She was a woman misguided, and to be pitied, and must think herself fortunate not to have become further embroiled with a man who it would be found had been utterly cynical when it came to the life of his wife.

Edward felt the shock as the judge's words beat into his brain — seven years' imprisonment. A callous disregard for his spouse's safety. No mitigating circumstances whatsoever. He saw Sir Redvers — that person's face rocklike and cold-expressioned as he looked in Edward's direction.

'We'll appeal,' raged his counsel. 'I'll be buggered if I'll lose this one.'

He did and lost, and Edward had the feeling that he would never be forgiven for his part in delaying his counsel's sprint up the ladder of professional success.

But Edward had no concern for Mr. Denton, only for himself just then as the full enormity of the cost of his impetuous protection of Ruth became reality to him. Seven years! Locked up in that echoing clanging place.

In the first month he had two visitors. Ruth was the first, the shine gone from her violet eyes staring at him, and in them the agony of her soul at his predicament. 'Oh Edward, I'm sorry, so sorry — I tried but . . . '

'I know Ruth.' He was calm and resigned in front of her.

'I'll stay in Daleford with Frederick. I'll stay until you're out.' She must have seen something in his eyes for she went on hastily, 'No, I'm not asking for anything from you now, Edward. Nothing. You must hate me.' At which he shook his head. He felt squashed and his emotions numbed. 'You'll have someone in the town — you'll know that there's someone not far away.'

Edward laughed shortly, bitterly, and shook his head incredulously at her offer. 'You can't wait in Daleford for seven years! Seven years, Ruth, seven!

No! I won't hear of it. I want you to go home please Ruth to Guernsey. If you really want to help me, take Frederick and forget about me. Don't let your life stand still worrying about me. You're still young and,' he looked at her and away, 'I think quite beautiful. You can make a happy life for yourself and someone else I'm certain.' He managed a desperate half smile. 'You won't be single long,' and he suddenly realised that it was perhaps the first time he had said anything complimentary and nice to her for many years. 'You will do that?'

She nodded with bowed head, then as if remembering something suddenly dug into the innards of her handbag, and brought out a photograph which she held up against the partition between herself and Edward.

He saw a child's face — Frederick's face — innocent, chubby and fair, with a mischievous grin, staring out at him from large round eyes. He realised that he had thought of him by name for the first time.

'He's our child, Edward,' Ruth whispered over the top of the photograph. 'Will you keep it?' and her eyes were willing him to do so.

'Yes,' and he saw the warder looking. 'Give it to him. He'll see I get it.' Poor Ruth, she never stopped trying.

Ruth rose, it was time. Pressed her lips to her finger tips and placed them against the grille, her expression holding a plea for him to do the same. He did, their finger tips touching briefly.

'I'll write to you,' she murmured and turned away hand to mouth, overcome, and he stared despairingly after her. Now his only link with the past lay in the warder's hands.

A week later he had a second visitor — William. The first time he'd seen him since before the visit to the cottage when he had heard his brother and Elaine together. William looked at him rather strangely, and gave an uncomfortable laugh. 'Thought I'd wait until you'd settled in before I came.'

Edward ignored the attempted joke in bad taste. It was too late to quarrel and he was still overcome at the thought of the sentence he had to serve. His brother looked well in a fine-cut suit.

'How are you then? Sorry you're in here,' William resumed, plainly ill at ease. 'I couldn't help you at all. Nothing I could do.'

Edward shrugged. 'It's all right.' He didn't want to go over anything with William. 'How are you? Are you still living with the ladies?'

'Yes, for now, but not much longer. She died you know — I mean Adeline — Miss Steck — collapsed and died very quickly.' He wasn't going to tell Edward what she'd been doing at the time. It wasn't his fault. He'd told her to take it easy and she wouldn't listen. Not that he'd minded. It was all she lived for, every night, that fleshy body. Insatiable. Just died suddenly beneath him. Just choked and fell still — very still. She was enjoying herself anyway.

Edward was staring at him, a funny look — far away and yet aware. Had Edward known about Elaine and himself? Perhaps not. Elaine had never said. She'd made a change — a young change from Adeline. Anyway he hadn't been the only one

— she'd had others. But he could have been the one with her that night, and he shuddered inwardly. Edward hadn't lost much, he thought, but he'd got himself into a mess — had been an idiot to ignore that call. He became aware that his brother was speaking.

'So what are your plans now?'

'I'm not sure. I might go back to Guernsey.' Hell! Two mistresses and they'd both died. He was unlucky. He remembered why he had come — the real reason. Must get a proper answer this time. Better say what he had to say quickly, visiting time was short.

Looking his brother full in the face he said, 'I've been thinking Edward, it's about time we decided what we're going to do with the old home. I mean I'm sorry and all that, but you're going to be in here for a long time. So would you agree to sell the property and we'll share the money? After all, why keep a ruin when it could bring money in? You don't need the money in here, but I do. I've no job.'

Edward eyed him, bitterness, humiliation rekindled and hopelessly lost in his life. 'No, I won't give my permission to sell, William,' enjoying his refusal of his brother. 'When I get out of here I'm going to do something with that ruin, as you call it. You must find work like I had to do.' His emotions fused, flared into high anger. 'When you were living off that woman I was working, trying to make a go of things. I didn't come to you for any help. I will not agree to selling,' and half turned away from the partition, set-faced. He'd had enough.

Sudden temper flashed from the other side as

William shot to his feet. 'Right, then, I'll show you. I'm going straight to the States. I'll get this thing settled once and for all. You can rot in here, you'll not get a penny of it if I can help it.' The warder was staring at them.

Edward rounded on him fiercely. 'Don't make things worse in my eyes for yourself than they are already. I'll be out someday, and I shall not forget that you helped to break up my marriage — the cottage — remember?' Then seeing the rigidity of shock come for an instant on his brother's face, he added, 'Yes, I know.' He hadn't meant to reveal that he had known but it had been forced from him by the argument.

'All right, that's enough. You'd better go Sir.' Edward and William stared at each other for long seconds, then the latter walked away and through the door without a backward glance. And Edward's bowl of misery was refilled once more, as he sat slumped and alone a few minutes later.

12

Ruth returned to Guernsey with Frederick, finding a place for them to live in Hauteville. She could not, she felt, face her aunt and the questions certain to be asked regarding the child — had to have time and quiet to think about her future — a future without Edward. No longer could she delude herself in thinking that he would at last be her true love and her husband sometime. She had, she realised, lived in a land of make-believe — a fantasy world, childlike in her naiveté that all would come right in the end. Not only that, but she had been indirectly responsible for one death at least, possibly two, in the dam disaster. Her utter foolishness had been paraded in the papers for all to read about. The public rejection of her in the court by Edward had been humiliating, and she had been shown to be a silly, obsessed, jealous woman. Oh! Why couldn't she have been taken as the guilty one, which she was? Damn fool Edward. Why had he to take her place? Twice now he had saved her; once on the quay side as a young girl caught up in the action of war, and now taking her place in prison so that she could go free. Damn him again, and them for not believing her. Edward did not have any real feeling for her, so why had he gone to prison for her?

But peace of mind and an easing of the tension that had beset her for so long were not to be Ruth's. In her fitful bouts of sleep her mind showed images of telephones, rushing waters and Elaine's face. Edward locking her out into the night, pointing at her with long accusing fingers. And the shell she had cherished all those years grew large in her nightmares, and everyone danced madly on it until it shattered into a thousand fragments, and gleeful vindictive eyes went round and round her as she tried to put the pieces together again.

Frederick was too young to understand what was happening. Strangers came and comforted him — took him away while his mother was being helped to come to terms with the new reality of her life. Mrs. Le Ney, astounded and uncomprchending that shc had been a great aunt without knowing it, rejoiced in the task of giving Frederick a new home for the time being until Ruth had recovered sufficiently to look after him again, and also deeply thankful to have her niece returned to the island again.

It took Ruth nearly three months to feel physically and mentally well again. Three months in which she almost came to terms with herself regarding her feelings for Edward. Almost, because still somewhere in her deepest heart she retained the spark which flared up in love whenever she allowed herself to dwell upon him. He had filled her life, and now she must concentrate on a new one without him. Yet she wrote to him every week without fail as soon as her health had improved sufficiently. She kept her letters matter of fact — news from the island, things she thought he might be interested in, and about Frederick. Of the ruin — the old Ormer Hotel she said very little, knowing how much it had meant to him, and there was nothing else she could tell him about it that he did not already know.

Seven years in prison. Perhaps a little less if he was lucky. Poor Edward. And Frederick, his son, would be a proper young boy by then. Whenever these thoughts filled her mind, Ruth was remorseful and deeply saddened. If only things had been straightforward and simple, she Edward and Frederick would have been a family living together, enjoying life. Although she tried very hard not to dwell on what might have been, occasionally her willpower was overwhelmed by a resurgence of those feelings and she despaired.

She found work part time in one of the island's hotels, in reception, and on the days when she worked her aunt would look after Frederick, but Mrs. Le Ney was now becoming too old and frail to look after him for long periods.

One fine but cold day in January Ruth was shopping with Frederick in town, then having completed it she walked along the esplanade with him, he holding her hand and often asking about and pointing excitedly at things in the harbour. He enjoyed coming with her and she loved showing him something of his adopted island. The winter covers on a few boats were rolled back, owners letting light and air into their craft, the promise of sailing yet to come in the Spring and Summer. Ruth turned to cross over to the bus stop on the other side of the road. A short line of cars slowed at the crossing. Halfway across Ruth glanced at the front one — a large maroon car. The driver was staring at her, his gaze following as she went by the front of his car.

On reaching the pavement she turned to look again, to see that he had his window down and was calling out to her. It was William! She mouthed an astonished greeting, but then as someone in the traffic behind hooted impatiently, he signalled to her that he would go on and turn around.

Ruth stood on the pavement with Frederick pulling at her hand. What was William doing in Guernsey? By the look of the car he was quite well off. Returning, he parked on Albert pier and then came across to join them. He kissed Ruth on the cheek, obviously as surprised and glad to see her as she was him. 'You're the last person I expected to see, Ruth,' he exclaimed. 'I couldn't believe it,' then looked at the chubby figure at her side.

'This is Frederick,' Ruth explained.

'Yours?' William asked, surprise already showing.

Ruth nodded. She didn't feel like giving any details there on the pavement.

William glanced about him. 'Look, how about having a drink somewhere or something to eat?' he suggested. 'There's Amarios just on here. We can have a chat.'

Ruth agreed readily. It would make a change instead of going straight back to the confines of her flat. She wondered how much William knew of her involvement in the Scarton affair; if he had been in Daleford at the time he would know almost everything.

They sat down in the warmth of Amarios looking out over the harbour scene — lovely even in mid winter.

'I thought you were living in Daleford, William.

How long have you been here?'

'About a month.' So he would know about Edward and herself — the whole affair. 'I'm sorry about Edward, Ruth,' he said glancing at her briefly and away to the window, 'and all that business. Must have been hell for you.'

She settled a restless young Frederick. 'A nightmare — and for Edward.'

'You're not still carrying a torch for Edward are you? I knew you were always keen on him, but he's going to be away a long time, Ruth.'

She shrugged. 'I shall wait.' It was all hopeless but she wasn't going to reveal to William what had been said between Edward and herself.

'What the hell did he want to do that for? I mean, I'm very sorry for him but he landed himself in a mess. He's only himself to blame.' William shuddered inwardly. It could have been himself up at the cottage when the reservoir wall gave way.

Ruth put her cup down, helped Frederick with his straw. The actions gave her time to think. If only William knew the truth.

William took hold of Frederick's podgy hand, wet from orangeade and looked at Ruth. 'And Frederick is yours?' Again he looked very surprised.

She regarded him squarely. 'Yes, mine and Edward's.' She couldn't keep the pride from her voice, but why should she? Frederick was the result of a union between the man she loved and herself. Frederick was the only thing she had from that association, even if love had been present in her but not in Edward.

'The dog! I didn't know he had it in him,' exclaimed William.

Ruth guessed by her companion's eyes that he was clearly trying to work things out as to where and when, and wondered if he really felt sorry for Edward, stuck away for years. She changed the emphasis of the conversation. 'Have you left where you've been living? I thought you were settled there, lodging with two ladies I believe.'

William nodded, looking displeased at something. 'Yes, one of them died. The other went into a home afterwards. The house was going to be sold.' William's manner made it clear to Ruth that he had been hard done by, and blamed them for him having to leave.

'Well you seem to have done all right for yourself. You've got a lovely big car, William,' she observed.

William frowned at some memory. 'Oh yes, I've got that — they let me keep it.' Actually he had misappropriated it. He had possession — some sort of law — probably be able to keep it. Anyway it was payment of a kind for his services in keeping her happy. He was sure she would have wanted him to have it, and wondered if she'd made a will. There'd be nothing for him he supposed. William gazed out morosely across the harbour, thinking that he could do with finding another Miss Steck.

'And are you working?' asked Ruth.

'No, but as a matter of fact I've got plans, Ruth,' and his eyes brightened and hardened. 'I've been to see the States and the solicitors over here.'

What on earth did he want to see them for? And

she waited expectantly for him to enlarge on the matter.

'Just simply that I'm damned tired of brother Edward's refusal to sell the bloody ruin he calls a hotel. I've asked him over and over again to agree to sell and share the money, but he won't. He has this stupid idea that he's going to rebuild it — make it into a viable proposition again. He's crazy. Stuck in there for God knows how many years, and he won't have a cent when he gets out. So how does he expect to be able to do anything with the place? I could be doing something with the money that's tied up there, it's no good to anybody just now. So I've been to see about overriding Edward's refusal and I've asked the solicitors and States to get together to give me permission to put the thing up for sale. They seem to think that this time I won't have any trouble in getting permission to do it. There's been no will found, and it's donkey's years now. There never was a will. Our father never made one I'm sure, and if he did it's been lost. I had a hard time over there, believe me Ruth. I hadn't a job — couldn't find one — while Edward lived in the lap of luxury with plenty of money.' He broke off to order more coffee.

Ruth gazed at him. He was bitter, felt he had been unlucky. As far as she knew he'd never looked for work, and had lived with those two ladies. Edward had worked hard, and had looked after her when she was having the baby, paid for things and given her money to pay for the flat and food. Now he languished in an English jail in her place. William was ungrateful, selfish, and self-centred in the extreme she realised; didn't know he was born. Ruth felt angry. How people changed, but perhaps William had always been like that.

She became aware that he was speaking again, something about staying in a guest house, but she wasn't paying much attention. Soon afterwards they parted, William offering her a lift, but she making the excuse of more shopping to do. She wanted to be alone, to think something over.

The winter sun lightened the old dark walls of Castle Cornet as Ruth later sat in the bus, hardly aware of Frederick's demanding babble, her mind full of something William had said. He was seeking permission to sell the former Ormer Hotel, and by the way he had spoken it appeared that the States would agree. He had been very confident. But the restoration of their old home had been Edward's life ambition. How many times had he told her with such enthusiasm of his plans for it? Bitter sadness swept over her momentarily. His one and only life's ambition should have been to love her. With an effort she pushed that emotion away. He did not and that was that. However, something must be done to help him. He could do nothing himself about stopping William from selling, but she could try on his behalf. Edward had given her her freedom, even though at the time she had not cared. Now she had a chance to repay him. He wouldn't allow her to love him, but he could not stop her from showing her feelings by helping him. But how? What could she do to stop the machinery of the States once it was set in motion?

Two days later in the early afternoon Ruth sat on

Moulin Huet, Frederick squatting happily with bucket and spade beside her. It was cold, overcast and they were alone. Winter's stark face was everywhere, without the makeup of Spring and Summer colours, flowers and people. She pulled her collar closer around her neck, and gazed at the sombre ruins of the Ormer Hotel for inspiration in her quest for help for Edward. How different that day before their lives were changed forever. The house had been alive, painted and burnished, windows sparkling like eyes in the sun. All those years ago. They had been children then, playing on the beach. Now a child of her own played on that same beach. The voice of Mr. Dorner echoed across the years in Ruth's memory, calling them from their play on that fateful day so long ago.

Her eyes strayed towards the drive, seeing again the Vicar's hasty arrival, the small unreal-seeming service of blessing by him before their frantic departure. She had jumped in beside him, the boys and their parents following.

The window into those far-off memories cleared under concentration. They had not followed immediately, she remembered. Mr. Dorner had not been ready. When she had looked back from the end of the drive, he had been shirt-sleeved, carrying something and hurrying down the steps that went from the garden to the beach. But she was sure he had not gone on to the beach itself. Her mind returned to the present, seeing those same steps and their rocky creviced side marking that end of the bay.

Ruth's thoughts were not idling now but

speeding. Mr. Dorner carrying something down the steps — something valuable with no time to take anywhere else. She was sure he had been holding a box or case as he descended those steps as the family waited. Jewellery? Papers? Articles of importance — taking something to hide. At high tides the water came part way up the steps; he would have known that. Whatever it was would not be near the bottom of the steps — more likely halfway and above.

Grabbing a surprised Frederick she hurried to the steps and leaving him within near sight at their bottom began to walk up them slowly looking for large cracks, hollows, holes in the cliff face. Mr. Dorner had not had much time. Whatever it was he must have placed it in the first likely spot which afforded cover. Over halfway and she had found nothing. The upper half also revealed nothing. Could she really have expected to find anything after all that time? The occupying forces had used the house, a gun emplacement had been built not far from the steps, and soldiers had been in and around the house for some years. If it had been found by them it would have meant nothing — just rubbish. Any jewellery would have disappeared. Furthermore, rocks could have loosened and slid, blocking the cavity into which Mr. Dorner may have placed whatever he had to hide.

The thought of Edward enclosed in his cell for the next few years made her retrace her steps again, her eyes searching even more keenly, her hands feeling every place which might have been used by his father. If only she could find something to encourage and sustain Edward during that time. She must keep on. If not that day, then other days until she had made as certain as possible that nothing remained of whatever had been hidden.

Frederick, with the beach to himself, was still quite happy, though once attempting to follow her up the steps, but she persuaded him to continue to play at their foot. Then once more she went up the flight, wriggling her hands up to the elbows in holes between rocks and fissures in the lower cliff face. There was nothing. Birds fluttered and wheeled as she looked up at them hopelessly. Arming herself with a piece of driftwood she began inserting the wood where her hands could not reach. Two-thirds of the way up she stopped. It had just occurred to her that Mr. Dorner had been a tallish man and could well have placed something above the line that she had been searching, and yet out of sight from above the steps.

Ruth began to poke into higher areas of damp moss and grass, into hollowed sections of the rock, filled with debris of the years gone by, then plunging the stick in, and soon a carpet formed on the steps from her efforts. Nine steps from the top she struck rock through the topping of earth. Tiring now and with Frederick getting restless below she felt she ought to finish. Definitely her last effort. Scooping the soil out revealed a boulder underneath. It moved when she pushed on it, sliding on something. More rocks she guessed, and stood on the next higher step. By stretching she found she could reach far enough to move the stone sideways, and by using her piece of wood able to strike whatever lay below it. The sound this time from the hole was now quite different — a metallic one. No thought of stopping now, and with heart beating faster with excitement as well as exertion she worked the boulder further away from the object that lay beneath. Her searching fingers found something with corners to it, and with rapidly tiring hands, pulled the object out until she could grasp it fully. A rusty metal box with a curved lid, patches of the original black paint still showing. There was no lock, just a clasp holding the edges together. This was it — the box that Mr. Dorner found necessary to hide when the family had fled that day. Ruth held it a moment almost reverently and with a sadness, despite her success at locating it. Barely an hour after he had hidden it, Mr. Dorner along with Mrs. Dorner had been killed on the White Rock pier, leaving this behind. Did it hold anything which would benefit Edward in the future?

Ruth collected a by now very fretful and impatient Frederick and went home. Frederick on the end of one hand, the box in the other. She too was impatient to find out what the latter contained. Soon afterwards it stood on the table, fragments of rust and pieces of earth surrounding it. The last time it had seen light had been a momentous day in the island's history. Now all had been and passed — a new world — a new island almost.

Ruth cried as she opened the box. She had liked Mr. and Mrs. Dorner. They had formed part of a world which as a child she thought would never change. Inside was a yellowed envelope and some papers loosely rolled together. She opened them out. They were the deeds to the building known as the Ormer Hotel. With unsteady fingers she opened the envelope while uttering a prayer for Edward. She saw that it was the last will of John Dorner and dated July nineteen thirty eight with the name of some high street solicitors beneath. The document remained folded in her hand for a moment. Should she look? She had no right; the solicitors should do that. Yet she had done the hard work, had persisted until she had succeeded. After all she could put it back and no one would be any the wiser. She was doing it for Edward. Her fingers hovered over the neatly folded papers. Suddenly she unfolded them, pressing the indented creases out.

Three pages and Ruth pored over them, oblivious to everything else. The will stated that should Mr. and Mrs. Dorner die before their sons reached maturity then the house, business and land must be sold and the proceeds held in trust until they had reached such age. Once Edward and William had reached twenty-one, then on the death of both parents Edward would be entitled to the property known as the Ormer Hotel. Ruth paused in triumph. It was Edward's property! He would be overjoyed and it would help him to bear his imprisonment.

She read on. Any monies from the estate would go to William the younger son, but in the event of Edward selling the property known as the Ormer Hotel, then the money realised must be shared between the brothers.

Ruth closed the box again, apologising inwardly to Mr. Dorner for reading the contents. But she had done it in the interests of his son — Edward — the man she loved. Depression followed the elation at finding the will. He did not return her feelings and she was wasting her time thinking that in trying to help him it would make any difference as regards his attitude towards her. However, she had the satisfaction of knowing that she had now repaid in some measure the debt she felt was owed to him. As for William — he was going to be upset and angry when he found out. No doubt he had in putting his case to Messrs. Haggard and Co. made sure that they were well aware of Edward's very prominent and less than gracious accommodation in England, but it had seemed to her during their brief conversation together that that he had showed very little compassion for his brother and his very much altered circumstances. William had been engrossed with thoughts of the money to be gained for himself. In a way he had altered; still happy-go-lucky, not too fond of work, but now revealing a cynical selfishness. Perhaps it had always been there, adulthood having just sharpened it into avarice.

Ruth took the box with its enclosed documents to the solicitors. She stated simply that she had found it near the beach, and having opened it seen their address on the will. Afterwards she walked out to face the coming years — years when often she saw Edward in Frederick's face and mannerisms, and she dreamed and hoped as passionately and fervently as ever that one day when Edward was free, he would come and join them and bring happiness and contentment into her life.

13

When Edward received the news of his right to the old Ormer Hotel, his utter despair was lifted, giving him the will to carry on — to survive. Ruth sent him a letter each and every week and he knew that she had searched for the will, the solicitors having told him that Miss Le Ney had brought it in. Staunch, loyal Ruth, reaching for him even in there. She had saved not only his old home for him but also his sanity, which before he had doubts that he would keep. Those letters assumed an importance to him beyond measure, keeping him abreast of happenings in the place to which he would one day return and never leave again. The new leisure centre on which work was soon to begin. The island attracting more foreign yachtsmen, and becoming more popular with holidaymakers. Her letters contained no words of love or endearment. They were straightforward and informative about what she saw and heard, the changes. About Frederick — how he was growing quickly and the things he did.

One other object helped him in his dreams of freedom and home — the Ormer shell cherished by Ruth for so long and left by her in his room at Scarton Manor that fateful evening. Sometimes he would put it to his ear and was certain that he could hear the murmuring sounds of the distant sea. And from the close-barred window of his cell he could see the landscape beyond the prison walls. Over the years the faint green of arriving spring — the rising haze beginning a summer's day; white in winter or a depressing heavy grey. And far beyond over the water to the south lay the ruins of the Ormer Hotel, one day to rise from his imagination into solid and habitable shape again.

The photograph of Frederick he placed so that he could see it when he awoke, the wicked yet innocent smile of a little boy ready to wreak the mischief that little boys had always wreaked. As Edward looked at the photograph one day he was surprised to find himself wishing that one of Ruth could be next to it. Then he thought of Maxime, his daughter by Elaine. The last time he had seen her had been just before the trial. There had been no communication of any sort between himself and the Scartons since. The name had been Elaine's choice — had seemed strange at first, but he had come to accept it, even like it, but no doubt he would never see her again. Those important early years from a baby to a young girl, with no part in them for him. It was the same regarding Frederick but at least he had a photograph. In his cell he retreated into a world where he drew and redrew plans for the restoration of his old home. He would have no means of fulfilling his dream, but the effort kept his mind alert — a vision for the day when he was free again. A balcony here, a tea-garden there, music in the evenings perhaps. Sheets and sheets of paper he filled with drawings, seeing each one being built and finished in his imagination.

The prison grew quiet one week. There was to be a hanging at eight o'clock in the morning. There was a tension beforehand, and afterwards an atmosphere of relief when the hands of the clocks had passed the hour. The next day at exercise Edward saw the green door, quite a large one at the bottom of one of the buildings, with a short slope leading to it from the yard he was in. Glances strayed to it frequently and he heard the chilling comment, 'That's where you part company from this earth.' Back in his cell Edward uttered a prayer of thanks that his crime had not warranted that journey so soon in his life.

Some five years later on a Friday in late Spring Edward stepped ashore in Guernsey. The prisoners welfare had paid for his passage and also given him money with which to pay for accommodation during the first week of his return. He lingered, letting the taxis go with their holiday passengers, standing on the edge of the quay looking towards the town in the bright sunshine, over the boats — so many of them bobbing gently, tinkling shrouds against their masts, in the twinkling golden reflections of the harbour water. The town, church and Castle Cornet, dark against the blue. The esplanade with cars and bustling with people. Colour and summer clothes.

He began to walk slowly along the pier, carrying his possessions in a small bag and savouring the smell of his native air. He crossed over to the raised pedestrian walk — over the road where his parents had died on that dreadful day. He hadn't meant to think or to look at the surface or try to remember where they had parked the family car. But he couldn't help it, his eyes straying of their own will. He was back where it all began and this time he hoped for good. Reaching the wall he leaned over, gazed into the carefree water below with a mixture of emotions he could not control.

Later he sat in the gloom of a coffee house deciding upon what to do next. Looking for somewhere to stay must be his first task. He had not told Ruth the exact date of his release as he could not face her immediately, and had wanted a few hours by himself beforehand — time to adjust. After finding accommodation across from Havelet and washing away the stains of his long journey he took the cliff path walk to Fermain. After that he would need a good night's rest before coming to terms with the huge problem that he would be confronted with when he began on his long-held ambition.

At Fermain he propped himself up against the sea wall, letting the bay's sounds and sights fill his mind. The sun was lowering now, hovering just above the southern cliff and pinking the front of the Martello tower. People were leaving the beach, a small column queuing at the water's edge for the boat back to St. Peter Port. Couples passed, arms around each other's warm flesh, and in the darkness to come some would stay to make love near the water. He hadn't held a woman for five years — a long time. Also fashion had changed in those years and his eyes were held by the bare tanned bodies.

He thought of Ruth. He would see her tomorrow. No doubt she would be very surprised. There had been times in prison when he had cursed her for being the cause of his predicament, but his anger had evaporated quickly. She had remained the one true friend through it all. And what was William doing now, he wondered? His brother had faded rapidly from his life after his first and only visit to the prison. Some bitterness still remained in him over the latter's affair with Elaine, but it was in the past now. His concentration must be in the present. He must make up for those lost years. Perhaps he and William could be on good terms again. After all years had passed since that argument over the property, and William would have had money left by their parents.

The next morning he called at Ruth's house but could not get an answer. Perhaps she was out shopping. He decided to walk down to Moulin Huet and look over the ruins of the Ormer Hotel which was now his, and call on Ruth again later. A feeling of pride and excitement had built up in him as he approached the bay. The day was breezy but sunny and this added to his mounting optimism. He was not a poor man at all he told himself. The property and the land it stood on were his. In a way he was well off.

A few minutes later, and for the first time in many years he stood at the entrance to the drive, gazing in shock at the state of the building on which so much of his hopes had been pinned. He sighed in dismay. It was much worse than he had imagined. Half the roof was off, the windows stared sightlessly without glass, and the door was missing to the side entrance. Graffiti had been scrawled on the lower walls, cans and bottles and old papers littered a wilderness of scrub and overgrown weeds and wild flowers. A collection of various pieces of fallen wood lay where the garage had been. In prison it had assumed a magnificence it did not possess. Was this the place his fertile imagination had created so many grandiose plans for? He leaned against the gate post, all his optimism drained from him. Where on earth was he going to get the money to pay for such repairs as the building obviously required? Since his last visit so many years before it had deteriorated badly. He had survived those years in prison on those plans, but his mind had played him cynical tricks and now he was presented with the reality.

He walked slowly towards it — drawn to it, as if his old home was in a masochistic way intent on showing him the full extent of its crumbling miseries and hurts. Sunlight split the gloom inside revealing the filth, and the smell of smoke and urine pervaded everywhere. Something fluttering caught his eye through the broken kitchen window, a line of tattered and dingy washing over what had been the vegetable garden — his mother's vegetable garden.

He heard a noise, seeming to come from the old dining room. In the near darkness he went forward slowly. Someone was inside. He pushed the door open. A woman turned from the fireplace, from which smoke billowed out, a pan in her hand, long tendrils of hair swinging around her face as she stared out sideways from between them at Edward. A long baggy blue pullover hung to her knees. They stared at each other. Edward's dream of home had never been like this.

'Who the 'ell are you? What y'doing here?' And she glanced out of the window as if expecting someone. Her arm remained outstretched, the pan held level. Obviously she had just been about to put it on the fire. Wary eyes stared at him from the tense heavy face.

The state of the place and the finding of someone there had left Edward with little more than a blind anger. His house — the family house where they had eaten and loved together. This filthy being using it, desecrating his memories. His shocked mind came to life. He moved towards her. 'Get out. I'm Edward Dorner. This is my house — I own it.' It could be a dream, he wasn't quite sure — it was very real.

Something like humorous relief glinted in the dirty features of the woman. 'Well Mr. Edward Dorner or whatever your name is, you go and find your own place — we found this first.'

Edward struggled to hold fast to any resemblance of intelligent reasoning he had left. 'This is my property and if you don't move out immediately I'm going to the police.'

'Oh my God, you don't expect me to fall for that do you, you barm can? You're like us. You ought to know a squatter's rights. They couldn't turn us out. Bugger off — find your own bloody cave. This is ours.'

She looked past him and Edward turned to find a creature as equally repulsive and dirty as she was. Large with a big belt and tight blue dirty trousers, and holding a bundle of driftwood.

'Hey Len, this joker says he owns this place. Telling us to get out. Marvellous innit? As soon as you find a good place, someone else wants it.'

The man came close. 'Looks like a mainlander to me. Get back and find your own squat, matey. This is nice and comfy for Liz and me. Now scram before I get the police and have you done for burglary.' He laughed at his joke, dumped the wood in the fireplace, then spat into the fire. 'You're not the bloody owner, and if you were you can't do anything about it; we've got squatters rights.'

It was the spitting that made Edward bring his fist up in a sudden surge of hatred. A satisfying thunk to the round uncouth face. The same fireplace from which light and warmth had been thrown into his childhood.

The other staggered and fell but was up again quickly, a knife appearing from near his hip. He pointed it at Edward, his unshaven lips quivering with murderous obscenities.

'No,' shrieked the woman and she hung on to his wrist. 'Let him go,' then turned on Edward. 'That's what you'll get if you come back here again. Get out and leave us alone.'

Edward stood his ground but, fearful of the knife, mustered all the self-control he had. 'This is my house. I was born here, grew up here. It was my home and now it belongs to me. I have come back to claim it. My solicitors will bear me out in what I say. You have no right whatsoever to be here.' His tone grew fierce as he went on contemptuously, 'And you're not Channel Islanders — your accent doesn't fool me. You've no rights of any kind in this house. I'm going straight to the States and my solicitor now. You'd better move out. I know your faces; I'll get you thrown off the island.'

He backed away slowly, courage stemming from the white heat of anger at being forced to leave. 'I'll be back, don't you worry, and I won't be alone so you'd better not be here when the police arrive.' Edward turned and stumbled away into the brightness outside, hardly aware of what he was doing. Down on to the beach of a thousand memories, and across it until he had found a place where he could be alone to think, collapsing into a private place of flat rocks, head in hands. Brave words he had uttered. Could he back them up? Were there such things as squatters rights? Or could he get them evicted? He groaned. It had been a bad morning and nothing like he thought it was going to turn out. The dreadful state of the house and then the shock of finding that disgusting couple living there. Despair filled him. He might just as well sell the thing. It would be much the easier way. Share the money out and walk away from the whole problem which the place presented. And yet . . .

He became aware of people passing him, spreading out across the beach, dressed in holiday wear. Looking down at himself he realised he was still wearing his dark grey suit, the one given to him by the prison authorities. Taking his jacket off he rose and wandered on a short distance wondering if Ruth had returned home yet. Did she know about these squatters? He continued to stroll, his back to the ruin of the Ormer Hotel, and nearer the water's edge, seeking solace from it. What should he do? Go straight to the States and the solicitor as he had threatened? The sooner he did the quicker the action against those trespassing thieves. Standing still he gazed out to sea, feeling drained of vitality and enthusiasm. Even when they had gone, the money needed for the task of just making the place inhabitable would be quite beyond him. He had no work and barely enough money to last him the week out once he had paid for his stay at the guest house. Whatever he decided to do about the house he must first get work — anything to enable him to keep going and give him time to think once more about his future.

Edward decided that he would walk up to Ruth's again, and if she was still not in he would go straight to his solicitor or perhaps the police first, although he shied away from the latter course — he had seen enough of them five years ago. They may not view his case sympathetically if they knew that he had just served a sentence for manslaughter. He raised dulled hopeless eyes seeing the Peastacks outlined clearly now, the early morning mist having lifted. Something white caught his eye on the headland to their rear. A large white building, and apparently very close to the edge of the cliffs. His sight sharpened in concentration, and he could make out coloured umbrellas, the gleam of metal and the occasional movement of people. He was puzzled and surprised. He'd never known of a building there before, but of course he'd been away a long time and things changed. He guessed it was a hotel, and a very large modern one judging from its design. Its position was just about opposite the ruins of the Ormer Hotel and somewhat above it, the cliffs rising higher at that the eastern end of the bay. There it was gleaming white and new in the sunshine, and his old home dark, broken and filthy on the other. He turned and made for the lane, his spirits as low as they had ever been in his life.

A car stood in the short drive of Ruth's home. Was it hers? His heart began to pick up its beat. Would she have changed much? He knew he had, and just then he felt wretched and no doubt looked it. He knocked, pushed open the door and called her name.

She came into the hall and saw him. 'Edward!' What a welcome was in that uttering of his name. All her emotions — past experiences. Clasping her hands on his tightly she looked at him a few seconds, then slid into his tight embrace, their lips finding each other's cheeks. Her body felt pliant and yet sturdy and as they drew away his hands fell and brushed her hips. He couldn't help it.

Grasping him by the hand again she led him into the light of the living room, then faced him again flushed and excited. 'You were going to let me know, Edward. I'd no idea you were coming. Oh, how marvellous. When did you arrive?'

'Yesterday. I had to find somewhere to stay first and what with one thing and another I didn't feel so good so I decided to come today instead. I did call earlier but you were out.'

'Yes, I work part-time.' She gazed at him. How pale and haggard and gaunt he was — a haunted look about him, the poor thing. She wanted to open her heart again to him. But no, they must be friends — just friends she had decided, but seeing him it was very hard to comply with the strict rules she had made for herself regarding their relationship.

Reaching up she kissed him on the cheek again. 'Welcome back, Edward. Look, you must be tired.

I'm going to get you a drink first, then you can eat, I'll make you something. We can talk afterwards.'

The Ruth whom he had last seen just after his trial had gone. She was a woman now he realised, not a girl anymore. Edward looked at her gratefully and warmly. Dressed in yellow, abundant strong fair hair with touches of grey — the loyal steadfast eyes though were just the same, and appearing to look into his thoughts. He remembered his mother once saying that Ruth Le Ney had eyes like a Guernsey Violet. He realised they were — funny how he'd never noticed them before. Sipping at the whisky she had given him together with a cup of tea at his elbow, he watched her as she moved about. She was beautiful he decided, a trifle heavier around the hips, but the folds of her dress around her thighs and the graceful calves drew his eyes. It was too late now. He'd had his chance years ago and he was surprised she hadn't married. But how good it felt to be with her. Her welcome so different from the one he had received when he had entered the ruins of the Ormer Hotel.

They sat across the table from each other. 'After I called the first time and you were not in, I went down to have a look at the old home,' and Edward went on to tell her all that had happened and concluded with, 'it was dreadful, and the place is an absolute shambles.'

Ruth nodded. 'Yes, I'd an idea someone was in. I used to go down occasionally, but I daren't tell you in my letters.'

'I'm going to see the solicitors and States about getting them out, and also see the will. I hope something can be done. They said something about squatters rights. I didn't know there was such a thing.'

Ruth regarded him. He still had those dreams about the Ormer. It must have been a shock for him to see it.

He leaned across, caressed her cheek. 'Thanks for everything, Ruth. I owe you a lot — for finding the will and everything. At least I can always sell the property.'

'No Edward, I owed you,' and she shook her head at the memory. 'It was all a horrible nightmare and I was such a fool.' Patted his hand. 'Don't let's talk about it — it's all over now. I'm just so happy to see you,' she said with intense feeling.

Edward wanted to embrace her but was hesitant after his treatment of her in the past. Instead he glanced about him. 'Where's Frederick?'

'He's at school. I fetch him about three thirty usually.'

'He'll be growing up now I suppose.' How strange, he didn't really know what age his son was.

'Oh yes, eight next in July — a terror,' then Ruth smiled proudly, 'but a lovely little boy. Actually not so little now.'

Edward remembered the photograph he received in prison. He still had it — the mischievous face, a real boy. 'Can I see him?'

Ruth looked surprised. 'Of course you can. You'll be staying today won't you?'

Just for a moment he saw the appeal in her eyes. She wished him to, and so did he. 'Thanks I'd like that, Ruth,' and sighed as he recalled the events of earlier that day, 'but if possible I'd like to get in touch with my solicitors about those squatters. I must get them out.' They would be on his mind all the time until they were.

'I'll take you into town,' volunteered Ruth, 'then we can pick up Frederick on the way back.'

Edward agreed readily. A good idea. It would get it over with. Then it would be exciting to see Frederick — his son. He was beginning to feel more relaxed in Ruth's company, no doubt in part due to the whisky. It was a comforting thought that he had a family, and was not alone as he had so often thought during the last few years.

Ruth cut him a piece of apple pie. 'I might have known you were coming — I baked yesterday,' and she looked at him with a smile.

Elaine had never baked him a pie of any kind during their marriage, he thought. Hers had been all gloss, shallow fires — erupting frequently, but diamond underneath, hard and glittering — blinding at times. Ruth, he had come to realise, had spirit, and of great depth, and when set in motion, powerful and constant. God, it would be nice to caress her, to feel her beneath his hands and body. All those years — a long time to be without . . .

Their eyes met as she turned to hand him his plate. A fraction of time, but he was certain she knew all that had been in his mind. 'Hope you like it,' she laughed shortly, suddenly, rather tensely. 'I know it used to be a favourite of yours.'

He couldn't blame her if she rejected what must have shown in his eyes. His attitude towards her had been dreadful at times over the years.

The pie tasted marvellous and he had devoured two pieces before he remembered something else that he had to ask her about. 'When I was down on the beach earlier this morning Ruth,' he said, 'I noticed a building, a large white one, on the opposite headland to the Ormer. It looked almost on the cliff edge. I don't remember it being there last time I was in the island.'

Ruth gave a quick shake of her head. 'It wasn't,' and looked away

'It looked like a hotel to me. Is it?'

'Yes it's fairly new — two to three years — I just forget. It's called the Two Bays.'

'They must believe that Guernsey is becoming very popular to build one of that size. It looks very modern.'

Ruth looked rather uncomfortable and Edward wondered why. He went on, 'I know the idea of a large international hotel with conference facilities had been talked about for years, but I should have thought they would have built that nearer town.'

'That hasn't been built yet, Edward. The one on the headland is privately owned.' Her expression puzzled him.

'Whoever they are it must have cost them something to build,' he observed and sighed when he thought of the ruin which was his, and its occupants. 'Are they Guernsey people or are they from the mainland?'

'From Guernsey.' Again there was that quick anxious glance at him.

'Anyone we know?' Not that he himself knew anyone with the kind of money needed to finance a place like that. He saw her hesitation.

'Yes — yes we do know the person — quite well.'

'Oh.' Edward was very surprised and intrigued, just couldn't think of anyone and waited.

'You'll never guess,' Ruth said quietly, then in an even quieter voice, 'it's William.'

'William! Our William!' Edward stared at her dumbfounded. It was indeed a day of shocks and surprises.

She nodded in confirmation. 'Yes, though I was hoping you'd find out for yourself, Edward.'

'But . . . ' He was mystified. 'How on earth did he get the money to buy that?' It was unbelievable.

'He said the money had been left to him. Didn't he go to live with two ladies somewhere not far from the school?'

Edward was beginning to understand. 'Yes he did for quite a while. Mrs. Prind and oh,' Edward patted his forehead to stir his memory, 'Miss Stack — Stike — Steck — yes that was it — Miss Steck and Mrs. Prind. He came to see me in prison, mentioned that Miss Steck had died. That was the last time I saw William. He went off in a temper. We quarrelled because I refused to sell the property and share the money with him. Said he was going to appeal and get it sold whilst I was in there.' Edward gazed at Ruth gratefully. 'But you found the will and saved the Ormer for me.'

'Well I didn't think it fair that William should do that,' but Ruth knew in her heart that it was nothing to do with being fair. It had been because she loved the man sitting opposite and still did so, 'Actually,' she went on, 'I think William has always been a bit envious of you, Edward. Anyway he's no need to be like that now — he's well off. Miss Steck left him all her money. I'm not just sure how much, but it was a lot.'

It must have been thought Edward, still staggered by the news that William owned the hotel on the headland.

Ruth regarded him. Poor Edward. William had accomplished almost at a stroke something that Edward had dreamed of for years — easily it appeared and without a penny of his own money she guessed. It must be a bitter blow to Edward to find his dream already created on the opposite headland by his brother.

'Are you certain that he owns it?' Edward queried.

'Yes I am as far as I can be. He told me himself and I've no reason to believe otherwise.'

Edward shook his head in wondering amazement then asked, 'I don't suppose you see much of him then these days?'

Ruth gave him a peculiar look again. 'As a matter of fact Edward I see him several times a week.'

'Oh, you mean he comes here?' and he could not help the sudden harder edge to his voice.

Ruth gave a quick understanding half smile. 'No — no, I go over there to the hotel.' She paused then stated quietly, 'You see I work there — for William.' Seeing the puzzlement, surprise, then a near anger in Edward's face she continued in explanation, 'After I came back here I had a breakdown. I couldn't work. Then when I got better I had to find work to support Frederick. I had one or two jobs which kept me going, then William had the hotel built and asked me if I'd like to work there. I had to accept — I'd really no choice, and he paid me quite well. Also he helped to pay for Frederick's schooling.' She saw the question coming. 'Yes, he's at a private school — Sausmarez Park way.' Ruth regarded Edward seriously. 'So you see I've had to be thankful to William. He's tried to help.'

Edward's anger died as quickly as it had risen. He could hardly blame Ruth when for years he himself had been turning her away, indifferent to her, and wanting her out of his life. And a breakdown afterwards; he wasn't surprised. She'd had a dreadful time. But her working for William! His mind balked at accepting that. He saw Ruth glance at the clock. 'Is it time to fetch Frederick?'

'Yes, he'll be waiting,' and Edward saw the smile of anticipatory pleasure — the proud mother. Of course during all those years when she had fended for both, a strong bond was bound to have been forged between them.

'Are you sure you want to come along, Edward?'

'Just try and stop me,' he smiled, feeling better after the time spent in her company. She'd taken him out of himself and shown him that despite his problems the world went on. He offered to drive her but she told him she would rather him relax and see the changes in the island as they went along.

It was warm, sunny and the lanes and roads seemed filled with colourful holidaymakers, their presence seeming to give the island a vitality that he had not noticed before. But of course it was now long after the war and holidays were big business.

And there were cars by the dozens.

Edward glanced at Ruth, her hair blown back by the slipstream of the open window. She drove confidently, seriously, sitting close up to the wheel. Small transverse lines across her throat revealed the passing years. His eyes slipped to her heavier breasts and the clearly discernible tops of her thighs beneath the thin dress. Yes, she was a mature woman now. The ingenuous girl had gone.

They drew up alongside a bus at the top of the Grange. Children's faces with sun hats and ice cream looked down on the car. He wondered what Frederick would look like now in the flesh, and felt a rising excitement. Going to meet his son. What would he say to him? How would he, Edward, introduce himself to someone who did not know him? Twice when Frederick had been a tiny baby Edward had seen him: in a nursing home where the birth had taken place, then in the lodging house where Ruth had stayed. Edward realised that in his excitement and anticipation of going to meet Frederick he had forgotten that he had intended to see the solicitors, but today his son came first. Tomorrow was another day.

They stopped outside some large open gates. A group of children were on the pavement, one already on the move towards the car before it had stopped. Ruth got out and Edward followed.

A fair-haired boy in a light blue and grey blazer, tie askew and cap a shapeless object in his fist went up to Ruth after a rather surprised glance at Edward. 'Hello Mum — you're late. I was going to go into town and catch a bus home.'

Ruth lightly cuffed his unruly hair in mock anger. 'I'm only a few minutes late, Frederick. Anybody would think you hadn't a moment to spare.'

Edward hovered nearby, noting their easy air together — long established. This was Frederick his son — tall for his years with a golden hue to his skin. The child in the photograph so long gazed at during those years away from the world. This was Frederick, conceived by Ruth near the path leading to Fermain. A lifetime ago it seemed.

'Edward, this is Frederick.'

A smaller hand in the too short sleeve was enclosed in that of the adult. Eyes that could have been transferred from Ruth's as a girl fixed upwards on him — a stranger's eyes, and looking at him without recognition. The photograph had come to life but several years later.

'Hello Mr. Edward.'

'No, it's Mr. Dorner,' Ruth corrected him quickly.

Edward felt the hurt, wanted to say, 'Tell him he is mine — my son.' His eyes held their message as they locked for a moment with hers.

'This is Uncle Edward from England. He's come to live in Guernsey.'

So she wasn't going to admit to Frederick that he was his father. Well, he couldn't have expected anything else, having had his chance many times in the past to assume his rightful title, but had spurned them. On the other hand he had married and stuck to his vows. Short of committing bigamy there was nothing he could have done about it. He smiled down through his disappointment. 'I've been wanting to meet you for a long time, Frederick,' and that was the truth. 'It's a lovely island — you're lucky to live here, Frederick.'

Frederick made a grimace. 'It's all right,' and turned to scramble into the car and fall on to the back seat.

They set off with Frederick standing up holding on to the front seats, his face between his mother and Edward. 'Two uncles — Uncle William and Uncle Edward,' he announced enthusiastically. 'Great. I didn't know I had another.'

Uncle William! Edward felt the hurt and this time a spasm of jealousy also. Perhaps Ruth took him over to The Two Bays Hotel occasionally.

'Sometimes I go out to golf with Uncle William — takes me in his Rolls Royce, and he has another car as well.'

Ruth shot a glance at Edward. 'William's taken up golf. Frederick sometimes accompanies him at the weekend when I'm working,' she explained.

'Have you got a Rolls Royce, Uncle Edward?' and the fresh hot face beamed into his.

No — he had bloody nothing but a pile of stones to his name. Aloud he began, 'Well, just at . . . '

Ruth came to his rescue, interjecting, 'Uncle Edward has just arrived and hasn't brought everything with him. He's just sort of looking around first. He'll see about cars and things later.'

'I haven't really made up my mind which sort, Frederick,' he said and Frederick nodded between them satisfied.

On the way into town Edward gained consolation for his lack of cars from the thought that the eager-faced youngster rubbing shoulders with him was his son, not William's.

They stopped outside the police station, Edward having decided to ask the police for help first as regards the squatters. He felt that he had nothing to fear from the former, having paid his debt for the crime he had been accused of committing. And in the last half hour from meeting Frederick he had begun to feel a new strength of purpose. He was not alone. Now he had a son, in the flesh, for whom to attain things. The police were very sympathetic when he explained his position and promised to send someone up to the property to investigate the following day and would report back to him.

In his room at the guest house Edward passed a restless night, fretful at the thought of the day that had just gone. William was uppermost in his thoughts. Once upon a time he would have welcomed success for his brother and been happy for him to have it. But now he was bitter and uneasy, remembering Elaine at the cottage, and William's affair with the woman who had been his wife. The humiliation that he, Edward, had suffered — he had been a joke between them. Elaine had been that way inclined to take lovers, but William being one of them had not helped matters. Now Ruth worked for him at the hotel, seeing him several times a week, and had admitted that William had been good to her and had helped her. Might he just try his hand with her? He seemed to want everything that he, Edward, had. In the darkness Edward smiled cynically at his own righteousness. He was concerned because William might have, or could have already made a play for Ruth. And yet, he himself had spurned the chance many times in the past to make her his own. There was absolutely no reason why Ruth should not fancy William and be grateful to him. After all she was not married to anyone, but the thought of Ruth and William together burned deep and painfully into Edward. So did the thoughts of Frederick's school fees being paid by William and in the past according to Ruth, some of his clothes. Frederick was his offspring, and the boy's education was his preserve, as were the clothes that were bought for him. He would choose with Ruth what Frederick should wear. And William taking him to golf. They boy should be on the beach — swimming, picnicking, sailing. Depression set in Edward then. Where was the money to change all this to pay for such things for Frederick? Nowhere — he hadn't any. The boy was a treasure, but Edward's rediscovery of him had come it seemed too late. But there was a solution and Edward was well aware of it, and in the darkness of the night he pondered on it very seriously.

He could sell the property — no doubt make a reasonable profit and give Frederick the benefits of such a decision, and at the same time free himself from the poverty he was in. He decided to give himself a week in which to see how things developed.

But still the modern white hotel belonging to William drew his eyes each time he ventured near to Moulin Huet. He had wanted to see what it was like inside, and yet he was reluctant to show himself to William in his position of a pauper.

During that first week Edward picked up

Frederick from school, and they would go into town and he would treat his new friend to ice cream, cakes or whatever took Frederick's fancy, then catch the bus back home. Once he took the youngster to the pictures and was forced to smile at Frederick's infectious laugh. On another occasion he took him swimming at Moulin Huet, and afterwards they walked together along its beach, overturning rocks, looking for crabs, searched for treasure trove in secluded small caves at the rear of the beach. On the return Frederick pointed at the ruins of Edward's former home. 'Mum says that's yours, Uncle Edward.'

'Yes it is Frederick, and I was born there.'

'She said it was once a hotel.'

'It was — once,' and he gazed at it sadly. There had been no news yet from the police.

'Are you going to make it into one again? Will it be as big as Uncle William's over there?'

Edward turned away from its ugliness. 'Oh yes,' he declared with an enthusiasm and optimism he did not actually feel. 'When I get things organised it's going to be a beautiful place just like it used to be.'

'Will you start next week then?' and the blue eyes stared up at him excitedly from under the unruly fringe. A fresh young mind that saw no obstacle to accomplishing the rebuilding in a week.

Oh, if only it were so easy. 'Well perhaps a while longer than that. I've one or two things to do first.'

'I'll help you Uncle Edward. It won't take as long then, and when it's finished you can get people to come and stay in it just like Uncle William's across there.' Then he added, 'Course, Uncle William's place is new. He didn't build it, but I can help you build yours.'

Edward was happy and touched at his son's remark. Patted him on the shoulder. 'That's very kind and thoughtful of you Frederick. I'll remember your offer when I start.'

They started off back up the lane, Edward well satisfied with the way his relationship with Frederick had developed during that week. They had got on well together. The boy seemed to like having a new uncle about the house. And so it appeared did Ruth, chatting and laughing animatedly with them on their return. But Edward knew it was only temporary — this almost happiness which had touched him once more, and gazed regretfully at them as Frederick told Ruth where they had been and the things they had done. This happiness, this family, could have been his long ago. His other life in England with the Scartons now seemed centuries ago. There, money had been his, but with only a passing fleeting marital happiness. Here in Guernsey he had no money, no work, but something else infinitely more valuable and lasting — the companionship of Ruth and that of his son Frederick.

But Edward was well aware that those intangibles would not bring him money. His week at the guest house was now over, and he did not have sufficient finances left to pay for another week. He needed a roof over his head until he could find work and pay for lodgings again. Once he thought about his old home, but the squatters were still in residence. Why didn't he borrow from Ruth until he found work? No, he couldn't do that, would not ask her. She had a hard enough time going out to work and looking after Frederick. There was however nothing to stop him asking her if he could stay with her for even just a week until his fortunes improved. He was loath to do it, but he had little choice. To his great relief Ruth made no fuss, said she understood and that he could have the boxroom until he found work. Edward was very grateful. Once more she'd been his rock on which he could depend and square up to the world again. Frederick of course was thrilled. 'Hey! Uncle Edward you're coming to live with us.'

'Well it's only until I find a place of my own before I start rebuilding the old hotel again.' He could sound important and affluent with Frederick, keep the pretence up. For Frederick it meant more swims, more exploring on the beach, and more stories about old Guernsey from the stranger called Uncle Edward who had suddenly appeared out of nowhere, and seemed to like him very much, and was very kind. His mum liked Uncle Edward a lot, he could tell. His friends at school were envious when he told them he now had two very rich uncles, and that the newest one was going to build another magnificent hotel where the ruins of the old one now lay, and that he, Frederick, was going to help and when it was built he was going to help to manage it and make a lot of money. His youthful imagination ran riot. The sooner he could help his uncle to build it the sooner he could leave school with all its annoyances and restrictions.

As for Edward, he too could not help giving rein

to his own imagination in front of Frederick. They would have a boat, and fish from it, and sail around the island, then perhaps to Herm, and Jersey, but always to return to the welcoming harbour of his rebuilt home with its new family inside.

14

After a week in which he had failed to find work, Edward was beginning to accept the fact that the only way out of his predicament would be to sell what was left of the Ormer Hotel. But then during the early evening as he scanned the Guernsey press for work vacancies, Ruth said, 'I saw William today at the hotel and I mentioned that you were back in the island but couldn't find any work. He was rather surprised, and said he thought you'd have stayed on the mainland — more chance there.'

'He didn't stay there,' stated Edward shortly. 'Came back here and used all the ideas I had,' and made no attempt to hide the bitterness he felt.

'Well, he said to tell you,' Ruth went on, 'that he might be able to find a job for you at the hotel if you'd like to go and see him.'

No! He wouldn't like, thought Edward, going cap in hand — the poor relation. He'd sell the Ormer first. William would gloat, and would not have forgotten that Edward would not sell the property when asked to do so. And Edward remembered William's fury and words at their last meeting when he was just beginning his sentence.

But a day later and Edward was thinking that he would have to go and see his brother. Put aside his pride, his envy and injured feelings. No longer could he go on staying with Ruth and not paying his way. In effect he was living on money which William was providing through her. Dearly he would have liked to have gone on living there, not wanting to go into a guest house again. He was surprised that she had not already asked him to leave — would only be doing what he had done to her in the past.

The next afternoon he caught the bus to the hotel. The gates were open under an archway with the hotel name curved along it — The Two Bays Hotel. A wide drive with fluttering flags atop poles led the way to the large chrome and glass entrance with taxis drawn up in front of it. Beyond the entrance to one side Edward caught a glimpse of a swimming pool and people around it. From the wall bordering the hotel drive he looked down and over on to the expanse of Moulin Huet and in the distance the dark remains of the Ormer Hotel.

Edward walked up to the entrance between the colourful lines of cars gleaming in the sunlight and into the shade of the foyer. A huge chandelier of crystal glass hung over the centre, and the reception desk in the shape of a large crescent of light-coloured wood confronted him. He waited to enquire from one of the smartly attired gold-jacketed girls behind it, and he was aware of the aura of a successfully run establishment.

His turn came. Had he an appointment?

No, he just wanted to have a word. Mr. Dorner had asked him to call and would see him. What the hell did he have to have an appointment for to see his brother?

Mr. Dorner was usually rather busy. What name was it?

'Mr. Dorner — Edward Dorner — I am his

brother.' Then disliked himself at the satisfaction he got from seeing the change in the girl's attitude and expression, his hypocritical basking in the authority of her employer.

A voice on the other end of the phone, then she turned to Edward. 'Mr. Dorner was just going out, but he can spare a few minutes if you'll go up.'

That was damned gracious of him, Edward thought as he went past the red and gold of the restaurant and along the softly carpeted passages with the coloured wall-lights and numbered doors. All this for riding a middle-aged spinster for a couple of years. He was surprised at his own somewhat lewd though correct and fitting observation. And Elaine? Burning humiliation swept over him again. That was in the past but his anger was always easily stoked by the return of memories.

He went up a short shallow flight of stairs which brought him to an almost circular hall with a domed ceiling of glass flooding the area with sunlight. Chairs and low tables to his left and right. In front of him was a door marked with his brother's name. Edward did not knock but opened the door and stepped inside.

William rose from a desk at the other end of the room, came from behind it. If his hand had moved, so would have Edward's which hovered hesitantly at his side. It did not, perhaps because the latter's recent thoughts were still etched upon the face.

'A long time Edward since we met,' and he motioned to the chair at the desk side, then sat easily on the other corner gently swinging a leg.

'Yes it is, William — a long time.'

William had put on weight, and there was now a slight wave to his hair, and he was wearing a well-cut light blue suit. He looked the part of the owner of a flourishing good class hotel. 'I didn't know you were coming today,' his tone implying that he would rather have known ahead.

'Just thought I'd pop in and see you.' He felt he couldn't broach the subject of employment immediately, feeling shabby and worried, whereas William looked confident and very affluent, and knowing full well what Edward had come about.

'What made you return to Guernsey? I'd have thought you'd have more chance of work over there than in a small island like this.'

'There was nothing for me over there afterwards.' Edward was reluctant to go back into the past.

'Yes, a bad job,' said William. 'There was nothing I could do.'

Edward suddenly remembered William saying the same words to him when his brother had visited him for the first and only time in prison. He shrugged. 'It's over.'

'Where are you staying?' asked William casually.

'I'm just at Ruth's for the time being. I haven't quite decided what I'm going to do.' A mocking voice inside his head told him he had no choices.

William looked surprised. 'At Ruth's! But I thought you were not on very good terms.'

Did he hear the slightest note of disappointment in William's tone? If there had been, it gave him a feeling of satisfaction. 'Oh, we get on quite well now. I suppose we're both older and perhaps wiser,' but he hadn't come to discuss their relationship with his brother.

'I'll be going over. I haven't seen her for a while — socially I mean. You know that she works for me a few days a week.'

'Yes she told me,' and he wished that he could tell William that Ruth was not coming any more.

'She was having a bad time. Something had to be done.'

'Yes, I suppose so.' He had been powerless and helpless to do anything for her at that time, but William's words stung him. And the less William popped over to Ruth's the better he would be pleased.

'How's Frederick?'

'He's all right.' Edward's tone was protective, guarded.

'Growing into a nice boy. We've had some good times together,' and there was a gleam of meaningful satisfaction in William's regard.

Damn him, thought Edward. Frederick's mine, and he's talking as if he owned him. Good times together — that hurt. But there'd be no more for William. The good times were going to be between Frederick and himself. 'Oh we've started doing a few things together already,' Edward said defensively. Then with a total pleasurable satisfaction of his own he went on, 'Yes, my son is a fine boy — be quite an athlete some day. Swims, runs well, and he's going to play rugby for the school team he told me yesterday.'

William's leg had stopped swinging and his eyes had narrowed fractionally. 'Yes, I'm sure he will,' and he shrugged slightly.

Yes — my son, thought Edward — something he, William, hadn't got, for all his philandering ways. Then he felt the deep soft carpet beneath his feet and was reminded sharply of what he did not have.

'You know of course that Frederick's attending the most expensive school on the island,' pointed out William, 'and the fees have got to be paid quarterly.'

No he did not know, had never thought of it, although Ruth had mentioned that William had paid the fees.

'I've seen to his schooling and to the cost up to now,' William informed him.

Edward nodded. 'Ruth did say something about it, and I'm very grateful, William.' His gratitude was given grudgingly however, unable to muster the surge of warmth that an act of generosity such as that demanded.

'I think they're due within the next few weeks again. Can you manage to pay them?'

Edward wasn't in the future going to have William playing such a large part in the upbringing of his son. 'I'll see to that now. No need for you to bother,' he said recklessly, at which his brother regarded him doubtfully and with some surprise. He'd had a feeling that William was enjoying himself up to then. 'I had some put by for a rainy day,' he lied with a confidence that had no foundation whatsoever.

'Oh well, in that case,' William waved a hand in a gesture of displeasure and slid from the desk to stand by the window looking out. Then without turning to Edward he asked, 'And what are your plans now for the future?'

'I suppose what they've always been. I want to get the old house on its feet again, make it into what it used to be — one of the best hotels on the island.'

William looked back at him sharply then laughed in amused disbelief. 'You're not still hanging on to that crackpot idea of yours are you?' He continued to stare at Edward for a few seconds then exclaimed, 'My God, you are — you're serious. I can't believe it. You must be crazy talking about resurrecting that old pile of stones. It'll cost you fifty thousand at least, probably a hundred by the time you've finished. Good God, I'd have thought a spell inside would have knocked all that nonsense out of you. You just can't be serious, Edward.'

Edward hadn't expected quite the damning of his idea that William had expressed, and was both astonished and angered. 'That nonsense as you call it kept me going for more than five years.'

'All right then, tell me where are you going to raise that kind of money? Daydreams like that need money to make them live you know.'

Edward felt he had no need to be told that. William had never really worked, having progressed on the backs of fortune and women. No doubt he had what he wanted, but he shouldn't pour scorn on another's dream. 'Don't worry. That one will live even if it takes me fifty years.'

Standing up he looked through the picture window down on to Moulin Huet and its quieter, smaller companion Petit Port. The view was very impressive he had to admit. Bobbing heads in the glittering sea, busy running children and people lying on the beach. The ivy foliage of early summer on the cliff tops and the green fresh land behind. And directly across in the shelter of the opposite headland, the lonely forsaken place that had once been their home, and was now the focal point of his dreams. No wonder William thought he was crazy and naïve. Perhaps he was. Putting too much importance on an overgrown ruin. There was the easy way out and that he guessed would please William.

Sitting down again he said, 'Did Ruth tell you that I found a couple of squatters living there? I've been to the police about them, but I haven't heard anything yet.'

William snorted dismissively. 'I told them they could stay. I was over there last year and they were in then.'

'You gave them permission?'

'Yes. I didn't think you'd be bothered about the place any more.'

'You'd no right to tell them they could stay there, William,' and his voice was harsh with a sudden annoyance.

'Well, the place could hardly be made worse just by the addition of two squatters,' William retorted scornfully. 'My advice is sell the bloody stone and land before it all drops into the sea. Of course if you want to be down and out for the rest of your life, you go ahead. It's your problem.' He paused then added, 'Ruth won't want to go on providing for you will she? She's enough to do keeping herself and Frederick.'

Edward tried to stem his rising anger. That was

rich coming from someone who'd lived blatantly and parasitically on a couple of women for years. His brother had a short memory. Then Edward remembered the purpose of his visit. When he spoke his voice was strained, thin. 'That's why I came to see you.' Why was he in such a mess that he had to ask his brother? Should never have been in that position. Began again with an effort, 'Ruth said something about you may have — er — some work for me.'

William left the window and sat down behind his desk and gazed at Edward. There was a clearly discernible gleam of triumph in his eyes. 'Well, how the mighty have fallen, eh Edward. I never thought I'd see the day when you came to me for a job. You were not so bloody keen to help me though were you when I asked you to sell the godforsaken place? I needed money then, but you didn't think of my problems.'

Edward endured the remarks and stared back. Some day his star would rise again. Thoughts came of William with Elaine, but he tried to keep his mind orderly and calm. 'You were free to work and earn; I wasn't. I had to keep something for when I came out, and anyway the will proves that I was in order.'

William leaned across the desk, his expression totally devoid of understanding and sympathy. 'Look, you damn well put yourself in prison. That was your fault. Anybody who does nothing to help his wife escape a catastrophe like that deserves to be put away. If I'd have been the judge I'd have had you for murder. As for the will, when I asked you to sell you didn't know there was one. You were just damn selfish.'

Edward stared aghast at William, shocked at the strength of the enmity that his brother was showing towards him. The bloody hypocrite didn't know the true facts. An overwhelming desire to confront William with the truth gripped Edward. To hell with the job. But he didn't, surprising himself and William no doubt when he said, tight-throated but levelly, 'I didn't come here to argue. You've got money now — you don't need the proceeds of the sale. I haven't any and I need to work, so if you don't want to give me a job I'll get out.'

William made him wait, eyeing him with an ill-disguised gloating satisfaction. 'All right, I'll give you one. Don't expect it to be much. This is my hotel — I own it. You were tops once, now I am. I've worked damned hard to get this.'

You bloody liar, thought Edward with a savage cynicism. Any work had been done in bed. Guessed that his brother was unaware that he knew the money had been left by Miss Steck. Grudgingly Edward had to admit though that The Two Bays Hotel was magnificent. It was well-designed, built, and obviously run efficiently, and if none of those requirements had been met, the money involved in the venture would soon have been lost. It was plain to see that William was very successful. He waited for him to say what the job would be.

'You can move the cars. The person who used to do it is ill — not likely to return.'

'Which cars d'you mean?'

'The ones that bring people here. Hired or their

own. They leave them at the entrance, and you park their cars for them.' His tone was only just civil as he continued, 'Report to the head porter at reception, get your uniform from him. Then go round to the gardener because you'll also give him a hand when he needs it. Eight o'clock sharp tomorrow — right?' He looked at his watch then flicked a switch on his desk. 'Miss Daley, tell Pearson to have the car ready. I'm going out.' He glanced up at Edward. 'You'll be on the payroll like the others. Think yourself damned lucky Edward, you caught me in a generous mood.'

A jumble of emotions accompanied Edward as he left, anger and humiliation uppermost at William's manner towards him. That was his brother, and yet they had grown so far apart over the last years. Surely there had not always been this underlying antagonism. He hardly recognised William now as the younger brother who had once been a playmate, friend and then a frightened youngster like himself during the war years. It had all gone wrong between them — envy, jealousy, single-mindedness and selfishness playing their parts. Edward went out into the sunlight towards the gates, depression heavy upon him. A car swished past from behind, startling him with its quiet approach. A dark blue Rolls Royce with William at the wheel, but there was no wave or glance, just the back of the car turning into the lane and surging effortless away.

So Edward began working for William at The Two Bays Hotel, parking the cars and wearing the regulation uniform. He also cut the grass on the surrounding lawns and dug rockeries over. But his interview with William and his lowly job had strengthened his determination to fight on until The Ormer was rebuilt and a going concern. Occasionally he washed the residents' cars and he was sharply reminded of his early days at the Scarton company in Daleford, when one of his jobs had been to do just that. Sometimes he would gaze across the bay and console himself with the thought that at least his old home was his.

His wage packet at the end of the week and marked Dorner E. contained a meagre sum. Edward clutched the envelope, smiled wearily and wryly, but small though the amount was he felt some independence returning. He could now pay Ruth for keeping him but he had resolved however that as soon as he had saved enough he would move out and into a guest house again, feeling that he had relied on her too much already. The fact that she worked for William irked him intensely, and also that both were employed by him. Life was strange. Never would he have believed that one day William would be doing just that. Sometimes Edward got a glimpse of her busily moving between the tables in the busy restaurant, but she did not discuss her work much when they met afterwards.

Working in the hotel grounds the following week he was surprised to see a blue and white helicopter standing on a pad some distance from the main building of the hotel. Then he recognised William as he boarded the machine with the pilot. Later he found out from Ruth that William had been attending a conference in Jersey of States committee members for tourism and hoteliers. The fact that

William was a member of such a committee surprised him. His brother was certainly in a prominent and influential position. He watched as it flew off in a south-easterly direction, and then looked at the spade in his hands and despaired of his own future.

One day Edward decided to see Mr. Haggard the solicitor, if indeed he was still in practice. He was — older, smaller but still very much the legal man.

'You've been out of the island for some years now I believe, Mr. Dorner,' he began.

'Yes, things didn't work out and I decided to return.' That was sufficient for him to know. The years had made a difference he noticed. It had been 'young Edward' before; now a more formal and polite address.

'You'll know of course that the will was found by your friend Miss Le Ney near the house. I believe you already have an idea of its contents.'

Edward nodded. He knew all about it. It had kept him going throughout those long years away from the world.

Mr. Haggard pressed a bell and Edward heard the door open behind him. 'Clarice, bring me Mr. John Dorner's will, please.' The door closed then opened again shortly and yellowed folded papers were deposited by a hand upon the desk. The solicitor spread the creased papers out in front of him.

Such a small missive Edward thought — his father's wishes, and he saw a signature. All that was left of the strivings of a man he had known as his father. No doubt when he had drawn it up he had had no idea the end would be so near. Had he sat where he, Edward, sat now?

'Your father insisted on keeping the will at home. That is why it has taken so long for the matter to be cleared,' Mr. Haggard said. 'Nobody knew where it was, although I suppose we could have drawn something up if it hadn't been found.' He paused then went on, 'The will was made in July 1938. Your father in the event of his death left everything to your mother, but of course the position changed when she died also.' He looked up. 'You are the eldest son I believe, Edward.'

'Yes, William is a year younger.'

'You are then the next in line as the eldest son, and the property known as The Ormer Hotel is inherited by you, which of course you already know, but for your benefit that is now confirmed.' Looking somewhat apologetic he hesitated. 'I am obliged to say though that it looks in a sorry state.' His hands fluttered in a backwards and forwards motion across the desk. 'Of course the Germans used it, but it will need an enormous amount of money spent on it to make it habitable. On the other hand it stands in an enviable position and the land alone because of that position is very valuable.' He glanced down at the papers and back to Edward. 'No doubt you will also know that there is one proviso in the will as regards the property and the land with it. If at some time you decide to sell, then the proceeds of the sale must be divided between yourself and your brother William.'

That was what William had wanted all along — one of the sources of the rift between them. 'There was also a sum of money from which William was the beneficiary,' Mr. Haggard informed him. 'Not a great amount but it all helps, although he had done very well I believe on his own.'

Suddenly Edward could not find it in himself to be enthusiastic and thankful over the confirmation of his ownership of his former home. All the money in the world would not make up for the loss of their parents. A high price had been paid for his acquiring the property.

The following Wednesday was Ruth's half day off and when Edward arrived at the house he found her waiting for him eagerly, taking him by the hand and pulling him inside. 'Good news for you, Edward. The Ormer is empty! The police took those people away — something about them having drugs on them. They'll be deported for it. The police came here but I told them you were at work.'

Suddenly the greyness of his existence had split. In a rush of excitement and relief Edward hugged her, aware of her pliant softness as momentarily she was pressed against him. But then he felt the muscles of her back stiffen as she drew away.

'That's wonderful Ruth — marvellous. Now I can begin to clear the place up. It will be a start at least.' The first step on the way to fulfilling his ambition.

Ruth turned away. He was not to see the sadness which swiftly replaced the pleasure at giving him the news. The Ormer was everything to him, the one thing he really cared about. No — there was Frederick. He was fond of Frederick. But oh, if only that look on his face had been for her and not a lump of inanimate and crumbling stone.

Later Edward hurried down to the Ormer, Ruth

having declined his offer for her to accompany him. Frederick was enthusiastic and would have done, but a friend had come to tea. When Edward arrived at the house he was relieved that Ruth had not come with him. The place stank. What a mess, and enough to daunt the keen enthusiasm with which he had entered. But his imagination countered that swiftly, seeing walls renewed, new windows, their shape altered, the place refurbished. Guests coming, music playing, light and chatter, the tea garden alive with people. Ideas came and went. Ten minutes he had meant to spend under what was left of its roof; instead it was near midnight when he walked up the lane to rejoin Ruth and Frederick.

The next evening father and son, armed with disinfectant, cleaning utensils and bags for rubbish, attacked the interior. Even Frederick with all his boyish optimism was appalled at the state of the building and its rooms. But once they had begun he found it great fun for a while, then leaving Edward and going to explore the house by himself.

Edward started in the kitchen partly because it was nearer the fresh air coming through the side door, and also because the evening sun entering it dispersed the gloom which had settled elsewhere. He worked hard after all the years of talking and thinking about it, coughing with the dust and plaster, filling bag after bag which Frederick held for him. The latter found an old German uniform button which he examined excitedly and then pocketed to show his mother. Edward told him something of the war and showed Frederick where the gun emplacement had been and that the house had been used by the occupying forces. How they had had to flee that day. The youngster's eyes were intent and fixed on him, punctuating Edward's story with exclamations of wonder. The light began to fade and they made to leave, Edward casting one last look around the old kitchen. It looked somewhat better after all that work but it still required a huge amount more. However it smelled cleaner and the point was a start had been made. They stood for some minutes away from the dust with his hand on his son's shoulder.

'Will you let me help you in your hotel, Uncle Edward?' the youngster asked. 'I could work for you here. I'd like to very much.'

Edward smiled at Frederick's confidence in the future. 'Of course you can, any time, but it's going to be a while before it's in working order again.'

'Well if we keep coming down like this, we'll soon get it done, won't we?'

'Oh yes I'm sure we could.' Such optimism was infectious. 'You've been a great help.'

'I could come tomorrow — leave school and just get this work done more quickly. I wouldn't mind leaving the school,' he added earnestly.

Edward chuckled. He hadn't done that much over the last years. 'It's a darn good idea, but you've got your schooling first then we'll see what happens.'

Frederick grimaced, and Edward knew what he felt like. There had been times in his early boyhood when the last thing he wished for was school. The sea and the beach had called strongly to him. They turned to go, the long oblong of white of The Two

Bays Hotel facing them across the bay up on the headland.

'We'll make ours as big as Uncle William's,' stated Frederick.

'Even if it's not quite as big it will be as good,' and Edward sighed inwardly. Brave words, but there was a deep abyss of wealth and time between the two buildings.

That night was hot and Edward could not sleep, his mind active and imaginative. What a fine real boy young Frederick was. In a short time a friendly camaraderie had sprung up between them. Wouldn't it be wonderful if some day Frederick could help him run the new Ormer Hotel. Father and son together. Edward thought of his own parents. What would they have said if they had known their grandchild had been helping in the beginning of the rebirth of the family home? They would have been thrilled and excited, and they would have asked about Frederick's mother. They liked Ruth — always had — a frequent visitor to the house. But then Edward heard his own mother's shocked voice, 'But Edward, you must give the child a proper name — your name — and honour Ruth. Marry her. She bore your child.'

Ruth. Edward's mind focused on her in the hot darkness of his bedroom. The feel of her when he had hugged her the other day. Momentarily she had moulded to him. He had felt the tips of her breasts, the mount between her hips through the thin material of her summer dress. The last woman he had slept with had been Elaine, always a traumatic unpredictable experience. So long ago he'd almost forgotten what making love felt like. His thoughts were making his body restless. Looking at his watch he saw that it was ten minutes past two and in five hours he would have to be up. A cup of tea would be nice.

Throwing a dressing gown over his nakedness he made his way quietly into the kitchen. The sound of the kettle grew louder — it was never so loud during the day. Then the click of the switch as it went off. Edward let the leaves settle in the small pot, then poured himself a cup, adding milk and sugar. Holding the spoon upright he stirred the liquid, then as it was almost withdrawn he allowed it to slide in again. The action fascinated him, scalding the tips of his fingers as the spoon went to its full extent. Thought of Ruth — so near and yet so far. A noise to his left. Startled he glanced up.

Ruth stood in the doorway, a hand to her heart. 'Thank goodness it's you, Edward. I heard something.'

'I just couldn't sleep.' He felt awkward and his eyes must still hold the desire brought on by his action with the spoon. How long had she been standing there? 'Would you like one?'

'No thanks, Edward. It may keep me awake.'

How formal their conversation was nowadays, he thought. In the past she had been at his feet — prostrating herself, eager for him to take possession of her. Not now. Her manner was matter of fact, occasionally withdrawn, and never showing very much emotion in their renewed relationship. He was aware of her gossamer-like pink gown loosely worn over her short diaphanous nightdress.

She moved and the overgarment parted slightly then closed, but not before he had glimpsed the blur of pale flesh and dark shadow underneath.

'I'll go back to bed then — ''night Edward,' and she turned away.

''Night, Ruth.' Her hair was tumbled almost to her shoulders, the rounded shape of a woman beneath the material moving away from him. He wanted to cling to her hips, stop her from leaving. 'Ruth,' he called. She looked back at him. 'I can make another cup if you'd like one — soon do it.'

She gave a little smile of thanks. 'I'd rather not. Hope you'll sleep now,' and slipped through the door.

Sleep now! How could he! He stared after her across the kitchen, knowing what he wanted, and it certainly was not the tea cooling on the table. Under that same roof was his son Frederick, born out of a union between himself and Ruth. His hungry body made his mind seek excuses, blunted his intellect. Surely he had a right — some sort of right towards her. Only once in their lives he had possessed her. There would be no harm in just holding her. She couldn't object. A kiss — not too much to ask of her. After all he had given five years of his life for her. Just a few minutes.

He stood in the narrow hallway outside Ruth's bedroom, his thoughts dwindling to nothing under the influence of his desire. He stared at her door. Beyond it was Ruth of the fair hair, violet eyes, and pale curving thighs. What was left of his common sense cried out for him to turn away in the tiniest of voices. Edward ignored it utterly. Turning the knob, he pushed the door open and stepped inside. The light from the hall illuminated the room dimly. Ruth was half bent, her back to the bed, staring up at him. Her loose-fitting pink gown lay on the bed and she was in the act of pulling off a slipper. She straightened, the short fine nightdress at mid-thigh, and even in the half light revealing the continuing upward line of her limbs and beyond. 'Edward!' Astonishment, alarm and anger were in the sound.

He took another step further, his hands slowly reaching out towards her. 'When I saw you just now — five years, Ruth. Just hold you that's all.' Hell, it was hot. He heard himself — inarticulate nonsense, but couldn't help it. What was he doing there? Out of control like a machine. 'Please Ruth,' he beseeched.

'No, you don't love me, Edward. It's too late — no more. Get out of my room.'

His eyes had lost their intelligence, were dulled, animal-like, and she pushed hard with the back of her legs against the bed to distance herself from him, but the bed moved and she overbalanced as Edward's hands sought her, falling backwards, her upper body upon the bed, her feet straining to touch the floor. Her head moved violently sideways to avoid his mouth. 'A kiss Ruth — a kiss,' he kept repeating.

She struggled to raise herself but he held her by the shoulders to the bed.

'No!' she cried. 'Not like this. You don't love me. Get off me Edward — no more — we were all right as we were. Why have you to spoil it?'

Edward hardly heard her, eager with a pent up

desire. Her nightdress was raised, his flesh reaching for hers. He caressed the soft shallow dome of her stomach, and she lashed at him with her free hand and swore. He'd never heard her swear before. It only served to excite him further. All those years she'd pestered him, knocking at his doors, having his child. The worry, the expense, the tension caused by her persistence. Five years for her — she owed him something. His body moved violently and Ruth shuddered and sobbed with helpless rage, muffling the sound of Edward's lust.

'Mum — mum, what's the matter?' The shock of the voice penetrated his brain. He glanced behind. Frederick stood framed in the doorway, and Edward's mind struggled to regain some semblance of reason. He'd forgotten about the boy.

Small hands clutched at him, pulling at his robe. 'Get off my mum, get off her. Mum, what's he doing to you? Get off — leave her alone. She's crying. You've hurt her, made her cry.' Frederick was screaming at him.

Edward withdrew from her and lurched backwards, hiding his extended body with his robe from the boy, but reluctant to leave.

Ruth covered herself and sat bowed on the edge of the bed.

'Are you all right, Mum?' asked Frederick trying to look into her face, then glancing at Edward fearfully.

'Yes, yes, I'm all right Frederick. Uncle Edward and I were just having a little quarrel,' she gasped. 'Go back to bed. I'm all right. Go on Frederick — go back.'

Frederick then backed away past Edward, his young face a jigsaw of swiftly rising expressions — doubt and alarm uppermost.

'Go to bed, Frederick,' urged Ruth again broken-voiced. 'Shut the door.'

Frederick closed the door slowly, reluctantly, the eyes looking at Edward accusingly through the narrowing gap still holding the shock of his discovery.

Edward stared into the near darkness seeing dimly Ruth's figure still huddled on the edge of the bed. What was he doing there? If only it could be a dream and the act not a reality. He heard her shuddering sigh before she spoke. 'You could have done that with any tramp in St. Peter Port,' and the words uttered in a monotone surprised and sickened him to the soul. The cold isolation they had put between she and himself was total. He stood there, his desire expended, and a chill coming over him, wanting to flee the room but held a prisoner of his own accord.

Ruth's voice came again, detached in the night surrounding them, its tone matter of fact, awful to hear. 'Now Edward, say you love me.'

'Oh, I'm sorry. Oh Ruth,' he struggled. It was all wrong — all gone wrong. 'I didn't mean — it was just that . . . '

'You wanted a woman and I was handy,' Ruth supplied for him.

Edward shook his head in the dark. 'No, not like that — it wasn't,' but he knew it had been. A glimpse of her flesh and he had lost his reason. He saw Ruth's outline against the window as she stood up.

'Then tell me you love me now.' The words were said dispassionately. She could have been asking him the time.

Edward's lips were prepared but the words would not come. He thought the world of her, and he knew that if she had asked him during his lust he would have lied very easily. But not now, and frantically he sought for some soft blandishment, some endearment as substitute.

'You can't can you? You cannot say you love me — you never have. I didn't have to ask did I? You never could and you never will.' It was as if she were telling herself something she already knew.

Edward heard the acceptance and its finality miserably; also the accumulated hurts imbued in her utterance. She would never forgive him for reopening those wounds of humiliating rejection. He heard her draw breath deeply, but her voice was a whisper. 'In that case you have no right here in my bedroom. Get out, and I want you to leave my house in the morning. It will be better for both of us.'

He was being dismissed just as he had dismissed her on numerous occasions. He was sorry, desperately so. Wanted to tell her but it wouldn't alter anything, not at that moment. Looking back he saw that she had her back turned to him. He had gone into her bedroom like a bull; he was leaving it like a mouse. Closing the door he returned bowed to his room, seeing the tea stood cold that he had been making when Ruth had come to the kitchen door. If only, as with a film, he could wind back his actions of the last half hour.

Edward's bed was not comfort to him — his mind a corridor of rushing whirlwind thoughts. Cursing himself for his behaviour in forcing himself upon her. What had possessed him? His mind had ceased to function. If only he could have restrained himself. After all he had decided to leave as soon as he could afford to live elsewhere. Just once a feeble excuse disturbed his self-recrimination. The flimsy nightdress and the glimpse of her had triggered his desire. A few minutes more and he would have been on his way back to his room with the tea. But he had behaved like a lout and a bully, and now he had to leave.

A flame of anger against her rose and died quickly. Why did she always have to insist on his loving her? He was extremely fond of her and could think of no one else he was fonder of. But it wasn't enough for Ruth. Perhaps he wasn't capable of what she called love. Even with Elaine he realised it had been a treacherous infatuation — he had mistaken it for love. He hit his pillow savagely. Why for once had he not lied to her, told her what she had wanted to hear? Say he loved her. She would have been overjoyed. After all in his faltering way he did. What a fool he'd been! Instead of being thrown out of her bed he could have been in it with her now. All would have been well for the sake of a few words — a few bloody words. And both would have been happy. God! Why had he got to be so strait-laced and honest about the fact that he didn't love her like she thought he should? The peculiar thing was that he had in effect just raped her, but it didn't seem to matter as much to her as the fact that he had been unable to say what she wanted to hear. He sighed with a desperate bitterness. William would have handled the situation better. He would have known what to do, would have lied without so much as blinking. Oh yes, William would have had no problem at all.

Edward's face burned in the darkness. In front of his son! How much had he seen and heard? His attempt to pull him away from Ruth. Edward felt that in a flash the friendship that had arisen between himself and Frederick had gone. The frightened shocked eyes had held nothing of it. He laughed savagely, tormentedly. A high price to pay for the transitory fleeting pleasure that he hardly remembered now, and nor had Ruth need to worry about conception again — ejaculation had been denied him by Frederick's intervention. He should never have gone to stay at Ruth's — it had been bound to happen sooner or later. Where could he go now that she had asked him to leave? The small family which had been his such a short time was now broken — he was alone again.

He fell into a fitful sleep in the later hours, to awaken tired and heavily depressed at the return of the night's memories.

15

Edward got through the following day with an effort, finding it difficult to concentrate on anything, and aware once more of the difference in his situation compared with his brother William's, and was glad that their paths did not cross that day. He had risen early and left the house without seeing Ruth and Frederick. Could not have faced them just then after what happened. Once whilst sweeping one of the terraces he leaned tired and despairing on his brush, and as usual his eyes fell on the ruins across the bay. A voice screamed in him, 'Sell — you fool — don't be crazy. Look at you — penniless and down and out. Put it on the market. Learn from William. Get the money and start elsewhere. Buy something that is already a going concern. Forget the rubbish about it being thc family house — get rid of it. If not the place will keep you poor. Do you want to work as a lackey for your brother for years to come?' It was with a new inner relief that he set about the remainder of the terrace.

That night Edward spent at the Ormer for the first time since leaving in nineteen hundred and forty, amid the dirt, the memories and with the wind blowing through its broken roof. Upstairs in the darkness in what had been a guest room overlooking the bay. From where he sat the deep dark blue with its pinpoints of stars joined the shattered edges of the roof. He heard music wafted on the breeze from

The Two Bays Hotel, and once stood at the cracked windows staring out on to the myriad of coloured lights stretching along the headland opposite — like a liner stranded out of the water. The place vibrant with life, money, love, laughter and between it and him the dim fine ribbon of gentle surf.

Later huddled in his coat he ate some sandwiches which he had purchased at the staff canteen, and drank lemonade from a bottle — lemonade at three in the morning did not have very much appeal. Cold water still ran from the kitchen tap but there was no means of making a warm drink. Unable to sleep he spent the time thinking about which firm he would engage to sell the property and how much he was likely to get for it. Then he must throw away the chains of his ambition and be free to enjoy himself. He had to admit that nothing but trouble had dogged that ambition since it had first taken root in his mind. Wondered if Ruth knew he was down in the old house. Perhaps she didn't care now — just glad to get rid of him.

It was summer and the dawn came early and he was glad. A new day and a new start. He would set the wheels in motion to bring about the sale. Meanwhile if he was going to spend some time in the ruin he must make his existence there as comfortable as possible. He could have a meal in the canteen at work and buy something to see him through the night. There was also one special purchase that he made — a small camping stove on which he could boil water for a hot drink and for shaving. And that night the dim glow from the stove placed in the kitchen and the bubbling water upon it served to raise Edward's spirits.

That week found him busy clearing up the debris of years from the downstairs rooms. If he was going to sell he must make the place look as presentable as possible. He and Frederick had made a start in the kitchen, and he sighed with deep regret at the thought that no doubt they would never get together again in their former happy relationship.

By evening what had once been the family room — the one where he had found the squatters — was beginning to look cleaner and smell better. The floor was visible and damp from the water he had brushed upon it. Old peeled paper from the walls and any other rubbish that would burn he threw into the fireplace. Then setting it alight he made himself a cup of tea and watched the flames leaping up the fire back for the first time in many long years. As he sipped and gazed at them something flared no less strongly inside him in response. In the cool and dusk of the evening the flames spread a welcoming warmth around him, and the lengthening shadows hid the harsh realities of the state of the room. This was his house, his fire, and the tea he was drinking had been made there. From that moment the house was imbued with life again — a reawakening after its nightmare slumbers. Later Edward stepped outside and walked around the building, oblivious to the ruin it actually was, seeing only the glow of the lessening fire through the ground windows. Damned if he would sell the old house. He could live there, clear and do it up as and when he could. Little by little it would take shape into what he had envisaged in his dreams. It would never be the large modern glittering palace that William's hotel was. That would be impossible, but it would be equally as good and successful, he was certain; comfortable, elegant and high class. It would take time, which he had; he was still youngish. Selling the place would be a mistake, and he may not be as well off as he had thought because according to the will he would have to pay William half of the proceeds from the sale. He guessed William did not need the money but he was sure that his brother would claim it as soon as he found out that their old home had been sold. It was therefore with a new optimistic eagerness that Edward returned after work to the old building, working late into the night until he fell asleep tired out with his endeavours to shorten the long task that would eventually result in the first guest coming through the doors of the new Ormer Hotel.

Over the next fortnight he concentrated on the kitchen and the old family living room, managing to replace the broken windows. Now there were two places in the house which were sound, and a barrier against the harsher weather to come. He also had locks fitted to the inside doors as it was still possible for anyone to gain entry elsewhere into the house. As the work progressed he would spread outwards, thinking of it as a military operation — his bridgehead established — a foothold gained and reclaiming more of the building.

There was no electricity so he used candles, and for the colder weather he made his largest purchase — a paraffin stove for extra heating. Driftwood he found quite often, but it could be difficult to light and reluctant to burn when wet. He was also aware that when the authorities knew he was living there they would want payment of some kind. The roof, or lack of most of it, was Edward's biggest worry. The winter storms to come would no doubt weaken and rot the remaining structure further, and was now the next major work to be tackled. Further interior decorating could wait. Any money he had now went on making the part that he occupied as near waterproof and comfortable as possible.

The following weekend he visited the boatyards in St. Peter Port, and in one he found what he wanted — a large tarpaulin that had been used as a yacht cover. It was torn in places but he could repair it, and obtained at a reasonable price, and for the cost of the petrol was delivered to his door plus an old but serviceable ladder which they threw in for what Edward thought was a generous figure. He made a vow on their premises there and then that if and when he bought a boat, then they would get the business. He smiled grimly to himself, not being able to afford an oar, never mind a yacht. Nevertheless the fact that he had now two further items which were to be used for the improvement of his home cheered him considerably.

Saturday evening found him up the ladder in one of the bedrooms trying to cover the joists with the tarpaulin, the latter being difficult and heavy to handle, but he did manage to get part of it to cover some of the gap in the roof. He leaned against the ladder for a moment, thinking that perhaps he would leave it at that and do the remainder the next day; it was a start at least. Through the opening he could see people on the beach, hear the occasional voice and the insistent murmur and movement of the sea. The tide was coming in, and a couple of yachts were still anchored offshore, lights showing on one in the dusk.

A voice came, but not from the beach — from inside. 'Uncle Edward.'

Edward turned on the ladder and looked down into the face of Frederick upturned to him.

'Frederick!' he exclaimed in joyful astonishment. 'What are you doing here?' Then he realised what a silly thing it was to say. Why shouldn't he be there? Frederick was his son. But after the other night he had not expected to see him again. 'I mean — I — just didn't expect you, thought you might have been busy with — er — homework.' To cover his embarrassment he prodded at his handiwork and then descended the ladder. But there was no such emotion on the youngster's features — only a keen-eyed inquisitiveness as he glanced up and around, his fresh face and fair hair contrasting with the dark blue of his guernsey. A boy on the verge of becoming a youth. 'Well, this is a pleasant surprise — good to see you, Frederick.' So he hadn't lost his son after all. He was here in the old Ormer.

Frederick pushed a large parcel at him. 'Mum sends these. I've brought them for you — she thought you might need them.'

Happy relief filled Edward. Neither had Ruth deserted him, she wasn't that sort — she'd forgiven him, enough to think of him anyway.

'Blankets and things,' stated his young companion, then gazed upwards. 'Do you want a hand to cover the other hole, Uncle Edward? If I help it won't take long,' he added with the optimistic enthusiasm of his age.

'That's kind of you Frederick but I'm going to pack up now. It's getting a bit dark. Probably put the remainder on tomorrow.'

'All right, I'll come down tomorrow,' said Frederick looking about him. 'It's the first time I've been in here. Mum always told me to keep away when it was empty.'

'There isn't much to see, Frederick, I'm afraid. There's such a lot to do before it's all finished,' Edward said as they went downstairs. There he took Frederick on a brief tour of the lower house in the gathering gloom, then they sat side by side on a packing case which Edward had found on the beach and now used as a chair-cum-table. Briefly he told Frederick of how the Germans had used the house as a look-out post and that there had been a gun emplacement at the front. The firelight reflected the excitement in the young eyes.

'This is much better than being at home. Why don't we all live here together? If we all helped we'd get it finished quicker,' but then his face dulled. 'I suppose you had to come to live here after you quarrelled with Mum.'

To which Edward was at a loss for what to say immediately. 'Well you see Frederick, this is really my home and I've always wanted to repair it and — er — your Mother was very kind and allowed me to stay until I felt I was ready to start. Of course we like each other very much, your mother and I, but . . . '

'She doesn't like you enough for you to stay in her room,' helped Frederick with a straightforward logic.

Edward was thankful for the suggestion. It sewed up the problem neatly as an explanation of why they had really quarrelled. 'Yes, that's exactly it, Frederick, but of course we're still friends.' Suddenly he experienced a further rush of embarrassment talking about Ruth. After all Frederick had witnessed him carrying out what amounted to a rape. Bending, he delved into the plastic bag in which Frederick had brought the blankets, along with tins of beans, spaghetti and meat, sugar, tea and coffee. 'You must thank Ruth — your mother' he couldn't get out of the habit of calling her that — 'for this. It's very thoughtful and kind of her, and thank her very much for me. I'm sure I'm going to manage a lot better now.' He really felt he would.

And the firelight lowered along the walls as they sat there, just as it had when as a boy he had spent many hours in that same room with his parents.

'I hope your mother isn't getting anxious about your staying down here,' he said. The last thing he wanted to do was to upset Ruth again.

The golden head turned to him. 'Oh no, she won't be,' he uttered confidently.

'Well, perhaps it's time for you to go back now, then no doubt she'll allow you to come again some time.'

Frederick saw the logic of that argument quickly enough. 'Yes, all right, and then I'll be able to come tomorrow, and we can put the roof on again.'

Edward stood at the end of the drive and watched him disappear up the lane. Afterwards he thought how simple his son made the continuing restoration of the house appear. And that night Edward lay in his blankets watching the last of the embers dying out. Life wasn't so bad after all. The visit of Frederick and the gifts from Ruth had once more strengthened his will to carry on.

The following week he saw Ruth several times at The Two Bays Hotel, never near enough to speak, but he was glad when she waved to him. He wondered if she would ever pay him a visit at his new home. The fact that she still worked for William continued to irritate him. His brother was now no doubt rich enough to settle an amount of money on her to enable her to live without going out to work. But then Edward realised that he himself would view that act with suspicion. The fact was that he felt a degree of jealousy nowadays regarding Ruth which was, he had to admit, rather strange considering the attitude he had adopted towards her earlier in their lives.

One person however became a constant visitor — resident almost of the Ormer — Frederick. Intent it appeared on bringing the old place back to life in a very short time. After tea consumed at an astonishing speed at Ruth's he then laboured, carried, and splashed paint, hammered this and that, and appeared to enjoy himself immensely. The whole of his school knew that he was actively engaged in the rebuilding of a hotel at Moulin Huet, with the help of a person known as his Uncle Edward.

A few days later and the tarpaulin covered the main hole in the roof, the ends tied to the remaining roof supports on either side. How it would last in the bad weather to come Edward couldn't tell. What he really needed was wood — good stout lengths of wood — and slates to renew the roof properly. But the price of that amount of wood was beyond his pocket. Perhaps some time he would come across some good secondhand timber and slates from a demolition firm. In the meantime he had to hope for the best, but at least now the rain would not pour in. Later in the worst months when he could not do anything externally he would be able to start clearing some of the other rooms. Until then he would concentrate on the outside, particularly the jungle of weeds and rubbish that had once been the tea garden. It had been on a terrace slightly raised from the drive area, the latter not quite so overgrown. This was because as Edward had discovered, a large part of the drive had been concreted and squared off, and used as a miniature parade and drill ground by the enemy forces occupying the house and surrounds during the war.

It was hard work, the years of neglect allowing nature to obtain a stronghold, and recent rain made sure that very soon both Edward and Frederick were wet to their knees. The young man had come armed with a rake and a pair of shears, but Edward did not dare ask from where he had obtained them. Near the rear of the terrace they found one of the original tables with its well rusted iron legs. The next object which they came across evoked even more memories for Edward — a rowing boat, its overlapping planks rotten in places, missing in others. They turned it over. The rowlocks were still in place and the ring at its stem head. The old family boat — *Seagull!* After all those years! The Germans must have brought it up from the beach and forgotten about it and over the years it had become hidden. It had been called *Seagull* because it bobbed up and down on the waves like one.

Frederick's face was flushed with the excitement of the discovery. 'D'you think it will float, Uncle Edward?'

'No, I don't think so, too far gone — it needs some new planks.'

'Is it yours?' Frederick gazed up at him from the one remaining thwart.

'It is now, but it used to belong to my father. He used to take us fishing and swimming from it. Sometimes we went to the other side of the bay and picnicked over there.'

'Gosh, I wish I had one,' and then he looked up from fingering the old wood. 'Where is your dad now, Uncle Edward?'

'I'm afraid he and my mother died quite a long time ago.'

'Oh.' Frederick's expression became solemn and wistful. 'I don't have a dad. I wish I had, then perhaps he'd take me fishing and picnics in a boat.'

'You have one. Didn't your mother ever say anything about him?' Edward was curious to know what Ruth had told Frederick.

'She just said that he was in England somewhere, and once I think she said he might be dead. Anyway he couldn't have bothered much about mum and me, just leaving us.'

Edward looked at his son and an emotion that he could not control engulfed him, and neither could he have stemmed his words even if he had wished to do so. 'Yes, you do have a dad — I've seen him today,' and he watched the young face in rising joyful anticipation.

Frederick stared up at him wide-eyed, body rigid suddenly. 'Where? In town?'

'No, he came here this morning.' Edward was savouring the expressions coursing swiftly across Frederick's face.

'Here? Before I got here?' The words shot out.

Edward nodded, not trusting himself to speak and wanting that particular conversation to go on for ever.

'Well, where is he now? Why didn't he stay and see me?'

'He did,' and Edward nodded at the house. 'He'll be in there in a minute or two.'

Frederick's body sagged. 'Oh, you're just kidding. I thought you meant it,' and the young face turned away sadly, his fingers plucking at the rotten wood on the boat's gunwale.

Edward patted him on the shoulder and stood up, his excitement almost too much to bear. 'I'll go and fetch him. You're going to be surprised.' Suddenly he had an idea. 'No, wait until I call then come to the kitchen door; he'll be there.'

Frederick shook his head. 'No, you're still joking Uncle Edward. Let's mend the boat then we can take it across the bay, see how it goes.'

Edward started towards the house. 'You never

know, perhaps your father will take you.'

'Well why hasn't he come out to see me now? He must have seen me. Doesn't he like me?' Frederick's tone was impatient and cross, disappointed. His uncle was taking the joke too far. 'Come on, let's mend the boat then we can do the garden afterwards.'

'You wait until I call,' said Edward as he disappeared inside, leaving Frederick standing morosely, hands in pockets, staring after him.

Edward stood by the table in the kitchen facing the door, his heart thudding away. Suppose he was doing wrong? What would Ruth say? But what wrong could he be doing? The boy had a right to know — to know that he had a father alive and caring for him. He took a deep breath and shouted, 'All right Frederick, he's here.' Suddenly it was serious. Heard the young eager footsteps. The box had been opened. Would it contain happiness? Too late now. Frederick stood in the doorway. 'Here he is just as I promised,' and he smiled in some apprehension.

Frederick gazed blankly at him. 'Where?'

Edward tapped himself on the chest almost in time with his heart. 'Here,' and he saw the dreadful disappointment on the face opposite.

'Told you you were joking, Uncle Edward. I knew my dad wouldn't be here.'

Edward leaned forward enthusiastically but rather hurt at the look which Frederick had given him. 'But he is — I'm your father.' His hand rested on Frederick's shoulder.

'But you can't be. You're my Uncle Edward; mum

said so.' His regard of Edward told the latter that he was going along with the joke but that he didn't think much of it.

'Your mother told you that because one day long ago we didn't agree on something and she became very angry and said that from then on that's what she would tell you to call me.' It sounded stupid but it was the best he could think of at short notice.

Doubt and bewilderment expressed themselves strongly on the boy's face. He glanced around the kitchen as if seeking help with his problem, then regarded Edward directly again. 'Why have you been away so long? You could have stayed with us.'

'Well you see Frederick, when you were young I had to go away to work — out of Guernsey. I was gone a few years. Your mother followed but wasn't happy so brought you back here to live with her. She thought it better to return here where her home was, and of course where she knew people.'

The gaze on him was unwavering. 'And where did mum have me?'

'In a town called Daleford in England.'

The fair head gave the slightest of nods. 'And when you came back she sort of still didn't like you enough for you to live with her always?'

'Yes, I suppose that was it, Frederick.' It wasn't as easy as he had expected it to be, and unprepared for the boy's questions. He should have realised that his statement wouldn't be accepted immediately. Some day he would explain about everything to him.

'She didn't like you very much the other day,' said Frederick, adding, 'She was mad with you wasn't she?'

Edward well remembered the embarrassing situation very clearly, and so obviously had his son, although this was the first time it had been mentioned between them since.

'I was sorry about that, but adults do have quarrels, Frederick, I'm afraid.'

There was a slight but growing light of concurrence in the young eyes. 'I think mum likes you a lot better now. She lets me come to help and sent those things for you,' he said with a strong logic.

'I'm very glad. It was very kind of her.'

'Some day she may ask you to come and live with us again,' Frederick suggested hopefully and optimistically.

'Yes, that would be nice, but it is more convenient here, Frederick, because I'm busy in my spare time getting this place ready. If I was at your house I should have to keep coming and going — I'd be wasting time.' He watched the young face considering.

'Maybe then, mum could come to live here and then we could all help. That would be great wouldn't it?' he enthused.

'I suppose it would, yes,' and Edward knew he would have to be careful about what he said, 'but I think your mother likes being in her own house. This is not very comfortable and nowhere is very clean yet.'

'Perhaps she wouldn't like it just now,' Frederick agreed, 'but we could ask her when we've done a bit more to it.'

'Might take a while yet,' and Edward smiled wryly

at Frederick's youthful disregard of the obstacles involved. A few years more likely at the rate the work was progressing. He became aware of the frowning stare, of the doubt and yet the joy waiting to be unleashed in the youngster's face.

'Are you sure that you're my Dad, Uncle Edward?'

Edward chuckled at his double title. It must be difficult for Frederick to comprehend. 'Yes, I'm positive.'

'Gosh!' exclaimed his son. 'Look — I'm going home now, going to ask mum — she'll know. I'll come back to help later.'

Through the open door Edward watched him dashing away to be lost to sight up the lane. What would Ruth say? Did it matter? He had a son, and soon Frederick would have confirmation that he had a father after all. A new excitement was building up in him. He had made a beginning on the house, and now a new beginning was being made with a family of his own — for the second time.

That night he thought long about the other member of his family — Maxime, his daughter by Elaine. What would she be like now? Was she still at Scarton Manor? She would he guessed be about two years younger than Frederick. Once he got settled and on to his feet he would seek her out and introduce himself before it was too late. He had nearly lost Frederick, so he must do all he could not to let that happen in the case of Maxime. Yes, he would get to know his daughter and she him. They would have so much to talk about. A terrible doubt struck him. Elaine had taunted him, saying that

Maxime wasn't his. She couldn't be William's! She mustn't be. No! She was his. Edward rose from his makeshift bed, hating William. Made himself a drink while the rain beat against the window and dripped steadily into the other parts of the house. Rather it be from a stranger, one of the other lovers she had gone with, if it had to be that way. William had been only one of them. And yet, had he not thought he had seen himself in the tiny face?

By the time daylight came he had convinced himself that Maxime was his. Perhaps she could come and stay at the Ormer Hotel when it was finished. A cynical voice inside him put a stop to such exhilarating thoughts. When would he be in a position to say it was finished? Five — ten — twenty years? Even if he went to court in order to obtain custody of Maxime, he wouldn't stand a chance in his present circumstances. But if he sold the building and land, and approached the problem of Maxime in a more affluent state, then he may have some success. Edward looked out through the driving rain. When the Spring came round he would decide once and for all. In the meantime he must work and enjoy the blessings that had been put within his reach. Frederick was one of them. Since the day when he had told the boy that he was his father, Frederick's attitude had altered towards him. During the first few days afterwards he had shown a shyness — a respect — even awe — that had not been evident in their previous easy-going relationship. For Edward, his son's use of the term 'Dad' was a thrill and satisfaction each and every time he heard it. In strident tone calling from somewhere in the house, or confidentially and quieter in close conversation. And as for Frederick it was a title which he appeared to enjoy saying morning, noon and night.

It was nearly Winter again, and the holiday makers had gone, the beach was empty, the sand undisturbed between the rocks. Only the constant washing of the latter by the tides remained the same. And the gales that blew only served to remind Edward of how much remained to be done to the broken building he lived in. Wood was needed — lots of it, and slates to repair the roof properly, the makeshift repair with the tarpaulin having been torn to pieces after one month. He continued to work at The Two Bays Hotel for William. That place also had quietened but conferences were held there quite frequently by business people from overseas which kept the place ticking over. Its restaurant had also procured a good name for food and was frequented by many island residents. Edward had to admit, albeit grudgingly, that William had made a great success. But a bitterness held him often when he sat in his one room and the wind howled through the remainder of the structure.

It was on such a night early on that he was greatly surprised by a visit from Ruth. He was sat listening to the radio, seeking to give his mind a rest from his problems when she arrived. She stood just inside his door a moment, regarding him from under the hood of her winter coat, drops of water clinging to its edges. Then she pushed it back from her face, her fair hair looking halo-like in the yellow light of a paraffin lamp.

'The outer door was open — I came in. I didn't think you could hear me,' she explained.

'How nice to see you Ruth,' but he felt awkward as he took her coat. It was the first time they had spoken together since their quarrel and she asked him to leave her house. He brought the only real chair he had up to the fire for her and smiled down. 'It's a long time since you were in here, Ruth.' He knew exactly when it had been and so did she.

'That day we left in a hurry — I remember popping in to the kitchen — you and William were upstairs grabbing anything you could. The vicar coming and the planes in the harbour.' Her face had tautened at the memory and she glanced at him. 'Sorry Edward, I didn't mean to . . .'

'It's all right, I've got over it — a terrible day but a long time ago now. Have you eaten Ruth? I have some food in the house.'

She nodded. 'I have thanks, but a cup of tea would be nice.'

'I was hoping you'd say that. I can manage that better than food,' he smiled in mock relief.

Later as he poured the tea he remembered the last time he had made one in her presence, shortly afterwards he had gone uninvited into her bedroom. Remembered what he had done, and his pulse quickened. Wondered why she had come. He sat down on the packing case on the other side of the fireplace, pleased to see her under his roof — very pleased. She looked lovely, the damp curls clinging to the sides of her forehead, the soft light masking the lines of life. A woman to grace any man's house — a real brick, he thought. Aloud he said, 'And how's the young man? In bed?'

Ruth's eyes warmed. 'Not quite. He wanted to come but I said no. He was doing his homework. I told him to go to bed when he'd finished.' She smiled adding, 'He'd live here if he could. He loves coming down.'

Edward nodded. 'I know, but he's a spirited little fellow — not so little now, a young man nearly. They don't seem to stay children very long nowadays.' He paused, wondering what the real purpose of her visit was, then he said, 'I hope you didn't mind me telling him I was his father. I just couldn't help it, I felt so sorry for him. Everyone at school had one except Frederick.'

'No, I didn't mind — I couldn't hide the fact for ever. I was wrong to try, and anyway it is the truth — you are his father. He was so excited — couldn't sleep that night, thinks you're marvellous.'

'I suppose that will wear off when he's seen more of me,' smiled Edward.

She looked at him across the fire with those frank eyes. In them was the same light he had seen so many times in her life before. The light that had been there on the beach when they were children, the same when he had covered her body in protection and during their school years — always — it never wavered. God! He didn't deserve that calibre of loyalty. But she did.

He heard himself saying, 'Sorry about the last time, Ruth, at your place. Couldn't help myself — you looked so damned attractive. I had no right to force myself upon you — and what Frederick must have thought!' He covered his eyes in an agony of memory, so missing Ruth's expression.

'He hasn't mentioned it since. He was very upset at the time, but children are very resilient. I explained as best I could. He seems to have forgotten about it.' She put out her hand in a tender sympathetic motion and in little more than a whisper said, 'You could do that every night my Edward if . . . ' then hesitated, 'if you thought enough of me to . . . ' Her voice trailed off.

But he knew what she meant. Having been hurt and repulsed so many times that she dare hardly utter the words regarding marriage. And she was prepared to humiliate herself again.

Edward stood up slowly, wanting her, his body rising. Bent over her, pushed her head back and crushed her mouth with his, feeling the swell of her breasts under his hand. His eyes strayed to the bed in the corner, but through his fingers he felt her reluctance to move from the chair. With a great effort he straightened and withdrew his lips, knowing that if he persisted the same thing would occur as before — another quarrel if he forced himself on her. He was drawn to her physically now, but was it enough? He kissed her on the forehead and sat down again looking into the fire, feeling rather embarrassed at his show of passion. 'I do think a lot of you, Ruth, have done for a long time now.'

Ruth regarded him lovingly, grasped his thumb with her hand — an action he knew well. 'We could be happy — I could make you happy — we can try.'

'It's whether I could make you happy that matters, Ruth,' and he was surprised at what he found himself saying.

'Let's try, Edward, please.' Her voice was longing, pleading.

Perhaps he did love her and didn't know it, or was the desire just to hold her on his bed the extent of his feelings for her? Could he ever feel more for her? Was he capable?

Ruth took his silence for disinterest, letting go of his hand and leaning back in her chair, then she sighed deeply, bringing her hands together in her lap and giving an almost imperceptible nod of her head as if a decision had been made.

'I saw William today,' she said quickly.

Edward was mildly surprised at her sudden change of topic.

'I mean — I had a talk with him.'

'Oh, is he all right?' he said offhandedly. Why should he care?

'Yes.' She was regarding him in a peculiar way. 'He's having a house built in Albecq — should be ready for next Spring.'

This time Edward was very surprised. 'For himself?'

Her expression still puzzled him. 'Yes — at the present.'

A stroke of envy pierced Edward. William must be doing very well. Albecq was on the west coast, rocky, residential and near Vazon. But what did she mean — at the present? 'Have you seen it?'

'Yes, he took me to see it. Very modern — lovely views. It will be very beautiful when it's finished.'

Edward was perplexed and irritated. 'Did he have to take you to see it?' Why couldn't William get on with his own life? There was no need to bring Ruth into the matter.

His companion focused an unwavering gaze upon him and the combined light from the fire and lamp revealed a sadness. 'Because he's asked me to go and live there when it's finished.'

Edward got to his feet, shocked, enraged. 'The hell he has — the cheek of the sod. What's he think you are? You're not going — you told him where to get off I should hope. The nerve of the man. God! How could he? He just thinks he can have anything.'

But Ruth just sat still waiting until he had finished, then she said very deliberately and quietly, 'He's asked me to marry him.'

Edward stood looking down on her, mouth working — no words coming, and shaking his head. At last they came. 'Can't mean it, he doesn't love you . . . ' His mind was stunned at her statement.

'Do you?' Ruth asked simply.

'That's not the point — I . . . '

'Oh but it is, Edward,' she interrupted. 'If you don't love me — don't want me, you've no right at all to say who shall have me.'

'Have you given him your answer?' he asked fiercely.

Ruth stood up, avoiding his eyes. 'No — not yet.'

'There you are then — you don't want to marry him — you don't love him.'

Ruth suddenly took his hands — hands which did not return the passion with which she grasped his. 'I came here first to see you. I'm a fool I know where you're concerned. I came to ask you for the last time tonight — the very last time.' Bent forward to look up into his face closely, beseechingly. 'Let's marry — you and I Edward.'

He was angry and at once jealous. In the past he had not wanted to marry Ruth, but it was clear to him now that he did not want anyone else to do so. This sudden attack of hers — this new attempt forcing him to make a decision had thrown his selfish and insular little world into confusion. 'But Ruth, I can't offer you a proper home, you know that. This is how I live. You wouldn't want to live like this.' He struggled to come to terms with her proposal.

'There's my house,' she said eagerly, fervently. 'Move into mine — sell this. We could even sell mine, and buy whatever you wanted then.'

The challenge had been thrown down — the sole purpose of her visit. He might have known — Ruth had never given up, but he realised that this was the end. William waited in the wings.

Ruth allowed him a few seconds of thought, then caught him completely off guard with the vehemence of her outburst. 'All right, Edward, stay in your leaking pigsty. I'll marry William,' she flung at him. 'At least he cares enough to ask me, he wants to marry me. And you'll lose Frederick. William will not allow him to come here like he has been doing. Am I so ugly? Anyway, I'm not going to humiliate myself again. You can go to hell. I've wasted a lot of my life thinking that some day . . . But you don't care, it just isn't there. You're too bloody obsessed with this building. Well I'm not competing any more. Stay here until you're a hundred if you wish and rot.'

Edward watched in a terrible dismay as she grabbed her coat and flung open the door, heard the outer one bang to and then he was alone again. He sank on to the bed — anger, hurt and jealousy exploding in his head. Some time later he was able to think again calmly and logically. Ruth had every right to marry whom she chose. Just because he had not wished to marry her did not mean that he should prevent her from marrying someone else. But then the devil popped up in his mind again. She was doing it to spite him, throwing in her lot with William. If it had not been William, perhaps he would not have minded so much, but he could not forget the former's affair with Elaine, nor his brother's attempt to get the family house sold against his, Edward's wishes whilst he had been in prison. William would have everything and his new home sounded wonderful.

He looked around his room in despair. Perhaps William and also Ruth were right as far as the property was concerned. And if Ruth did marry William it was possible that he would not see a lot of Frederick. Gradually the boy's interest and enthusiasm would be channelled elsewhere, and he, Edward, would become the distant figure again of an uncle. And William in bed with Ruth. The thought cut like a knife through him.

16

Winter came with its biting winds and driving rain, and the water poured in through the exposed roof, and Edward began to think very seriously about how long he would be able to continue to live there.

One night in January a gale blew up and the seas pounded into the bay and along the coast. Before midnight he heard a ship's hooter several times and not having yet retired to bed, he threw on his heavy coat, grabbed a hat and went out. There was nothing to be seen in the bay, but then a flare lit up the sky over the small headland behind the house. The hooter sounded again, coming from the same direction. Edward battled to reach a point where he could look out to sea from the higher ground, and in the blackness towards Saints Bay several lights moved up and down sharply to his right, and another flare rose into the storm. He glimpsed a shape — a ship in distress off the rocks. He shivered partly from the cold and partly from knowing the terrible danger the crew were in. He wondered if the St. Peter Port lifeboat had been alerted, but he couldn't see them being able to do much on a night like that, doubting that they would be able to reach the stricken vessel. He had no phone, nor had Ruth, but surely someone else had seen the flares, and perhaps the crew had managed to get a message out already. The poor souls — they were so near and yet so far. Regaining the shelter of his home — such as it was — he felt thankful. His position was nothing compared to the perilous one of those being flung about near the rocks out there.

When the dawn came Edward was back on the headland. The wind, although still strong, had subsided from the gale force it had been. Waves still beat and broke into sheets of spray rising far enough to wet his face. The ship lay on its side about a hundred yards out amongst the rocks, but it was what surrounded the vessel and littered the rocks that astonished him. Wood! Turning the scene into a pale moving platform — a mass of planks. Caught between the rocks and even halfway up the cliff where they had been flung by the force of the storm. The cargo had been wood and now it was floating free everywhere. There was no sign of human movement near the vessel that Edward could see, and no other craft in sight. Perhaps a rescue had been effected during the night, but he doubted it — no one could have survived that.

There it was. Wood, tons of it — all he needed for the roof and floors of the Ormer. Just for a moment he thought of the price that must have been paid. How many lives to bring it within his reach? He had no idea. It would be in the paper, but he prayed that none had perished. It wasn't his fault, but the offering would be received gratefully. But how to get the wood home? At low tide he might be able to drag some around over the rocks. It was also possible at the next high tide that it would wash some into Moulin Huet, the wreck itself being nearer to the latter than it was to Saints Bay.

All the next day at work he was on tenterhooks

wishing for the time when he could get away to claim some of the wreck's cargo. No doubt a lot of people would visit to gaze on the scene, and maybe gather some. But he was fortunate in being on the spot. If some of the wood was washed into Moulin Huet it would be much easier for him to reach. The tide was out and it was dark when Edward arrived on the beach that evening. It was still blowing, a fitful moon giving seconds of light showing isolated pieces of wood along the foreshore. But there were larger piles nearer the water's edge, and also against the rocks at the base of the low cliffs of the headland. For the next two hours he laboured dragging pieces up the steps from the beach to the back of the house, where it could not be seen so readily. It was tiring work but when he had finished he went to bed in some excitement and satisfaction. Another step in the rebuilding of the Ormer Hotel.

On his next day off he spent a lot of time following the tide out and seeing for the first time the large quantity of wood which had been washed up. The wreck of the ship attracted a lot of people that weekend to Saints and Moulin Huet Bays, so he made a note of the whereabouts of several piles amongst which were suitable lengths and widths of wood. He would return later when the people had gone and before the tide turned. Later he read the newspaper reports about the foundering of the coaster during the storm. It had been bound for a northern French port and had been swept on to the rocks on the island's south coast. Distress signals had been received and the Guernsey lifeboat had put out, but had been unable to get near enough to effect a rescue owing to the high seas and the proximity of the rocks. A helicopter had then been brought in and had winched two crew members to safety, but others were missing.

It was getting dusk when he returned to the beach again, and alone as far as he could see. He must hurry because the tide would be on the turn and he wanted to obtain as much wood as possible before it covered everything again. Making his way towards a certain pile that he had seen earlier, he came upon a pool left by the tide and enclosed by rocks. It contained wood, one fine flat piece in particular looking just right for the making of a new door. Although he wanted some for the roof first he couldn't resist clambering over the rocks and hooking his fingers under it and raising an end. The eyes in the purple face looked up into his from the water, the hair in a floating fringe! A cry of fear and horror jerked from Edward as he let the wood go and stumbled away. Within a few yards his mind had steadied. The body must be that of one of the crew from the ship — washed ashore. What should he do? Go and find help and report it? By the time he did that it would be nearly dark and the tide well up. And the police — they would question him — perhaps up at the house. They may see the wood that he had already collected. He decided that he would let the body stay where it was. Within an hour the tide would refloat wood and body together. There was nothing he could do — the man was dead, and perhaps after the next ebb tide he would be found on another beach.

Edward went home — he did not have the

stomach for seeking and gathering suitable pieces of wood any more just then. From a small bottle of whisky he poured himself a large measure, then tried to erase the memory of the face in the water from his mind. He failed because in bed later he had a nightmare. The man in the water was coming up the steps from the beach, looking in the windows, trying the doors, and calling out for the wood from the doomed ship to be returned. At last he stood in Edward's room, water cascading from him, his hands outstretched and enfolded in seaweed.

The former awoke screaming out; 'I'll bring it back, I'll bring it back to you,' and it was some time before he could bring himself to realise that it had been a terrible dream, and that the floor was dry, the doors unopened.

By the next day the body had gone with the tide as he had hoped, but the incident had upset Edward and he was very wary of where he sought for wood. What he was looking for now were planks that would be suitable for replacing the rotting floors in the other rooms, sufficient timber having been collected for the roof.

The following afternoon after work he raced back to change and then hurry down on to the beach. He had about three hours before high tide. After searching diligently for a while without finding just what he required, he then saw a large amount of timber some twenty-five yards from the cliff face at the rear of the beach, about six feet high, caught high and dry on the rocks. From the headland earlier that day he had seen the enormous collection of wood remaining near the wreck, and no doubt this particular one had been deposited after the last tide; he hadn't noticed it before. On inspection he saw several long, wide and thick planks, and wanted as many as possible. It had been a bright winter's day, with a viciously cold wind, and now the sun was lowering. Another hour and it would be dark and he could hear the sea increasingly loudly.

A cluster of tall rocks lay immediately behind the mound of wood, and clambering on to one he found he could look down upon it. Spotting a piece he leaned forward, one foot resting for balance on the top of the pile. Suddenly the whole thing moved and he fell sideways to land face down on the sand and trapped under the planks by his legs. Cursing himself for being a stupid clumsy ass he tried to free himself. He couldn't — his legs immovable under the weight of wood, the right one beginning to hurt. And the light was fading. He shouted but knowing as he did so that he had not seen anyone else on the beach. He was just out of sight of anyone on the main stretch of Moulin Huet even if there had been someone about which was unlikely. He had wanted absolute privacy during the claiming of the wood. Now he would have given anything to see just one person, and sighed helplessly against the cold sand at the irony of the situation.

By straining his neck he could make out the lights of The Two Bays Hotel on the far headland. William would be in his fine office, or in his equally fine and comfortable flat above, while here he was trapped under a pile of old wood on a chilly deserted beach. His brother had been right — right all along. Their home should have been sold. He cried out with all his lung power, but the only reply came from the carefree gulls: struggled violently again but he remained pinned by the legs. If only Frederick would come. He hadn't been down much since Edward had quarrelled with his mother again. It wasn't the boy's fault; Ruth was keeping him away. Frederick had been enthusiastic and wanted to help with the gathering of the wood and had done so on several occasions, but had mentioned that his mother would be mad if she knew. And the white streak of breakers along the shore was drawing nearer. Rampant fear took him. He was going to be drowned — a foot of water or less would be enough. The amount of wood above him would require several feet of water before it floated and released him, and by that time it would be too late.

He remembered when he and William were children. The warnings by their parents not to climb on to the rocks in the bay. How three girls had been drowned long ago when after climbing on the Cradle rock the tide had come in. They had not been able to swim ashore and were drowned. Now it was almost certain he was going to join them. An irrational fear fixed him. What if the drowned seaman's body floated back in with the tide and looking for him — the dead face against his, then they going out on the ebb tide together.

Edward felt very cold and his mind drifted mercifully. He hated William — something to do with a girl called Elaine. Where was William? Why hadn't his mother and father called them in? It was getting dark — didn't like them out on the beach when it was dark; it was past tea time. Ruth must have gone home. Thought he heard someone shouting, waved an arm as vigorously as he could. Must be his father, and hoped he wouldn't be too angry. After all he'd only been making a den with the wood.

He felt his hands being grasped by warm urgent ones. A face came into view in the gloom, bringing Edward into the present. Frederick! He was so cold he could hardly move his mouth.

'Dad, going for help — can't move it, won't be long.'

The shoes and trousers bounded away speedily, lost to Edward's sight in seconds, but his mind stayed in focus. Frederick — young Frederick. Thank God, he must have traced him on to the beach in some way. Gone for help. How long? The waves were a white wall now, noisy, crashing to flat water which retreated, but then returned so much nearer to his head. There was no feeling in his legs now — no pain. Was the sea only about a foot away now? It was difficult to judge — he was down and nearly out. Where had Frederick gone? Oh damn the boy — he'd forgotten, probably in bed reading comics — he was fond of comics. The sand was rough and very cold and now wet from spray.

Suddenly movement about his head, lips on his cheek — a woman's voice — Ruth's! Good old Ruth — could rely on her. He felt the vibration from the wood above him, frantic speech and movement, gasps of effort. The water touched his outstretched hand, icy and remorseless. Just for a moment his mind slipped again. Didn't the sea know that he was its friend? Born within sound of it, had played in its placid blue warm waters, fished and swum in them. Admired it, and longed for it when he was away. Someone pulling at his shoulders — he felt himself move, then the weight gone from his legs, his hands trailing along the sand as he was dragged clear and up the beach, and placed with his back against a rock.

His thanks came in inarticulate grunts against Ruth's bosom as she half straddled him, pressing his head against her, praying her thanks, while Frederick hovered above in terrified relief, repeating, 'Just in time Dad — just in time.'

Ruth slithered down Edward to rub his legs, and he was conscious of the endearing and encouraging words she used all the while.

Between them they got him to the house, and once there he began to recover quickly but Ruth insisted that a doctor see him, dispatching Frederick on swift young legs to the hotel at the top of the lane, to ask them to phone for one. She then helped Edward to bed and made him a hot drink.

'How did you find me Ruth?' he asked with heartfelt gratitude.

'It was Frederick. He came down, you were not in the house, but he saw all the marks in the sand where you'd been dragging the wood. He heard you calling. Saw your hands.' Her tone was becoming brusque, cross. 'It was a near thing.'

He sighed and blew out his lips at the memory. 'I thought I was done for, The wood collapsed on me,' then he made to get out of bed protesting, 'Look Ruth, I'm feeling better now. There was no need for a doctor.'

Ruth stood up from where she had been sitting at the foot of the bed, and Edward was astonished at the sudden change in her expression. 'Oh yes there is, Edward Dorner — for your head, you bloody idiot,' and her voice was strained with anger. 'When are you going to stop this playing about in this godforsaken house? You must be mental. Look what's happened. You could have been killed — you stupid clown. You nearly got yourself killed. What's so important about this place that you have to do all this? To hell with the damn thing.'

Edward stared at her astonished. She'd been so loving only a short time ago. What had come over her?

'You don't understand Ruth,' he muttered.

'Don't I? Oh yes I do. A stupid ambition — a selfish bloody ambition. You don't care a damn about anyone else,' she raged at him, 'or anything except for this broken-down mausoleum. It's all you care about, but it's time you woke up and thought about other people for a change.' Contemptuous scorn sounded. 'Humping pieces of wood around in the dark. If you can't afford to have the place done properly — leave it, because if you don't you'll end up in a lunatic asylum.' She clenched her fists making a downward motion of helpless frustrated torment. 'Oh, why the hell do I bother with you? You're not worth it, never have been.' Then she left him, banging the door to behind her, and he heard the pots in the kitchen being moved furiously, then he thought he heard her crying. Edward slumped back on the bed, swamped and shocked by this sudden and violent outburst from her.

The doctor arrived and after examining him pronounced him unharmed apart from bruising to his legs which would take some time to wear off. He advised Edward to rest at home for a couple of days and keep warm. Then Ruth left with the doctor who was going to drop her off at her home.

'Thanks again Ruth,' Edward called after her.

She looked back at him from the door. 'Goodnight, Edward,' she said shortly, her tone and expression calm and composed now.

Afterwards he sat staring into space from the bed. Unbelievable the way she had changed. So nice to him when he had just been rescued, but then losing her temper completely soon afterwards. Always saying she loved him — it was a bloody funny way of showing it. Mad that he still bothered with the house — she was jealous of it. Ruth never changed. How could he marry her when she hated and begrudged the time he spent getting the place fit for her to live in if he married . . . . . . That trend of thought stopped abruptly. Marriage. She'd got him thinking about it now. She was attractive, there was no doubt about it, even as she grew older. Her eyes had flashed like sapphire and diamonds. But he wanted to be able to support her properly. He couldn't do that until he had the place finished and visitors paying money to stay there. Then Edward remembered with a shock what she had told him not so long ago. Was she really going to marry William? Certainly not if he had anything to do with it. Hellfire! he'd marry her himself first. But then he laughed with bitter cynicism. Bluff, bravado, that's all he had to offer. William had the money, fine property, and no doubt meant very seriously to marry Ruth. He locked the door and the lights from William's hotel twinkled mockingly at him from across the bay. His legs were sore and he realised he was lucky to be alive, and ought to be deeply grateful for that. Frederick was the one he had to thank for finding him. His son — must thank him again when he saw him, and buy him something special.

He settled into bed. Pity Ruth couldn't have stayed the night, but she couldn't very well leave Frederick alone. In any case he didn't think she would have wanted to, being so angry with him. Perhaps he could have calmed her down but it was doubtful. The only way he could please Ruth would be to marry her, and he'd have to be damned quick to do that; William was after her.

The following week he went to look at William's new house at Albecq from the outside. He was impressed and envious. Two-storied with a balcony to each window and a veranda to the front and sides. In fresh new granite with a red roof, and a new lawn was being laid at the front. The view was magnificent, overlooking the rocks and sea, and in the summer the glorious sunsets would imbue the walls with a pink glaze. The building must have cost a great deal of money.

Edward went home and sat brooding. Ruth was going to live there, married to William. But she didn't love William he was sure, so why was she doing it? To spite him? Surely she wouldn't go to that length, and yet . . . No! he couldn't accept that — not Ruth. Perhaps after all it was just for money, the comforts and things that it could buy and security. Women liked security. He hoped William played fair with her. There'd been rumours at work that he wasn't averse to inviting attractive women up to his flat. He was a bachelor — why not? But would he still do that when Ruth married him? Edward thought there was a chance, and he did not want to see Ruth hurt. No! he damn well didn't.

His attempts at repairing the roof over the next few days were half-hearted, and nothing seemed to go right. Ruth was on his mind all the time, and his legs ached clambering about the roof. If and when he did manage to get the joists fitted correctly, hundreds of slates would be necessary to complete the job. Where was he to get those from? Slates did not float, and no one was likely to deliver a load unless he paid for it, and then it would need a skilled hand for it to be done properly. In the evenings by the fire he slumped in his chair, depressed and imprisoned by his indecisiveness.

The reality of the coming marriage of Ruth to William was brought home to Edward when he saw the Sale notice outside her house. He would miss her very much although she would not be far away; the island was very small, but she had always lived up the lane. And Frederick? He would go with her and people would think that he was William's son. Edward wondered anxiously if he would see less of him as a result. Suddenly he remembered the rowing boat they had found together on the site of the old tea garden, and his promising Frederick that he would get it repaired and then during that coming summer they would go out in the bay in it.

He must get it fixed as soon as possible; didn't want Frederick to slip out of his life. But neither did he want Ruth to go out of it, and he was damned if he was going to let her.

That evening Edward paid her a surprise visit. She greeted him with a sad pleasure in her eyes. It was the first time he had been inside the house since she had asked him to leave after they had quarrelled. But then they seemed to quarrel at frequent intervals during their adult lives. He thought she had been crying.

She led him into the living room. 'How are your legs?'

'Just a bit stiff at times, but the pain's gone now, thanks.'

Funny he thought how after each quarrel when they met again, everything was normal, then everything seemed to build up again. She was wearing a red housecoat and her hair was untidy and tumbling about its collar.

'Where's Frederick?'

'He's up at his friend's — Roger. He's got a new snorkelling outfit and Frederick's becoming very keen. He'll want one I suppose.'

Edward had seen them — a thin tube showing just above the water, the swimmer just under the surface and able to breathe. He would buy one for him and read up on the business. In the coming fine weather he and Frederick must do things together. 'I haven't seen you at work recently.'

Ruth glanced at him quickly. 'I don't work any more.'

He was surprised but then he realised that he

shouldn't have been. Something white and brocaded hung over a chair back.

'My wedding dress — I — I've been trying it on.' Their eyes met. 'It's next Saturday,' she said quietly with a slight falter.

Something pierced his being. So soon! He hadn't realised, too wrapped up in his own affairs. Had put it out of his mind, hoping it would not happen. 'You're going ahead with — with everything?'

'Yes.' Her whispered reply was firm.

'No! no, Ruth — put it off. You can't marry William.'

'But I am, Edward, it's all arranged.'

'Why? Why are you doing it? You don't love him,' he flung at her.

Ruth sighed despairingly and slumped sideways into a chair away from him. 'Look, we've been through all this before. It's no good, I've promised to marry William, that's all there is to it. Don't let's quarrel again,' and she pushed her hands outwards in a gesture of finality.

'No it isn't,' he cried hoarsely in a rising anger borne from his own frustration and helplessness at the situation. 'You can marry me instead — yes marry me, that's it. I want you to marry me instead, Ruth.'

Ruth looked up at him and gave a bitter short laugh. 'Oh, Edward, I'd have given anything to have heard you say that. All those years. You're too late, it's no good now.' Her voice rose and thinned with an anger of her own. 'You've had your chance, God knows. Where were you these last few weeks? The banns have been read in church. Were you there to object? No, you were not. You know why? Because you love that house. You don't really want to marry me, you're only offering now because you can't stand the thought of me marrying William.'

He gazed fixedly at her. She was right partially, but not totally. Maybe it was too late. 'But why Ruth? Why? I could understand if it was someone else.'

'I don't have to give you a reason, Edward.' Suddenly she leapt to her feet facing him, her eyes blazing accusingly into his. 'All right Edward, say you love me and mean it. Go on,' she demanded.

He drew back and away, their impact searing through his hesitancy even then. 'Why,' he exclaimed flinging his arms sideways, 'do you always have to talk about love? It's only a word — just a word. One word shouldn't mean so much. Let me marry you. I'll make you happy. Tell William you're calling it off,' he entreated.

A sad haunted look flicked into and out of her eyes, superimposed on the fading rancour. 'No I can't go back now. I promised, and besides . . . .' Her regard left him, sliding away with other thoughts.

Edward waited confused and furious with himself. 'And . . . ?'

'No, it's nothing,' she shrugged.

Edward stood there, drained and unable to think of anything else to say that might persuade her. Better if he left. Then he remembered something. 'Are you going away?' he asked tonelessly.

She nodded. 'Yes, we're flying to some island in the Mediterranean for a week. William doesn't want to leave the hotel for too long.'

'What about Frederick?' Surely he wasn't going to go with them.

'William wanted to take him, but he didn't want to go — he'd rather stay here.' Ruth cast a worried glance at Edward. 'I was wondering — would you mind looking after him? You could stay here if you wish, he's too young to be by himself.'

Edward was relieved that Frederick was not going to accompany them, couldn't have stood the thought of him going on a holiday with William.

'Of course,' he replied quickly. 'You didn't have to ask, I think we'll stay at my place.'

Ruth sighed her relief. 'Oh, I'm glad that's settled, everything's such a muddle. The reception is at the new house, so Frederick can come down with you afterwards.'

'When are you leaving?'

'About six — to Heathrow.'

He moved towards the door.

'Will you come on Saturday?' Her voice was very quiet from behind him.

His reply was equally so. 'I don't think so, Ruth.'

'You'll wish me well, then.'

Edward turned but his face averted, gripped her hands and kissed them in turn. 'Always Ruth.' He couldn't manage anything else and set off down the path.

'St. Ann's, eleven thirty, dearest Edward if you change your mind,' she called after him in a breaking voice.

Back at the Ormer his mood was black. It was all his own fault. She had turned him down. What had he expected? She was right when she had said he had had enough chances, and that he had waited until she was nearly married to William before he decided to ask her himself. Trouble was, they had known each other a long time — too long.

The next day he saw William and told him he wasn't going to come into work again — that he was resigning.

William was hugely surprised. 'Don't be an idiot. I thought I'd given you quite a good job; it brings money in. What's the matter, don't you like it here? Have you found another job?'

'Not yet, but I will. I've one or two things in mind.' He wasn't going to let William think his was the only work he could get.

'Wouldn't it have been better to have waited until you'd found another one?'

'No, I've made up my mind.'

William frowned heavily then shrugged and regarded him directly. 'You know I'm getting married, I suppose.'

'Yes, I saw Ruth last night — she told me. Didn't look very happy to me though,' and he enjoyed the expression which appeared swiftly on his brother's face.

'What d'you mean?'

'Looked more like she was going to a funeral rather than a wedding.'

William smiled thinly under Edward's goading. 'Oh, just nerves. I thought about asking you to be best man, but I didn't think you'd care to do it somehow,' he said offhandedly.

William was damned right — he wouldn't.

'Coming to the church?'

'No, I don't think so.'

'You should — going to be something special. The dress cost a thousand pounds.' His tone was arrogant and self-satisfied.

'Can you make her happy?'

'I've never known a woman I couldn't make happy.' William's tone had moved to the boastful, and sexual inference shone from his gaze.

'This is marriage,' pointed out Edward. 'A lot different to loving and leaving. You're sure that she's just not another acquisition?' Remembering his own marriage and the fact that his brother had helped in the eroding of it.

William's features tensed, but his delivery was even when he spoke. 'Ruth informs me that you've asked her to marry you several times, but she's refused you.'

Edward was taken aback, couldn't hide it, and William made no attempt to mask his satisfaction at this. Ruth had her pride but it had been only last night when he had asked her to marry him, and he wondered if she had already spoken to his brother.

The latter did not await a reply. 'Ruth's had a raw deal and I'm going to make it up to her.' He looked reflective through his gloating. 'You know, I'm surprised you didn't do the right thing years ago and marry her. After all she's had Frederick by you. Damn fine boy, Frederick. I've got plans for him.'

Edward had kept his calm up to then and had been determined to keep it, but William's talk of doing the right thing and his plans for Frederick goaded him into sudden anger. 'Don't talk to me about doing the right thing. What the hell d'you know about doing the right thing? That's a bloody laugh, William. You didn't do the right thing by me, you with Elaine. I know what happened up at the cottage. You didn't think I knew, but I did. I'm not stupid, but you thought I was. You helped to destroy my marriage to Elaine. All right, she wasn't an angel, but we had a chance together, but you were one of those that helped to wreck that chance. And keep Frederick out of it. Any plans there are for him I'm going to be the one to make them. He's mine. Keep your hands off him.'

What little of the mask remained on the features opposite slipped, revealing in face and tone uncaring and savage contempt. 'The trouble with you, Edward, is that you're just plain bloody jealous of all that I've achieved here. This hotel, my position in the community — I've earned it. As for Elaine, I was hardly breaking anything up; it was in pieces when I came along. All right I did see her. Do you know what she used to call you? Her little waif and stray — hobble-de-boy! All you thought about was work. Dull as the godforsaken weather up there, she used to say. She said you were pathetic, and how you managed to give her a child was a miracle. At that time I was just what she wanted.' His eyes glowed at the carnal memories.

Edward was staggered mentally. The whole affair was in the past, but the jibes and barbs reawakened memories of his shortcomings. He sprang up, face set in flushed and bitter resentment, his finger a rod at his brother. 'Two can play at marriage breaking, William. So you watch out. You'd better take good care of Ruth and soon, because she isn't going to be with you for long.' He made for the door, slamming it behind him, and hurried unseeingly out of the hotel. He had not meant to lose his temper and had made a mess of things as usual. The division between himself and William had grown wider over the years, and he realised then that they were now enemies.

Edward changed his mind and went to the church to see Ruth marry William, seating himself right at the rear in the last pew. It was Saturday March the twenty-ninth and the daffodils danced joyful at the Spring in the cool wind outside. But inside he was utterly miserable. No work, no money, his home still in ruins and the woman he should have married coming down the aisle on his brother's arm. A mature woman now, she looked lovely, the gown revealing her fine rounded shoulders, the head-dress having small flowers matching the violet of her eyes. Serious eyes moving left and right, accompanied by a small smile as she recognised someone. William had a swagger to his slow walk, and his smile was one not so much of pride but of triumph. Edward edged nearer to the aisle — he wanted her to know that he had come. He leaned outwards. Ruth was a yard or so away. Then she saw him and the smile which had only touched her lips until then expanded and brightened her whole face. As she passed she mouthed her thanks silently and then was gone, her arm through William's, and Edward was twisted inside himself as he gazed after her.

He joined the assembly of admiring and well-wishing guests as photographs were being taken, swallowed up in the midst of people he had never seen before. The bridesmaids, all of them in light blue, surrounded the couple as they posed, and Frederick joined them looking smart in his tail suit and quite the young man. Edward felt proud of his son and his spirits lifted a little, yet retaining a sadness that, as the bridegroom's brother, he was not arranging himself with the groups for photographs. Perhaps it would be a good time for him to slip away. Ruth was pleased that he had shown himself, that was all that mattered. He eased himself between the guests towards the gateway but then felt a tap on his shoulder, and a guest pointed at Ruth who was beckoning towards him. A photograph. The bride and groom, bridesmaids and the groom's brother. Ruth wanted it, but certainly not William he guessed. Smiling amongst the bridesmaids he was relieved when the group separated.

'Come to the reception please, Edward, at the new house,' Ruth whispered, and then she was deluged with confetti with guests surrounding her and William. More photographs, and then they were speeding away.

Edward didn't really want to go to the reception, but Ruth had asked him so he would attend just to please her — it was her day after all. His own feelings must be put aside. He hung around for a while until many of the guests had set off to follow the bridal couple. Someone gave him a lift and as they drove away the headstone in the corner of the churchyard caught his eye. What would his parents have thought about the whole sorry business? Their two sons estranged, adversaries quarrelling over Ruth. He sighed. It was today — the problems had to be faced; there was no retracing of steps.

The newly-weds were having more photographs taken on the lawn when Edward and the others arrived. The sun was breaking through, the clouds dappling the ground swiftly, and towards Cobo, Edward saw the breakers and glimpsed the coloured triangles of the board-sailors. Inside, William's new house was staggering in its opulence and design. The smell of new carpeting and furniture, and the splendid gallery above the main lounge with its full-length windows overlooking the gardens and sea beyond.

There was food of all kinds, champagne, wine, anything any guest could wish for, and music — from a magnificent white grand piano, but never did William so much as glance in Edward's direction, though Ruth did, searching for him in the throng of people present. Once she was able to speak to him. 'You'll come and see us, Edward? Don't stay away — please.'

He nodded. 'All right.' The last thing he wished to do was argue on that day. 'You look marvellous, Ruth,' and he meant it.

Her eyes glowed at his compliment. 'Glad you came, Edward.'

'I hope you're happy, Ruth.'

'I'll try,' and she touched his hand. 'It's like a dream — very strange. I'm a little frightened, Edward.'

'Don't worry, Ruth, I'll be around. It's your wedding day — you enjoy it.'

People were pressing towards them. 'Love you Edward always, bye,' and then she was captured and escorted elsewhere, the expected smile returning to her lips.

Sadly Edward gazed into his drink. Strange words for a bride to utter to a man other than her husband. He was sad for Ruth and couldn't understand the whys or wherefores of it all, and his hand tightened around his glass each time he saw William's arm about her waist.

Then a puzzled but excited Frederick found him. 'I'm coming to stay with you, Dad. I didn't really want to go with Mum and Uncle William.'

'Glad you're coming, Frederick. Hope you're not too fed up with helping me repair the house. You can give me a hand with it if you feel like it. Bring your friend Roger down, but if you'd rather go with him sometimes it's all right by me.'

Frederick was pleased. 'Oh, don't worry,' he said earnestly, 'we'll give you a hand,' then after glancing at the bridal couple across the room he looked directly at his father. 'I can't understand why Mum should go and marry Uncle William — can you?'

'Well Frederick,' replied Edward with a frowning sadness which he just couldn't hide completely, 'neither do I,' and as far as he was concerned that was the truth.

Speeches were made and William gave one. In it he said that he was brought up in a hotel — had always wanted one of his own. The old family home would never rise again, being a ruin, but a new one had arisen nearby in its place — The Two Bays Hotel. Together with his dear wife Ruth, they would make it attain new heights of efficiency. He thanked his friends and associates in the hotel and tourist industry, and the States for their help. The accent in William's speech was on the hotel rather than his marriage to Ruth.

It occurred to Edward that that was exactly what he himself had being doing for years and he gazed at Ruth with fresh eyes. Realised just what a rose petal complexion she had and how statuesque she looked at William's side. What a fool he'd been all those years.

Then William and Ruth led the dancing on the small specially constructed floor in the main lounge, and Edward could hardly bear to see his brother holding her close. Instead he wandered amongst the guests, meeting and being introduced to people he'd never seen before, and he began to realise what a lot of powerful and influential people William now knew. One of them told him enthusiastically that William was going to be elected president of the States tourism bureau. 'Yes, your brother has drive and a willingness to get things done. In fact he's done a great deal already to raise the standard over here. He's been instrumental in getting conferences to the island that would otherwise have gone elsewhere. A lot of new business is coming in — he's full of ideas.' Then the other's eyes sparkled with something quite unconnected with tourism and suchlike. 'I must say, I like his wife, Ruth. What a beautiful creature. God! he's a lucky man — lucky in business, lucky in love. How does he do it?' In conversation later he asked what sort of work Edward was in and the latter replied that he too was in catering, and then slunk away dispirited and depressed.

Before Frederick joined him that evening Edward walked the length of the bay. He couldn't get the thought of Ruth being in bed with William out of his mind. Caressing and penetrating the flesh that had borne Frederick — their son. He himself had enjoyed Ruth twice, but only briefly on each occasion. Once long ago when she had enticed him on the Fermain walk, thinking that he was serious about her. She had conceived Frederick from that incident. The other, when she had stood in the kitchen entrance at her home, and lust had overcome him then. Now she could stand anywhere in sight of William and he could caress her any time he wished. The important difference was that William had married her; he Edward had not.

The self-torture continued as he made his way back to his house. Ever since the day he had discovered Elaine and William at the cottage in Daleford he had felt a sense of inadequacy where his brother was concerned. There was no real reason why he should, but it had persisted. The remarks made by Elaine which he had overheard when she and William had been together. The leaving of the large amount of money by Miss Steck to him in her will. He must have pleased her very much for her to be so generous. And now, Ruth.

On his return to the Ormer, Edward made a bed up savagely in the kitchen so that Frederick could have the bed sitting room, seeking to drive away the jealousy gnawing within himself, a jealousy which had appeared to be without a foundation or so he had thought. Hell! he was so mixed up he was like an adolescent.

However, that week with Frederick helped Edward to free his thoughts elsewhere — on to his son. They swam, Edward trying his hand at snorkelling, Frederick amused at his first clumsy attempts. They rowed around to Petit Port one gorgeous day and picnicked there. Sometimes they did a bit more towards the repair of the house. Once when he was sitting watching Frederick swimming, he thought about the latter's further education. It would cost money, he knew, and so did all the other things he would have liked to have given him. William had the money and Frederick would be living with him and Ruth. William would then have more control over his life. If he, Edward, wished to continue having some influence on Frederick's upbringing, then being in a state of poverty would not help. And having seen the trappings of wealth and all it could bring at William's new house, it was becoming clear once more that if he wanted any of his own, he would now have to sell his property. As Frederick grew up he would begin to make comparisons — it was only natural — and Edward did not want to appear always as the poor relation in his son's eyes.

Edward left the estate agents with both misgivings and relief. He had done it! Had been assured that the price he would obtain would be a good one, and that a buyer would probably be found within a week. But had he done the right thing? It was only later when he began to ponder over what he was going to do in the future that another problem revealed itself. If he wished to buy sound property in a nice location, whether it be a hotel or a place to live in privately, then he would be buying in the same market. And from the properties he had seen for sale on the island and their prices, then he was going to have to pay as much or more than he would receive for his own. True, he would have a sound property or going concern, but the hotels he could afford — and also have some capital left to put aside — were in locations much inferior to that enjoyed by the Ormer at Moulin Huet.

Within the week Edward had cancelled the sale and had found work in a small restaurant on the harbour front, waiting on tables for the remainder of the season. It was a lovely warm, blue-canopied day, the masts of the yachts in the harbour tracing gentle arcs in the sky, and the tinkling music of the shrouds joined those of the seabirds. Boats were leaving for Fermain and Herm. Edward gazed thankfully upon the scene — he loved the island. Perhaps it was the weather, but he felt more cheerful and confident; doubts had gone for the time being regarding the property. Money would be coming in again, and he felt free now that he was not on William's payroll.

Edward's decision for the umpteenth time to carry on was helped by a number of holidaymakers who climbed the steps from the beach at Moulin Huet and stood gazing at where the gun emplacement used to be during the war years. They were surprised when he appeared. Obviously they had thought the place was an empty ruin, but he found himself explaining on that and subsequent occasions about the house, and that it had been part of the German fortifications around the island's coast. His optimism in the future grew. The first visitors to set foot in the old hotel grounds. He became quite used to showing people around — at the concrete look-out with its gun slits, and also where the small parade ground had been. After the first visitors had shown interest he made sure that the sites were kept clear always.

Towards the end of the summer he had even started serving visitors with refreshments as they sat on odd chairs at makeshift tables on the original tea-garden terrace. The house was coming alive again. After all those years of doubt and struggle. There was no way now that he would ever again change his plans for the old hotel. It was still going to be a hard long way to the time when guests could actually stay there, but he had noticed in the town that there were shops already selling books about the occupation. Perhaps it would stimulate interest in his house. Whatever happened now the fact remained that people had sat once more in the tea-garden and taken refreshment, and looked out upon the beauty of the bay and its surrounds.

17

One afternoon, about a month later, he had a visit from Ruth. He was outside painting the window sills when she drove up in a new-looking car. Watched as she got out and approached. She was in yellow, and he admired again the way she walked. The first time he had seen her since the wedding. They kissed each other's cheeks and he smelt perfume — he'd never known her use it before. His hands held her waist for seconds, a delightful too short-lived sensation. 'Nice to see you, Ruth.'

'And you, Edward.'

He ushered her inside. 'I was just going to have a break.'

'Look, let me make it,' she volunteered. 'I don't get much practice now.'

He wondered what she meant and observed her as she busied herself. She looked smarter, more sophisticated than she used to do.

'How d'you mean? Don't tell me William makes it.'

Ruth glanced round at Edward. 'No, we have a cook and a maid. William engaged them soon after we were married, so you see I don't get much chance of doing anything myself.'

They sat opposite each other and Edward was surprised at the feeling that he had — almost a shyness. Ruth was another man's wife now and here she was in his house. A small thrill of satisfaction took him. Looking at her over his cup he asked, 'And how are things?' Meaning her marriage, but couldn't quite bring himself to say it.

Ruth took another sip before answering, laughed shortly, lightly. 'Don't I look well?'

She did certainly and Edward hoped that it wasn't all due to William. 'Are you happy?' He hadn't meant to ask, dreading the answer.

Ruth gave a brief close-lipped smile, an almost imperceptible shrug. 'William's very good to me.'

Edward gained a sudden vicarious pleasure, but then the feeling faded very quickly. His brother's hands would know Ruth very well by now, whether she was happy or not. With an effort he thought of something else.

'I haven't seen Frederick for a while. Does he ask about me much nowadays?'

'He couldn't stop talking about the fun he had when he stayed with you that week we were away. William didn't like it too much. He's trying to get him interested in golf, but I don't think Frederick is so bothered.'

Another spurt of satisfaction ran through Edward. William wasn't having all his own way with Frederick. It struck him then how the roles were now reversed. Ruth as William's wife now visiting him. The curve of her thigh just visible before it continued up into the shadows of her skirt. Suppose he now made love to Ruth. Some sort of revenge. Just to think about it was very gratifying. Life was strange the way things worked out. 'You're looking very well, Ruth.' Actually he meant beautiful.

She arose under his hands. 'No, please Edward.

I'm married to William. I didn't come for . . . ' and she turned away.

His expression must have been read very easily. She was loyal even to William. 'Why have you come?'

She looked back into his face. 'To see you, Edward, that's all. The fact is you haven't been to see us.'

'Well, the truth about the matter, Ruth, is that we don't get on, I think you know that.' It was a huge understatement. 'Things have got worse between us. He'll do his damnedest to make sure I don't make a go of this place.' Obviously Ruth did not know of their recent quarrel or the present extent of the enmity between them. 'It goes back a long way, Ruth.'

Ruth looked out of the window. Yes, she knew. Just like her feelings for her companion went back a long way — those feelings had brought her there today. Her fingers touched the article in her pocket that she had brought for him. It would benefit him far more in the long run than any brief fleshy contact on the bed nearby. She tolerated William, she had married him — tolerated his strutting in the bedroom and the violent intrusions into her body. He provided wealth, and a home for Frederick. She had married an old friend who acquired things. There was more to love than a length of flesh, and there was no more real communication between her and William than there had been when they were children. Edward had not understood, but he would soon. An excitement began to rise in her, and she found him watching her. His face had filled out a little, but it was still a lined and troubled one. How she wanted to make those worries disappear. If she had anything to do with it, they would — very soon.

'Does William know you've come here?'

'No, he's at a meeting of the hoteliers association, something to do with safety, fires etc. He's secretary now, did you know?'

Her companion shook his head disinterestedly. 'He seems to be in everything.'

Ruth heard the ill-concealed jealousy and envy. Dearest, dotty ever so slightly pompous Edward. She could hardly wait to see his face when he found out the real purpose of her visit. Regarded him with a sudden cheerfulness. 'Now I want you to tell me how you're progressing with the house — I want to know.' She didn't really have to ask, having seen already, but she was going to change all that.

Complete surprise had settled on Edward's face. It was no wonder she thought. The last time she had been there she had been offensive towards him about it — a damned ruin she had called it amongst other things, and had done her best to persuade him to leave it. 'No, really,' she smiled encouragingly, 'I do want to know, because I think you can do it,' a glow of pleasure lighting up her face.

'But I thought . . . .' He hesitated, stared at her in puzzled doubt.

'No, I've changed my mind.' She took his arm. 'Show me what you've been doing.'

Edward conducted her around the building, pointing out his work here and there and at the pale wooden joists of the roof. Ruth chilled at the sight of them — that wood had nearly cost Edward his life.

The slates had loosened and already fallen from them. He saw her looking.

'Some day I'll have someone to fix them properly,' and he laughed with a bitter discomfiture.

Ruth observed that some windows had been replaced and the ground cleared around the house of the once all-enveloping weeds and grass. Apart from that and the one room which Edward used as a bed sitting room, it was a mess. He would never in the next ten years get anywhere near making it properly habitable. As for his ambition of restoring it to its former use as a hotel — he hadn't a hope. Not by himself. A thrill of anticipation ran through her at the happiness she was going to bring him.

They had reached the drive again and Edward was leading her to where the old tea garden used to be. He pointed at it. 'D'you know, a couple of weeks ago I had people sitting here and I served them — for the first time. Nothing great, just teas and coffees, a few biscuits. They seemed to enjoy it. I had about eight people. They admired the view, then I told them about the war, all I could remember. They were very interested.' His whole being seemed to kindle with the remembered happy satisfaction that the incident had given him.

Ruth was delighted for him and congratulated him, but there was, she knew, going to be much more success in his so far long drawn out venture. She tugged at his sleeve. 'Let's go inside. There's something I want to talk to you about.' Her breathing had become shallow with excited anticipation. Inside the kitchen she turned to him eagerly, brought the folded paper moist from her hand which had guarded it so closely, and thrust it at him. 'Now Edward,' she uttered, 'you don't have to worry — you can go ahead.' Her gaze was direct and eager to observe the first signs of his rising delight, as he looked at the cheque between his thumbs, his lips moving silently above the figures upon it.

'What's this, Ruth? I don't understand.' His expression was almost accusatory.

'A cheque of course — from me to you.' His joy, she knew, would break from his features in a moment, held her breath.

A flash of irritation showed, a half shake of his head. 'From you to me? What d'you mean?'

'In plain English, Edward, I have given that to you. It is yours to spend on the house, from me.' It was the figure within the cheque that had shocked him, she guessed, and soon his gratitude would be overwhelming as he caught her up in his arms. 'It's all right, I can afford it,' but still joy and gratitude remained absent from her companion. Looking into his face intensely, her words rushing with her enthusiasm, she went on, 'Now you can have the roof done — all of it, professionally, and the floorboards renewed. Decorations — the lot, just as you've always wanted.' Her face was still flushed with the pleasure of her gift to him.

Edward, stern and unsmiling, dropped the cheque on to the kitchen table. 'I can't take that.'

Ruth looked at the cheque, then back at him, searching his features. 'Why not? What's wrong with it?' Her gift was not being accepted in the way she had thought it would have been. The warm glow inside her was fading.

Edward glanced at her coldly. 'I'm not accepting any of William's money.'

'It's not William's money,' she retorted.

A mirthless smile came and went on Edward's face. 'Oh, I know what's his is yours now, but it is still coming from him indirectly, and he certainly wouldn't give me any.' He paused, eyeing her, then continued, 'You'd better not let him know that you've been trying to give his money anyway. You meant well, and it was kind of you but . . . .' He shrugged.

Ruth was exasperated, her voice strained when she replied. 'You never think do you, Edward — never. Why in hell's name can you not stop bringing William into everything? God, you're a fool!' she exploded. Always — always they argued and quarrelled. It should have been such a marvellous moment and occasion. She had been anticipating the joy of it for days now. 'You've always got to spoil it. Listen to me and don't interrupt. When I married William I stipulated that any money that was mine I should keep separately from his. That money there,' she said, pointing at the table, 'is mine from the sale of my house — my house,' she repeated very deliberately. 'It has nothing whatsoever to do with William.'

Edward's shoulders slumped, and he passed the back of a finger across his forehead. 'You're so blasted right, Ruth. I'll have to start thinking before I open my stupid mouth. I used to do, but lately — I don't know — I'm sorry Ruth. Of course, yes, you did sell your house.' He regarded her for a few moments with a great and tender affection, then went on, 'You're a saint, Ruth — far too good. But that's your money. Put it back in your pocket.'

Picking up the cheque he glanced at it before holding it out. 'Five thousand pounds! That's a lot of money.'

'No it isn't. Not for what you want to do with the Ormer. Take it. It means so much to me if you would. It's your dream, Edward. Let me help you to realise it. Don't refuse it — please.'

Edward shook his head jerkily, impatiently, half turned away. 'I can't Ruth — I can't take it. Now put it away and buy something really nice for yourself. Don't think of me.'

Ruth ignored his outstretched hand, and he dropped the cheque on to the table again. She had meant to keep calm, but frustration, disappointment and anger welled up in her. 'Don't think of you, Edward Dorner. That's rich. God! I've never thought of anything or anybody else all these bloody years you've been going on about restoring this place, but as soon as you're offered money to do just that, you refuse it. What the hell do you want? I don't think you know yourself. I'll say that for William — he accepts what he's given. He wouldn't turn down five thousand pounds.' She grabbed the cheque, grasped Edward's hand and rammed it into his palm. 'I'm not leaving this place with it,' and stared wide-eyed into his face with unrestrained fury. 'Did you ever wonder why I married William? Did you? Well, I'll tell you. I married him so that the money that I had could go to help you spend on this place. I married him so that you couldn't say I was trying to buy you into marriage between us, but I love you, and I will always, so you damn well take it, Edward Dorner, and the next time I come to this house I expect to find some improvement. If it hurts your stupid pride too much then you can always return it when the place is full and you're rich.' Abruptly she turned away but then looked back. 'There's just one other thing — the matter of your son, Frederick. He's growing up now into a young man. I'm sure he doesn't want to see his father living like a tramp for the remainder of his days. William isn't all that bad and Frederick could be influenced. He's your son, but shame and your poverty could keep him away. Swallow that pride Edward. Be sensible — don't be a damned fool.'

Long after the sound of her car had faded, Edward remained standing there, his thoughts in disorder. She had been truthful, yes, shown him to be a blundering fool. The depth of her love for him, her sacrifice so that he could have the money to fulfil his ambition. Hell, he felt an inch high. For her to go to those lengths for his sake. She had also given a warning that Frederick could be influenced. He must learn to accept, that's what she had said. A woman of immense inner steadfast strength which he couldn't match. Ruth — she had been aptly named — something in the Bible about the same kind of loyalty.

He became aware of the piece of paper in his hand and gazed down at it. The cheque moved slightly, stretching at its creases as if imbued with a life of its own, the figure clearing as it did so. What he could do with that amount! Learn to accept. The words came into his brain again. A gift from the woman who loved him. Use it. Straightened the cheque out. Already he felt lighter mentally, something had left him. Now a gradual buoyancy of mind was seeping into him. Coming alive. So would the house now. Accept — accept . . .

Edward leapt in the air and the battered ruin of the building resounded with his yell of delight. Later he drank a large toast to the woman who loved him and had made possible the coming rebirth of the new Ormer Hotel.

A year later, and work on the building was well under way. But the progress had been dogged by seemingly endless interruptions from one States body after another. The kitchen was found to have faults in it according to the health department. It seemed all right to Edward and the contractors but nevertheless it had to be altered, and even then approval was only given grudgingly by the inspectors concerned. The greatest blow financially and in retarding the day of completion was the fire department's insistence that a fire escape had to be provided. But again Ruth came to his rescue to pay for the extra work that had to be done. Edward remembered that William was on both committees, and guessed that he had played a major part in making things difficult for him, but he must wonder where the money for the restoration was coming from. Bitter satisfaction ran through Edward. By the coming Spring he should be ready to open. Only two rooms at the cliff end of the house remained to be furnished. They could be left for now. Occasionally he would walk around his rising dream, hardly believing that it had come true. The new terrace had been laid, the veranda restored with large windows which would open in hot weather and adjoining the dining room. In a corner of the latter was a piano. Laughter, music and happiness for the guests was to be the order of the day. At the end of the newly tarmacked drive was the hotel sign with the name in silver on a blue background. And the tea garden with its newly laid lawn and bordering hedge was the final touch in the fulfilment of Edward's long-held ambition.

A week before the hotel opened Edward had a further visit from Ruth. She was thrilled, and shared his pleasure and pride as they surveyed it.

'This is all due to you, Ruth,' he said with a lingering look of gratitude and something else. The years were there, he knew, but she did not show them, wearing a simple blue dress and white cardigan against the Spring breeze.

'No, Edward,' she protested, giving a wry smile. 'A lot of it is owed to yourself. You persevered and hung on. Most of the time I was telling you to get rid of it.' She shook her head in mock shame. 'The things I called it — I hope it forgives me.' Her voice softened as she gazed at him. 'And I hope you'll forgive me too.'

Edward smiled. 'I'm sure it has done already. It owes everything to you, and I have nothing to forgive you for, you know that.' He hesitated, looking at her in a way that surprised her as he went on, 'And anyway there will not be a more attractive woman coming to visit us than you, I'm certain.' Edward surprised himself with his utterance, but the sentiment just fell easily from his lips. No wonder Ruth glanced at him with something like astonishment — quite unlike him really.

'That's a very nice compliment to pay me, Edward, but,' and she sighed, 'I'm getting on now — not young any more. I'm a mature married woman.'

He thought he detected an underlying sadness with her last remark and her words made him realise that he himself was not a young man any more, but in some quite foolish way he'd always thought of Ruth, William and himself as remaining in a time frame of somewhere between twenty and twenty-five, which was ridiculous.

Edward opened a bottle of wine and they drank to the coming opening of the new Ormer Hotel.

'When is the date?' asked Ruth.

'A week tomorrow — Monday.'

His companion regarded him speculatively over her glass. 'Would you mind if I tell you what I've heard about business recently and for the coming season?'

'Of course not, no, go on,' he insisted, seeing the flash of doubt appear. After all she had her ear by marriage to the trade, and what she had to tell him would be useful when he started. William would be furious if he knew, but that didn't matter.

'Well, it seems the hotel trade is going through rather a slack period on the island. Visitors are coming — a lot of them in their own yachts from all over, but they're no good to the hoteliers. They spend a lot, but it's in the town shops on provisions, chandlery, drinks — that sort of thing.'

Trust it to be the time when he was ready to open his hotel, thought Edward in some anxiety.

Ruth carried on. 'Don't worry too much, Edward, because from what William's been saying, self-catering is becoming very popular with many holidaymakers — particularly families. They find it cheaper and they can please themselves as to their meal times.' She gazed at him sympathetically. 'I didn't want to put a dampener on things, but I thought you ought to know.'

'I'm glad you have told me, Ruth. I can plan ahead now and make some alterations. I suppose that's part of being successful in business — being aware of changes and being ready for them.' All the same he didn't feel quite as confident as he had been before her arrival.

'William's worried,' observed Ruth. 'He hasn't had anything like the number of bookings for this year.'

Edward, in all honesty, couldn't say he was sorry. It was time something disturbed the smooth workings of his brother's life.

'But of course he still has the conferences and weddings taking place there,' Ruth pointed out.

Edward was conscious of a note of discontent in her voice. He leaned over, refilled her glass, though she waved her hand over it.

'I shouldn't have any more, Edward. I mustn't go back home drunk.' Her eyes strayed away. 'But perhaps it wouldn't matter,' and there was now a sad resignation in her tone which surprised him. Something wasn't quite right. Her intensely frank eyes could never hide anything. Was William treating her properly, he wondered?

He clinked his glass against her again in a toast. 'To you, Ruth, for all your help. I will make a success of it, whichever way the industry goes, for the faith you've shown in me.'

'You know I didn't do it for business reasons,' she stated simply.

Yes, he knew well enough. Perhaps it was the wine, but she looked softly, yet sturdily feminine and also very vulnerable. William's wife. Hell! He just couldn't get over the fact on some occasions, and this was one of them. He rose quickly as if to shake the image off. 'Let me show you the rest of the rooms,' and he took her by the arm. She smelled of fresh spring flowers. 'It's a bit different,' he smiled, 'from the time when you came and I was eating from a packing case and sleeping on the floor.'

'I'm glad for your sake, Edward.' It was said quietly, without a return of smile, and he sensed unease in her.

He escorted her through the newly-painted and decorated rooms, proudly showing her the dining room. Then the upstairs with the blue and gold carpets and the new ceilings overhead. Showed her one of the bedrooms overlooking the bay. It had a double bed in it and he laughed rather awkwardly. 'I may be old-fashioned but I've kept one room with this in.'

He turned to find her looking out across the bay towards The Two Bays Hotel. 'Is William over there today?' He saw her nod, and her shoulders drop in silhouette. Suddenly he was sorry, very sorry for her, but not quite sure why, and his arm around her seated her on the bed. She didn't seem to care, leaning against him as the mattress gave under their weight. Conscious of the line of her thighs against his — her closed eyes. He kissed her tentatively and comfortingly on her cheek. She remained still — very still. Turning her head he found her lips, and she did not resist, they being loose and pliable under his, but with little response. He was only half aware of this as they swayed backwards, his fingers undoing then brushing apart the skirt of her dress.

Ruth's mouth formed a soundless 'no' and she fluttered an arm vaguely, but that was all. Her flesh was his, supple and pliant, her pale thighs rounded vertical columns. She made a muted sound in her throat. A savage triumph overcame him. William's wife was beneath him. The tables had been turned. He bent and kissed her still lips in his passion. Through the window he could see William's hotel and make out where his office was. Kept his eyes on it as he made love to a limp and supine Ruth, and enjoying his command of his brother's wife. A savage satisfaction twisted his face. This is your wife, William, I am doing to her what you did to mine — now we're even.

The violence ended and he looked down and saw her face as if for the first time. Tears were glistening from under her eyelids and he slid sideways from her and brought her close, muttering his apologies. 'Oh, hell, I'm sorry, Ruth, I didn't mean . . . '

Her head moved against him, her words muffled. 'No, not you . . . '

'But you're crying. Don't cry, Ruth, I'm very sorry.'

Again he felt her shake her head, then she murmured, 'William's seeing another woman.'

Edward swore at his brother — at himself. So that was it. Oh God, and she had come that afternoon for comforting and refuge. What an uncaring unthinking idiot he had been, using her to score in some obscene game against his brother. An empty revenge. He remembered the sad look he had glimpsed earlier.

Ruth tilted her head up at him, heavy misery filling eyes, her voice husky in her despair. 'My life's in a mess, Edward. I'm so fed up. What can I do?'

Gently he straightened her clothing to hide her limbs from his shame and conscience. He was deeply upset over her. She'd been hurt too many times and he'd done his share. After the lust he was spent. What remained was love, and for the first time he was fully aware of his real feelings towards her. He kissed her eyes tenderly. 'Leave him, Ruth, come to me. I'll look after you always. Divorce him and marry me please, Ruth.'

A wistful little smile and such a longing came to her face. 'Oh dear Edward, so very gallant of you, but William's my husband — I married him. It's too late, Edward.'

He looked away. The price she had paid. That fine room and all the rest of the building, just for him.

'Perhaps I shouldn't have married William.' Ruth's voice came again. 'I'd made up my mind to make him a good wife, but it was foolish of me — a mistake. He must have known I didn't love him.'

Edward held her head close to him. 'Well, I do love you, Ruth, I do. I'm not just saying it.' All those years when everything else had taken precedence. Elaine's brittle beauty, money, the hotel restoration. And yet he had given five years of his life to protect her. No one did that if they did not think very deeply about someone.

Ruth stirred against him, brought a hand up to touch his face and let her fingers linger on his lips. 'After all those years, Edward, you've finally asked me to marry you, and you really mean it.' Sighed heavily in sad regret, 'And now I cannot.' She paused to gaze at him lovingly. 'But you've made me so happy by asking me and I know now that you do mean it.'

He clutched her to him, so that she could not see his great emotion. Then controlling himself he said, 'This is your home. I'll be waiting here any time for you, dearest Ruth. I've a lot of making up to do. I've been the must stupid undeserving idiot in the world. You can't possibly forgive me, but at least you know how I feel about you.'

A vitality had returned to Ruth's eyes. 'I can manage now, Edward. It will be easier for me, no matter what happens.'

'Divorce him, Ruth,' but even as he said it he knew she wouldn't.

Later just before she left he gestured at the house in all its splendour of reconstruction. 'I'll never be able to repay you for all this.'

Ruth turned to him, her face alive with her feelings for him. 'You love me, Edward, that's all that matters,' she said simply. But then suddenly serious-faced with some new worry, she took his hands in hers, pulled at them in a supplicating pleading movement. 'Be a brother again to William, Edward,' she entreated. 'I know he wronged you, but each one of us is to blame. We used to be friends — the three of us. We went through such a lot together. The games we played on this very beach, once we had no cares.' She gazed at him intently with encompassing eyes. 'You will try, for my sake?'

'Yes, I will, Ruth,' he promised. How he had no idea, but he would try. She was right though; each held a portion of blame.

That summer guests came and stayed at the new Ormer Hotel. Chatter and the chink of crockery was heard in the dining room and so was laughter. The piano was played morning and evening. Luggage from everywhere came into and went from the hall. The two extra rooms Edward used for people wanting self-catering — he had remembered Ruth's information. Once more that end of the beach was busy and colourful. Happy voices floated up and around the hotel.

And on the promise of a summer's day when the sea mist was rising above the water, he would stand in the background on the tea garden terrace and marvel at the miracle that had happened.

That year Frederick went to work at The Two Bays Hotel for his stepfather William. Occasionally on his day off he would visit the Ormer and give Edward a hand. The latter was not happy with the arrangement, but could not offer his son the year-round training and employment that William could, whereas the Ormer, being smaller, was quiet out of season. Edward grasped eagerly at this precious time they had together and watched with pride as Frederick, tall, blond and handsome, went about the place. Sometimes with the unthinking honesty of youth and the first arrogance that little experience spawned, he would hurt Edward by remarks such as that he had not realised how small the Ormer was until he went to work at Uncle William's hotel. That Edward should see the ballroom and the swimming pools — indoor and outdoor. About the wealthy people who stayed there, and how a new part had been added which was solely for others who wished to self-cater.

Edward listened and consoled himself with the thought that at least it was his son and not William's informing him of those things. He was also made aware that all was not well at home. William resented the fact that Frederick spent time — even the short time he did — at the Ormer, and Ruth arguing that he had every right to see his father. Edward was careful not to say anything regarding the problem, but he was very troubled on Ruth's account to hear about it, not wanting her to be upset and worried.

In the meantime he wrote to Scarton Manor, Yorkshire, to Miss Maxime Dorner. Perhaps the fact of having Frederick under his roof prompted the longing again to have his daughter under it some day. He writhed in mental agony under the thrust of Elaine's taunt that the child may not be his.

As he stamped the letter he realised that it would no doubt be intercepted by her grandparents when they saw the postmark, but it was a chance he had to take. He remembered writing many years before and often, but had had no reply to his enquiries. He fell to thinking about her, and about what age she would now be. Who did she take after? Was she dark or fair? His pleasant contemplations were shattered by a dreadful thought. Had Sir Redvers and his wife acquainted the young Maxime with the details of her mother's death and the trial, and his subsequent imprisonment? He allayed his fears partially by trying to convince himself that they would confine information given to Maxime as to how and where Elaine had died. It all seemed such a long time ago, and a time in his life that he would dearly wish to eradicate from his memory.

As soon as he had posted the letter he began to wonder whether it might not have been better to have addressed it to Maxime Scarton instead of Dorner. No doubt they had done their level best to make sure her father's name was never referred to. If there was no reply he would write again, using the name Scarton. He mentioned to Ruth that he had written to Maxime and immediately wished that he had not. The look in her eyes as she returned to the past . . . What a complete idiot he was — never thinking. After all it was a child by another woman. Jealousy of the dead could smoulder on.

The next time he saw Frederick the latter was looking very worried.

'It's Mum,' he told Edward. 'I don't think she's very well. I thought I'd better let you know.'

'What's the matter, what's wrong?' He hadn't seen her recently and had meant to do, not yet having visited her in her new home. She had asked him to.

'I don't know. The doctor's been, but I think he

was puzzled and he's coming again.'

'Is she in bed?'

'Sometimes, and she's not eating much.'

'What about — er — Uncle William?'

'He gets a bit ratty. He thinks she's putting it on — I've heard him say.'

'Tell her I'll be up in the morning, Frederick.' Felt uneasy. Was William still playing around outside the marriage? Was that the trouble? He should have gone up before this — he had promised.

In bed that night his thoughts were on Ruth. Frederick had been worried — very worried. And Edward felt ashamed and angry with himself. Only a few weeks ago he had confessed his love for her, and then just hadn't seen anything of her. He'd been busy, but that was no excuse. If he really loved her he would not have let such a time elapse before seeing her again. Was he deluding himself? Did love rear itself in him only when they were together? He couldn't interfere too much, but he should have kept more of an eye on her. Having sworn his love, then out of sight — out of mind. What sort of love was that?

He squirmed in mental anguish. She was more important than his feud with his brother. He would visit her more often. He must.

18

When Edward saw Ruth the next day he was very concerned for her health. She was up and sat in a chair, but in the time since he had seen her last she had become thinner, and seemed listless and disinterested in her surroundings. She was alone, both William and Frederick being at The Two Bays Hotel. She was happy to see him, and thanked him for coming, then stared out of the window. He found it difficult to talk to her, had never known her like that in all the years before.

'Have you and William got together yet?' she enquired once without looking at him.

'No,' then he added hastily, 'but we are going to do. We must stop this nonsense of quarrelling.' He said it more for her sake than in any real belief that they could agree to settle their differences. Ruth didn't pursue the matter. 'I'll call again tomorrow, Ruth.' She appeared to have forgotten he was there. He kissed her on the cheek, touched her hair, 'I love you, Ruth.'

Half turning her head towards him, she lifted a languid hand and fingered his cheek for a moment and a little smile came and went. An expression that told of disbelief.

Edward returned to the Ormer a very concerned and worried man.

The following day he received a telephone message from Frederick to say that Ruth was in hospital to where she had been taken that morning. Would Edward go after two o'clock, as Uncle William was already there with her? The doctor had been called during the night and had then made arrangements for her. Frederick couldn't say what was wrong. They were doing tests on her — he didn't know any more. He sounded very upset, and Edward did his best to comfort him.

One o'clock and Edward was outside the door of ward three. An hour early, but perhaps they'd let him in beforehand. They didn't, and he turned and twisted impatiently, peering through the window into the corridor of the ward every few seconds. Figures of nurses and white coats appearing then disappearing quickly. He tried to catch an eye but to no avail. It must be two o'clock by now. Was the clock wrong? It must be — so slow. A small queue began to form behind him. William had been with her that morning and Frederick of course. He felt a hurt. When she wanted help, he hadn't been there. Of course he was not to know, nevertheless . . . He sighed angrily.

Then it was time and like a sprinter from the block he was in and enquiring as to where Mrs. Ruth Dorner was. Strange that — he would have said the same thing if they had been married.

A side ward, a few minutes only allowed he was told. It was shadowy inside, the curtains half drawn shutting the bright world out. Ruth was lying in bed and turned away from the door. She raised her head slowly with an effort as he approached. Dim as the room was he was aware that her eyes were gravely serious dark circles from which vitality had gone.

'Ruth,' and bent over her, grasped her hand in his. 'What's the matter? What the hell's wrong?' Worry made his voice brusque.

'Hello Edward,' she breathed, shrugging with her eyebrows and making the smallest sideways movement of her head.

'Not like you, Ruth.' Or was it? Perhaps he had not noticed the change coming. 'What do the doctors say?'

'Don't know, Edward.' Was there something accusatory in her stare? 'Are you all right?'

He nodded impatiently. 'Oh yes, it's you I'm bothered about.' His tone became uncomprehending. 'I mean — what — what are they treating you for?' Her shape was small and obscure under the stretched sheets.

Ruth's gaze slid away and she was silent.

'Have you eaten?'

'I think so — I'm not sure.'

'Are you comfortable?' He played with her pillow and touched her hair gently. The pressure of her hand increased against his. Edward was puzzled by the absence of drugs or medicines on the locker next to her bed.

'Perhaps a couple of days rest, you'll be all right then,' he said with a cheerfulness he did not feel.

'Yes,' and it was a whisper.

'Perhaps a holiday — a change,' he suggested. Just a case of being run down, he thought, and strain over the last years. What with marriage and helping him — they must have taken their toll. But she frightened him the way she looked now.

'D'you want anything — a drink?'

She moved slightly in the bed, murmured, 'No, I'll be all right thanks, Edward.'

It seemed an effort for her to speak.

Behind him the door opened. The efficient face above the apron. 'Long enough for now, please.'

Edward leaned over, kissed Ruth on the forehead, gained the impression that she had already said goodbye to him. 'I'll be in this evening. Don't worry Ruth, you'll be all right.' Optimistic words. He wasn't sure, at a loss and alarmed.

Outside in the corridor he realised that in that alarm he had not reiterated his love for her. He saw the doctor who seemed very young and remembered the saying about policemen. When doctors also looked very young were you getting old?

Was he the husband?

No, brother-in-law. It sounded strange. Should have been the husband but too late.

The papers flipped on the other side of the desk. So far they hadn't been able to find anything wrong. The patient had been in a collapsed state, rock bottom and exhausted, but otherwise no other disease. Should be all right after quiet and rest.

Edward went away somewhat relieved, but still troubled.

On his second visit that evening however, great anxiety returned, Ruth appearing no better. William was just leaving when he arrived.

'Don't stay long,' he said curtly and brushed past Edward. The latter stared after him angrily, then calmed himself. Ruth was the important one.

One week later he and William stood opposite each other at Ruth's bedside. She had not improved, and if anything was worse. When she did speak in reply she was distant and vague and Edward had the dreadful feeling that she was drifting away from them. God! What was happening? Why couldn't something be done? He glanced across at William. 'Have you had a word with the doctor?'

'Of course I have.' William's brows were one line and his tone edgy.

'Well what did he say?' His own was just as short and impatient.

'They don't know what's wrong.' He breathed out deeply. 'But I do.'

'Oh.' Edward stared at him in some surprise.

'It's all through you — you and your blasted place. She's worried herself sick over you. That's all it is.'

Edward was shocked at the outburst. 'No — no, it's not true, you know it isn't.' Even as he denied it though, he knew there was a measure of truth in his brother's accusation.

'You know I'm damned right,' grated William. 'You've taken all her money.' He nodded at his brother's expression. 'Oh yes, I know all about that. I hope you're bloody satisfied at what you've done. By hell, she's paid a big price.' His face twisted contemptuously. 'It must be great living on someone else's money.'

Edward reeled and flinched inwardly under the attack. No words would form in his brain for several seconds, then he retorted fiercely, 'You've some room to talk — a short memory you've got. Where did you get your money for your hotel from? I'll tell you. From living on an elderly spinster old enough to be your mother, sponging on her for years. Don't talk to me about living on someone else's money, you're an expert at it. When I was lying under cars trying to make a living you were lying on her and getting paid for it.' He paused for breath as William glared at him across the bed, then carried on, 'It didn't end there did it? You had a go at my wife. Remember Elaine? Yes of course you do. How much did you get from her, or was that just for love?'

Taut and leaning they faced each other across a Ruth forgotten by both. They were not to see the flutter and widening of eyes beneath them.

'You may have married Ruth, but it's me she loves — and I love her,' Edward stressed savagely.

'Took you a long time to find out. Seems to me you only thought of it after I married her,' William threw back cynically.

'If I'd have married her, I wouldn't be seeing someone else behind her back.' Edward hadn't meant to reveal what Ruth had told him, but it was out and he watched the insolent smile fade from William's face. He pressed on. 'Yes, she knows.' His voice grew louder in his anxiety and anger. 'And that's why she's bloody ill now.' He glanced down at the figure in the bed. 'Oh, what a selfish bastard I've been. How I love her — I do,' he choked. He saw her eyes widen and her lips move.

Another voice joined in, an urgent admonishing one. 'Please will you not quarrel in here. The patient will not be helped by such noise. I'm sorry but you will have to leave now. The doctor would like to see the patient's husband — Mr. William Dorner.'

Shamefacedly and apologetically alike they left

the room to part in the corridor without speaking, William accompanying the sister to see the doctor, and Edward upset and miserable to make his way home.

Once there he locked himself in his private quarters and sat staring out into the night, and blaming himself for the state which Ruth was now in. He should have seen it coming on; a breakdown had been inevitable. Too engrossed in his own world. God! please help her. How small and weak she had looked and helpless. She had been a pawn between William and himself. A loyal, faithful girl. She only wanted to be loved — that was all. What a mess they'd made of it between them. The thought of Ruth being ill had never crossed his mind. He'd neglected her. Love. He spat the word mentally. He knew nothing of it. Empty words about love. Empty perhaps until the present. But now they didn't seem to matter to her. There was no sleep for him that night. He rang the hospital twice. Her condition was unchanged.

Two days later after visiting Ruth, Edward was taken aside by the doctor.

'I would like your help Mr. Dorner please. I've had a word with your brother — Mr. William. I was wondering if you could shed any light on the cause of Mrs. Dorner's illness. She's not unfortunately making the progress we had hoped for.'

'I'll do anything I can to help of course.' He had prayed until his mind had gone blank.

'Well, when she was brought in she was very distressed and we couldn't make any sense of what she was saying, but a name did crop up several times

— Elaine. Your brother says that she did know someone called Elaine, but he wasn't able to tell us much about this person.'

No, he wouldn't thought Edward with a bitter cynicism. But he himself must do all possible to aid her recovery. If it meant revealing some of the past he must do so, but mention of prison must be avoided. It would not do his business any good if it became known. 'This is in the strictest confidence?' he asked grave-faced.

'Of course,' the doctor nodded reassuringly.

'All right, I'm a bit involved,' he began. 'Elaine was someone she knew many years ago. This person Elaine was trapped when a dam burst — she was in a cottage in the path of the water. A telephone call was put through for someone to get a message to her. Ruth — er — Mrs. Dorner took the call, but didn't pass it on.' Then very definitely and firmly he stressed, 'There was no way in which Elaine could have been saved even if the message had been passed on. The water had already swept her and everything away.'

The doctor nodded in a way which suggested to Edward that the information would help. 'Now, I'm going to ask you something which I hope you can answer to help us further. It is strictly between us as I've already said. I've no wish to pry into anything private, but I do feel that it may have a bearing — from what you've told me — on Mrs. Dorner's case.'

'If it will help Ruth, that's all that matters.'

'Thank you. Now all I want to know is — was the act of not passing the message on deliberate on her part, or did she just forget?'

He saw Edward's hesitation. 'It is to help the patient, Mr. Dorner, that's all we're bothered about.'

'It was deliberate,' he answered quietly and steadily.

The doctor tapped his top lip with his pen as he continued to gaze at Edward, then went on, 'In that case I'm sure we can do something for her, Mr. Dorner. It's quite possible that she's still suffering from a guilt complex, probably suppressed during the intervening years.' He looked decidedly hopeful. 'Well that's something else we can work on,' then confided, 'she had given us cause for anxiety over the last week.'

And as Edward left he reflected that the doctor's last statement echoed his own feelings. However, after the consultation he left the hospital in a much more optimistic and cheerful mood than when he had entered.

Edward paid several visits the following week, and making sure that they did not coincide with those of William. He was determined that a repeat of their quarrel over Ruth would not take place.

A worried Frederick joined him on several occasions, and after one took him by the arm, gravely anxious, and asked, 'What's the matter with Mum, Dad? Is she going to be all right again?'

'Yes she is, Frederick.' He tried to sound positive. 'Already I think she's looking brighter, don't you?'

His son pulled a doubtful face. 'Perhaps a little, I'm not sure. She doesn't say much does she?'

'That's because she's still weak. One thing we will

have to do when she's better is to look after her — all of us. We must never let her get like this again. But I'm sure she's going to be all right, so don't worry Frederick,' he added encouragingly.

Later when Edward thought about Ruth, he too wasn't so sure. To him she appeared not to have improved much. She still seemed distant and lost, and once asked him where William was, why were they not there together. The fact that William had been separately did not satisfy her. He had held on to her hand, as if by doing so he could banish the terrifying feeling that she was slipping away into a dark abyss at the side of the bed.

The next day on William's instructions she was moved into the most expensive private ward available and a top specialist called in to help. Then later Edward received a call from the hospital saying the specialist — a Dr. Le Marquand — would like a word with him regarding Mrs. Dorner. He was puzzled as to why he should be asked. Why not William — her husband? But perhaps he had already seen him. Whatever they wanted him for, he was glad to attend if he could help Ruth in any way.

Edward arrived at the appointed time at the hospital and was shown into the consulting room. He was very surprised to find William already there. 'Oh, I'm sorry — I didn't realise you had . . . ' and turned to go.

The man behind the desk called and waved for him to come in again. 'It's all right, Mr. Dorner, it was arranged that you should both be here. What I have to say concerns you both.' Edward took a seat in front of the desk alongside William under the observing gaze of the consultant — a middle-aged lean man, of eagle nose and dark hair which had waves in it too deep to be natural. His eyes were prominent and sharp behind thin rim spectacles. Putting his hands flat on the paper and cards in front of him he said, 'Right gentlemen,' then addressed William. 'Now let me begin by saying that you, Mr. Dorner, are paying me a large sum of money to find out what's wrong with your wife and to help her to become well again. I like to believe that I earn my fees and sometimes in the pursuance of that ideal I have gained a reputation for being straight and calling a spade a spade.' His glance moved from one to the other. 'You will understand then that what I have to say to you may appear possibly offensive, but we are here with only one person's interest at heart. That is correct is it not?'

Edward nodded firmly and William uttered his agreement, though neither looked at the other.

'Very well then,' continued the consultant, 'you are both I'm sure men of the world and successful in it. No doubt you will have found out that to become successful you will have had to use your intelligence and common sense — call it what you will.'

Edward wondered what he was getting at and was further surprised when the speaker went on, 'You're both familiar with the Herm suite where the patient is.'

'Yes, of course,' replied William frowning, and just as puzzled obviously as Edward was.

The doctor regarded each man seriously for a moment, 'Behind that door is a very sick woman. You know that as well as I do. When she was admitted to the hospital she was suffering from a combination of things, but only one of which was physical. She was run down and at a low ebb; the others were of a psychological nature.'

William looked astounded. 'Psychological — her mind! But I don't understand. How could that be? She has no money worries, a lovely home and clothes — she lacks for nothing.'

'Yes, Mr. Dorner, her mind,' echoed the man behind the desk. 'Your wife's case has something of a jigsaw about it, but a jigsaw where you do not see all the pieces. You have to search for them and then they present themselves. Sometimes you think you have all the pieces and the right ones, but then you find you are wrong and have to build again. Between the three of us we have the ability to complete the jigsaw and promote a complete recovery in Mrs. Dorner. Both of you share one piece, I hold another and you,' he said looking directly at William, 'as the husband — one more. The strengthening of her body is already taking place, and I'm quite satisfied with her progress.'

'Are you sure?'

The consultant eyed him then carried on, ignoring William's look of nonplussed irritation. 'As for me, acting on the information given to my colleague, I have been able to make the guilt complex she had recede.' He focused his attention on William again and spoke very deliberately. 'For your part as the husband I advise you to seek and keep the company of your wife. A woman withers if she is not loved, Mr. Dorner.'

Edward cringed inside himself — he too must

take some of the blame for that, while William looked upset and angry, exclaiming, 'Look, I think you've gone a bit too far. You've no right to . . . .'

'Haven't I?' interjected the other. 'I thought the object of you coming here was to get your wife well again. After all I did warn at the start of this consultation that I might be thought of as giving offence. You must understand that it is for your wife's health that I am saying what I consider necessary.' Suddenly he leaned across the desk, his tone harsh and forceful. 'My God man! Don't you realise you've had a beautiful woman there — will be again? Court her — treasure her, and watch her flower again.'

For a moment William sat staring at the specialist, set-faced and flushed, and Edward thought he might get up and walk out, but then his brother somewhat unexpectedly admitted, 'Yes, you did, and I acknowledge that — you're quite right. I really must spend more time with her.' He gave a quick excusing half smile. 'Business takes up so much of my time you understand?'

'I'm sure it does, Mr. Dorner,' and the others tone held just the faintest of cynical sarcasm. 'But remember from now on she must come first.' He gazed at him steadily. 'No doubt you could ease off somewhat now. Another thing, just supposing you were to become ill, have a breakdown and not be able to look after your wife.'

William laughed shortly. 'Me! No fear of be being ill. I've been very fit all my life — that's not likely to happen.' His tone was boastful, certain.

The doctor shrugged then glanced at Edward.

'Now what I'm going to say next concerns you both — very much so, and is perhaps the most important thing I shall say to you today in relation to Mrs. Dorner. Together you hold the last piece of the jigsaw to her full health. If you do not act on my advice, you could lose her. To be blunt — she will die — no matter what medicine I prescribe for her.' He nodded at their shocked faces and went on, 'It appears that you are not on good terms with one another. Now, I don't care a damn what's happened between you in the past, but when it affects a patient of mine then I do bloody care. You imbeciles! You quarrelled over her bed. Where was your intelligence? Left outside when you went in to see her, no doubt. Has it ever occurred to you that that is one of the reasons why she is as she is today?'

He banged the desk top once. 'You must unite in front of her, be friendly to each other when you see her.' He paused, shaking his head in a kind of despair. 'I don't want to know what the trouble is between you — it cannot be worth a life — and that's what it amounts to in this case. But one thing is for sure, you've got to get it ironed out and settled if you want Mrs. Dorner out of this hospital, and to stay out. It's up to you.' He stood up. 'Now I'm going to tell you what you're going to do — together,' and he emphasised the last word. 'You're going out of here, out of the hospital and into town to buy the largest bouquet of flowers that you can have made up. You will return here to me, and then we shall go to the patient's room, and I shall stand at the door, and you gentlemen are then going to smile at each other while standing at the same side of the bed. You will then present the flowers to Mrs. Dorner. And remember, between you you hold the balance of whether she improves or not. Now get out of here. Don't let me down and, much more important, don't let Ruth down.'

He did not close the door on them immediately but watched them disappear round a corner in the corridor. A peculiar relationship between the brothers and the woman, he thought. Successful in business and yet so lacking in communicative ability. Getting the Dorner men together had been a long shot. It may work. If it didn't, then as regards Mrs. Ruth Dorner he would have a real problem on his hands.

It was raining when the two very chastened brothers left the building. 'Damn rain,' said William.

'I don't know what's happening to the weather,' said Edward. Each was very glad of the vagaries of the island climate. They had spoken together calmly, finding fault, but not with each other. They sat side by side in William's car and drove into town, parked on the Esplanade and found a florists in the High street.

William gazed around the shop. 'Blast if I know anything about flowers. Do you, Edward?'

'No, I can't say I do. Perhaps roses — they always seem to look well.' William had called him by his first name for the first time in years. The whole business didn't seem real. Here they were in a flower shop together and speaking normally to each other. There was strain, but they were talking.

'Well, shall we have a mixture of colours?'

'A good idea, William,' he smiled. 'We'll play safe,

otherwise we'll get into trouble — you know what women are,' and he laughed awkwardly, realising that it had been rather a stupid thing to say in the circumstances that had existed between them. He pretended to busy himself inspecting the flora nearby, suddenly annoyed at himself for his thoughts — don't spoil things.

The bouquet took the two to carry it, and watched by passers-by they placed it in the car.

Edward wasn't easy with a silence between them as they began the return. 'Nice car you've got here, William,' he observed, glancing at his brother. Was this the person that he had at times felt hate for?

'You get used to it, I suppose. Can be a bit difficult threading it through traffic — I like it.' But there was a note of pleasurable pride at Edward's comment. And Edward kept his fingers on the bouquet — a link between the three.

Out of the car again they approached the hospital entrance carrying the large array of flowers between them. Suddenly William staggered, wobbled, and Edward with his free hand clutched at his brother's arm instinctively to steady him. Afterwards it occurred to him that it was the first deliberate physical contact between them for many years.

William glanced downwards. 'Must have tripped over something,' but when Edward looked there was nothing, only smooth tarmac. Then he remembered William's rather jerky walk to the car when they had left the hospital earlier, but forgot about the observation when they reached Ruth's room and found the specialist, Dr. Le Marquand, there in conversation with her.

He affected great surprise when he saw them, though some of it must have been genuine when he saw the size of the bouquet. 'Well gentlemen, you certainly don't do anything by halves — quite magnificent.' Nodding approvingly at Edward and William, he moved towards the door then looked over his shoulder when he reached it. 'I'll leave you now, Mrs. Dorner, in the capable hands of your menfolk. Must be very flattering to be the object of so much attention.' His eyes rested momentarily on the brothers before he closed the door, his expression leaving them in no doubt as to what was expected from them.

And remembering their instructions they stood together at the same side of the bed, Edward allowing William to be nearest to Ruth; after all he was her husband. Edward observed her anxiously, and noted an awakening of delighted surprise as she gazed from the flowers to them. Her face was still drawn, but there was a faint tinge of pink to the skin now, and life stirred in her eyes.

Ruth touched and fingered the petals in the huge bouquet, its crown resting on her pillow, then she gently placed her face amongst the flowers — the white, the red, the yellow and the unusual purple. A tear emerged and showed halfway down her cheek. An arm gathered the brothers' heads down to her own. A kiss for each of equal pressure. 'Dear William, dear Edward. How kind. Much too much.' Other tears joined the first and fell away. 'And you got these together? You went together?'

'Of — of course.' Edward spoke first. 'Neither of us know much about flowers, so we thought two heads would be better than one.' Through his emotion he managed a smile. 'I think we did quite well.'

Ruth glanced in awe at the flowers. 'For me — all these?'

'You're the only woman in our lives, Ruth,' William stated and his voice was no steadier than Edward's had been.

Edward pretended to inspect the flowers very intently and closely. Didn't want to make an idiot of himself. Ruth lay back with a sigh and immediately two pairs of eyes were fearfully peering down on her. She lifted her hands, and they took one each, and a very slow relaxed smile appeared over her features, the lines and creases of illness as if by magic smoothing and stretching away. Her eyes closed.

'Are you all right, Ruth?' Edward asked anxiously.

A little nod. 'Oh yes I am — now, and thank you both. What a lovely glorious surprise.'

'Perhaps we'd better go Edward, d'you think?' and his brother agreed.

A gleam showed between her lids. 'You'll come tomorrow — together?' she murmured.

Edward spoke with wet eyes. 'Try and stop us.'

The smile appeared again, but her lids remained closed as they tiptoed out.

The next few days saw a remarkable change in Ruth's health, from her bed to a chair, from the chair to busying herself in her room, and then short walks along the corridor. A new vitality shone from the violet eyes and the cheeks, although still pale, began to round. An urgency to get out and catch up with life was coursing through her. And Edward and

William were there to see it occur, making sure that they visited her together once a day, with William seeing her alone at other times. Frederick played his part also, being present as often as he was allowed and helping to bridge the gap when awkward silences occurred between his father and Uncle William.

And Edward who not so long ago had railed bitterly against a God that would take his new found love away so quickly, prayed his soul-felt thanks for her recovery one night. His love had blossomed too late. She belonged to William, but he had learned his lesson, and would never make the mistake of taking her for granted again. It was to be hoped that William felt the same.

He began to visit them at their house at Albecq, and saw the difference in Ruth who was more contented, and in William who was spending more of his time at home with her and relaxing.

As for Ruth, she delighted in seeing them together. Then one weekend about a month after her return home, she and William spent a weekend in Jersey to celebrate her full recovery. It was cool and bright and being late in the season they had some places to themselves. They went for walks and took rather self-conscious photographs of each other. Sat in cosy hotel bars and looked out towards Guernsey. They held hands, and splashed bare foot in the water at St. Brelades. A bird sat in Ruth's palm at Rozel, and she ate a box of expensive chocolates in a very short time.

Edward was happy — happy that Ruth was well and would be enjoying herself. He was also aware of another improving relationship. Having forced himself to be pleasant and cheerful towards William for Ruth's sake during her illness, he found that it had become something of a habit. The lessening of the tension and erstwhile hostility that had existed for so long was a good feeling. The awkwardness that he had felt must have been apparent at times though; it had been too soon to forgive and forget entirely. His mind however was becoming freer of the grudges and grievances of the years past, and he suspected that it was true for William also. The latter had even mentioned about recommending people to stay at the Ormer, if they wished for a smaller quieter hotel. How strange that it had taken Ruth's illness to bring about such a change.

And in another part of the island of Guernsey, a certain Doctor Le Marquand poured himself a drink at the end of the day and made a silent congratulatory toast to himself — he should have been a damned detective!

19

But Edward was to see a troubled frown again on Ruth's face not long afterwards. He had called one evening as he had begun to do usually once a week. It pleased Ruth, and William, although he didn't say, appeared to welcome his visits. Edward was careful to go when they were both at home. He had come to terms with his love for Ruth, and had no wish to go behind William's back. His chance had come and gone long ago, and he accepted the fact now.

On that particular evening he could see that she was worried about something, and it was only when William left the room briefly that Edward found out what it was.

'It's William,' Ruth said in a low voice. 'He's become quite unsteady at times when he's walking. I haven't said anything to him about it and he hasn't to me. What shall I do Edward? I don't want to upset him.'

Edward regarded her. He could be flippant and ask if his brother was drinking more, but Ruth's anxious and serious countenance prohibited that. 'Give it another month Ruth,' he suggested, 'see if he improves. If not just mention it to him — let him see you've noticed, and ask him to see his Doctor. It'll be something and nothing I'm sure.'

Ruth brightened at this. 'Yes I'll do that, Edward, because he seems well enough otherwise.' She seemed relieved and comforted by his advice, though Edward couldn't stop an undercurrent of jealousy coursing through him at her concern for her husband.

On his way home however he thought about William and was far from sure that his brother was suffering from something and nothing. He himself had noticed William's unsteadiness and he recalled him stumbling once when they were at the hospital to see Ruth, and he had also lost some weight. Then he fell to wondering if William would ever visit him at the Ormer. It would have been nice to show his brother around and let him see what had been done, and the transformation that had taken place over the years. Some day perhaps.

Another month went by and Edward heard from Ruth that William was no better but no worse, and that she had persuaded him to visit the doctor as a precaution. The fact that William's condition had not worsened was encouraging, Edward thought, and told her so.

But then an incident occurred which, for the time being, drove everything else from his mind. He had decided to keep the hotel open over into the new year, and close for a month in January or February. A lot of hoteliers closed down until the following Easter. However it had been noticed there had been a trend for people to take short breaks in what had been considered the quiet part of the year. While no one could expect Mediterranean weather, walkers could enjoy the beauty of the cliff paths on cold but bright invigorating days. The island tourist industry was also opening museums concerning the occupation, and places relating to the matter were being shown on the maps. Also a new leisure centre had been opened — the island was catching up with the times. So it was that Edward in the middle of December was checking the guest list. Occasionally Frederick liked to give a hand when the regular staff were off duty or on holiday, and he would take the bookings if Edward or the usual receptionist were not available. Frederick had seen the building as a ruin, helped his father from the very beginning as a youngster. This had made the bond between them even stronger and given him a deep affection for the place.

Edward's finger ran down the list of guests already there. There were eight in all. Not bad for the time of the year, it kept things ticking over. Then he turned to the small pile of letters from people wanting future reservations, and those who had already telephoned and written to confirm their holiday.

He picked up the top one, the writer's address embossed on the pure white paper. The letters growing larger than the page. Scarton Manor, Daleford! And below the few penned lines the name that set his heart pounding. Maxime Scarton! His lips formed the name. He skimmed the words — confirmation of arrival on Saturday the twelfth of December. It was now Monday. She would arrive the following Saturday. Shock, joy, rampant emotions made the letter shake in his hand. He had written some weeks before and in the worry and trouble of Ruth's illness he had forgotten. And now a reply to his letter. After all those years. One had reached her. Deep down in himself he had doubted if he would hear from her, but he had — it was a miracle.

Edward hurried up to his room, sank down in front of his fire and gazed in wonderment at the signature. Traced it with his finger. Maxime Scarton — his daughter — a tiny thing when he last saw her, a world away; from another life almost. A faint smell of perfume from the paper. The few lines — neat, feminine, slightly backward sloping writing.

Steadying himself he read it again. 'Dear Sirs,' — a disappointment took him — so formal. 'To confirm my previous enquiry. Hope to join you in time for dinner.' He frowned, not having seen one, but of course if he'd been elsewhere when the enquiry came, it would have been dealt with by his receptionist or Frederick. Neither would have attached any undue importance to the name. Edward looked again at the signature — Scarton. Why not Dorner? That was her proper name. But then she would have been brought up with the name of Scarton, perhaps not even knowing she was a Dorner. Yes, that was it he decided. Her grandparents would have made certain that she never heard the latter name. This would explain the formal note of the letter. He was a stranger to her, and she was coming to his hotel as a guest. She was being correct, and businesslike, but once she was there in the new Ormer he would be her father, and all formality would disappear.

Edward returned to the letter several times that day. She was going to surprise him, that is why she had kept all the details about herself until they met. She would be excited just as he was, and by

Saturday he would be hardly able to wait until she arrived. He looked at the register of guests booked for the following week. There it was — Miss Maxime Scarton, and departing the following Wednesday. Only four days! Huge disappointment gripped him. Four days. What could they do in that short period? There was so much to say to her, to show her. His island, and hers he hoped some day. Oh! There would be so much to talk about. Then he reasoned and understood. If she worked she would only have so much time off. Perhaps with it being winter she had to return sooner. What did she do? The fact that she might be working surprised him. Being brought up by the Scartons, he thought that they would perhaps have raised her as a young woman of leisure, like her mother. Elaine's image flashed before him. Dark, sophisticated, spoilt and rotten morals. Was Maxime dark? He guessed she would be and tall perhaps. She would be pretty enough. Would she have a little of his looks? He wanted to tell everyone, but decided to wait until she came, and then he would surprise them all. Imagine their faces when he introduced her to his staff. How proud he would be. A thought jolted his happiness. Should he tell Ruth? She had known that he had a child by Elaine. But it was another woman's child, albeit by marriage. He guessed that as far as Ruth was concerned Maxime just did not exist, and in all the intervening years she had never asked about her or mentioned her name — did not want her to exist. Another face came before him — William's. No! She was his. The new-found understanding between himself and his brother did not go that far.

But Edward had to tell someone beforehand so he told Frederick, and his fingers were clumsy with excitement as he turned the leaves of the hotel register. Frederick had been preparing to go home and looked mildly puzzled as his father's finger indicated and then rested on one particular name. His parent's eyes held a feverish light. 'See that name, Frederick.'

He bent closer and nodded. 'Yes.' Gave a little shrug. 'Miss Maxime Scarton,' he read out. Just a new booking, that was all. Looked at Edward again enquiringly. 'Nice name but . . . . . . ' A thought came. 'Oh, is it someone on television coming — an actress — it sounds a bit theatrical?'

'No.' His father shook his head smilingly, obviously enjoying the suspense he was creating.

'All right Dad, go on tell me. You're bursting to tell me anyway.'

The eyes clung to his. Edward hesitated then, 'Didn't know you had a sister, did you Frederick?' and waiting to catch every change to come in his son's face.

'A sister! I've got a sister!'

'Well, a half sister really,' the older man qualified, beaming happiness.

'But — I mean — my name — Dorner. She's Scarton. After all this time?' Bloody hell, his life was full of surprises.

His father's hand rested on his shoulder. 'Now you know, Frederick,' he said in delighted satisfaction. 'Look, come over here and I'll just explain. I know it must be a bit of a shock.'

Damn well was, but not a bad one Frederick thought. The dining room was empty and they sat at one of the tables. His father gave a wry smile, looked a bit uncomfortable, then began, 'It's a long story really. You see, your mother and I as you know never got round to marrying each other. She came back here and I stayed in England and found work. I met this girl from a family called Scarton. Thought I loved her enough to marry her. We married, but it didn't work out. We had a daughter, Maxime, and she is the one who is coming to stay here, but for only four days — worse luck. Her mother died when she was young.' Frederick saw the flinch flash across his father's features. 'And then her grandparents brought her up as far as I know. They would never allow me to see her, and they didn't answer my letters. But I kept writing and now she's confirmed in a letter that she's coming to stay here.' The anticipatory excitement returned to his father's eyes. 'She wanted to surprise me obviously.'

'But she didn't enclose a personal letter to you with it?' Frederick thought it rather odd.

'No, as I say she must just want to wait until we meet. We shall have so much to say to each other.' His father regarded him a little anxiously. 'You don't mind? I mean that you have a relative you didn't know about.'

It was a bit strange certainly, but rather exciting also. He smiled. 'No of course not — I'm rather looking forward to meeting her. Just takes a bit of getting used to — the fact that I've got a half sister popping up in a few days' time.'

His father nodded at him understandingly. 'Yes I

suppose it does. Sorry I had to spring it on you like that. I've never mentioned her before.' His expression became reflective — a glance back into some memory. 'I thought that part of my life had been finished with.'

Again Frederick caught the glimpse of something unpleasant in his father's memories.

Then the latter got up, smiling cheerfully again. 'This calls for a toast, Frederick,' and his son watched as he poured out two wines from the dining room bar and returned with them. They touched glasses. 'To Maxime — the lost but now found again addition to my family.' It was said with a flourish and pride.

'To Maxime,' returned Frederick.

Creases deepened in the brow opposite. 'It might be a good thing if you didn't say anything to your mother about Maxime just yet.'

As he went home Frederick thought that it wouldn't have done any harm — couldn't see why his mother would object to Maxime's coming. Still, his father had requested him not to say anything, but it would be rather hard, keeping something like that to himself. It wasn't every day you found out you had a sister — well a half sister that you didn't know you had. Quite exciting really.

That night in bed Frederick lay deep in thought about Maxime — the new figure to come into his life shortly. He couldn't help thinking that it was rather strange that she had not written a proper letter or telephoned his father. Just a formal booking for four days' stay at the Ormer. Perhaps as his father had suggested she was saving everything until they met. The old man was on a high — just waiting for Saturday to arrive.

Frederick wondered about the death of Maxime's mother. His father hadn't said how she died. And why had they hindered his attempts to see his own daughter? All sorts of questions pushed into his mind and out again unanswered. He thought of his own mother. His father had said he had not got around to marriage, but she was sweet on him. As he had grown older he had realised the fact by the things she had said and let slip. But sad at times — very sad. Had cried when he had been younger — he'd seen her. Remembered when his father had come to stay with him, though he knew him then as Uncle Edward. That night when they had quarrelled he had been young and hadn't understood that people could be angry with each other and still be in love. When he had pushed open the door of his mother's bedroom, the sight had shocked and frightened him. His father holding her down as she struggled, her white legs spread and he embedded between them. Looking back he remembered them frozen into a tableau at his interruption as both had stared at him, then the sound of flesh withdrawing. The embarrassment that had doused the rage between them temporarily.

The young man smiled with the arrogance of his age. He would not be shocked or frightened any longer, having made love himself. Why on earth his father and mother had not got together and married he just didn't know, but they should have done. Instead she had married Uncle William. It didn't make sense. Frederick's eyes closed contentedly. His parents did not quarrel any more.

Saturday came and found Edward almost ready for the arrival that evening of his very important guest. He had thought of putting her into his bedroom, but it occupied a position at the rear of the building and the outlook was rather restricted. Instead he had prepared one of the rooms overlooking the bay for her. The carpet had been pulled up and a new one in powder blue had been relaid, and a delicately made dressing table put in place of the usual guest furniture. Colourful curtains and matching bed linen were added also. Drawers were lined afresh and scented, the windows cleaned again and the woodwork polished. As a final touch he had a large box of chocolates placed on the corner of the dressing table and he agonised for a while over what he should write upon it. 'From your Father' sounded pompous and old-fashioned. 'From Dad — welcome,' a little better. Finally he decided on just 'Welcome'. He could put into words what he felt later.

Sometime around four o'clock he put on his best suit and his favourite shirt. A good impression must be made on his daughter. Perhaps she would like dinner in the hotel's dining room that evening, but on other occasions she would dine with him in his room. A separate table for one had been made ready in the dining room for her, but in case she wanted to dine alone with him he had everything ready in his room also. On both tables he had set a bottle of the best wine he had in stock. As far as food went she could choose from the evening menu, or if she preferred something else it would be made specially for her. As an afterthought he had a bunch of flowers ready to present to her. His welcome for her was complete. A glow of happy and overwhelming excitement began to take hold of him. His world was becoming beautiful. He would introduce Maxime to Frederick. His children — son and daughter, his family under one roof. How fortunate he was. Then he spent an hour making a list of places he was going to take her. Show her the island. How proud he would be to escort her and tried to visualise her, but it was all guesswork. His mind turned away from a likeness to Elaine although the latter's face had blurred somewhat in memory with the years.

Edward looked at his watch every few minutes. The boat would be in about six o'clock. If she were flying she would be in earlier. For the umpteenth time he made a tour of the Ormer.

At four thirty the telephone rang in reception. Edward was nearby wondering if there was anything he had forgotten to do before Maxime's arrival, and vaguely aware of the receptionist's voice in the background. 'The Ormer Hotel.' A short silence then, 'Oh, I'm sorry — yes, I see — arrange some other time. Very well Miss Scarton. Oh! one moment please, Mr. Dorner is here. Hello — hello.'

Edward's feet were swift when he heard the name of his daughter. Perhaps she had arrived earlier than she had expected and was calling to tell him. Miriam the receptionist still held the instrument, and Edward heard the constant buzzing and stared at her.

'I'm sorry Mr. Dorner, she must have put the phone down.'

'Perhaps she ran out of coins,' Edward suggested eagerly.

Miriam looked at her employer's face and felt awful. 'I'm sorry Mr. Dorner, I'm afraid she's not coming. Unforeseen circumstances, she said. She'll arrange a visit later.'

'Not coming! But of course she's coming. What d'you mean? Maxime is coming today — she arranged to come today.'

'I'm so sorry, Mr. Dorner, but that's just what she said. I was going to put you on, but the phone went down.'

'Nothing — just that?'

Miriam nodded helplessly, watching the vitality and anticipatory excitement drain from her employer's face.

'Not coming!' His tone was incredulous as he turned slowly, his gaze becoming distant.

'Can I get you anything Mr. Dorner?'

'No — no thanks Miriam.' With heavy awkward steps he hunched away to his room, to slump into his chair empty of energy — everything. And the flowers he had bought for her continued to look gay and colourful.

Later when he thought about it he realised he had set far too much store on Maxime's coming, and after all people did cancel for one reason or another. Her grandparents could be ill or she herself could be unwell even though she had made the call. It was the brevity of both the message and also the original booking of the holiday which was puzzling, and now hurtful. Surely she could have just waited long enough on the phone for him to just have a word with her, after all those years. Instead it had all been so impersonal. Edward did not understand, but he clung in hope to the fact that she had said she would arrange to come some other time. He sighed despondently. Whoever got the room now would think themselves lucky.

In the meantime reception received another call from someone just off the plane and the room was taken.

When Frederick found out he was surprised and sorry for his father. Maxime's coming had meant so much to him. He felt disappointed himself, had been looking forward to meeting the new female member of the family. On the other hand it could be a good advertisement for the hotel if it was thought that all the rooms were like the one that had been prepared for her.

As was his custom at dinner Edward went into the dining room and stopped at each table briefly to wish his guests good evening. He had not felt up to doing it, but he made himself, remembering the days when the possibility of even one person dining at the Ormer was a far off dream. Business was business and his feelings had to be hidden.

The fire was burning brightly and the dining room looked cosy and welcoming. There were about a dozen people in. Automatically Edward's glance went to the table that had been reserved for Maxime. A young woman occupied it, dark haired in a green dress and bending over her plate. He was mildly surprised — a coincidence that another young woman should be seated there. On his reaching her table she raised a serious face in reply to his greeting and hope that she would enjoy her stay. Just for a moment he thought he'd seen her before, wasn't quite sure where; something about the eyes.

As he left the dining room he glanced back to find her gazing after him, and he responded with a quick smile. Perhaps she was a little shy and taking time to settle in. A wave of depression enveloped him. If Maxime had been seated there — how different. He would have sat opposite her, they would have been absorbed in conversation. Asking her about her room, did she like it. Seeing the pleasure and happiness on the young face. Introduced her, and would have announced with great pride that she was his daughter. Plans for the following day. His dream faded, it was not to be. Sometime in the future perhaps, but he had the feeling in his present mood that it could be never.

The following morning he saw the same young woman going out. Quite a striking young woman, and well-dressed. Somewhere near Maxime's age. Mentally he shook himself. It was no good dwelling on Maxime. Must put her out of his mind and get on with running the hotel.

At dinner that evening he paused again by the young woman's table. 'Is everything all right? Enjoying yourself?' He enquired politely.

She glanced up. 'Yes.' If she said thank you it was inaudible to him.

'And your room?'

'It's very nice.' Her voice lacked enthusiasm, but

her large dark eyes were now deeply observant of him — disconcertingly so.

'Oh good.' Her manner was not conducive to further conversation, but he persisted in explanation. 'As a matter of fact that particular room was made ready for my daughter's coming from England, but unfortunately she had to cancel.' Edward shrugged and smiled pleasantly. 'So you've got it instead.'

At that moment her next course arrived and he moved on. She made him feel uncomfortable, he did not know why, but she was difficult to talk to and he was rather put out by her lack of enthusiasm for her room — it had just been 'very nice'. All the effort that had gone into preparing it. Maxime, of course, would have loved it.

Edward saw her walking by herself along Moulin Huet beach the next day. She seemed a lonely sort of girl, though not as shy as he had first thought, and sophisticated, but he couldn't quite place her accent. This was rather a rare occurrence as he prided himself on being able to tell where visitors came from without looking at the hotel register.

On the second evening just before dinner Edward developed a bout of sneezing and realised he was without a handkerchief. Slipping up the stairs quickly, his footsteps were quiet on the carpet. Turning on to the passage leading to his room he was surprised to see a woman leaving it. She started when she saw him and he saw that it was the young woman who was staying alone.

She laughed shortly, nervously. 'Lost my way — thought that was my room.' Stared at him and in such a way that he guessed she was lying.

Edward had forgotten her name for the moment and recovering from his surprise said, 'Oh, it's easily done,' and pointed down the passage. 'Go to the end and turn right.' She wore a crimson dress and her dark hair framed her face in a page boy style.

Edward gazed after her. She was attractive, even beautiful. A memory long dormant stirred, revived by the colour of her dress. Stirred, that was all. He glanced around his room. Nothing was out of place, but suspected again that she had lied. A guest usually put a head into a room if they were not quite sure which was theirs, but she had been fully into his room. Sometimes he did not bother to lock his door. What on earth had she been looking for? Also when he thought about it, she had made no apology. Having found a handkerchief he went downstairs, still puzzling over the incident. She had looked to be dressed for dinner, had probably just left her own room, rather than looking for it as she had said. He glanced at the register again. 'Mary Scrivener, Old Hall, Dove Road, Kent.' It meant nothing. And that night in the dark he dreamed frighteningly of Elaine standing looking at him from the door, and wearing the crimson dress he had seen on the young woman guest.

The daylight and work restored his common sense, until the afternoon at about two thirty when he happened to glance out of the dining room window on to the terrace. For a moment he was held rigid. The figure — staring at the building — Elaine! No! it couldn't be — she was dead years ago. The figure moved out of his sight and Edward sagged in absolute relief, realising that it was the young lady visitor. He sat down — he had to — must get a grip on his imagination. In a way he would be relieved when that particular person had gone. Her departure was to come sooner than he had expected because on referring to her booking he saw that her stay was of only four days duration. She would be leaving the next day.

The following morning after breakfast he was in the hall when she appeared carrying her case which she placed in the reception area. Dressed in a long green winter coat with high collar and attached scarf flung over her shoulders, and matching large beret tilted fashionably forwards over her dark hair. An elegant and striking young woman, Edward thought as he bade her a cheerful good morning.

The guest he knew as Miss Scrivener nodded serious-faced with a barely perceptible return of his greeting and stared at him.

'So you're leaving us today?' he said conversationally as he made out the bill. He was conscious of her continuing stare at the top of his head as he bent over the desk. She was too solemn, had a lovely face, and should smile more. Looking up he met her gaze which to his great astonishment held an ill-concealed hostility. He handed her the bill. Her eyes left his to glance at it. Could he have been wrong? Or was she displeased about the service the hotel offered? Opening her bag she brought out notes and placed them in front of him.

'I hope that you have enjoyed your stay in Guernsey with us, Miss Scrivener,' Edward said as he obtained the necessary change for her and handed it over.

'I did not come here expecting to enjoy myself, Mr. Dorner,' she stated coldly, the dark eyes a shade wider and maintaining their intent gaze upon him.

Edward was nonplussed, feeling that she was rather a peculiar young woman. He had not offended her as far as he was aware, yet he had the feeling that she thought he had. It would be more prudent, he decided, not to seek the reason for her strange remark. Usually people went on holiday for pleasure and to enjoy themselves. 'Have we ordered a taxi for you, Miss Scrivener?'

'Yes.' She half turned away, and Edward was glad of the respite. Her manner was rude and offhand.

Stepping from behind the desk he bent to pick up her case. 'I'll put it by the door for you, ready for when the taxi arrives.' Two words had broken into his consciousness, pounding and repeating for attention. Four days — four days! Had not someone else arranged for four days? Just coincidence surely that another young woman should have arranged the same length of stay — Maxime.

Edward placed the case near the entrance — the coloured airline label attached to the handle settling horizontally beneath his eyes. What was written there in bold letters riveted his crouched body and exploded his reasoning. Miss Maxime Scarton, Scarton Manor, Daleford, Yorkshire! His mind was unable to take it. His finger ran along the words. They should read Miss Mary Scrivener from Kent. Surely that's what they did say — must do. Maxime's cancellation had affected and upset him more than he had realised. And yet the name and address remained as he had first seen it on the label. The initials M.S. — the same — the four days' booking. He stood upright slowly and turned, a hundred questions fighting in his mind, but only one word broke from his lips as he stared back at the woman still standing by the reception desk and watching him. 'Maxime!' He took a step forward. 'Maxime!' She didn't move but remained poised, eyeing him intently, hands to her sides.

Utter joy smothered his reason as he raised his arms to her. 'Maxime — my daughter.' Moved quickly towards her, and she just as quickly stepped backwards. Edward hesitated fractionally, confused. She was here — had been — now she was going. Why? But his great and joyful shock had rendered him insensitive to the rebuff. He made to embrace her. 'Oh Maxime.'

She recoiled away and in her haste almost falling. 'Don't touch me,' she flung at him through clenched teeth, and brushed the air at her sides with her arms as if even that, where his had been, was repugnant to her.

Even then Edward's mind refused to acknowledge the expression on her face for what it was. 'After all these years. Oh Maxime. How well you've grown, into such a beautiful young lady. I didn't recognise you. Such a long time.' Pointed at her case then looked at her in utter bewilderment. 'You're leaving? We haven't been together — spoken. You didn't say — why didn't you . . . ?' Was this reality? Something was wrong. She had cancelled but now she was here and had been for four days under an assumed name.

He felt sick and helpless in his ignorance of what was going on. Clung to a hope and a malicious voice laughed in his head — a feather of a hope. She was an impostor — yes, that was it. 'You're not my daughter — Maxime Dorner. You can't be.'

'No, I'm not. You're quite right. I am Maxime Scarton — Scarton,' she repeated vehemently. 'Dorner means nothing to me. The man who called himself my father went out of my life years ago. He was never in it, do you understand?' Her voice was rising.

Cold had gripped Edward's being and a new all-pervading shock replacing the erstwhile joyous one. He sought refuge in movement. 'Let me take your case upstairs again, Maxime. Some misunderstanding. I know we . . . .' and bent to her case.

'Leave it. Don't touch it.' The sound cut across the space between them like a whiplash.

Edward gazed at her, stunned and miserable at what was happening between them, not believing. 'Why then did you come?' he asked in a flat and hopeless tone. In the background the sounds of the hotel going about its normal business — voices from the dining room and the chink of cutlery.

An overwhelming enmity showed on the face opposite. 'I wanted to see at first hand the person responsible for my mother's death.'

'No!' The cry jerked hoarsely from him. 'No! I didn't, it's not true. You don't know.'

'You wanted her dead so you could carry on with that other woman,' she flung at him fiercely.

Edward's head was shaking his denial before the words would come. 'You can't know. How could you? You don't. You were too young. It's not true.'

'I found out — old newspapers. And the jury thought so. My grandparents told me everything, and they knew. You should still be in prison. D'you know my grandfather died? He wasn't old. He died of a broken heart after losing my mother.' Rage and revulsion twisted her face.

'No — they couldn't. The water killed her. She would never have got away, even if a message had got through. The wall gave way.' Surely to God she could see he was telling the truth.

'You made damn sure that she didn't get away,' Maxime said savagely. 'She didn't have the chance. If she'd had that warning she may still have made it.' Her voice was climbing again. 'How can you say it wasn't you? You admitted it at the trial.'

Yes — he had. Desperately he tried to halt the roller coaster of recrimination and accusation they were on. Pain in his heart and mind he stumbled over his words in his eagerness. 'There were things — things that happened — I — I didn't reveal them then.'

'All right, just for the hell of it, tell me who it was,' she challenged angrily, and the eyes which should have been looking at him in new-found affection were glittering hard and accusing.

Edward was faintly aware of people in the background, then his surroundings became a blur as he focused on Maxime. The past had come alive in the shape of his daughter — revengeful and bitter. Whatever he said he realised would be construed wrongly. Ruth must be kept out of it, and in any case Maxime was so prejudiced and so alienated from him already that it would not have brought them together again. It was obvious that already he had been judged for the second time and found guilty. 'Damn you Maxime, it was the water — nothing else made any difference.' His voice was strained and hoarse under his breaking control. It couldn't be real, this public slanging match between them. Staring, listening faces on the periphery of his vision. Maxime had become Elaine, screaming at him all those years ago. He could see her in front of him, taunting him about his sexuality, his ordinariness, how she was sick of him. The hurt of those years returned again. Wounded, he wanted in turn to savage someone — even a memory. 'If she'd been as quick getting out of that bed as she had been getting in, your mother might have had a chance. She used that cottage with her lovers. She was a tramp. I loved her once. Oh, I don't care what you think Maxime. In fact, I don't care a damn if I never see you again.'

Maxime blanched under his attack. 'No! She was never like that.'

Edward laughed harshly, bitterly, relishing the cruelty. 'Wasn't she? She was a tramp — a beautiful one I'll grant you. I used to stay in at night to watch you whilst she went out. See the evidence in those papers you've obviously been so fond of reading.'

Maxime stared at him and he saw hate there. 'You're still lying. You had a woman coming to the house.'

'There was nothing in it. I sent her away.' Edward suddenly was totally drained, empty, his protest lacking conviction. He could sense Maxime thinking of ways to discredit him further.

She swept air with her arms. 'Look at this place. You didn't work for it. The money came from my mother. You haven't earned it.' The loathing poured out. 'All those years, those sanctimonious letters you sent. Oh yes, I got them — they made me sick, and so do you.' She laughed — a terrible sound. 'Did you really think a tarted up bedroom and a box of chocolates would make me fall into your arms, dear father?' and the latter words were spat out.

Somewhere a horn sounded. He felt her brush past him and the air as the door opened, and then he knew she was gone.

Later when Frederick called he found his father in a dreadful state. All he could get out of him was that Maxime had been and gone after a violent quarrel. Frederick decided the best thing would be to ask his mother to come down — she may be able to help more than he could.

Ruth drove fast, to the side of the man she loved, having been given only the bare details. Her whole being had recoiled at the mention of Maxime, Elaine's daughter, but Edward needed help and all the hurts and jealousies were of long ago. But she couldn't understand. Maxime at the Ormer! Edward had never said anything about her going, rarely mentioned her name. She had left William at home after telling him that Frederick wanted her urgently which was the truth. She was worried — very worried about William and had wanted to talk to Edward about him and what was to be done, but first she must find out what had happened that day at the Ormer.

Edward slumped, distraught, in Ruth's enfolding arms on the couch.

'Oh my dearest. What's the matter? What's happened?' She was alarmed and sickened to find him like that. 'Frederick said something about Maxime having been here,' and she felt him nod against her.

Then haltingly, in utter despair, Edward told her what had happened.

'Why didn't you tell me that she was coming?'

'I didn't want to hurt you. After all she is Elaine's daughter. I couldn't risk you being ill again.'

She stroked his face, great and tender feeling in her words. 'Oh Edward, it's in the past. I'm stronger now and over that. You should have told me, we could have faced it together.' Her heart poured over him; all he'd thought about was shielding her again. 'But why had she such ill feelings towards you? You haven't seen her since she was a child.' Suddenly Ruth was furious. Maxime had no right to do this to him. 'I wish I'd been here.'

Edward left the shelter of Ruth's arms, buried his face in his hands. 'Just as well you were not — it was dreadful. My daughter, and she's gone forever. I'll never see her again, Ruth.'

Absolute incomprehension took Ruth. 'And she'd been here for four days and hadn't told you who she was?'

'Yes,' he sighed deeply in painful recollection, 'under my roof. Something I'd dreamed about. My two children together with me here.' His head moved from side to side. 'And I didn't know.' A shudder took him. 'But to find out who she was just as she was leaving . . . ' Edward turned dulled shocked eyes on Ruth. 'She hated me — hated me.' He shivered. 'I'm cold, Ruth, I feel cold.'

Ruth's heartfelt sympathy surrounded him as gently and compassionately she guided his shoulders back against the couch and pushed it nearer the fire. Then she poured some whisky — a lot — and placed it in his hand. 'Take that — I'll make a tea.'

Poor dear Edward. What had the bitch been trying to do? Ruth replaced the empty glass with a cup of tea. Edward sipped at it then spoke in a slightly firmer voice. 'I was ashamed Ruth, today of myself and of Maxime. The things she said to me — the things I said to her. It was awful — a nightmare.' Then looking up at Ruth and holding her elbow, he uttered gratefully, 'Thanks for coming, Ruth. Sorry to drag you into this. You've enough on your plate without my problems.'

She kissed him tenderly on the forehead unable to speak.

Edward looked into the fire and murmured, 'I've been down before, but this was different, a terrible blow, Ruth.'

Ruth regarded him in huge and helpless sympathy. He was sorely wounded, had really taken it to heart very badly, and she again felt a rage inside her at Maxime for what she had done. He must have been so excited — too much so for his own good as it had turned out. Ruth thought she knew the reason as to what had brought on such extreme ill feeling in Maxime for the man who was her father. She was proved correct when Edward told her that Maxime's mind as a child had been poisoned against him by her grandparents, Sir Redvers and Lady Scarton. Sir Redvers had since died and she had also blamed Edward for that.

He finished by saying, 'Thanks Ruth, I love you. You'll excuse me — I just feel so tired.' Misery stared from his eyes. 'I'll be better tomorrow. I'll come up to see you and William.'

She shook her head adamantly. 'No, I'm coming down here again.' A kiss on his cheek, a caress of its sunken contours and she left him.

Downstairs Frederick told her he would stay and keep an eye on his father. Then Ruth went home leaving one worry to confront the other of William's worsening condition, of which she had said nothing to Edward, judging it better not to do in the circumstances in which she had found him.

That night when he did bring himself to dwell on the incident Edward realised that he was mourning the loss of a daughter that he had known only for a very short time. A small face in her cot and then her dramatic appearance some twenty five years later. Sir Redvers had died a few years after Elaine, but there was no doubt that he had said enough before his death to have instilled the seed of hatred that had finally manifested itself during the visit of Maxime to the Ormer Hotel.

20

When Ruth saw Edward the next day she understood once more what a shock the affair had been to him. He was haggard and strained of face, and unshaven. There was a stoop to his shoulders which she hadn't noticed before. She realised then that they were both getting older. Only that morning she had observed in the mirror her own increasing wrinkles around mouth and neck and the furrowed brow above them.

He was pleased to see her again — very pleased, and embraced her but without an accompanying kiss, and although he was still obviously very upset, his demeanour was some improvement on the day before. She wondered whether the refounding and ownership of the hotel had brought him the happiness that he had expected and for which she had wished so hard and long for him.

They sat in front of the fire in Edward's room holding hands and middle-aged. Ruth wanted reassurance, help, and a shoulder to lean on, and wondered if it was the right moment to bring up the matter of William's health. However to her thankful relief, her companion gave her the opportunity when he enquired, 'William across at the hotel?'

'No, I've left him at home.'

'Oh, taking a day off is he? Does he know you've come here?'

'I told him I was going shopping.'

'Is he all right — getting over that problem he had?'

The winter sun was yellowing a corner of the room and it illuminated her features as she regarded him squarely. Edward saw that her face, open and frank as it had ever been, was troubled. There was an unease about her. Faint red lines clouded the whites of her eyes, but the light violet remained as vivid as always.

'I had to come to talk to you, Edward. I'm worried about William.'

Edward frowned and remembered. William's problems had been forgotten under the weight of his own recently. 'He's no better?'

Ruth shook her head. 'We were going to wait a month to see if there was any improvement and then he was going to go back to the doctor.' She sighed. 'Well he isn't better after a month — he's no different.' Pushing a stray hair back from her forehead she went on anxiously, 'They gave him tests — all sorts and not very pleasant for him I believe. At the end of it all they've told him that he has some sort of nerve disease — I cannot remember the name.' Ruth returned her gaze to Edward fully, dismay and perplexity showing. 'They as much as told him that there's nothing they can do.' Her voice broke and fell away. 'It's — it's progressive,' and she sank back, her head resting against his shoulder.

Edward put his arm around her swiftly, tightened it protectively and resisted the vicious imp of bitter satisfaction at his brother's misfortune. Snuffed it out, ashamed that it had ever risen inside him.

Flaming hell fire! William with something like that! God! They'd been at loggerheads a long time in the past, but he'd never have wished anything like that on his brother. Something from the women William had had? Aloud he asked, 'Are you sure about this, Ruth?'

She nodded against him. Her voice when it came was weak, resigned. 'Yes, all the tests were positive, and from what they said it had been present for some time.'

'I'm sorry Ruth, I am — very sorry. What blasted bad luck.' There was silence a few moments, the warmth from the fire comforting. Life was like a bloody switchback, Edward thought. First you were up, doing fine, but just over the horizon there was always another dip. 'How's he taking it?

'Not so good. He's raging inside himself about it. Takes it out of me, anything and anybody. He can't understand, refuses to believe that it's happened to him.' Her voice became deeply compassionate, sympathetic. 'I don't blame him — it must be awful to be told you have something like that.' Ruth remembered their early years. William had always been the happy-go-lucky one — never really caring. Then as he had got older he had gradually changed. With success had come impatience, avarice, and until recently a belief that only his hand should be in every pie. Now though she was sorry for him. She had always been very fond of him, he also having formed part of her life for so long. He had been good to her, providing a fine home and lifestyle for her and Frederick. Her heart had never been his however and she wondered sometimes if he cared.

She had been his in the sense of being possessed; that was what really mattered to William. But the pride in bed had now deserted him. The long instrument of pleasure had gone, would not do his bidding and he had nothing left to give. Love had never been a part of their association. She sighed deeply and grasped Edward's arm. 'What can we do Edward? Is there anything we can do? I feel so helpless.'

Edward forced himself to ask the question, his delivery hesitant. 'I mean — they've said it's progressive, but well, will it be slow?' He tried to add optimism. 'I believe something like that can go on for years.'

'They just said it was progressive — that's all,' Ruth replied in a monotone.

'I wonder if they said anything to William?'

Ruth was silent against him for a while. When she spoke it was with sadness and a catch in her voice. 'He's mentioned having a will drawn up.'

Oh the poor sod! Edward had never thought that he would be thinking in those terms of his brother. If he was thinking of making a will then things must be pretty desperate for him. He did his best to comfort Ruth. 'Look, it may not be as bad as it seems. You do hear of people being wrongly diagnosed or they suddenly start to improve. William's case could be like that.' He had a feeling though that the specialists were usually right when it came to the serious illnesses.

Grateful lips pressed against his cheek then Ruth stood up. 'I needed someone to talk to, Edward. I feel better now that I've told you. Will you come up and see him soon?'

Edward didn't hesitate. 'Yes I will — this evening. I'll settle things here and then I'll come straight up. Don't say anything, just let him think I popped in.'

She nodded and grasped his hand and pressed it to her heart, then bent her head and brushed his knuckles with her lips. Something she had done before in the past. He didn't like her to do it — he wasn't worth homage of that sort. Nevertheless, his arm was around her waist as he walked her out to her car, conscious of the still good figure and the hair salon's blonding masking the growing greying atop the slightly more angular face and fuller chin.

After Ruth had gone he sat staring into the fire for a while. For the second time in a fortnight the cruel hand of apparent unreality had touched him. First Maxime and now William. William, whom he had never known to be ill in his life before. Suddenly it seemed that he had a very serious complaint. Edward felt very worried — he didn't like the sound of it at all. His world as he thought he knew it was changing rapidly. Ruth's words regarding William came into his mind. 'What can we do Edward?' and he had noted the 'we'. Their lives had always been interwoven. The thought came that things could have been a lot different for him if she had not had such an influence on his life. Maxime would have been a daughter to him and Elaine would have gone off anyway: perhaps he would have continued to live at Scarton Manor. Five years of his life would not have been lost. On the other hand he would certainly not have been the owner of the Ormer Hotel; he had Ruth to thank for that. It was all conjecture and in the past.

Two hours later he was entering Ruth and William's home — that lovely house, the huge picture windows almost hidden by the heavy long curtains. A large modern artificial coal effect fire with regular leaping flames in the stone fireplace. To one side was the gallery above, the subdued lights gleaming cosily on the bedroom doors opening off it. Ruth rose from her seat, a new fresh and warm welcome on her face, but the flames revealed the strain behind it.

William was sat in a high-backed leather chair by the fire, and Edward was surprised to see a stick hanging from it, its crook curled over its top. A glass of amber liquid stood on a table near at hand.

'Just thought I'd pop in — I didn't get up last week — had rather a heavy cold,' he excused himself to William

'And you're feeling better now?'

Edward couldn't remember the last time William had enquired about anything to do with his well-being, but his brother seemed genuinely pleased to see him. Sometimes Edward had wondered. 'Yes thanks, William, I seem to have thrown it off. And how's things with you — any improvement?' He took the opportunity to observe the pinched face, the whole form appearing thinner, and trousers loose fitting about the thighs. The other's blue eyes held the look of a man struggling to come to terms with life after a shock. Edward thought his own must have held very much the same expression after Maxime's visit.

'Just when I think I'm making progress I get a

relapse. Have bloody good days — some bad ones.' His speech was jerky.

'I thought you were doing well this week, William,' joined in Ruth encouragingly.

William looked sharply at her, spoke irritably. 'You know I'm not, Ruth. I know whether I am or not.' He looked at Edward. 'She keeps saying that, but I should know.'

Ruth threw Edward a quick glance of resignation. 'I'll go and make a coffee for us.'

William nodded after Ruth. 'She means well. I can't be easy to live with now.' Pointed at his glass. 'Have one?'

Edward joined him in a whisky then leaned forward. 'What the hell's gone wrong, William?' and mindful of not letting his brother think that Ruth had told him anything. He'd go raving mad if he knew.

'Damned if I know. The doctor thinks he does — some bloody sclerosis or other.' His voice took on a savage resentment. 'Who do they think they're kidding? Me? Fit as anything. You know. Then they tell me I've got that. Must be out of their idiot minds. Almighty God,' he exploded, 'when I think of the money I've paid them to tell me that.' Glared away across the room, fingers tight around his glass, then his gaze returned to Edward again, the eyes seeking reassurance. After a moment he raised his glass and gulped the remaining liquid. 'It's my legs — they feel like bloody rubber,' he informed him in a calmer tone.

Dismayed, Edward regarded his younger brother — younger by a year. He appeared to have aged swiftly in the last few months. Edward remembered the time long ago when they had just arrived at the school in Daleford. William was being bullied and he had defended him. This time the enemy was much more formidable. What could he do to help?

William was talking again. 'I've had the Rolls altered so that all the controls are round the steering column.' His eyes came alive. 'Absolutely marvellous, everything to hand.'

Ruth appeared with the coffee. 'Is he telling you about the Rolls, Edward? D'you know, I'm sure he thinks more of that car then he does of me,' she said in mock reproof.

Edward smiled. 'I can't believe that, Ruth, though I must admit it's a beautiful car.'

'Gets me out of the house,' said William, 'bit more independent.'

'You're too independent, William,' Ruth remarked, placing his coffee on the side table.

'How often d'you get across to the hotel now?' Edward asked.

'A couple of days a week. Just to keep my hand on things. Frederick keeps me informed of everything. Done well — picked up the business quickly — good brain.'

'He's busy getting ready for New Year's Eve,' put in Ruth, there's a large party coming over from Jersey.'

New Year's Eve! Edward stared at her. He'd forgotten. Christmas had come and gone — such a miserable one as he'd never had before. Decorations and tree had gone up, but his heart hadn't been in the occasion. Now it was the New Year approaching in a few days. An idea came. 'Why don't you both come down to my place and spend New Year's Eve with me? There's plenty of room. I've only about half a dozen booked in.' He looked from one to the other. 'How about it? What d'you say?'

Ruth was enthusiastic. 'Yes, why not, William? It'll be a change and you haven't been down to the Ormer for years.'

William gazed at them over his cup rim, a light of interest showing in his eyes, but when he spoke a note of doubt was present. 'Should really show myself over at the Two Bays — busy time.'

'Oh William, you can manage it,' urged Ruth encouragingly. 'You said yourself Frederick's very good and he's got enough staff surely.' She waited expectantly for his agreement as he pondered. Then smiling through her impatience she suggested, 'All right, if you must, why not just go across for an hour. Show yourself, and then we'll go down to Edward's? Will you? Please, William. I think you ought to.' Then a mischievous sparkle flared in the glance she gave to Edward. 'Who knows, you may just be able to give him a few tips on how to run the Ormer.'

Edward was glad to see that sparkle — it had been missing for so long.

'Yes, I will. Why not?' exclaimed William suddenly. 'Yes, let the damn place take care of itself. The Jersey crowd can have it for a night.'

So it was arranged and Edward left soon afterwards. William was pleased he had been and Ruth was certainly. It must be very difficult for her. Beneath her smiles he sensed the strain she was under. As for William he was much worse than he had expected. It was upsetting to see his brother like that. However, the thought that they would all be together on New Year's Eve was a joyous one.

The last evening of the year was both a sad and happy time. When the three had entered the Ormer, William looked about him. 'Hellfire, Edward, it's a long time since I was here. The day we left with Mum and Dad.' And Edward glanced away. Had he seen a glistening in William's eyes? They were almost boys again. Then together with Ruth they chatted with the guests and drank with them and someone played the piano. Edward was happy, forgetting all about the problems that had beset them recently. All three under the roof of the Ormer for the first time in forty years! Soon the clock hovered between that year and the next, and then they joined hands and sang with the guests.

At just after one o'clock Frederick appeared with a crowd from the Two Bays Hotel. They had insisted on coming over when they heard William was there. The Ormer Hotel was filled with laughter and talk and music. There was dancing and Ruth took part and the violet eyes shone as they used to do. To Edward in the joyous confusion it seemed a symbolic joining of the two hotels. And he hoped an omen for the times ahead.

When at last things quietened down, Ruth and William said a late and slightly incoherent good night, and disappeared into their room. In bed Ruth prayed her thanks for the miracle that had brought Edward, William and herself to sleep under the one roof for the first time since they were children, and dared hope for another to heal William.

* * *

There was no turning back now, Ruth thought as she walked into a room at Scarton Manor to meet the young woman by the name of Maxime Scarton. She had lied to effect the meeting by saying she was an old friend of the family, having recently returned to England. It was not a complete untruth. She had flown in from Guernsey after telephoning first. It was something she had vowed to do at the earliest opportunity in the New Year after seeing the anguish caused to Edward by the visit of Maxime. Ruth was determined that the latter should know that her father had always been innocent of the affair of which she had judged him so harshly.

Ruth felt a slight shock as Maxime came forward. She did have the look of Elaine — a more serious looking Elaine. Her expression was puzzled, and she did not extend a hand. 'Your name — I cannot remember anybody of that name. I asked my grandmother — she has no recollection either.'

'I'm not surprised. It is not my real name. I am Mrs. Ruth Dorner.' She saw the eyes flinch and then widen.

'Dorner! His wife? Get out, go away. I have nothing to discuss with you.'

Ruth heard the contemptuous dismissal in the words and it angered her. 'Not until I've told you what I've come to say, then I shall go.' She was determined to remain calm and dignified. Being older should confer that upon her she hoped.

'He's sent you over to plead for him has he? Well it's no good. You might as well understand straight away, it'll make no difference whatever you say,' and she turned away.

'I am not your father's wife — though God knows I've tried hard enough. No, I'm married to William, your father's brother.'

Maxime looked sideways at her. 'I want nothing to do with anyone of that name — it makes me sick. I don't know what you've come for and I don't care,' and she moved to the window, her back to Ruth.

'Don't turn your back on me, Maxime Dorner.' Ruth's voice was sharp across the space between them. 'What I have to say is important to you whether you think so or not. It's just as important to me that you hear it. So you might as well listen and take in what I'm going to tell you. I'm here until I have done so.' Moving alongside the younger woman she spoke at her profile earnestly and gravely. 'My maiden name was Ruth Le Ney.' Saw the other's swift half glance and carried on. 'You'll have read the old papers and accounts. I loved your father — always have. I would have done anything to make him mine. I tried that night. In my mind I wanted your mother dead, I admit. I took the telephone call, not your father. No one believed me. But I was guilty, he was innocent. No matter that the water was already sweeping the cottage away when the call was made, I was guilty in my mind. I wanted her dead.'

The other rounded on her angrily, accusingly.

'Well I don't care for your confession or your stupid love for him. You admit that you loved him and like the papers said you were just trying to protect him. I'll never forgive him. You were in it together. He knew he was guilty — he as much as said so. I have read the papers and also I know what my grandfather said. Now go back to that island and tell him that sending you was another mistake.'

With a great effort Ruth contained her fury. 'Your father does not know I have come,' she said with only the slightest tremor in her voice. 'I came to acquaint you with the truth, something which has been in short supply during your life as regards your father. It matters nothing what you think of me. What does matter is what you know of your father. And I tell you you know nothing. You talk of not forgiving, you silly misguided girl. God! you should get down on your knees now and pray for forgiveness for what you have done to your father. What d'you know about forgiveness? Your father was — is — a gallant man and you're not worthy of being his daughter. He went to prison for five years to protect me. I like to believe that it was because he loved me. But that's nothing to do with you.' It was obvious that Maxime was taken aback — stunned by the growing vehemence of Ruth's words and manner.

'He was seeing you at home when my mother was alive. Is that like an innocent man?' she retorted.

'No. I wanted to see him. He never wanted me. Threw me out. I was totally to blame. In those days I was stupid, besotted with him. It was always going to be he and I. Then he married your mother. I couldn't take it. And I can prove that I was there that night, but your father did not know until he saw me by the phone. If ever you see him again just ask your father about a shell he found — an Ormer shell on his table. I left it there that night. I knew he didn't love me then.' The fire was dying away in her voice as she continued, 'In our differing ways we both owe your father. I for his shielding of me, you for the last twenty odd years when he hasn't had the daughter's love that was, and is, rightfully his.' Suddenly Ruth grasped the younger woman's hands, her eyes wide with only a deep longing and hope in them, her voice trembling with the fervour of her heartfelt entreaty. 'Maxime, I beg of you to be a daughter to your father. Please, please undo the wrong you have done him. Be part of his life again. Hate me if you must but never Edward.' Then impulsively she placed the lightest of kisses — the brushing of a butterfly on the cheek of an astonished Maxime. Hurried from the room. Leaving the house she thought it had always been an unlucky place — full of jealousies, hurts, rages. One more act had been played out there — the last as far as she was concerned.

21

It was Spring again and Ruth knelt by the side of William's wheelchair near the cliff walk at Icart Point. The doctors had been correct unfortunately in their prognosis and the weakness had progressed. It had become very difficult for him to walk even a few yards, so he had purchased a folding chair which could be stored in the boot of the car and then used when they could not get any further by car. She knew that he was too proud to go into public places often, so he liked to be taken to spots on the cliffs where it was quiet and sometimes they would picnic.

Ruth tried to keep her sadness away from William, forcing herself to be cheerful and to think of things to interest him apart from the running of his hotel which he still took a keen interest in. Often he was morose, awkward and savage in his tilting at a fate that had handed him such a cruel blow. Afterwards he would apologise to her, saying that he hadn't always been in such a state. She remembered that he used to laugh a lot when he was younger, caring for life and occasionally uncaring for others. Now he needed constant encouragement and bolstering.

Sometimes Edward, when he could get away from the Ormer, would accompany them, pushing William into places she would have found impossible to reach. It was hard work she knew but Edward seemed determined and pleased to help.

Once she found him a short distance away, sat on the grass, head in hands. He was dreadfully upset about William she realised but had never shown it in front of him. Very often the refreshments on those trips included alcohol, and then she would have to drive on the return, the brothers masking their differing heartaches lolling in the back.

William stared out to sea from his wheelchair on the cliff top behind his hotel. A blue hazy day with a fresh wind whitening the waves below. Nearby were Ruth and Edward. Such a lovely day, and he flaming well couldn't walk — couldn't do much of anything nowadays he thought bitterly. The administration of the hotel he could direct from his office, but he hated being seen in the wheelchair along its corridors and open spaces. In any case Frederick kept it functioning smoothly. He was useless at home — useless in and out of bed now. Ruth didn't seem to mind. Perhaps she didn't care — never complained, but he was a burden. Had been bloody surprised when she agreed to marry him — she'd always been stuck on Edward. William remembered the other women in his life — he had been fortunate with them. His mind drifted to Miss Steck and her companion. A world away now. He'd been king of the castle then. She'd been game for anything; sex and fantasy had been a reality. A mind-blowing shock from a staid appearing spinster. He had lived on her, Edward had been right, but she had not minded, wanting to keep him there always. Her will had turned his world the right way up. From the money had grown his huge and successful hotel behind him together with the lovely home on the west coast.

Elaine came into his thoughts. Well brought up but with no morals. Edward had blamed him, but she'd gone off the rails long before that. He himself had no real feelings for her other than sexual. Miss Steck on the other hand had been deprived of men — she'd had every right to be greedy. His other affairs on the island flitted into and out of his mind quickly, none being of any consequence. He'd paid them off if they looked like making trouble. Smiled inwardly with a dreadful bitterness at the final cost.

William glanced behind him with pride at The Two Bays hotel. Known throughout Europe as a top class place. But he couldn't acknowledge the greetings of guests and celebrities in the restaurant now. Never went in, unable to bear to be seen as he was. He sighed. His will had been made. There was nothing else to do. It was Hell. Ruth and Edward had stuck by him. They'd be all right. His hands moved.

Edward saw the wheelchair beginning to roll down the slope towards the cliff edge. At first his mind was slow to react. It couldn't be. The brakes were on, he himself had pushed the levers. The chair was running away — it was! Gathering pace. Edward started after him, William's stick in his hand. He had taken it off the back of the chair in case his brother had wished to stand for a moment. The handles of the chair stayed just out of reach as he dashed headlong after William. Caught the rear support with the crook of the stick and held on desperately. The chair veered and slowed, and Edward, falling full length, was dragged along. The chair overbalanced and fell, taking his brother with it towards the cliff edge. He scrambled on hands and knees, lunging for William's jacket shoulder. His fingers gripped and held while the chair clattered and slid sideways the last yards and over the edge.

'He tried to commit suicide,' Edward told a shocked Ruth later. 'I know for a fact that the brakes were on — I put them on — I'm certain I did. There were two and it's highly unlikely that they would both release at once.' He could hardly believe that it had happened but it had. William must have felt in a bad way to attempt to kill himself.

That night he remained with Ruth and William much longer than usual, the latter being taciturn and sunk in his fireside chair in a deep depression, bruised but otherwise not badly hurt. Ruth was upset, blaming herself for not understanding his problems sufficiently. Edward did his best to comfort her, but when he finally left it was with misgivings, aware that Ruth like himself thought it was quite possible that William would try again.

It was dawn before he dozed off, but by then he had decided on a course of action. Ruth and William must be persuaded to come and live with him at the Ormer Hotel. Ruth would have the benefit of company other than William's and be drawn into a more cheerful and optimistic world than the one she had become used to during her husband's illness. He could help her look after his brother and they could keep an eye on him much more easily. And very important, Edward thought, William would be returning to the family home. The number of guests he took in could be cut so that

Ruth and William could use those rooms. As for Frederick — he was a young man and William's flat at The Two Bays hotel would be a bachelor pad and office combined. But he would know and had always known that the Ormer was his real home and he was welcome at any time. Edward felt certain that it would be of benefit to all concerned if they accepted his offer. But would they? William's pride had not quite vanished yet, and Ruth was now used to being in a spacious modern house. So it was with some doubts that he hurried to see them soon after breakfast was finished, and the Ormer running smoothly into another day.

To his great and utter delight and relief, William agreed, while Ruth did not need any persuading. William however insisted that their home should be kept going. Edward understood. It was a reminder for his brother of happier and healthier days when it had first been built.

A week later Edward and William were sitting on the veranda of the Ormer Hotel overlooking Moulin Huet. Across, atop the headland was the white outline of The Two Bays hotel. In between holidaymakers were scattered along the beach, and in the water the white sails of a yacht being furled as it entered the bay. The Pea Stacks were clearly defined and all was blue and green — a perfect Guernsey day.

Edward glanced at his brother. Since coming to live at the Ormer the latter's depression had begun to lift and he was taking an interest again, not only in his own establishment, but also the Ormer, his mind being occupied with something other than his disability. He had his off days which was only to be expected. But Edward was very pleased — they were both home again. And Ruth was happier and more content, welcoming the chance occasionally to give a hand when needed in the running of the hotel.

Edward saw the binoculars at William's side and smiled inwardly but with a sad compassion. His brother had not changed much. The lovely limbs and costumes on the sands below still drew his attention.

The subject of his thoughts turned to him. 'Sorry about the business on the cliff, Edward. I was a bit down that day.' He shrugged. 'Well, more than a bit — a hell of a lot.'

'S'all right,' murmured Edward. 'All I could do. Could hardly let you go over the edge.' Momentarily he had been surprised. For the first time in his adult life William had apologised to him over something.

'No need to worry,' William assured him. 'I'm coming to terms with things. I won't try again.' A sad wry smile appeared. 'Well, not with the chair. I'll use the car next time.' They chuckled together, then were quiet for a while before William spoke again, and this time regarding his brother with great seriousness. 'I want you to promise me that you'll do something for me when I'm gone.'

Edward was alarmed and sad all over again. He couldn't envisage a time when William would not be around. 'Nonsense. You'll probably outlive the rest of us.'

'Give me the credit for knowing my case better than you do, Edward. I'm under no illusions now,' his companion admonished him.

With an impatient movement Edward slumped back in his chair. 'All right but I don't want you talking like that. Well, go on, what do you want me to promise?'

'That you'll marry Ruth when she's widowed.'

Edward twisted irritably to face his brother. 'Look, she's married to you. Can we talk about something a little more sensible?'

William's stare was grave and steady. 'You know what I mean Edward. Damn you,' he exploded suddenly, 'she's loved you all her life. For once you bloody fool do the right thing by her.' Saw the protestations rising to Edward's lips. 'God almighty! Have you forgotten? Any man who goes to prison for five years for a woman as you did must flaming well love her. All these years you've shied away from the fact.' William paused, letting his words penetrate, then he demanded, 'Well — your word, Edward.'

Edward nodded. 'I will.'

'But not a word to Ruth,' William warned.

'Yes, all right, but I hope to be ninety when I do for your sake.'

William smiled with a knowing and sad satisfaction, and their hands clasped.

A few days later Edward, whilst throwing out some old clothes, found the Ormer shell deep in the pocket of a jacket. He showed it to Ruth. 'D'you want it?'

Ruth looked at it, remembered all that had happened. 'No, throw it back on to the beach.'

They watched it fall and bounce and settle to become lost again. From childhood to adulthood it had accompanied her but she did not need it now. Marriage to Edward may have eluded her, but at least she was living under the same roof as the man she had always loved.

THE END